THE FIRST ORDER

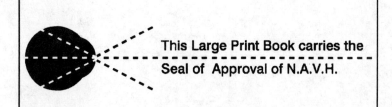

This Large Print Book carries the
Seal of Approval of N.A.V.H.

THE FIRST ORDER

JEFF ABBOTT

THORNDIKE PRESS
A part of Gale, Cengage Learning

GALE
CENGAGE Learning

Farmington Hills, Mich • San Francisco • New York • Waterville, Maine
Meriden, Conn • Mason, Ohio • Chicago

GALE
CENGAGE Learning®

LIBRARY OF CONGRESS CATALOGING-IN-PUBLICATION DATA

Names: Abbott, Jeff, author.
Title: The first order / Jeff Abbott.
Description: Large print edition. | Waterville, Maine : Thorndike Press Large Print, 2016. | © 2016 ¦ Series: Thorndike Press large print thriller
Identifiers: LCCN 2015044746| ISBN 9781410486769 (hardback) | ISBN 1410486761 (hardcover)
Subjects: LCSH: Large type books. | BISAC: FICTION / Thrillers. | GSAFD: Suspense fiction.
Classification: LCC PS3601.B366 F57 2016b | DDC 813/.6—dc23
LC record available at http://lccn.loc.gov/2015044746

Published in 2016 by arrangement with Grand Central Publishing, a division of Hachette Book Group, Inc.

Printed in the United States of America
1 2 3 4 5 6 7 20 19 18 17 16

For Dan Sloan

Me and my nation against the world.
Me and my clan against the nation.
Me and my family against the clan.
Me and my brother against the family.
Me against my brother.
— Somali proverb

There is but one mind in all these men, and it is bent against Caesar. If thou beest not immortal, look about you: security gives way to conspiracy.

— William Shakespeare, *Julius Caesar*

■ ■ ■ ■

PART ONE:
IF I AM DEAD

1

Manhattan

"It will be the most dangerous assassination in history. You are to kill the Russian president, Dmitri Morozov, when he comes to meet with the American president in two weeks. The client will pay you twenty million dollars." Mrs. Claybourne said it all in a rush, holding the gaze of the man she knew as Philip Judge.

Slowly he shook his head.

"I am completely serious," Mrs. Claybourne said. The two of them were alone in the room, a table between them. The entire office had been fitted to counter any attempt at audio surveillance. Her smartphone lay between them, an app on it constantly scanning the room for bugs. She had pasted special privacy film on the windows as a barrier. It would protect against any snoopers using laser microphone technology to read the vibrations of the glass from their voices and decipher their words. Sound-masking equipment had been installed on the doors, walls, and ductwork, playing a low-level hum to baffle any eaves-droppers. The empty office had been leased through a shell company for the next year, although it would remain empty after this meeting.

In the midst of humanity-packed Manhattan, they were utterly isolated and un-watched.

And she was not joking.

The smile vanished from Philip Judge's face. It was a handsome face, she thought, despite the sharp edges of mouth and cheekbone and chin. He wore a well-cut black suit, Italian, with a silver tie. Only the slight scar on the left side of his throat, a hard line, marred his good looks.

"This is the one you've waited for, Judge, the one you've trained for. The one you've made all your sacrifices for. You will need never work again."

Judge shook his head. "You want me to kill Dmitri Morozov. No, thanks. Can you recommend a good bar around here? I could use a drink, since you've wasted my time."

"Did you not hear me?"

"I did. I just did not believe you." He

stood, straightening the suit jacket. "I could have stayed another day in Copenhagen, enjoying that lovely city."

"Please. Sit." She gestured at the chair. "I assure you I am serious."

"The first order of business in my work," he said, "is don't get caught. Morozov is an impossible kill. At least impossible for me to survive," Judge said. "I don't believe in martyrdom. Good day."

"Please, sit," Mrs. Claybourne said.

Judge, after a moment, sat.

Mrs. Claybourne's poker face wasn't as effective as she believed it to be. She was in her late forties, in an impeccable dark suit with a soft blue scarf, her brown hair stylish and short, with a streak of gray through it. Her voice was calm and measured. But for all her meticulous reserve, Judge thought, she's scared.

He cracked another smile, to ease his refusal. "I appreciate the compliment. But no."

"You said *impossible.* Let's just explore it for a minute."

"There's no point. The Russians would never give up hunting me. Ever. I could never work again. I could never have a moment's peace. And frankly, I'm ready for some peace."

The teakettle whistled. "Let's have tea and talk it through." Mrs. Claybourne stood, walked to the office's small kitchen, prepared two mugs of oolong, set the cups on the table, and sat back down at the table. She glanced at him. He had not moved a muscle in her absence and was lost in thought. That beautiful brain of his, she thought, can't resist chewing on the challenge.

"Thank you for not leaving while I was gone."

"That would have been rude."

She sipped her own tea. "I know you don't often read the papers or news sites. So: The Russian president has been invited by the American president to have an economic and peace summit at the vice president's ranch near Houston. President Morozov will first visit Washington, and then go on to Texas, close to two weeks from today. He's also been specifically invited to bring his inner circle — the men who help him run Russia."

"Those men are all billionaire oligarchs," Judge said. "They've been targeted again and again by the West with economic sanctions over the past couple of years. They won't come to America."

"Actually, they will. A source inside the

State Department has confirmed this for me. This will be a singular moment in history," Mrs. Claybourne said. "And the sanctions are being lifted. Relations between Russia and America have been abysmal for too long, and now there is an impetus to improve them. The Americans hope to make the Russians less of an authoritative government, and to open up new markets there. The Russians need Western markets and they need the West to not be undercutting Morozov's legitimacy."

"Then that ranch will be more secure than Fort Knox," Judge said. "I'd never get close. The Russians in that inner circle are all ex-KGB. They are not soft American executives; they are robber barons. They have their own private security force, mostly ex–Special Forces people. Add to that the American Secret Service. Drones in the sky. A security perimeter greater than any bullet's range." He stared at her. "Not to mention the elephant in the room. A Russian president killed on American soil? It would likely mean war." He paused and took a deep breath. "I don't have any desire to cause a war," he said.

"Ah, yes, your rule book." She smiled but he didn't smile back.

"Tattered and worn and it's only on one

shelf." Here he tapped his temple. "It dictates that I care about the aftereffects of a kill. Every death causes a ripple."

"And the ripple here is that Morozov dead might open Russia to a more moderate leader. One who will not micromanage and manipulate Russian democracy for his own gain and greed, and put the world at greater risk of conflict." She spoke with confidence. "If such a result fits into your sacred rule book, eases your decision, and helps you sleep better."

"Who's hiring me?" he asked her.

"You know better." She sipped at her tea.

Judge got up and paced the room.

Dmitri Morozov had been president of Russia for two years, the immediate and controversial successor to his older brother. Viktor Morozov had ruled Russia for nearly twenty years, robbed the nation blind, slashed freedoms, built up (at least in his mind) a Russia that was a counterbalance to the decadent West, and made himself a billionaire off the country's resources. He called, without irony, his Russia a "careful democracy" — one careful not to criticize him or his inner circle. One careful to check rights, to control all media, to return Russia to its former glories. And one careful to shape and name enemies of the people —

journalists, Muslims, gays, atheists, musicians, intellectuals, business leaders who argued for openness and fell out of favor, the individual-obsessed West — all supposedly dangerous forces that the Morozovs, to save Russia, would defeat. Viktor, however, could not beat the Reaper. He'd died from cancer, from chain-smoking. His younger brother Dmitri, who was nicknamed the Little Czar and who served as premier, stepped into office as his successor. The Morozovs weren't czars, but they were close. The Russians kept electing them, again and again, for the sake of stability, and Morozov and his blood circle of billionaires ran the country like their own private company. "Russia, Inc.," as Judge had heard critical Western journalists refer to it.

He stopped his pacing. "Why only two weeks' warning? It wouldn't be enough time to plan."

"That is the time frame."

Twenty million, he thought. Freedom. The rest of his life to live in quiet perfection.

Mrs. Claybourne leaned forward. "Approach the challenge as you see best. You get five million up front, so hire the help you need. If you need to recruit and pay a team, you can. If you choose to act alone, that's your concern."

"It can't be done," he said. "Not on American soil."

"He has to die on American soil."

Die on American soil. He felt a little tickle in the back of his brain. An idea, looking to breathe, struggling for life. A bit of room to move.

Mrs. Claybourne watched him. "You were not my first recommendation to the client. I felt a team approach was best and you work alone. We approached another professional assassin. She and her team thoroughly studied the situation, but she could not see a way to it being done."

Judge raised an eyebrow.

"That said, once I described you to the client, you were the only candidate of interest. You speak fluent Russian. You can pass for an American. And you don't exist. The man with no past." He blinked at this. "And you are a superb mix in your thinking: methodical, yet intuitive, and still able to cope when disaster strikes. You are right: To approach this as a conventional assassination will be to fail. You will not be conventional."

"I would need to know how he moves. Where he will be. Where he is going. Without that . . ."

"I can offer you one more advantage, one I did not share with the first candidate for the job."

"I'm flattered."

"I trust you in a way I did not trust the other. Our long history . . ." she began, but then she stopped for a few moments. "We have someone inside President Morozov's inner circle. Someone who could apprise you of his movements, his habits, his security detail, even the last-minute changes. You would have regular contact with this person, if needed."

"Who? One of the billionaires?"

"I cannot say. The contact has only a code name. Firebird."

"That's a nice, generic Russian symbol," Judge said. He thought: I'll bet the contact is the client. But he said nothing.

"I can serve as a conduit, or you can talk to Firebird directly via text. No face-to-face, obviously, and we'd use encryption and masking technology to protect you both."

"I need to know who Firebird is." Everyone inside Morozov's inner circle could afford a twenty-million-dollar kill fee. They were all billionaires several times over who controlled the most important aspects of the Russian economy and were in turn controlled by Morozov.

And one of them apparently wanted Morozov dead.

"I don't even know," she said.

Judge knew his life would be in the informant's hands. It was an unsettling thought. But Firebird, if exposed, was dead as well. "An informant inside is not such an advantage."

"It's up to you to make the most of your advantages. After all, you don't exist, do you? Not like a normal man does."

His skin felt cold. He would have to say yes or no.

"Just so you know . . . if you take the job and kill Morozov, but are killed in turn, the remaining fifteen million would be placed in escrow for your named heir."

"An heir, for a man who doesn't exist." He finished his tea. "I think we both know you'd just keep the money."

"You wound me, Mr. Judge," Mrs. Claybourne said. "Everyone has someone they love. Perhaps even a man who doesn't exist. A wife? A child? A parent?" She paused. "A sister? A brother?"

He didn't look at her for a long moment; then he set down the mug and met her gaze. "Not having someone to love is how I can do what I do," he said evenly. "No one can be a target for revenge. What if I undertake the job and decide, after further deliberation, it cannot be done?"

She frowned. "You will present me with an itemized list of your expenses, and you will be paid a reasonable fee for your time. You would refund the remainder of the initial five million payment. But . . . I beg you not to decline. You're my best hope, Mr. Judge. I do not want to disappoint Firebird by refusing this most generous offer."

It was a threat and he ignored it. He would not be bullied. He had killed fearsome, powerful men and women before, but Morozov was an entirely different level of target.

"Call me when you've decided," she said. "Since you're in town for another job, I would suggest you complete that one quickly, and then give your full attention to making your decision. Time is already short."

He'd thought she'd cancel the job she'd brought him here to do in light of this much greater offer, but no. Fine. He stood.

"Thank you for the tea." They didn't shake hands. He turned and left the soundproofed office. He headed to the elevator and a minute later he was on the streets of Manhattan. He walked, thinking, watching

21

for watchers. He got on and off the subway five times, took a cab to Bryant Park. No one was following him. He got out of the cab and headed down the street and saw the name of a bar he recognized.

The Last Minute. Well, that seemed an apt name, given the decision he faced. He almost couldn't go inside. *What if . . . Why did you come here?*

He ignored the impulse to turn away and he walked inside. The bar was handsome with an old-school feel, rich mahogany and a patterned tile floor. Well-dressed office workers and a few tourists drank martinis and craft beers. He sat at an empty table. A handsome older gentleman in a bespoke suit — the manager, Judge assumed — saw that he hadn't been served, stopped, and glanced for a moment at Judge's face. Judge thought, I'm no one. I don't look like anyone you know. And . . . don't let *him* be here.

If he could take this risk, he could take any. Including the Morozov job. Walking into this bar was the most terrifying step he had taken in years. He felt his thundering heart grow steady in his chest.

"What may I get you, sir?" The manager spoke with a slight Haitian accent. He wore a small, elegant name pin that said BER-TRAND.

"I'd like a martini. I don't even know how to order one properly. Whatever is the most classic way, please. And with your best gin and whatever else is in it."

"Vermouth, sir."

"Yes, that. And olives, or lemon twist, or whatever. You pick for me."

"Very good, sir." Bertrand went to the bar.

Judge surveyed the room. In the back of the bar there was a staircase, roped off from the public. He had been trained to spot surveillance and he could see cameras, tiny, hidden, watching the bar. He moved his chair around the table to the optimum position to keep his face off tape. He wondered how long the tapes were kept before being erased with a new day's recording. *If he walks in . . .*

It was madness to come inside this bar. Yet so was the Morozov job. Sometimes you embraced the madness. He had, and it had made all the difference in his world.

He sat very still, watching the stairs for feet coming down them, but they remained empty.

He's not here. You've gotten this out of your system. Drink your drink, and never do this again. Ever.

Bertrand returned shortly, carrying a chilled martini with two olives speared.

Judge tasted it. Icy steel. "That is excellent," he said.

"Thank you, sir. Would you like to run a tab?"

"No, thanks. I'll pay my tab now."

Bertrand nodded and, a few moments later, brought Judge his bill and left it with a polite smile.

Judge turned his thoughts back to the proposal. He thought of various political assassinations through history. The Kennedys, Lincoln, Gandhi, Martin Luther King, Benazir Bhutto, Archduke Ferdinand and his wife, Sophie. Nearly all the assassins ended up dead or in prison. Even Gavrilo Princip, the archduke's killer, a teenager too young for the death penalty, rotted away in jail from sickness and malnutrition; he'd lost an arm to skeletal tuberculosis. Judge wondered if it was Princip's shooting arm that died before he did, because then there was some karma. And Princip had known, from his prison cell, that he'd caused the unprecedented suffering of World War I. Princip's cheap little bullet had claimed far more victims than the archduke and his wife. Judge might ignite a war, too, but he didn't think he'd get to ponder how he'd changed the fate of the world from a prison cell. He'd most likely be dead.

But he hated to think that he couldn't find a way.

To strike from a distance on American soil, via a rifle or a fired weapon, would be incredibly difficult. To strike close, with knife or gun, would be suicide. You'd have to penetrate that inner circle; then you'd have to vanish during the moment of greatest suspicion. His escape route would have to be laid carefully: not only a way to get physically away from the scene, but also a way to disappear. Multiple identities would need to be created — fallback upon fallback upon fallback — even more than he had now.

Twenty million dollars. But Mrs. Claybourne's client Firebird could eliminate him as well. He would be the world's greatest loose end. Judge would have to protect himself on every front.

His mind danced.

He drank the martini with slow appreciation. He would think about the problem purely as an intellectual exercise. But he could not let it distract him from tomorrow's job. He finished the drink and stared at the glass on the small granite-topped table, lost in thought. If he had left even two minutes earlier, perhaps he would not have gotten the inspiration. But then the loud foursome at the table next to him were talking about attending an off-Broadway revival of Shakespeare's *Julius Caesar* starring three famous film actors as Caesar, Brutus, and Mark Antony.

Judge had little interest in theater; he would rather read a play than sit in a darkened room with strangers. Crowds made him nervous when he didn't need them for cover. And people mentioning, even for a moment, a play in which a leader is murdered in the simplest of manners when Judge was puzzling out an impossible assassination — it struck him as a troubling omen. He left a handsome tip for Bertrand and headed out into the evening. Life roared all around him, and he was pondering death. Three minutes later, as he was walking through Bryant Park, the idle conversation of the theatergoers shook a thought loose in his head.

He saw, with the sudden certainty of the songwriter who hears in her head the first strains of a beautiful new melody, the beginnings of how it could be done.

2

"Where was he held captive? Answer me!" Sam Capra gripped the man's neck and held the combat knife to the man's throat.

The answer was a gasp. "The village doesn't even have a name anymore."

"Then the GPS coordinates. I want an exact location."

The man tried to jerk away from Sam's knife, reaching toward his own gun on the table. Sam lowered the knife — a 5 7/8-inch Böker Applegate-Fairbairn, double-edged — to the man's groin and he froze.

"I don't want to hurt you," Sam said, "but I will. I have very little to lose right now. You tell me the coordinates for this village."

The man whispered the coordinates.

"Thank you," Sam said. He heard a noise, feet outside the door. One was not often alone in the *katchi abadis* — the slums of Islamabad where thousands were crammed

27

and piled atop one another in dried-mud-and-stone hovels and makeshift shacks, criminals and refugees and outcasts packed together unwillingly. This was the Afghan Basti, a shantytown of thousands of escaped Afghans and poor Pakistanis. "The Brothers of the Mountain. Are they still using the village?"

"It's . . . it's a place to sleep, only, on a smuggling route. No one lives there. It's cursed."

"Why did you talk about the Brothers of the Mountain on your phone?"

"How did you know . . . ?"

"The American NSA has very big ears."

The man blinked as if he didn't understand. "The Brothers . . . They're not extremists. They're businessmen. Heroin."

Sam steadied the knife. The room was cramped, just a table and a chair and a small filthy stove. Two cots in the other room, buckets to carry water, and to Sam's surprise, a modest amount of heroin stored in the next building. These guys didn't live here; this was a working space to move cash and drugs. But there were lots of people nearby, and if the man yelled for help . . . Sam would have a very hard time getting out of the *katchi abadis* if this man's friends came to his aid. Most of the people in the

28

Afghan Basti were honest laborers just trying to survive and avoid deportation to Afghanistan. But many criminals, and worse, hid among them. A few weeks ago a Pakistani narcotics agent had been captured while undercover here, and tortured for days, left headless at the gates of the fences the government was building to keep the *katchi abadis* isolated from the rest of the city.

"Six years ago, were you there? The Brothers of the Mountain took two Americans. They killed them . . ."

Then a second man came through the doorway, his gun raised. Sam moved more quickly than the second man, who was pivoting, trying to get a bead on Sam in the dim candlelight. Sam whirled, the first man now his shield, the combat dagger back at the throat.

"Shoot him, Adnan," the first man urged. "Shoot him dead."

"Cooperate," Sam said, "and you both live. Don't, and you die. This is a simple choice."

"Let's all stay calm," Adnan said, teeth gritted. He kept trying to lock his aim on Sam's head, but Sam kept the first man positioned so he wasn't willing to take the chance. "Let him go."

Then Sam noticed the hat the man was wearing. It was a beret, with the blue Islamabad Territory Police badge stitched at the front — but riddled with bullet holes, ragged, and stained. An obscene and brutal fashion statement. I killed a policeman, it said.

"I will cut his throat," Sam said. "Put down your gun, raise your hands. I'll let you both live if you cooperate."

"Put down the knife," Adnan said. "Or I'll blow your brains out."

Sam let the blade bite into the man's throat, just enough to draw blood. "Put the gun down. I got what I came for, and now I'll go."

"You will die here," Adnan said. "It's just choosing how you die. Slow or fast."

"He'll die fast," Sam said. "Put down the gun."

Sam could see the decision play across Adnan's face: the certainty that even if he put the gun down, there was no way for Sam to get out of the Afghan Basti without being caught by Adnan's friends. So Adnan nodded, very slightly, toward the hostage and set the gun down on the table next to the doorway.

"Raise your hands, away from the gun," Sam ordered.

Adnan hesitated but finally did, his right hand against the wooden support frame that climbed to the ceiling, his left up in the air.

"He asked about two Americans, six years ago, in the Hindu Kush. Aid workers," the man Sam held said. "He wants to go to the dead village."

"The aid workers," Adnan said. "The two men. Yes."

Sam froze.

Adnan decided to press, to unnerve. "Ah. I wasn't there. Sorry. I only heard the stories. About how they cried, wept, begged for their lives . . . I don't think you'll easily make it there. I think you better let him go; otherwise, you will die. You have nowhere to go, much less that place." He tapped at the police beret, as if it evoked a memory.

Sam yanked the man off balance and threw the combat knife, straight like a spear, none of that showy spinning. It thunked hard into the wall, piercing Adnan's right hand to the wood, and he screamed. Sam set his feet, wrenched the man backward, and broke his neck. The man dropped soundlessly, eyes open and staring. Adnan kept screaming in agony and shock and didn't have the presence of mind to pull the knife out of his hand. Sam picked up Adnan's gun off the table and shot Adnan through the head.

It was over in ten seconds.

Voices raised in the neighboring shacks, men yelling. Sam slipped through the window. The skyline of the Afghan Basti was a jumble: stone huts of varying size, roofs mostly of dried straw, some of tin, haphazard wires strung along improvised, jigsaw streets. The air reeked of waste and garbage. Sam ran, jumping from roof to roof, aiming for the broad wooden planks that held the straw in place. If he missed . . . The night was falling, lights coming on in the more fortunate shacks.

A bullet zipped close to his ear.

He jumped, landing on a straw roof that parted under his weight. He fell onto a stone floor, an old man in the corner hollering in rapid Pashto. Sam scrambled out the door, desperate to get back onto the roofline and away from the crowds. In the street, people lined up with buckets at a single water faucet, some staring at him, others yelling and pointing, calling to his pursuers.

He ran through the street, past vendors, past old women, and vaulted up back onto the roof. The edge of the slum lay close, and he could see the cleared land where the authorities were laying out the frame of a massive fence, a wall to keep the poor refugees and the criminal and extremist elements away from the cleanly planned city of Islamabad. As if you could seal away darkness and despair as a cure.

On the roofline, on the higher, taller shacks ahead of him, lights gleamed as the sun faded below the horizon. Behind him, men roving on the rooftops, hunting him.

And he was silhouetted against the glow.

They opened fire, careless of the danger to others, intent on the kill. Bullets parted the air around his head. One light shattered just ahead of him. Sam hunkered low and ran, seeing a mass of cables ahead. They were tied to cars parked in a flat lot to his left. Much of the electricity here was run off automotive batteries. He grabbed the cables, yanking hard; a flash sparked, and the lights illuminating him went dark. He heard angry calls. He swung down the bunched cables, using them as a rope, stepped onto the roof of an idling car, and jumped to the ground.

An angry man tried to grab him, yelling in furious Pashto. Sam punched him hard and bolted for the open area where the fence was being slowly erected.

A soldier stopped him. Sam slipped him a paper with the stamp of the Pakistani interior secretary. The soldier let him pass, and Sam ran into the night.

A kilometer away on the road, a Mercedes pulled up to him and he got in.

"They're sending the police into the Afghan Basti," August Holdwine told him. "Well done, you."

"Don't," Sam said.

"Please tell me you got what you needed."

"I did. Thank you."

"Did you kill anybody?"

"Only the people who tried to kill me." Sam leaned back. His normally dirty-blond hair was dyed black, and he wore contacts to turn his eyes the rich dark hazel seen in many Afghan faces. "No one will know I was there."

"We don't need an incident. I called in every favor for you on this. Getting the NSA trace on the Brothers of the Mountain chatter, getting you that pass, letting you stay at a safe house . . ."

"These men knew where my brother was held. And . . . killed." He hadn't told August his suspicions that his brother was still alive. "It's in the Hindu Kush. So I need to get to Kabul. I assume the CIA would be willing to investigate a lead on two missing Americans."

August, Sam's oldest friend from his former days in the CIA, said nothing for a

34

minute. "I could call Bob Seaforth, but I heard he's leaving the CIA soon. He's in Kabul."

"Thank you." Sam stared out at the night as they drove through the carefully laid out streets of Islamabad, back toward a safe house in a wealthier district. "I think I've overstayed my welcome."

"I don't think you were at all welcome in the *katchi abadis,*" August said.

Danny, Sam thought. I'm going to find you. Dead or alive. For six years he'd thought his brother dead, until he'd found a burned file in an abandoned secret prison, and his brother's picture, time-stamped well after his supposed murder. He had told none of this to August, just that he had a lead on the group that had kidnapped and executed his brother.

It was only an hour-and-fifteen-minute flight from Islamabad to Kabul, but he knew that direct flights ran only five times a week, usually on Thursday and Sunday, and cancellations happened as a matter of course. After six years, he was so close, and any delay seemed agonizing, but he'd have to calm himself, spend the night here, and figure out his next move.

"You haven't mentioned your son," August said.

35

"Oh. Daniel's fine." Sam's voice was distant.

August glanced at him in the rearview mirror but said nothing.

At the safe house, Sam washed the black dye out of his hair, removed the dark contact lenses, restoring his eyes to their normal green color, and put the clothes he'd worn in a burn bag to be destroyed, so there would be no trace of the killer who came into the Afghan Basti. He thought about the two men he'd killed, that if they'd just not fought him he would have tied them up and let them go. About why people chose to die, why people chose to live. His brother was a man the world thought dead and yet . . . there was a chance.

August came to the door as he was getting dressed. "Seaforth said come to Kabul and you two can talk. Frankly, I'm surprised."

"I'm still a pariah to a lot of the agency," Sam said. Being accused of treason, and your wife actually committing it, were bad for the career. His name being cleared had not changed his refusal to rejoin the agency's Special Projects team, a secret group focused on fighting overseas organized crime where it threatened national security.

"If he wants to help me, he must have his

36

own reasons." Sam expected the CIA to take his information, push him aside, and handle it themselves. But the fact he had once been wrongly accused of treason and forced out of the agency gave him a certain traction in his dealings with them. They owed him. But that, he knew, would not last forever, and their help depended on the capriciousness of the person he approached. Bob Seaforth was a good man, but he was not someone Sam considered a friend eager to do him favors. "But if he doesn't help me, I'll go into the mountains alone."

"What about your son, Sam?"

"I told you. Daniel's fine."

"He won't be if you end up dead in a Pakistani slum or a Taliban village," August said. "Daniel already lost his mom. I know you want to find your brother, but he's likely dead and if he isn't . . . Well, he doesn't need you."

"What's that supposed to mean?"

"You have a wonderful kid at home who needs his father." There was a steel in August's tone that Sam had never heard. "A kid who's been through so much . . . He can't lose you."

"I'll be careful."

"This is not healthy."

Sam turned and stared at him. "If it was

your brother, you'd have to look for him."

"If it was my brother, I'd tell the CIA what I knew and let them find him."

Sam finished dressing. "I have my reasons."

"You need to worry about being a father more than a brother," August said.

"Look, I appreciate your help . . ."

"And this is the cost of it. You, listening to me. Have you told your parents or Leonie that you're looking for Danny?"

"I can't. Not until I know."

"Where do they think you are, Sam?"

"I told them I was checking on my bars in Europe." Sam's voice went flat.

"So you're lying to your parents, to the woman who takes care of your child. What do you think your parents would say about you being over here where they already lost him?"

"I . . . I have to do this. I have to find Danny."

"Why? If he's dead you can't bring him back. And if he's alive all these years, why hasn't he contacted you?" August let the awful question hang in the air, unanswered. "Maybe you can't bring him back either way."

Sam didn't look at August. He just stared at the floor. Finally he said, "I know what

I'm doing. The sooner I find him, the sooner I'm home with Daniel."

"Grab your bag," August said. "I'll drive you to the airport now."

3

Afghanistan

The MI-8T helicopter rose into the bright
blue sky from Bagram Air Force Base and
roared east. Its tail markings indicated it
belonged to a humanitarian relief agency
based in Morocco, which it did not. Inside
the security team of ten soldiers watched
their young passenger, sitting in the back of
the chopper, staring at his phone. His face
was gaunt, as though whatever played on
the screen was a private nightmare.

He was a mystery.

Sergeant Will Allen, the squad leader,
watched the young passenger out of the
corner of his eye. He guessed the passenger
was in his midtwenties. They'd been roused
to take on this unexpected escort duty on a
day they thought they'd have off to watch
movies or read books or exercise. Instead
they would now have tomorrow off, and
spend today flying Seaforth, a senior intel-

ligence guy, and this young passenger out to a "Sleepy Hollow" — an abandoned village in the mountains of the Hindu Kush. It should be a "milk run," an easy, no-stress operation, but Allen knew that milk runs could turn deadly. You had to expect the unexpected.

This passenger was the unexpected.

Allen played a game in his head, and he thought the rest of the squad did the same: trying to figure out who the young passenger was and if today's trip was another example of "combat tourism," where they escorted a dignitary to a safe, insulated spot far from danger where he inspected the locale while wrapped in a bubble of protection, had his picture taken, and then went home to tell his audience that he understood the situation in Afghanistan, having been "on the ground." Such VIPs were usually older. And this guy wasn't a famous actor or musician here to entertain the troops. He seemed too young to be in Congress. Maybe an aide to someone important? Allen decided he wasn't a media guy because they — newspaper reporters, photographers, TV hosts — always mentioned who they worked for, and often wore a bulletproof vest with Press on it. So maybe an administration appointee, Allen thought, from a think tank or a university, some desk-bound geek who had read books and blogs on terrorism or the Islamic world or Afghanistan's endless misery but never risked the reality. Those guys were nicknamed "Fobbits" because they never left the Forward Operating Base, lest their safety or opinions be challenged by reality.

After the passenger's initial firm hand-shake and hello to each squad member, thanking each of them for his help today, he hadn't tried to make small talk or buddy up to the soldiers like a guy who had never known a moment's danger sometimes tried to do. The passenger carried a reinforced Pelican backpack, the kind with metal plating to make it crushproof and waterproof. Maybe a photographer? He wore a dark-navy baseball cap with no insignia. Lean, with darkish-blond hair, a boyish face, but a gaze that seemed older than his years. As they had departed Bagram he sat silently, staring ahead, not even making small talk with Seaforth. After a few minutes he took out his phone and seemed to be studying something on the screen, his mouth a tight line of anger.

Allen was impressed with how clean and nice the MI-8T was on the inside. The CIA guys always did it right. He asked Seaforth,

"Where are we headed, sir?" as the intel chief came back from conferring with the pilots.

Bob Seaforth was fiftyish, thick hair graying, with the stern face of a demanding schoolmaster. He had been at Bagram several times before, although Allen was unsure of his exact title or area of responsibility. Did he work for the CIA, or one of the many other intel agencies? He kept those details close. Seaforth surveyed the squad. Allen saw the young passenger put away his phone, and he gave Allen, after a moment, a polite nod.

Seaforth said, "Gentlemen. Several years ago, two young American humanitarian workers were kidnapped near Kandahar. Danny Capra, the son of longtime relief workers who'd served all over the world, and Zalmay Quereshi, an American whose parents emigrated from Afghanistan after King Zahir was deposed in 1973. Both were twenty-three years of age. Zalmay Quereshi was fluent in Dari, Pashto, and Arabic and worked for charitable organizations as a translator. Capra and Quereshi were college friends. No ransom demands were made to the government or their families" — here Allen saw Seaforth glance at the passenger — "and our sources could not determine which tribal group had taken them. A few weeks later, a video was sent to the American embassy, showing the two prisoners and a few men in balaclavas. Only Capra spoke on the video; Quereshi was gagged and blindfolded."

Allen glanced at the passenger. He sat, listening, staring at the floor of the helicopter.

"The group who had taken them called themselves the Brothers of the Mountain, a group that we had not heard of before, and haven't heard much about since. The speaker briefly demanded that all Allied forces leave Afghanistan. Danny Capra gave a short statement echoing that demand. Then his throat was cut" — Seaforth's tone lowered — "and he was pushed to the floor, out of camera range, and decapitated. The executioner momentarily raised Capra's head, but with its face turned away from the camera. Quereshi's throat was then cut and he was shoved out of camera range. Their bodies were never recovered."

The squad was quiet.

Seaforth glanced back at the passenger, whose face betrayed no emotion. "This is Sam." Sam nodded again at the men. "He brought us new information last night as to the location where the two men were held.

First break in the case ever."

"How do you break a case like this?" Allen asked. He didn't expect an answer.

At this, Sam, the silent man with the boyish face, looked up at Allen and met his gaze. "With a Böker Applegate-Fairbairn combat knife."

One of the younger soldiers made a kind of half-laugh, half-cough that he smothered in the sudden silence. They had seen civilians try to impress soldiers with their toughness, and fail. Sam said his words in a tone that did not try to impress. He had answered the question. Allen, though, gave him a slight smile.

Seaforth said, "The NSA picked up phone chatter in Pakistan, mentioning both the Brothers of the Mountain and this location. We're going to a long-abandoned village in the Hindu Kush. For a number of reasons of state and national security, this excursion is classified, and you will not talk about it." His gaze met each of theirs. "That's why we're flying on a helicopter marked as belonging to a humanitarian agency. That's why the records will still show you all were off duty today. You were chosen because you're a top squad, and your leader vouched for you all that you could keep your mouths shut until the time comes, hopefully very

soon, when this can be spoken of. Gentlemen, we need to bring these two Americans
home." Again he glanced over at Sam. "I
can't give you orders, but that is what I need
you to do, and that is what I respectfully
ask of you."

"Then that's what we'll do," Allen said.
"And we'll keep our mouths shut."

The squad seemed to gather themselves
as one, with sudden purpose and focus. So
this wasn't combat tourism. This was important work now.

"So this is to recover the victims' bodies,
if possible?" Allen asked. He wondered why
the recovery of long-dead prisoners had to
be top secret. This would be big news back
in America.

"This is to take an initial look. Find
evidence to confirm the story. If we find the
bodies we'll bring them back today. I had
the appropriate forensic gear loaded on the
copter. If not we'll bring another team
tomorrow. Your job, gentlemen, is to secure
the village and to protect this young man
while he gathers the evidence we need to
find these Americans."

Allen glanced again at Sam. He seemed
awfully young to be an intelligence agency
field operative — Allen thought of such
people as older, in their forties, a bit world-

weary and grizzled — but in a world of suicide bombers and cyberhackers and ever-younger and more vicious drug lords, perhaps the agency needed a kid like Sam, a peer to the new, younger, bolder breed of criminal. He was lean and spare, but Sam had an intensity about him that made Allen think he'd be good in a fight. He wondered what kind of hellhole this kid had gone into to find the execution locale. Prying information from hostile Afghans or Pakistanis was a difficult and delicate job. But this kid had done it. Allen's respect for him, and curiosity about him, inched upward. He wondered what happened to the man who had faced Sam's blade. This Sam looked like he might flick the knife over a throat and not blink.

The helicopter roared over a mountain pass. A teenage boy looked up from the shade of overhanging rock, where he'd been reading the book his uncle brought him back from Pakistan. He'd come up to the pass to get away from the nagging of his grandfather. It was a beautiful, clear day and he loved the quiet, which had been broken only by the groan of the wind and the sound of the approaching helicopter. He raised the binoculars he wore and read the markings. A relief agency from Morocco. He wondered who they were coming to help. Then he watched its descent, lowered the binoculars, and hurried down the trail toward his own village. His uncle had given strict orders that he be told of any strangers or visitors heading toward the village of ghosts. He stopped only to reposition the AMD-65 rifle he wore on his shoulder. It had once belonged to an Afghan policeman his uncle had killed. The boy eased the weapon to the center of his back so he could run faster.

The helicopter pilots took no chances; they descended toward the village in a "yank and bank," a stomach-churning, nose-high descent to minimize the risk of taking a shoulder-fired missile. The helicopter corkscrewed downward and Sam fought not to vomit.

The MI-8T settled on a flat clearing above the village and the squad disembarked, dividing into two teams. Allen told Seaforth and Sam to stay aboard the copter with the pilots until they had done a recon and secured the area. The soldiers were armed with M4 carbines, one man on each team lugging an Mk 19 grenade launcher.

There were outposts like this scattered throughout the Hindu Kush, built on the steep slopes, the roofs of one stone structure serving as the terrace of the next one up. Sometimes such settlements were used seasonally, depending on how high up the mountains they were. The soul of a village was its people, and people had long left this place. Maybe no one cared about it anymore. Or, Allen thought sourly, maybe it was cursed, blighted. Which would take some real doing, in this country of unending grief.

The squad worked methodically through the deserted village, down the stairstep pile of buildings, the mountain air cold and sharp against their skin. Allen couldn't help wondering if they'd find headless corpses in one of the rooms. But they didn't.

After the sweep, Allen returned and gestured Sam and Seaforth out of the copter. "Sleepy Hollow is both hollow and sleepy," he said. "No one's here, and it doesn't look like anyone's been here in a long while. Where to?"

Sam said, "I just want to walk through all of it first. Then if there's a room with red-painted walls —"

"We found that," Allen said. "Follow me."

They traipsed through the village, which had at most fifteen buildings, with one steep road down the mountain snaking through them, some falling in disrepair, others holding as firm as the mountains themselves. Sam breathed in the air extra hard, as though he could catch a scent, breathe in a memory.

"Why is this place abandoned? Do we know?" Allen asked.

"Well, war, generally," Seaforth said. "But there was also an accusation made long ago against the village that they had allowed Soviet prisoners to escape, to buy their freedom, during the war with the Russians. More likely the Russians forced their cooperation under threat of death. Regardless, the nearby villages and the rebel forces did not take any news of collaboration kindly."

"So they killed the whole village? Even if the village had no choice?" Allen asked.

Seaforth shrugged. "Yes, they did. This is a bad place; you can feel it."

"It was used as a way station in smuggling," Sam said. "Opium."

"Well, there's no drugs here now," Allen said. He pointed at one of the bigger intact buildings. "The room with the red wall is there."

In the front room in the building, one wall was painted red. The red of blood, the red of fear and terror. Old, abandoned brackets were mounted on the ceiling.

"That's where they put the lights for the

cameras," Sam said quietly to Seaforth. And for the first time, Allen heard the kid's voice shake. He reached out and touched the kid's shoulder. He did it before he thought about it. Sam looked back at the soldier with gratitude and nodded, and the steel came back into his gaze. And he went to work.

Sam went to the wall. Allen followed, stepping onto a thick plastic sheet that covered the floor, anchored into place by four heavy hooks in each corner. Allen wondered why someone had laid a carpet of plastic down over the dirt. Why did dirt need to be protected?

Bullet holes marred the red wall; Sam, aloud, counted four.

"I thought you said they cut their throats," Allen said.

Sam knelt in front of the bullet holes and he opened his rigid Pelican backpack. He pulled out a camera and photographed the wall. Allen glanced down into the backpack: a camera, a ruler, a heavy knife, an assortment of brown paper bags and envelopes, a marker pen, a laptop with a jumble of cords, and what looked like a medical kit. Sam dug out the bullets from the wall with a tool that looked like a tweezer and, to Allen's surprise, he put each bullet into a plain coin

51

envelope. He wrote with the marker on each.

Then he stood and paced off the steps from the wall. He stopped and looked at his phone's screen. Over the kid's shoulder, Allen could see the execution video playing: another young man, blindfolded, a knife at his throat, a few men standing behind him.

In front of a red wall, with four bullet holes in it. The shooting had happened before the execution.

Allen glanced at Seaforth but the older man just watched the kid. He got up again, looked at the room. As if calculating, putting people in it who were no longer there, watching shadows, watching ghosts.

He went into the back room. Concrete had been poured on the floor, and there were three sets of chains leading from the center of the room, shackles at the end.

"Three prisoners?" Seaforth said.

"Accomodations for three. Doesn't mean there were three." Sam took photos from every angle. Then he walked the perimeter of the walls and knelt by a stone on the far side. He ran fingers along the stone and then he gasped and stopped. He took a picture.

Allen and Seaforth stepped closer and Allen saw initials scratched into the stone:

DWC. ZAQ.

"Are those initials . . . ," Seaforth began.

"Yes. Danny's and Zalmay's." For a moment he leaned against the wall, as if exhausted. They had tried to leave a trace of themselves here. A sign. He took pictures of the initials, forcing his hands to be steady.

"Sir?" one of the soldiers said, coming into the room. "We just found something, in another building. You better come see."

"American soldiers, at least ten of them," the boy's uncle said. A team of his men were close behind him as they peered down into the village.

"So not a relief agency," one of the men said. "Unless they are checking it out to set up camp?"

"Not how they operate," the uncle said.

"Why are they here?" the boy asked. "Pretending to be something they're not?"

No one answered him, and this stung. He thought it a fair question. And after a few minutes his uncle moved forward, the men following, fanning out as they had practiced in case they ever needed to reclaim the village of ghosts.

It was a hole in one building's floor, covered with a thick, worn wooden door. The door had been made flush with the floor and Sam saw strands of cloth caught in its hinges. A carpet that had covered the door had been pulled to the side.

"I pulled the carpet," the soldier said. "It just seemed odd, that everything else in the room was gone . . . but that the carpet was still here."

"Check for booby traps," Seaforth said. "I want to open that door."

The soldiers did, with care, and found no telltale signs of wires or triggers along the door's edge. Allen waited for Sam to go outside but he didn't move from his position. In fact, he knelt to pull the door open, waiting for a nod from the men checking it for traps.

The door creaked open. Stairs led down into darkness. Allen flashed lights into the pit. It was a room, a large one.

They went down the stairs. Sam ran his flashlight along the shelves and froze. On the shelf lay what looked like strips of skin.

Sam picked up one of the strips. It looked like Caucasian skin, gummed with blood. It was horrifyingly realistic. He studied it.

"What is that?" Allen asked.

"I think it's latex," Sam said. He put it in one of his brown envelopes, sealed it, and marked it with a pen. On the table lay a

54

scattering of what looked like hair, and the hacked remains of a wig of dark hair.

"Wigs are generally forbidden in Islam," Seaforth said.

"Yes," Sam said. "If made of human hair, or if the purpose of wearing one is disguise or deceit." He put the strands in a brown envelope and marked it with the pen.

He put the flashlight up to the top shelf. Heads, molded out of plastic, a half dozen of them, empty of wigs. Sightless eyes stared back at Sam and Allen. They were not crude models, but carefully sculpted to look realistic in proportion and with a range of skin colors. Sam felt cold. The heads were of very high quality, the type that might be used in Hollywood special effects. They had been carefully crafted. One had a false neck with a narrow tube underneath it, dried a dark red inside the plastic.

"What is this place?" Allen quietly asked. "How did a guy in the middle of nowhere have stuff like this?"

"It's a theater," Sam said. Below was a box, with a return address in Pakistan scrawled on a label. The name on the address was Mirjan Shah. He pulled the box toward him. It held recordable DVDs and their cases. The DVDs were still on a spool. Sam photographed the box and the address.

"Can someone look at these and see if they're blank or recorded?" Sam asked. One of the soldiers took the box back toward the copter, where a laptop awaited. Sam ran a finger along the shelf. Dust and dirt.

"A laptop," Seaforth said. He pointed to a table. Sam picked up the laptop, an old Windows model. The hard drive had been removed from its bay. Nothing to be recovered. Sam slipped the laptop into the backpack.

A soldier who'd been stationed outside entered the building. His face was pale under his helmet. "At the back of the village is a shed, and beyond it are mounds. Marked. I think they're graves. Two of them."

And at the word *two,* Allen saw something break in Sam's face.

The mounds, barely evident except to an eye looking for graves, lay fifty yards behind the village. They had been marked with a simple wood stake, weathered and worn.

Sam wondered if he was standing on his brother's grave. All the hope bled out of him. What if there was another reason Danny's picture had been in that prison file in a forgotten corner of the Brazilian jungle? What if he had never been in Brazil? But

56

only here, buried in this alien, lonely quiet?

Allen brought two shovels from the copter. He ordered his squad to keep a perimeter up; this was still a very dangerous place to be, and they wanted no surprises.

"Sam, let me," Seaforth said, reaching for one of the shovels.

"No," Sam said. "I'll do it." Then Allen and Sam rolled up their sleeves and dug.

The graves were shallow and Sam carefully removed the soil. A musty scent rose from the graves, despite the dry, cold air. Allen braced himself for a stench but it wasn't ripe; it was more like the smell of rich dirt.

Under the final layer of dirt lay a cocoon of cloth, spanning the close-together graves. Dried blood marred the canvas.

Sam and Allen lifted the canvas and eased it onto the ground. "Let's unroll it . . . ," Seaforth said.

They did, slowly. Two bodies lay inside, mummified by the arid mountain, with the waxy decay of adipocere present on the faces. They looked misshapen, nightmares of death. The faces were not recognizable.

"They both have their heads," Sam said. "Those aren't the clothes my bro . . ." He took a steadying breath, turning his face into the cool mountain breeze. "Those aren't the clothes that Danny Capra was wearing in the video." His voice was steady again. He knelt by his trusty Pelican and put on latex gloves.

"You're right," Seaforth said. "They're not. Is one . . ."

"I think this one is Zalmay," Sam said. The clothes appeared to be the same as those Zalmay wore in the video. The throat, even decayed, bore the mark of a slash.

The other corpse was also dressed. Sam eased open the shirt the corpse wore and cut away the bottom of it. He inspected a care label and then placed it into another evidence envelope and marked it. Then he took the scalpel and prodded at the corpse's stomach, where he'd pulled the shirt away.

Seaforth watched. "Bullet holes, maybe?"

Sam gave no answer. He cut an inch away from the hole; Allen tried not to gag. Sam dug out a bullet. He put it in another coin envelope.

"Here. Shot to death. And that looks like a knife wound in the shoulder."

"Maybe they were wounded when they were captured," Allen said.

"The knife wound that appears to be missing," Sam said, "is a cut throat." Sam removed an RSID — a rapid stain identification — blood detection kit from the

Pelican. He clipped off a bit of the fabric of the canvas, using a disposable scalpel from the kit, and applied the reagent to it. He stood and measured the canvas with his eye. Then he looked again at the screen of the smartphone, backed up the video. Stared again.

"What is it?" Allen asked.

"This canvas was on the floor in the video. It must have been over the plastic." He moved to the opposite corner of the canvas and repeated the RSID blood test. "It'll tell me in ten minutes if this is human blood," he said.

"Is there much doubt?" Allen asked.

"Yes," Sam said. "There is." He sank to his knees by the grave, his face grimed with dirt. "He's not here."

Seaforth glanced at Allen. "We have body bags in the copter. Would you please have the men bring two? We'll bag them and then go. I don't think we should stay much longer."

Allen stepped away and spoke into his mike. Two dead bodies, but clearly . . . one that was expected to be here wasn't.

They collected the bodies, zipping them into thick cadaver bags with fabric handles on the sides. Sam sealed them with tamper-resistant zipper pulls that would maintain a chain of custody. The grave, empty, looked forlorn. He looked at the RSID blood test results. One sample confirmed human blood; the other sample said it was not human blood. One man had bled on that canvas; another had bled fake blood.

Zalmay was dead, and Sam's brother wasn't here.

The execution video — at least Danny's part — was a fake. Why did the extremists kill Zalmay, but not Danny? Why make the world think Danny Capra was dead?

The soldiers were carrying the bodies toward the copter, Allen and Sam and Seaforth following, when the thud sounded behind them.

Allen turned and saw it: an RPG-7 grenade, skidding across the dirt toward them. But it didn't explode.

The soldiers reacted as one, those not carrying the body bags raising their weapons and firing, calling out to each other, laying down suppressive rounds. Sam could see the militants, above the landing zone, trying to work their way down the jagged rocks above the village. They retreated as the Americans responded with force. The man holding the grenade launcher retreated behind a shelf of stone. The others were armed with old Kalashnikovs, sputtering and roaring.

The men carrying the two body bags ran, drawing weapons, covered by the rest of the squadron. Allen started to shove Sam and Seaforth — they were civilians, after all — toward the chopper, covering them. Sam drew his Glock 9 millimeter.

"Run, just run!" Allen ordered.

The squad, Seaforth, and Sam clambered aboard the MI-8T. The copter lifted up from the dusty ground.

"Missile!" the crew chief yelled and Sam saw flares streaming out from below the helicopter in case it wasn't another RPG but a laser-guided weapon. But the flares would do nothing to protect against a rocket-propelled grenade. The copter veered violently in evasion, throwing Sam into Seaforth. The body bags, unsecured, slid hard along the floor. The silence was intense: no one screaming, every man bracing himself for the impact.

And then crowding into Sam's thoughts, his son's smiling face. He closed his eyes.

The evasion worked: the copter climbed hard, aimed west, and steadied. Allen took command, making sure every man was uninjured and had his gear. The copter appeared undamaged, but it would have to be thoroughly checked on arrival.

"Just mountain punks," Allen said to Sam and Seaforth. "They like to shoot at anything." He sounded far calmer than he felt. "They know this isn't a military copter. Our job is to get you back safely, and these bodies. Otherwise we might have stayed a bit longer, made some new friends."

Sam nodded and he and Seaforth secured the body bags. Sam kept his hand in his pocket. He had one more job to do.

The boy watched the flares dissipate, the American copter speeding away. His uncle gathered the men. One was hurt, a bullet through the shoulder, but he would survive. They marched back to their own village in silence. At home the boy told his aunt of their adventure. She glanced at her husband.

"We ran them off!" the boy said with glee.

"They dug up bodies? Why?" the aunt asked.

"Maybe their people," the boy said.

"Maybe," his uncle said. He turned to the aunt. "Bring me the box in the cupboard. At the top."

She did and he opened it. A satellite phone, with instructions that had been left for him, a preprogrammed number to call, with an offer of money. The uncle put the phone in its charger and let it power up, and then he dialed the one number in it.

In case anyone ever came to the village of ghosts, there was a man who wanted to know.

The ride back to Bagram was quiet. Sam returned from the back of the helicopter, where he had excused himself to have a moment to gather his thoughts. He handed Seaforth a smartphone with a scuffed protective case. "Is this yours, Bob? I found it on the floor back there. You must have lost it during the evasion attempt."

"Oh, thanks," Seaforth said. In the chaos he hadn't noticed he didn't have the phone in his pocket. He tucked it back into his jacket. Sam sank onto the seat next to him and clutched the Pelican backpack close to his chest, as if overwhelmed in thought.

"Sam," Seaforth whispered. "Your brother . . ."

"My brother is alive," Sam said. "The question is why? What did the Brothers of the Mountain hope to gain from faking his death? They needed the world to think he was dead." They? Or Danny? The question stabbed at his heart.

"Then they had a use for him."

Sam said nothing. The bullet marks in the wall. The latex shreds that looked like skin, the blood that maybe wasn't blood, the clipped hair left behind on the floor. The elaborate heads straight from a special effects studio. A hard drive taken, without its laptop. A box of DVDs, proven to be blank, abandoned in a place that barely had electricity. But there had been a shipping label on the box. Mirjan Shah. It was a thread. The truth was hidden in these impossible clues. Forensics tests would tell him more.

"If he's alive, he let you think he was dead." Seaforth could not imagine putting his family through that kind of hell.

"Maybe he had a good reason," Sam said.

"I cannot imagine what that would be."

"I think one is Zalmay," Sam said. "The other one . . . The clothing tag on the shirt is written in Russian. Why was a Russian here?"

"Another captive? We'll search the records, but I don't recall Russians being taken at the time Zalmay and Danny were. The Russians stayed out of Afghanistan at that point. Maybe they were old clothes. Prisoners don't get to choose what to wear."

"It's odd his captors had Danny talk, isn't it?" Sam said.

"Why?"

"Well, Zalmay was of Afghan descent. His family had fled Afghanistan, and then he'd returned with the conquering Americans. A traitor, right? A symbol they could have used. Yet they gagged him." Sam stared at his feet. "You would think their ire, their hatred, would be at him. Not Danny."

Seaforth said, "A lot can happen in those weeks of captivity."

"I once spoke to a former CIA ops chief who claimed my brother's execution wasn't what it seemed to be. He said, and these are his exact words, 'Your brother. In Afghanistan. Wasn't a bunch of Taliban hash smugglers that killed him. It was a Nine Suns job. Initiation . . .' "

"Nine Suns doesn't exist anymore. It fell apart." Nine Suns had once been a dangerous syndicate of top criminal bosses around the world, working together when needed for common purpose against law enforcement, the people behind the destruction of Sam's life in the CIA, who had kidnapped his family and framed him for treason. Sam had — eventually — rescued his infant son from them and exacted a devastating revenge. "And that man was trying to cut a deal with you. He'd have told you any lie to get your cooperation."

Sam glanced at him and Seaforth said, "Yeah, I know about what you went through with certain rogue elements in the agency.

I'm sorry."

"If you're sorry, then help me, Bob. I want to talk to the analyst who was responsible for intelligence in this area during the time Danny and Zalmay were taken."

"She's retired now. The Magpie — that was her nickname. Margaret Granger. She lives in New York now. I'll ask her to meet with you. But what she shares with you, Sam . . . it remains confidential."

"Of course. Thank you."

"We'll send the remains to my labs in New York; we'll put a rush on them. I'll escort the evidence there myself." Bob Seaforth was the Eastern European chief for Special Projects, the shadowy division of the agency that Sam had once worked for. "I assume you'll come with me?"

"I'll follow you in a day or so. I'm going to Budapest and then New York."

"Why Budapest?"

"I have another lead there. I can keep working while you're running tests. I can't lose momentum on this."

Seaforth studied Sam. "You thought we might not find your brother's body there, didn't you? This isn't a total surprise."

Sam said nothing.

"We did you this favor, Sam, because we owed you and you brought us this new

66

information. Exactly what kind of work are you doing now?"

"I own some bars. I'm out of the spy game."

"But you got this village as the location. You found information. How?"

"You don't want to know. Truly."

"Hmmm." Seaforth didn't sound convinced. "But if your brother's alive . . ." Seaforth's voice was cold. "It might not be a happy family reunion. One wonders."

"Wonders what?"

"What happened to Danny Capra here during his captivity. What he became. What they made him into. Why he wanted you, and the world, to think he was dead."

Sam had no answer; he stared out the window.

When they landed, Allen told Sam he had to go file a report, since they had been fired upon. Seaforth told him he didn't. There would be no report, not yet. After a moment Allen nodded and the squad headed back to their quarters. Allen stayed behind and offered Sam his hand. Sam shook it.

"Whoever you're looking for, Sam, I hope you find him. I can tell you can't talk about it. But I wish you luck."

"Thanks. Where do you hail from, Sergeant?"

"New York City. The Bronx."

"There's a bar near Bryant Park, in Manhattan. The Last Minute. I own it. When you're home you go there, ask for Bertrand, tell him Sam sent you. He'll give you drinks on the house and if I'm there, and I often am, I'll tell you the whole story. If I know it by then."

Allen nodded and walked toward the command post. Sam watched him go. *And what story will you tell him? You have no idea how this will end — and you're not even sure how it begins.*

4

Long Island

The next morning, Judge followed his two targets from JFK Airport to a small town on Long Island's interior, quiet, moneyed. He would have liked more time to study them and their habits before striking, but Mrs. Claybourne had insisted he come back from Copenhagen early, before the Germans arrived, presumably to make this grandiose offer of the Morozov hit. And the money was good for dealing with these two targets. The two men stopped in front of a small German-themed bakery on the town's main street. Judge watched them drive down the street; he didn't follow. They turned onto the street that led toward the address Mrs. Claybourne had given him.

He turned the opposite way on the street, in his mirror seeing the men walk into the house with their pastry box.

He parked one street over, in front of a

house under heavy renovation. The work crew was not on duty. That would not raise suspicion, a car close to a house where a contractor or a new owner might be visiting.

He walked past the residence; it was a nice, large house and it made Judge wonder if the neighbors knew how the targets had paid for the hardwoods, the vaulted ceilings, the elaborate stone walkway.

In the window he could see them talking, laughing, glad that their travel was over. One glancing over his shoulder, toward the back of the house, laughing again. Answering someone. Judge stepped back where he couldn't be seen. Placed his earbud in his ear, dialed Mrs. Claybourne.

"Problem?"

"I think there's another person in the target house. Aborting."

"Do not abort."

"It could be an innocent."

"There are no innocents in that house. Do not abort. There are three targets. You will be paid accordingly."

Why didn't she warn him of this before? He felt anger well up in him and he pushed it down. *Do the job.*

Inside the house he could hear loud chatting, gestures: they were talking European soccer.

He slid a lock pick into the back door. Mrs. Claybourne had gotten him the house plans from an archived web page from when it had been sold months ago. There was a mudroom, then a laundry room, then the large, expansive den where the targets waited, and to the right was a big kitchen. He could smell coffee brewing. The other person, if there was one, was in the kitchen.

He pulled a woolen mask from his pocket and lowered it over his face.

The door opened. No alarm sounded. He slid the lock pick back into his pocket and pulled out his suppressor-capped gun. He went into the mudroom, tidy, scented of cleanser. Then the laundry room. It smelled of soap and mint. The washer rumbled. Laundry from their travels already being done.

Laughter from the den, the murmur of television.

He stepped into the den. The first target had his back to the room, watching a recorded soccer match on the television. In the kitchen, a woman's voice asked, in German, "Boys, do you want any more coffee?"

And the two men both said, *"Nein"* as one, in bored voices, the way that brothers

71

might, although Judge knew they were not brothers.

The second target glanced over, saw Judge, and opened his mouth to speak.

Judge fired, drilling a 9-millimeter bullet an inch behind the man's ear, another through the neck. The other target had risen and turned, and Judge hit another sweet spot, the medulla oblongata. He fell before he could even scream.

Six seconds, relatively quiet. The soccer game was punctuated by cheering for a goal.

Silence from the kitchen. Caution made him position himself off the entrance to the kitchen, against the wall. He saw the gun first, as she headed through; she must have kept a weapon in the kitchen. *Well, they were hired killers. Why not?*

He grabbed the gun — it was cold, as if it had been in the freezer — and yanked her forward, hammering a blow on the side of her head. She sprawled on the couch, whirling to face him. Eyes wide in shock, but not frozen with fear.

"I'll do the job," she said in English. She repeated it, first in perfect Russian, and then in German.

He froze.

"I'll do the job," she repeated. "I'll find others who are willing to tackle it."

He stared at her, not answering. He heard the ever-polite tones of Mrs. Claybourne: *We approached another professional assassin. She and her team thoroughly studied the situation, but she could not see a way to it being done.*

This wasn't just a hit. It was housekeeping.

"The job?" he said. "Morozov."

"Yes. OK, look, I'll do it. I'll do it for half the price."

"I'm not in charge of negotiations," he said. "What's your name?"

"Marianne."

He'd heard rumors of her. German killer for hire, known for training younger men and women as her backup team, then taking a cut of their earnings when they went solo for the first five years. She supposedly called her charges her "kids." Never arrested. She was too good.

"The job is difficult, but I'll find a way," she said. "I have all the research still on my laptop."

He glanced toward the laptop, on the coffee table, and she hurled herself toward one of the men. He didn't hesitate; he shot her, once. She sprawled, her furious expression slackening. He checked her for a pulse — gone — then searched the man she'd reached toward. He had a Glock in his belt.

This was what happened if you declined the world's most dangerous job. You declined to live.

He called Mrs. Claybourne back and touched his earpiece. "It's done." He removed his mask.

"Three?"

"Three."

"There's a laptop there. Retrieve it for me," she said.

"I've decided I'll take the big job." He walked out of the back of the house with the laptop, jumped into the neighbor's backyard, and went out onto the street toward his car.

"I'll tell Firebird that you're a go," she said. "Crack the laptop. There should be information there that's useful to you." She paused. "I hope you have a better imagination than Marianne and her team."

He hung up.

I need to know who Firebird is, he thought. I need to be able to protect myself better than Marianne and her assistants. His hands were steady as he put them on the steering wheel to head back to Brooklyn.

Back at the small apartment Mrs. Claybourne kept for him in Brooklyn, he turned on the news. There was no report yet of a triple homicide in Long Island. Marianne's team probably did not socialize at all with the neighbors. The bodies might not be found for days. He left the news on. In case the story broke quickly, in case someone had seen him leaving in the morning quiet.

He showered, came out and watched twenty more minutes of news that did not mention the killings, then crawled into bed and slept for a few hours.

He awoke. The decision, now made, energized him. He could do this. He would.

He opened up the stolen laptop. It was passworded. He powered up his own laptop, plugged in a flash drive loaded with a password cracker, and modified its parameters to include variants of German words. He slipped the flash drive into the stolen laptop's port and let the cracking program begin to batter against its defenses. He made a late lunch, an omelet and hash browns and strong coffee. He finished eating and sat on the bed and began to think hard on the kernel of the idea he'd gotten when he'd left The Last Minute. Julius Caesar. Morozov. He closed his eyes. He sat in total silence. He felt no urge to talk or check his phone or surf the Internet or watch TV. His stillness was remarkable and frightening.

In his mind he began to build plans. Tearing them down, tossing them aside, beginning again when they did not satisfy. He did not hear the New York traffic, the laughter in the hallway, the distant honk of a taxi. His thoughts consumed him like fire.

When the password program breached the laptop's defense and beeped, he opened his eyes, stretched, and then started to read all the research on Morozov and his circle that Marianne had done, to see if his plan could stand up to reality.

A chiming alert from his phone disturbed him. He checked it, as he received very few calls. It was an automated notice, telling him that a message had arrived at a particular voice mail account he had set up years ago. He accessed it and listened to a man from Afghanistan describe the arrival of a squad of Americans at the village of ghosts.

He listened to the message five times. He wired money to an account in a bank in Kabul for the caller. Then he resumed his quiet sitting, but his heart pounded.

Someone is looking for me. How much time do I have left?

When Mrs. Claybourne got off the phone with the man she knew as Philip Judge, she

76

drafted an e-mail — in Russian — to an account Firebird had given her. The account was one that would scramble and forward any e-mail sent to it, to a long chain of addresses, making it impossible to trace. And then their communications would be at an end.

She wrote a short one, then thought Firebird might appreciate more detail. She didn't delete the first e-mail, which simply confirmed the job. She moved the brief confirmation to the Drafts folder, knowing that she might write a long one and then decide the shorter one was better. This was a difficult client who had to be handled with great care. A single misstep could mean she and Judge would end up like Marianne and her team. She wrote a confirmation that Judge would take the job, that he had dealt with existing loose threads, and that he would be in touch as appropriate, confirming all safeguards previously agreed upon. She encrypted it and sent it on its way. Then she deleted it from her Sent folder.

Then, at just that moment, her daughter called from Montreal, crying. It was jarring to move from planning an assassination to dealing with a distraught teenager who was homesick and hated boarding school. She kept telling her daughter that school in

Montreal was for the best, but her daughter had locked herself in her room and could not be consoled. The conversation lasted for forty-five minutes. When she hung up with her daughter, after listening to tears and recriminations, she felt exhausted. Mrs. Claybourne then had to phone the school doctor about her daughter's depression, then the headmaster, who seemed inclined to argue with her, and finally she called the Toronto-based parents of her daughter's roommate and in icily polite tones suggested that perhaps *their* daughter could quit teasing *her* daughter. She thought, You people don't even know what I could do to you. That I could send one of the world's best assassins after you if your kid can't quit picking on my kid.

An hour later, emotionally spent, she got off the phone, forgetting about the first, shorter draft to Firebird that had joined dozens of other draft e-mails in her folder. She went into the kitchen and poured herself a coffee.

She had made a critical mistake.

5

Budapest

"I appreciate the help," Sam Capra said.

"You're most welcome," Jimmy Court answered.

The gentleman tied to the chair did not participate in the pleasant exchange. He hung his head down. The men were in the upstairs apartment above the Café Chosen bar, on Budapest's hip and eclectic Kazinczy Street. They'd lured the man here with a free drink e-mail for ladies' night and he'd come alone. One drink, spiked, and he didn't feel well and no one in the bar paid any attention to Sam and Jimmy helping him up the stairs.

"I remember you," Sam said. "Do you remember me?"

The man, who was fortyish, balding, with a small uncorrected gap between his front teeth, looked up and nodded.

"You were a guard at a private prison in

Brazil that unfortunately shut down a few weeks ago," Sam said.

The man's mouth trembled.

"Well, I guess, technically, I shut it down." Sam had led a massive escape from the prison, a dark hole on no map where those who were threats or annoyances to the powerful criminal interests in the world were stashed. People they didn't want to kill, or didn't want to kill yet. Some were relatives, some were friends, some were rivals who would consider unending imprisonment worse than death. The prison's matron, a psychopath who called herself Nanny, squeezed information from the prisoners that was then usefully sold to various criminal groups or back corners of governments. "But I remember you."

The man looked at the ground.

"It took a while for me to find you. Most of the prison's records were destroyed. I mean, I was very lucky to find this fragment of a photo in the wreckage." He held up the photo, with his brother Danny's face on it, but didn't show it to the guard. "And some of my fellow prisoners heard you talk over the months you were there. That you lived in Budapest. That you have twin teenagers. That your wife died of a rare cancer four years ago and that's why you took such a difficult, faraway job because it paid insanely well. Those are enough breadcrumbs to find a man." Sam smiled.

"I know nothing."

Sam kept a gun holstered on the underside of the desk. He had one in every bar, hidden at every desk. He cleared the gun from the holster and aimed it at the prisoner. This was a tranquilizer gun but the former guard didn't know that. His eyes went wide with terror.

"Please don't kill me. Please . . ."

"I'd like to get you home before your twins are home from school. I mean, I don't want to be at your house when they walk through the door." He gestured slightly with the dart gun. Sam would never hurt the man's children, but this man didn't know it. What the Hungarian did know was that Sam had killed every guard that stood in his way in the prison break. "But you were at that hellhole when this man was there." Sam turned Danny's picture so the Hungarian could see it. "Do you recognize him?"

"Yes. He was a prisoner there. Number twenty-six."

"Number twenty-six." Sam's voice didn't sound like his own. He saw, to his surprise, a concerned glance from Jimmy. Jimmy wasn't exactly a friend and he'd been surprised Jimmy agreed to help him today. He put his gaze back on the former guard's face. Sam well remembered being stripped of his name, the number "47" written in heavy marker on his forehead, on his prison overalls. "Did you know his real name?"

"No."

"Do you know who sent him to the prison?"

The man's lips thinned. "They told us nothing special about him but . . ."

"But what?"

"Two prisoners died while he was there. One strangled in his bed. The other, a neck broken, found dead in the library. Both of them were hired killers, I heard. Sent to the prison by Russians for failing in contract jobs."

"Are you saying . . . prisoner twenty-six killed them?"

"I'm telling you what I know. He was only there seven months. Sometimes he was taken away . . . to another part of the prison."

"Another part?"

"The unfinished part. I mean, it had a roof, but the cells weren't built out. Prisoners weren't kept there. I heard Nanny let people stay there. I always thought it was people who wanted a place to hide, because no one would ever find you there."

"Was he the only person there?"

"Him and another man. Tall, big guy. Looked like a soldier. Dressed all in black, even in the heat of the jungle. I don't know the man; I never heard him speak. I only saw him at a distance. I escorted Nanny to the empty part of the prison once, as her security. She told me to wait outside. But in one of the big rooms, when she opened the door, I saw they had shooting targets set up in a room. And there was a gym — mats on the floor, weights, boxing equipment, weapons, targets on the wall." He shrugged. "It looked like a training facility of some sort. But the only two people I saw were this big man and twenty-six. When he was over there, twenty-six didn't wear chains or the uniform with his number. He didn't even look like a prisoner. Then he was gone for good."

"Did he leave with this soldierly man?"

He shook his head. "One day Nanny and another guard took him, and he was gone. My friend who escorted him took him to a woman in Buenos Aires. He saw her, for just a moment, although Nanny dealt with her while he waited. Said she was well-dressed, had a noticeable streak of gray in her hair."

"Where's this guard that escorted him during the release?"

"He was one of the several you shot during the escape." The guard stared down at his lap.

Sam swallowed the taste of bile in his mouth. What was done was done. "It wasn't very common for prisoners to be released. I was told by a friend inside that he was the only one."

The former guard nodded. "I've told you all I know. Please . . ."

Sam jerked his head at Jimmy and they stepped into one of the apartment's bedrooms. They shut the door behind them. "My God," Jimmy said. "That's an incredible story."

"Someone kept Danny alive and . . . trained him at the prison. He was there not as a prisoner but . . . a guest."

"Who killed inside the prison when someone needed killing. Maybe you should leave this alone."

"No. Never. Let's focus on how we can find him. A woman, who traveled to Buenos Aires, presumably from America, six years ago, on a certain date. Presumably alone, but who would have paid for an extra ticket flying back."

"That's all data mining," Jimmy said. "We

could access the major credit card data-bases, see if we find a pattern."

"Does that description of the woman sound like anyone in the underground economy? A broker, a handler of some sort?"

Jimmy shook his head. "Did your brother ever show a proclivity for violence?" he asked.

"No!" Sam said, suddenly and sharply.

"So yes," Jimmy said. "Sam. Let's be honest. He killed two men and was trained further at this prison. This mystery woman with the gray streak collects him. Perhaps she's acting as his manager, his handler. She's like you."

"What do you mean?"

"She has a cover, as do you in owning the bars. A person who handles money, payments, arrangements, they can't really live off the grid. She has a business; she has to be able to explain her income and tie it to legitimate concerns. So when you travel, you do it as you. So would she."

"How would you find her?"

"We have . . . relationships with the credit card companies. We can find out. Give me a few days." Jimmy paused and then said quietly, "You loved your brother, but you didn't know him. That's a shock. Like if I

85

thought I didn't know Mila."

"I did know my brother. He saved my life once."

"Where?"

"Burundi." Sam froze. He never discussed that day with anyone.

"I know we're not truly . . . friends." Jimmy made a sour face. "And we never will be. But someone has to tell you the truth, Sam. If Danny's alive, and he's kept away from you, then maybe you should honor his decision. No good can come of chasing after a man who doesn't want to be found."

Sam went back into the room. The man tied to the chair stared up at him and started to babble, "I didn't know the prison would be the way it was, and then I was stuck out there, too; they wouldn't let anyone walk away . . ."

Sam untied the former guard and shoved him out of the chair. "Go home to your kids, mister."

"But know this," Jimmy said, in that clear, upper-crust voice that could be so unsettling. "You keep your mouth shut about our little talk."

"I will, I will," the man jabbered. Sam took him down the back exit stairs and watched him leave, hurrying down the street. The guard looked back once and gave a pathetic little wave of gratitude.

Sam went back upstairs. He put the gun back in its hiding place in the desk. "Will you and Mila help me?"

"I'll help you find your brother. But for that help, I want you to do me a favor."

"What?"

"I want you out of my and Mila's life," Jimmy said quietly.

Sam went to the kitchen and poured himself a glass of water. His stomach twisted. August thought he was hurting his family with this search; now he was being asked to give up his best friend. "State your terms."

"You give me back the bars, all of them. You no longer work for the Round Table. And you don't ever see Mila again."

Mila was Jimmy's wife, Sam's closest friend. She was the person who had brought him into working for the Round Table, a secret alliance that, in Jimmy's words, tried to be a force for good in the world. It was so secret that Sam didn't know who he worked for. This didn't trouble him when they gave him the resources to find and save his son; he'd not cared to ask a single question. But now he felt uneasy not knowing exactly who backed him. Sam was their pocket spy, using the many bars around the world the Table gave him as a cover. Each bar operated as a safe house and provided a way, he believed, for the Round Table to finance operations and move money around the world. Mostly the Round Table had left him alone, except for Mila helping him out when he'd gotten pulled into dangerous situations.

"I know my wife loves me. But you are a temptation to her."

Sam set down the glass, his face coloring. "Mila and I have *never* . . ."

"Your brother for the bars. And you don't tell Mila of our arrangement. You tell her you're quitting because of your kid, and you say nothing to anyone, ever, about the Round Table. And if I don't find your brother, our deal stands, because he is clearly dangerous and finding and detaining him is no small undertaking. I am putting myself and my people at risk to find a killer. But I have the resources and contacts to do it, and you do not. Yes or no?"

"Yes." Sam could hardly hear his own voice. "I agree." He was giving away his livelihood. His work. His closest friend. Fine, if that was the price to find Danny. He'd find another job to support himself and his friend Leonie and his son.

Jimmy offered a hand and they shook on

it. "Your hand's a bit clammy," Jimmy said with a smile. "You feeling all right?"

"Fine."

"Good. I'm heading on to Vienna. I'll get Mila started on searching for this woman and your brother."

Sam walked Jimmy downstairs to the bar. Café Chosen was what the Budapest nightclub crowd called a "ruin bar," one of the trendy spots set in once-derelict buildings, of which Budapest had more than a few. Riotously mismatched furniture — a constellation of oval plastic tables, a line of Lufthansa airline seats, a set of leather chairs — stood in odd formations along the wall. The bar itself was neat and tidy and modern, specializing in a collection of Hungarian and Czech and British microbrews. It was casual, not trying to be refined or arty like so many Budapest nightspots. It was therefore terribly hip, as if by accident rather than design.

And it would no longer be his. Nor The Last Minute in Manhattan, or Adrenaline in London, or the Tsar Lounge in Moscow, or the many others.

"Thanks for the help, Jimmy," Sam heard himself say.

"You're quite welcome." And Jimmy turned and left, heading out onto Kazinczy

Street among the pub crawlers and revelers.

Sam watched him. The price to find his brother had just gotten much higher. Finally, he'd made a deal with his own devil.

6

En Route To Vienna, Austria
Jimmy thought as he drove from Budapest to Vienna, listening to his favorite Bach concerto, I am going to get everything I want.

The next two days would be critical for his future, his life . . . everything. Sam would be gone. He hoped Sam saying to Mila *I don't want to do this anymore; I need more time with my son* would be convincing. Mila was unusually attached to the Capra toddler, a constant thorn of worry for Jimmy. That child was the bond that Sam and Mila shared, having saved him together, and the bond he couldn't snap unless Sam was absent from their lives. Best to make a clean break. She should not see the Capra child — he usually thought of the kid as *it* — again. If he could give her a child of their own, then perhaps her attachment to Sam's son would diminish. But that had not happened and Jimmy felt a sharp annoyance that he could not arrange nature to suit his interests.

He clenched the steering wheel. He rang Mila on his cell phone.

"Yes?"

"Hi, it's me. I just helped Sam find a lead on his brother. We need to do everything we can to help him." But only help him so far. Smoke and mirrors here. He had no intention of finding the talented Danny Capra.

"I see." He had hoped for *Oh, darling, that's wonderful* and instead he got her instant suspicion for doing a good deed where Sam Capra was concerned. "I hope this is a new détente."

He explained about the search for the woman who'd come to Buenos Aires to collect Danny Capra and he gave her the specific date range. "Could you drive to Oxford and set up the safe house? And see if the hacker can meet you there? I'd prefer to run this operation from one location. I want to know everything the hacker finds."

"Why not use Sam's bar in London?"

Because soon it won't be Sam's bar anymore and I have my own secrets from Sam, so let's keep him at a safe distance. "I just would rather use the Oxford house. It needs stocking. I think I'll call Razur to do the

92

hacking. And then you can help with the fieldwork." Because Razur, one of the top criminal hackers in London, would do whatever Jimmy told him to do, including creating a false alias for Danny Capra, and a digital and credit history that would lead to a faked death for the false name. One good enough to convince both Mila and Sam of its veracity. Let Danny Capra — under any name — be dead again. Razur was very good and very determined. "Can you take care of that for me?"

"Of course." Then she was silent for four long beats. "Is there something you're not telling me, Jimmy?"

"No, why?"

"Just something in your voice."

"Sam's story about his brother . . . it's heartbreaking, darling. I know he and I have had our differences, but we can't let him do this alone."

"Jimmy, I'm glad you see it that way," she said in a rush, "and I'm so glad we can help him. Thank you."

"Of course. I love you and I'll call you later."

"I love you, too," she said. He hung up.

Something like guilt swam around his heart and he pushed it away, concentrating on the drive, turning the Bach concertos on the radio up louder, thinking through his plan.

He reached Vienna. He headed for the city's eastern side. He stopped at an apartment that he had rented under a false name. He went inside and shut the door. Food first, then a phone call to Razur to plan the grand deception. He was searching in the refrigerator for a snack when the door opened and three men rushed in. He saw the face of one, a thick-chested man he knew, and he thought: No. No. Not now.

"Let's not have a scene, Lord James," the man said, in a soft Scottish accent. "Makes it harder on you and everybody."

You can just bluff your way through this, Jimmy thought. He offered a wry smile. "Have you taken leave of your senses? I'm on a mission."

"It does not work that way today, Lord James," the Scotsman said. "You are hereby detained under the orders of the chief of the Secret Intelligence Service. Keep your hands up, don't resist, or I have official permission to shoot you in the leg."

"Just the leg?" Jimmy said.

"Yes, my lord, nowhere else. Please don't make me." So polite. So formal. It told Jimmy how bad the situation was. Because his colleagues in the service never used his title.

So, with a smile of surrender, Jimmy obeyed, his heart crashing in his chest. He thought he was ending the life Sam Capra knew; instead his own was ending. The men cuffed him and dragged him into a chair and they called their bosses back in London. At the Secret Intelligence Service, commonly known as MI-6, Britain's spies.

"What am I charged with, may I ask?" Jimmy asked.

"Formal charges will depend on how well you cooperate, sir." The Scotsman tilted his head. "You've got a lot of explaining to do about your extracurricular activities. You're supposed to spy for Her Majesty. No one else."

Jimmy's skin went cold. And with his life as he knew it dissolving before his eyes, all Jimmy could think of was Mila. What would they do to Mila?

7

London

After Jimmy's call, Mila pondered the unusual fact that her husband wanted to help Sam Capra. Odd. Maybe he was softening toward Sam. She might as well drive to Oxford and set up the safe house. The home in Oxford had been in Jimmy's family for the past few years, last owned by a distant cousin who had died. So he said. Dead, like the rest of Jimmy's family. She packed a bag, and headed to the parking garage where she kept her Audi.

She left a window cracked in the car as she drove. The cool evening breeze in London felt wonderful. She loved London and felt a dizzy happiness that she was here and not in the small town in Moldova, where she had been raised. She loved it as well, but London was opportunity and life and energy. It was home.

Sam. She had helped him save his child,

and now she could help him save his brother. Life was odd. How, she thought, unlikely it was that the schoolteacher from rural Moldova and the boy who wandered the world with his relief-worker parents, both turned intelligence operatives, could have become such friends and allies.

She decided to give Sam a call when she got to Oxford, an hour and a half away. She didn't notice the car passing her and staying ahead of her on the M4, and she could not know about the second car a kilometer back, tracking her own car's movement on a tablet computer's screen.

Five minutes after she walked through the front door of the Oxford house, she was making chamomile tea when two armed men burst through the kitchen door.

The first man through the door had his gun leveled at her. "Freeze!" he said. But she ran out of the kitchen into the den to give herself cover, grabbed the heavy crystal ashtray Jimmy kept on the side table by his favorite chair, and threw it, baseball hard, at the first man's head as he gave chase. He dodged, the gun's aim dropping, and she kicked him in the face. He went down, cursing in anger and surprise, and she ran down the hallway toward the purse she'd tossed on the bed.

The second man caught her by the shoulder and yanked her sideways, dragging her back toward the kitchen.

Unhesitatingly, she rammed her head into his nose as he tried to pinion her arms. He staggered back, nose bloodied, and she tried to kick out his knee. She missed, but broke free of his grip. She bolted into the bedroom, threw herself onto the bed, and raised the whole purse toward her pursuer because there was no time to pull the gun she kept inside free. She aimed as he charged at her, calculating for the interference of the leather in the trajectory, and fired. He took the bullet in the chest and kept coming down the hallway.

Vest, she thought, and as she fired again he landed on her, two hundred pounds of muscle. The air rushed out of her. He picked her up and threw her into the wall. Her ribs screamed.

"Stop resisting, Mrs. Court," he said. "We don't wish to hurt you."

She aimed a fist at his throat. He blocked it and said, "I regret this," and slammed a fist down into her temple. Colors exploded. He put his big knee in the small of her back. He snapped plastic cuffs on her and said, "Behave like a professional, please, Mrs.

Court, and don't make me hit you again," and she went still. The way he said her name was mocking.

The other man came in, his eye squinted shut where she'd kicked him. "She shot at you?"

"She hit the vest." Both had English accents.

"Well." The man she'd kicked leaned down close to her. "You'll regret that, you will."

"It was self-defense." She tried to twist to look at them and couldn't.

"Secure the rest of the house," the man with his knee in her back said.

The other man vanished. She heard footsteps upstairs, him checking. "Clear!'

The man she'd shot at said, "The house is secure, ma'am." Then he listened to his earpiece. "Yes, ma'am." He searched Mila to make sure she had no further weapons or phones on her. He was respectful, not rough. He picked up Mila as though she weighed next to nothing and carried her upstairs to one of the two guest bedrooms. He opened the closet door. Gently he set her down on the floor.

"You wait here for just a bit, Mrs. Court, and then we'll have a very nice chat." He leveled a look at her, opened his shirt, and picked the impacted bullet off the vest. He gave her an oddly kind smile. "Good try, that was. But life's about to change for you, so I'd advise you to cooperate."

He closed the closet door on her.

Who were they? If they wanted her dead, they'd just shoot her, yes? So they were what? Police? One of the intelligence services?

She could hear their voices, beginning to search the house first. *They want to be armed with information. Then they'll question you.*

She wondered if Jimmy would make a deal for her. Or just walk away from her, forever. It was unsettling to not be certain what your husband would do. But this wasn't a normal life they had chosen.

She put her head on her knees and listened to the people searching the safe house, listened to the slow dismantling of her life.

Whoever they were — the Round Table was over. And she had no way to warn Jimmy or Sam or anyone else who had worked for them.

8

Brooklyn

Night and day had ceased to mean much for Judge. His mind was full, churning, dissecting, and thinking about the research amassed by Marianne and her team and his own findings. He'd read it all three times, then connected the laptop to his printer and began to cover his bedroom wall with photos and articles.

He was retraining his ear. His Russian was a bit rusty. On his laptop played Moscow's Radio Russia, streaming news and talk shows via the Internet; on his table and in his refrigerator was leftover Russian food — pierogi, Georgian lamb soup, herring and potatoes — from a restaurant in Brighton Beach. It was a fifteen-minute taxi ride to Brighton Beach, but he'd been eating all his meals in restaurants there, eavesdropping on the conversations in the mother tongue in one of the largest enclaves of Russian immigrants. He'd spent the morning reading Russian language blogs and tonight he'd watch Russian movies, pirated on the web.

You had to immerse yourself in the story you were going to build.

Judge had printed out Marianne's analysis of the circle surrounding this particular Caesar. *Caesar, czar.* The words were so close, and with good reason. The only people who could kill Julius Caesar were those closest to him. Firebird, to be useful, must be one of that inner circle.

There were two key oligarchs who had stayed close to Dmitri after he rose to the presidency. One leaned toward the West; the other was much more hostile. All the others seemed to line up behind one of these two, so Judge decided to focus on them.

The lead pro-Western oligarch was Yuri Kirov, who ran Zvezda, one of the major oil companies in Russia. Like both the Morozov brothers, he was ex-KGB. Fifty-six, worth twelve billion. Widowed and had not remarried, with a daughter, Katya. Yuri had the look of a former boxer, thickly muscled, with a granite face that could take a punch; in his photos he gave the impression of a rough-and-tumble, unpolished man. He ran Russia's oil concerns with what one business magazine profile called "street cunning." For a man who controlled much of the world's energy resources, he kept a low profile. Now and then he would assent to an interview with a Western journalist, rare among the inner circle. He sometimes publicly disagreed with Morozov, something no other oligarch did, but the Russian press pointed to this as openness in Russian society. Western commentators thought it was a pose.

His daughter, Katya, was in her twenties and Judge had found several pictures of her in the Western press, at movie premieres in Hollywood or London, often on the arm of a handsome young actor or athlete. One photo caption called her "Russia's Sweetheart," apparently for her prominence on the celebrity photo pages. Kirov wanted to sell oil to the outside world, especially the United States, China, and Europe — Katya enjoyed being splashed on the pages of celebrity magazines. The Kirovs' interest in the West seemed pragmatic. Judge stuck a picture of him on the Western side of the circle, with Morozov at the center. He put a picture of Katya next to him, to the side.

Now for the side that favored a Russia that was less engaged with the West, hungering for a return to its former imperial glory.

Judge taped up the picture of the other key oligarch, Boris Varro. He ran one of Russia's largest banking networks and had used that power to acquire a majority interest in a huge natural gas enterprise. He was the most unlikely member of the circle. His mother had been Russian, his father Cuban, a high-ranking member of Fidel Castro's Dirección de Inteligencia, with many friends inside the KGB. His parents had made sure their son Boris was born in Moscow, not Havana, and that he had Russian citizenship. He was also ex-KGB. Varro was an expansive, highly social man, famed for his elaborate parties. Handsome still, with a crown of silver hair. He worked hard, one pundit noted, to be accepted as Russian. Varro, Judge guessed, had figured out that if he was going to ally with a parental homeland, Russia offered a brighter future than Cuba. He had served as a KGB operative in Latin and South America, given his fluent Spanish. He was fifty and worth nine billion. The joke was that he would soon return to his father's homeland and buy Cuba outright. He was, ethnically, the closest thing to an outsider in the circle. He married a Russian opera singer, Maria, and had two sons, Stefan and Anton. Anton was dead; he had gone missing six years ago on a trip to Dushanbe, Tajikistan. He had been sent there as a Russian envoy . . . by Dmitri Morozov, who was then the president's brother. A ransom was demanded, and paid, but Anton Varro was never found. A crime lord in Dushanbe was soon gunned down in the street, and rumor had it that justice had been paid.

His surviving son, Stefan, was his father's protégé and was often photographed with Morozov at social functions or with Katya Kirova when she was in Moscow. He was handsome like his father, but where there was a liveliness in Boris's eyes, Stefan's looked cold, calculating. Little was written about him in the Western press. And he had access to his father's money. People who had been problems for Stefan and his father had ended up dead or had disappeared.

Was this about revenge or misplaced blame? Morozov hadn't killed Anton Varro. And Morozov protected the Varro family. The journalists in Russia who had dug into Varro's past were either dead or dissuaded. One had been arrested for nine months, charged with financial malfeasance, a common tactic for those who peered into the past too deeply. Varro was quick to label dissidents as traitors.

But . . . Judge believed Firebird was most

likely either Varro or Kirov. They were the two most powerful — the others followed in their trail. And because of their power, they were Morozov's rivals.

And do they know what you've done for them already? He wondered. *Do they know you've stood in the shadows for them? Do they know you exist?*

There was one additional picture, and he was unsure where it belonged on his chart. He printed it out from the files and stared at it. She was a striking woman, with a strong, intelligent face, eyes of piercing blue, beautiful red hair.

Irina Belinskaya. She had been termed — by one reporter who later was shot dead in a Moscow elevator — the most dangerous woman in Russia. He read a profile of her from a London paper. She was former high-level GRU, Russian military intelligence, special-forces trained. She owned a private security firm that counted several families in the inner circle as their most important clients. Her husband, Sergei, had been a longtime right hand and protector of the Morozovs, killed a few years ago in a car bombing in Moscow. His murder was blamed on Chechen separatists. Popular rumor asserted a bloody vengeance: that Irina Belinskaya had personally hunted down and assassinated the men responsible for her husband's death — and their families. She had done nothing to dissuade the rumors and blithely told this London paper she had no comment. She had used that steely reputation to build her business, to win over the inner circle, who might never have entrusted their safety to her otherwise.

She was their protector. She ran security. There would be, of course, government security for President Morozov, but Irina Belinskaya protected the billionaire inner circle. Her operatives were the highest paid in Russia; the competition for their jobs was fierce.

He looked at Irina's picture, but he saw Sergei's face. Laughing in the mountain moonlight. Handing him his life. Giving him a future.

And now, giving him a way inside the inner circle.

He sat and he studied the pictures on the wall. Thought over what he had read. What he already knew. He could trade on his past six years to find a path inside the circle. He only had to get close enough to kill, and then get out. To be part of the group, for a moment, then vanish. All for twenty million dollars.

He called Mrs. Claybourne. "I'm leaving

New York. You won't see me again."

"I understand. Good luck. We won't talk again until it's done," Mrs. Claybourne said.

He left the pictures up on the wall. They didn't matter anymore and if he died perhaps they would be a tantalizing clue to the investigators. Who had this man been? *I've been whoever I wanted to be. Whoever I needed to be.* But once, he'd had one name, and he'd had a bit of ego, of self-regard, and for some reason he didn't want to tear the pictures down. And perhaps, if Firebird turned on him the way he had on Marianne, then this would be a smoking gun. A clear indicator that Morozov's killer was backed by either Kirov or Varro.

The map to killing Morozov was in his head. He packed his bag, tidied up the apartment, and walked out the door. He had never felt so alive in his life.

9

Oxford, UK

When the man she'd shot at finally brought Mila downstairs, the busted door was already repaired. No sign there had been a fight. An older woman sat at the dining room table. The bullet man pushed Mila into a chair. The other man — with a black eye from her kick — went and sat by the woman. The curtains were closed. She realized she didn't know whether it was day or night outside now.

The woman — fortyish, plain-faced, elegant in her movements — watched her with a stern gaze. Mila had taught school once, a lifetime ago, and she knew the stare. She'd used it herself.

The woman put Mila's cell phone on the desk.

"You're probably thinking it's best you don't say anything," the woman said. "I'm here to tell you that now is the time to talk."

Mila watched her.

"It's just so awkward for us, dear, when it's one of our own and not a grubby little hacker or a hireling or a religious extremist. Those we know how to deal with. You and James, though, you're a challenge."

Mila frowned.

"We don't really have time for the usual dance," the woman said. "I'd lay out the evidence, you'd get a solicitor in love with the press, we'd say we couldn't comment, and then the press would waste gallons of ink. Much of it would smear us. Amazing how an organization can be blamed for the shortcomings of an individual. It's grossly unfair. So that's not what is going to happen here."

Mila stared at her hands, cuffed. *You knew this day would come. You knew you might be caught. Here it is. Every day you dread, eventually that day comes. Life is just the days in between the dreadful times.*

"I'm not here to judge you. I'm here to make you the offer of a lifetime."

Mila looked up at the woman. "My husband already made me that offer."

"Your husband." She made it sound like the opening line of a curse. "You may call me Charity, Mila. Of course not my real name. But a virtue to which I subscribe,

110

and one that you quite desperately need at the moment. Speaking of real names: Do you even know what your husband's is?"

"Jimmy Court."

Charity shook her head. "That is not his real name. He's lied to you, Mila."

"He has not lied to me," Mila said.

"So. Mila Court. That's *your* name, is it? Also not real. You traveled to the United Kingdom several years ago on an Australian passport as Mila Cebotari. Born in Sydney, the daughter of Romanian immigrants, educated at local schools, graduate of the University of Sydney with a degree in education. All that is a lie. But your papers are extremely good forgeries, and I'm so curious to know what helpful souls gave them to you. Tracking your movements two weeks ago in Australia, we've found your aunt and uncle, who appear to be the one aspect of your life that is not a complete lie. Regrettably, they also have been given fake documentation for Australian citizenship . . . and are therefore felons."

Mila felt a thickness form in her throat.

Charity steepled fingers in front of her chin. "If you cooperate, we can shred and burn the file on your aunt and uncle. Your poor relatives will be left alone, both by MI-6 and by the Australian authorities, who don't even realize these elderly illegals live among them. Otherwise . . . they won't do jail well at their age. It will crush them."

"Do you often threaten old people?" Her rage at threats against Aunt and Uncle felt hot and bright in her heart.

"I don't discriminate based on age," Charity said. "They get mail from an elderly relative in a small town in Moldova called Harpă. Our man in Moldova visited and learned that a few years ago, a couple matching their description suddenly left town, along with their niece, a schoolteacher named Mila."

Mila felt her heart shrink. Her shock was slowly burning into anger. Good. She knew what to do with anger.

"I'm sure you told your aunt and uncle not to correspond with anyone back home, but the elderly are sometimes difficult, aren't they? Especially when they've been pulled from a small town where they've spent their whole lives and then dumped in a massive city in a foreign culture thousands of miles away. And you're not there much to keep them company. Your husband's kept you so busy."

Mila stared at the table.

"So, back to Moldova, this schoolteacher Mila, the local gossips told us her sister

Nelly vanished a few months before Mila did. Took a job at a nice hotel in Israel, although the Israelis have no record of Nelly entering the country on a work permit."

Mila looked again at the cuffs.

"Whispers that Nelly had been taken by one of those awful gangs that promise decent jobs to young women but are just traffickers who sell them into prostitution. Horrifying. You know, there I sympathize with you. If someone had done that to my sister . . ."

Mila, with a gaze of ice, met Charity's smile.

Charity continued: "One of those gangs, well, their Moldovan contact vanished. Then one of the gang's houses in Romania was blown up. Two young women who'd been trafficked there told the police that, and I quote, 'an angel had gotten them out of the house and killed the gang members.' Then days later, an Israeli brothel got shot up, and the girls were set free. Almost as if some brave, enterprising soul followed Nelly's trail from Moldova to Romania to Israel, dealing out revenge." Charity smiled.

Mila said nothing.

"Is that how you met the so-called James Court? Did he help you in dismantling a human smuggling chain? At least that's a noble deed. Perhaps his only one."

One of the men brought her water and she drank from the glass.

"Your husband — when not working under a false name like James Court — is supposed to work as an operative for the Secret Intelligence Service. He is a spy, sworn to protect his country. Did you know that?"

Mila shook her head.

"Jimmy, as you call him, has been running unsanctioned operations on the side, using the name James Court, using his resources as an intelligence agent to run an entirely separate organization that is highly illegal. And using you, an illegal alien with no standing, here under false pretenses." Silence filled the room. The man she'd shot, who'd brought her water to drink, looked at her with a mix of pity and loathing.

Charity opened another file. "Your alleged husband was detained in Vienna several hours ago by his fellow operatives of the Secret Intelligence Service."

And it gave Mila the barest sliver of hope. *You didn't take him here on British soil because it would raise too many questions from his colleagues. You couldn't grab him here because you don't want the rest of the service knowing about him.*

"Are you familiar with the term *the Round Table*?"

"That is a large piece of furniture in the King Arthur stories," Mila said.

"Ah, but there's a modern one, a name for Jimmy's little spy network. Selling our secrets to the highest bidder? To our enemies? What?"

"I swear to you," Mila said. "We have never hurt Britain."

"I'm afraid I'll need more than your word. Your cooperation could offset the many penalties you are facing for being in our country as part of a huge fraud, *Mrs. Court.*"

Her words might hang her husband. But if she cooperated, then Aunt and Uncle would be spared. She had no choice. Her voice didn't sound like her own. "The Round Table is a kind of exchange, between intelligence agents in different countries. Favors were done for Jimmy, and he did favors in return. Sometimes in trade, sometimes in payment."

"Information?"

She glared at her. "Yes, we worked outside the rules that bind you. But we broke up criminal rings. We ended terrorist threats. We . . ."

"But you were apparently paid for this so-noble work. Who were your clients?"

"I don't know. He kept our funding from me."

Charity stared at her and then closed her file folder, and it felt like the closing of a door. "We want all the information product he's collected. We want all the funds. We want to know who his partners and his clients are. Considering the pull of his family . . ."

Mila blinked. "His family."

"You don't know his family?" Charity said. Her smile was, for the first time, cruel. "Well. We'll let him tell you all about *that.* What a conversation it should be. Your husband was in Vienna; before that he was in Budapest. We lost him there before we found him again in Vienna. What was he doing in Budapest?"

Meeting Sam. But she said, "He did not tell me."

"A few days before Budapest, he met briefly with a man in Copenhagen. Our trackers picked him up there." She opened a laptop, slid it toward Mila, hit a button. A video played. Jimmy, walking across a square she soon recognized as Copenhagen's Højbro Plads, stopping and talking briefly to another man. A man she'd only seen in pictures. The man looked like Danny Capra. Sam's missing brother. The security video wasn't totally clear — only because she'd seen Danny's picture so recently did she recognize him. *Jimmy knows Sam's brother.* Her stomach felt like it would fall through the floor.

"You know this man?" Charity asked.

"I don't know his name. I saw his picture once . . . it's hard to say . . . it's blurry."

"He's a client?"

"I honestly do not know," she said, and that was the truth.

"Your husband made a substantial deposit in a Swiss bank account ten minutes after this conversation with this man," she said.

Why was Danny Capra giving Jimmy money? It had to be about Sam looking for his brother. But Danny didn't want to be found . . . and Jimmy would make sure he wasn't. She realized it all in a bolt of shock. "You say you have Jimmy. Ask him."

"He's not talking."

"I can't tell you what I don't know."

"Your husband is an embarrassment. We don't plan on airing him as our dirty laundry. But we can make him vanish." Charity leaned back in the chair. "The Americans have dark corners where you can lose someone. Forever."

"Please . . . ," Mila said, and she hated herself for pleading.

"But we would be lenient if you would help us. We need one of his clients. Find him for us." She tapped on the picture of Danny Capra.

"Bring him to you?" Shock inched through her chest. "What, you're going to set me loose to find him?"

"Yes."

"I could just run," she said, like it was an option when she knew it wasn't.

"You want to see your husband again, Mrs. Court. You want your aunt and uncle to keep their safe lives in Australia. Run and I promise you charges will be brought against them. You took down the scum who took your sister. You can find this man for me."

"You don't want to send your own people to hunt down this contact because you don't want an official history," Mila said.

"History, for you, is what I get to write," Charity said in a cold, flat voice. "You two could be painted as heroes or traitors. I'm giving you a chance to be a heroine to your adopted country." Her voice softened. "Have you been happy in Britain?"

"Yes." The happiest she had ever been. It was all gone now.

"Do this and you're safe. No prosecution. British citizenship, for real. A future, here."

And then her stare softened. "I know you love him, sweetheart, but he's been a dreadful liar to you."

"Jimmy . . . will tell you everything, if I ask him to."

"He wouldn't talk. Not even when I threatened to have your aunt and uncle arrested by the Australians." She shrugged, as if helpless. "He's not talking. You talk to him."

She produced another phone, punched in a number. Held the phone up. "Put him on speaker," she said to whoever was on the other side of the line.

"Darling." Jimmy's voice carried through the air. Mila closed her eyes. She remembered him walking up to her in Sydney, a month after she'd hidden herself and her aunt and uncle there, with a million-dollar bounty on her head. Jimmy offered her hope. A new life. A real way for Aunt and Uncle to stay in Australia. A sense of purpose when she'd failed to save her sister. One word. He'd cut through her steel, through her fear, to her heart.

"Yes," she said. "I'm here."

"James," Charity said. "Your so-called wife faces possible deportation if you do not cooperate with us. I assume the human traffickers she burned in Moldova will be thrilled to have her back in her homeland."

He laughed. "You won't send her back because then you'd have to explain. You don't want the attention. Anything happens to Mila, you will never get a word from me. Ever."

"I trust you," Mila said. Because she had to say something to him. "I love you."

"I love you, too."

Charity closed the line. Mila thought, Is that all he has to say to me? "If I were him, I'd be talking like mad to get you free," said Charity.

"He and I understand each other," Mila said. "We always have."

"Do you really love him?"

Mila blinked. "Yes."

"Get me this man, and I can write the history of Jimmy and Mila Court so that it was an undercover operation, sanctioned. If we know who the clients are, then we can deal with the problem. We can know the damage. But if we don't . . . then you and Jimmy pay the price."

Sam was searching for his brother. She could help him. But then she'd have to steal Danny from Sam to free Jimmy.

Take Sam's brother from him, just when he'd found him.

She stared at this woman she felt was

destroying her life, by inches, with this soul-crushing choice. "Once a man sat across from me in a schoolroom and told me that my sister had been forced into prostitution, and if I wanted her back I had to find and deceive three innocent young women, to be sent to replace her."

Charity waited.

"It was in that moment I decided to kill him. And I did. I killed them all. That's what happens to people who carry out threats against those I love. I'll do as you ask. You will do as you promise."

Charity smiled and slid a bag across the table. Mila opened it. Cash. Clothes, from her own closet here. Credit cards and a genuine UK passport in the name of Mila Cebotari. Her car keys. Four burner phones, a laptop that no doubt would report back to them where she was and what she researched and where she went.

She didn't stand up. She wanted to ask *So who is my husband, really, and why do you want to spare him the publicity?* But she was ashamed she didn't know. The humiliation burned like a fever, a wound.

"Report in twice a day. Call the number preprogrammed into the phones. When you have the client you'll tell me where and when to come apprehend him. You have ten days, because my patience doesn't extend further. Beyond that, it will be out of your hands. Vanish and the Australians arrest your family. You may go."

She got up and left the house. She walked out, without another look at these people.

Find and bring them Danny Capra and everything will be all right. Well, hardly anything. But Jimmy will be free. She owed him. He had saved her life, her family. The choice was clear.

She got in her Audi. She didn't search it; of course they'd put a tracer on it. But she realized she had one advantage. She was unofficial. She was secret. Charity was keeping her that way. Which meant Charity did not have limitless resources. Charity would rely on digital traces, not on warm bodies following Mila.

She had to make her one advantage work. First she had to find Sam and convince him to help her. Of course they would listen in on the phone. So she wouldn't use it. She and Jimmy had hidden gear and cash in several spots around London. She would call Sam using a burner phone.

I'm sorry, Sam, she thought as she drove back toward London. *I must take away what you want most in the world right now.*

10

Paris

Sam landed in Paris and spent a day there
tending to his bar and making phone calls.
He had not heard from Jimmy and that
made him uneasy. Jimmy might not look
very hard for Danny. Sam had not heard
from Seaforth. His need to maintain momentum drove him. He wasn't going to
wait, so he called Jack Ming.

In his bar in the Saint-Germain-des-Prés
neighborhood, he sipped a coffee and
waited at a back booth. Five minutes later
Jack Ming arrived and slid into the booth
opposite him. Jack was one of the top hackers on the planet, a young American who
had helped Sam bring down the Nine Suns
criminal syndicate — the same people who
had gotten Sam's wife to turn traitor and
had kidnapped his baby. The syndicate had
told Sam he could have his child back if he
hunted down and murdered Jack Ming, the

one man who could expose their inner workings. Instead Sam rescued his child, spared Jack's life, and turned him into an ally, and the two of them, with Mila, burned Nine Suns to the ground. Afterward, Jack had to drop out of sight, for his own protection and that of his wife, Frédérique, a Senegalese student. They'd thought of settling in New Zealand, but Frédérique preferred a Francophone country. They'd decided to hide in Paris, under new, legitimate identities that a French intelligence agency had provided them, in exchange for occasional hacking work from Jack.

Paris and marriage, Sam thought, looked like they agreed with Jack. He'd gained some needed weight, looked happy and healthy. He wore a well-fitted dark suit, no tie. This was a serious upgrade from his sloppy graduate student attire.

"You're a dapper man," Sam said with a smile. "How's your lovely wife?"

"Great. Better than great. Ricki's pregnant." Jack's normally serious face broke into a wide smile. Sam thought, After all the hell they went through, Jack and Ricki are happy. Maybe I can get there, too.

"That's fantastic, Jack. Congratulations." He remembered the immediate excitement he'd felt when Lucy told him they were going to have a baby. Lucy. He made sure not to let his smile at Jack dim.

"How's your son?" Jack asked.

Too far away and is he even wondering where I am? I need to call him, to hear his voice. "Talking, walking, just being awesome. I'll see him . . . soon. But I have a job for you."

Jack raised an eyebrow.

"I need to know what it would cost, first," Sam said.

"For you, free."

"No, Jack, no more. You already did free work for me. We're even. I insist on paying you."

"We'll never be even. I am alive, and I have a wonderful life because of you, Sam."

"And you have a child on the way. I'm paying. I insist."

"We'll see. Tell me the work, first."

Sam described his hunt for the woman who collected his brother in Buenos Aires. Jack took no notes; he would, Sam knew, remember every detail. "It will take some time. Credit card charges of that vintage are kept in an archive database. Usually for seven years. I could also try to access the record through the airline's database, if she got frequent-flier miles from her purchase.

But they may not keep that record for years."

"Do your best. Question number two. The eavesdropping app you gave me? I forced it onto a man's phone a couple of days ago. How easily will it be detected?"

"It's masked as part of the e-mail program, so you should be fine."

"He's CIA Special Projects."

"Oh, wow." Jack frowned. "Well, I can't test against their top-secret detection protocols. I wrote the app for a French intel agency and their protocols didn't find it on the sweep. Do you want to tell me why you're spying on Special Projects?"

"Because they are helping me, but I need to know it's for the right reasons."

Jack considered. "I assume if you need to spy on them you may need to steal from them."

"That sounds so wrong."

He pulled a pair of car keys from his bag, with an Audi logo. "Not actual keys." He pressed the end of one and a flash drive emerged from the key's thick housing. "It will copy data at a much higher rate than a conventional flash drive. It also includes a program to crack passwords." Another flick and the key resumed its normal appearance.

"Thanks."

Jack nodded. "You're welcome. I'll find out what I can on this woman."

"Give my best to Ricki," Sam said. "I'm so happy for the two of you."

On his cab ride back to Charles de Gaulle Airport Sam thought of calling home to hear Daniel's voice, but he decided instead to activate the app he'd placed on Bob Seaforth's phone during the helicopter flight back to Bagram. He felt guilty . . . Seaforth had helped him. But no one helped in intelligence work without expecting a payback. Always there was a trade, an exchange, an agenda.

Seaforth's phone was turned on, and the eavesdropping app activated. Sam slipped earbuds into place. He could hear Seaforth's voice. He was with a group; Sam heard three voices other than Seaforth's, chatting, all younger-sounding. A nasal-sounding man, a woman with a slight Southern accent, another man with a raspy hoarseness to his tone. They chatted about weather, the coffee, asking Bob why there were only six doughnuts instead of a dozen in the box on the conference table.

A meeting, Sam thought. If there were more people in the room, they were being silent.

Sam closed his eyes in the back of the cab, listening through his earbuds.

Seaforth's voice, quiet and commanding: "Let's begin. You three read the file on Sam Capra."

Sam sat up suddenly, then eased himself back down.

Young man, nasal voice, New England accent: "Yes. What a mess he is. I'm not clear on what we're supposed to do about him."

Seaforth: "I want to know what he knows. We've dangled a trail for him to follow and I want to see what he does."

Woman: "Why waste our time with someone radioactive?"

Seaforth: "Because he's going to take us to someone interesting, Romy. Right now I just want digital eyes on Sam. I want to know where he goes. I want to know where he stays. I want to know who he contacts."

Romy: "Julian scooped up his data."

Nasal voice, again . . . Julian: "He flew from Budapest to Paris; today he's booked on a flight to Atlanta, then on to New Orleans. His parents and his child are there. We have a trace on his parents' home and cell phones. He has not called them."

Romy: "Psychologically, that's interesting. He has news on his brother and yet he says nothing."

Julian: "It's not news you tell over the phone."

Raspy-voiced man: "I would."

Julian: "We looked at his parents' phone patterns. There's not a lot of contact between Sam and the parents. Not even once a week. Not e-mail. The mother is on social media and primarily posts about relief work. Do you know the effort it takes on Facebook *not* to talk about your kids?"

Seaforth: "Would you say they're estranged?"

Julian: "At least a tension. Probably related to the brother's disappearance. Some families get closer in tragedy, others splinter."

Raspy-voiced man: "He owns a house in New Orleans, bought in his own name." Sam heard a noise that sounded like paper being shuffled and rearranged. "A woman lives there, as caretaker to his son. Her name is Leonie Jones. She has a CIA file. She was a forger, an information broker, a specialist in creating identities for people who needed to vanish. She was forced into working for a criminal syndicate called Nine Suns, which is currently dormant and presumed broken up — Sam Capra dealt them a fatal blow after they kidnapped his son, and they've not found value in reassembling. She was given the Capra baby for safekeeping. Safe to say she grew very attached to him. Sam didn't show her the curb when he got his son back; she's the only mother figure his son has ever known."

Romy: "They should have a reality show."

Seaforth: "Are they intimate? Do their e-mails, texts, et cetera, suggest it's a romantic relationship?"

We were together twice, Sam thought, while chasing Daniel's kidnappers, and we decided it was a bad idea. But sometimes he thought of those moments with Leonie with a confused longing. They hadn't really tried for a real relationship. They had put each other into a limbo.

Julian: "No. It's friendly but it's mostly about the baby. Textual analysis indicates she is devoted to the Capra child."

Romy: "He also got a live-in babysitter who knows he's ex-CIA, that he has a particular skill set that he is willing to sell and use. If he's Batman, she's Alfred. Keeper not only of the child, but of his secrets. She could be forging identities for him to use right now."

Seaforth: "Prakash, you said his parents are in New Orleans as well?"

The paper shuffling sound again. Prakash, the raspy-voiced man: "Alexander Capra and Dr. Simone Perrault Capra. Former

130

bigwigs with an Episcopal relief agency. He's a financial guru, she's a surgeon. Very dedicated to their work. In fact, their e-mails to Sam are always about work, rarely about him or his life. They've retired but they serve as consultants to global charities. Speaking engagements, pro bono work. Simone Capra comes from serious family money due to timber and oil in Louisiana and east Texas. That was the explanation given when Sam bought the bars, that this was family money. If he doesn't tell them about his brother on this visit, I assume he won't until he has proof."

Seaforth: "What might Sam do if he finds his brother alive? Let's figure him out, misfits."

Misfits? Sam thought. What an odd term to use in an agency meeting. He heard papers shuffling, the squeak of a pen on a dry-board.

Romy: "Do we have DNA results yet on the bodies in the grave?"

Seaforth: "Not yet. I have a government lab extracting DNA from the teeth we brought back. I should have results tomorrow."

Government lab? Not a CIA Special Projects lab? It was an odd choice of words, Sam thought.

Seaforth: "Back to Sam. We have his psych profile from when he was hired by Special Projects. His emotional anchor was more his brother than his parents. The Capra boys were dragged all over creation, from one disaster or poor country to another. Odd that the parents didn't leave them behind, but they thought the world was a classroom. Sam's world centered on his brother."

Seaforth: "If Danny's alive, he might have spent his time with the extremist movements for the past six years. Maybe he was recruited, brainwashed, deployed."

Romy: "But these guys were heroin smugglers, not terrorists."

Seaforth: "Or they were both. We don't know what happened in that village. Not yet."

Romy: "You want us to watch Sam in New York? It's only the three of us."

Only three of them? Sam thought. Weren't these people part of Special Projects? Along with the comment about using the government lab . . .

Seaforth: "No."

Julian: "What if we do need to run an operation against him? As teams go, we are small and the plates are large. We've got the summit with the Russian leadership, the situation in Syria, the Estonia problem . . ."

Seaforth: "And every other intel agency will be focused on those. The Church is different. We're old-school. We're in the people business. Sam Capra and whoever he's been working with matter," Seaforth said. "We stick on him for now."

The Church? Sam thought, sitting upright. What the hell was this? Seaforth had gotten CIA resources to help him . . . but didn't work for the CIA?

What was the Church?

Julian: "Speaking of the Russians . . . what says our source there?"

Seaforth: "Nothing new to report."

Romy: "Where's Sam going when he comes to New York? We need an address."

Seaforth: "He's going to see the Magpie."

Romy: "Crazy old woman. She gets people killed."

Another awkward silence.

Seaforth: "Danny Capra is our priority. Run your work and we'll talk again tomorrow."

Sam shut off the app as the taxi pulled up to Terminal Two at Charles de Gaulle Airport. Seaforth wasn't CIA, but he was still government. So what was he? A secret group, a task force, a new department in a back corner of an agency? And clearly, he was going to interfere in Sam's search for Danny.

Sam went through customs as if in a dream, dazed. *The only person in this world you can still trust is Mila.* He didn't remember he wanted to call Daniel until the plane was taking off into the bright afternoon.

11

New Orleans

Landing in New Orleans in the evening, Sam felt exhausted. His mind spun with thoughts of Danny, like a ghost in his brain. Until he saw his son, Daniel. Leonie met him outside Louis Armstrong Airport, Daniel strapped into the toddler seat, laughing and calling for his daddy.

At least he remembers your name, Sam thought. He got into the backseat instead of the front, and he could sense the resentment rise from Leonie, in the driver's seat. Because he could have sat next to her after kissing Daniel hello, and now she was just the person driving him and his kid. From nanny to chauffeur.

She deserves better than this limbo we're in, Sam thought. Fix this. He didn't know how. So he began to tickle Daniel's toes and fingers and in the rearview he saw Leonie smile.

"By the way," she said, "your parents are waiting for us at the house."

"Oh," he said. He loved his parents but he had not wanted to see them while trying to prove that his brother was still alive. It would feel horrifically awkward, face-to-face, him suspecting that their greatest wish was true and not being able to share it with them. What would you say? *Hey, y'all, Danny might be alive. He just never called us in six years or let us know.* He could tell them nothing until he knew the truth.

He wished, for one moment, that he hadn't come here. But Daniel smiled at him, and that made his reservations melt away.

"I didn't ask them. They called me this morning and I said you were coming home and they said they had to see you. I couldn't say no."

"OK. I know it's a hard situation for you."

She didn't answer and she drove them to the house he'd bought, off St. Charles Avenue.

"How many days are you home for?" she asked as he pulled Daniel from the car, the child giggling. He nestled the boy against his shoulder.

"I go to New York tomorrow."

"Don't blink, Daniel," she said. "You'll

miss Daddy."

Sam's mother, Dr. Simone Capra, opened the front door, an uncertain smile on her face. His father, Alexander Capra, stood behind her, his hair now silvery with gray, but still a tall, wiry man.

"Hello, sweetheart," his mother said. Sam kissed her cheek and let her kiss his. He shook his father's hand and was a little surprised to get a strong hug from him. He loved his parents and he knew they loved him, but since Danny's death there had been a distance. His parents were reminders of loss, and he was one to them. They were caught in the nightmare together.

His mother scooped up Daniel from him. "Your dad made cocktails, if you want one. Old-fashioneds."

He went and got his bag and Leonie had vanished — or retreated — into the kitchen, which smelled of roasting chicken. His father handed him a drink. He thought: This is cozy. Something's wrong.

"Sit," his father said.

So he did, all of them with a cocktail in hand, and his mother said, with Daniel on her knee, "Why were you in Afghanistan?"

He had started a fortifying gulp of the old-fashioned and he nearly choked. "What?"

"Why. Were. You. In. Afghanistan?" she

said, enunciating carefully.

"What . . . why do you think I was there?" He'd told no one, not even Leonie, that he had gone to Kabul.

"A friend of ours from United Global Relief saw you in the Kabul airport."

His heart shifted in his chest. "Did your friend come up and say hi to me?" he said mildly.

"No, he saw you at a distance; you were boarding a flight at the last minute one gate over. But he was sure it was you. You ran past him."

"It wasn't me."

"He took a picture, Sam, and texted it to us," Simone Capra said.

You could have told me that before, he thought bitterly, but he kept the bemused smile in place. "Let's see this picture."

His father showed him the phone screen and, yeah, it was Sam, at a distance but standing in profile, about to board a Turkish Airlines flight to Istanbul, with continuing service to Budapest. It was him. The text read:

I saw Sam in Kabul airport — is he finally going into relief work like the rest of the family?

"It's not me," Sam said, handing his father back the phone.

His father shook his head. "Sam, look at the photo; that is you."

He couldn't tell them — that there was a chance Danny was alive. That there was a sliver of hope. It would be too cruel. He would have to carry this burden alone. He looked at his parents. He loved them so much but he could not, in that moment, have told them so.

Daniel got down from his grandmother's lap onto the floor, suddenly fascinated with a toy train.

"Is it Danny?" his mother asked. He noticed how tightly she was gripping her untasted drink. "Did they find his body and call you?"

"Mom, if his body was found they'd call you, not me." They didn't know he was CIA. They had never known.

"Well, maybe," she said.

"Sam," his father said in a gentle tone. "What's going on?"

"It's not me and I have zero intention of continuing to argue about it," he said. He tasted his drink again. "What else is up with y'all?"

"You are lying to us," his father said, a surprise, because his father was the quieter one; it was his mom who loved to argue. Steel in his tone. "That is you in the picture. You were in one of the most dangerous places in the world, where we lost your brother, and you don't get to shrug this off. Not when we have lost him and not when you have a child to answer for."

"At least I didn't drag my child there with me," Sam said, before he thought. He couldn't look at them for a moment and he stared into his drink.

"Sam," his father said, quiet again.

"OK. That's fair," Simone said. "Maybe let's all take a deep breath, OK? Alex? Sam?"

Sam did as his mother suggested and took a deep breath. His father kept his gaze steady on Sam.

Simone said, "But please don't lie to us. Why were you there?"

This was going to be a dividing line. A before and after, in his life. "I used . . . I used to work for the CIA. It was classified. I stopped working for them after Lucy . . . after Lucy got shot."

He only heard the grandfather clock ticking in the hallway. Lucy was shot at the so-called Yankee Stadium incident. A helpless victim, they thought, their lovely, quiet daughter-in-law who had been in the wrong

140

place at the wrong time. That was what the world was told, and there was no reason to disbelieve it.

"It wasn't random. Someone tried to shoot me and Lucy was hit."

His parents stared at him. The ice in his father's drink rattled. Daniel jumped up onto Sam's knees, wanting attention. Sam touched his son's hair and stared at the top of his head.

"Lucy and I both worked for the CIA," he added. "That was where we met. Not at church."

Simone took Sam's hand. "Baby, why didn't you tell us?"

It was so hard to say. "Because of Danny. I joined the CIA because of Danny."

"Oh, Sam," his father said. He reached out and touched his son's shoulder. Sam saw tears in his mother's eyes. He had not seen her react with such emotion since Danny was taken.

"I left the CIA after Lucy got hurt. A few weeks ago the CIA got new information on a village where Danny and Zalmay were taken after they were captured. In the Hindu Kush mountains. A CIA contact took me there. We found a grave."

They hardly dared to breathe. Leonie stood in the doorway to the kitchen. Sam could see tears in her eyes, her hand pressed to her mouth.

The only sound in the house was Daniel singing a Wiggles rhyme to himself and the ticking of the clock in the hallway. "We think we found Zalmay's body. His parents don't know anything about this yet. The identification tests aren't finished; probably we'll know tomorrow." It was all he could bear to say. "But not Danny's body. It wasn't there."

"Well, what does that mean?" Simone whispered.

"I don't know. I guess they took his body somewhere else."

Simone paled.

"Why would they do that? What reason could they have?" Alex asked. "No body. No body could mean . . ."

"I don't know, Dad."

Alexander Capra put an arm around his wife. She set down her drink on the coffee table. Her surgeon's hand, normally steely and controlled, quivered. Daniel toddled toward Leonie and she scooped him up, saying, "Come help me, sweet boy, OK, you sit with me and make me laugh." They vanished into the kitchen.

"Are . . . are they going to keep looking for Danny?" Alexander asked.

Well, I am, Sam thought. He wondered

what his parents would think of him, if they'd known he'd snapped the neck of one man and shot another one in the head to escape with the location of the village. That he'd threatened the Hungarian guard's family, even when he didn't mean it. Would they turn away in surprise or shock? They were devout Episcopalians who had devoted their lives to healing and helping and he . . . hadn't. They were good and he was . . . not.

If Danny hadn't been killed on video, if Sam hadn't wanted to avenge him, what would he have done with his life?

Would he ever have entered the CIA? Would he ever have met Lucy? Would he have Daniel, the whole center of his life?

His parents mourned what they'd lost; he realized that he mourned the life he hadn't chosen.

What did they make Danny into was Seaforth's question. Sam wondered instead what Danny had made *him.*

No. He had no time to waste on *what if.* What was done was done and he had to find his brother. Not to ask him those questions.

But to love him and forgive him and try to bring him home.

He answered his father's question. "I don't know that they have any new leads based on finding Zalmay."

"Maybe . . . ," his mother started to say. "Maybe . . ."

"Don't, Simone," his father said. He couldn't deal with hope, the sudden awful curse of it brewing in his wife's mind.

"If his body wasn't with Zalmay's . . . he could be . . . alive . . . maybe still a prisoner somewhere . . . oh, Danny, *Danny* . . ." And Sam saw how this was its own fresh hell.

"We don't know that," Alexander said. "The video . . . he died. We saw him die."

"Then where is his body?"

"Mom," Sam said, "we only know what we know."

Simone stared at Sam, as though his face had suddenly come into focus. Then she leaned forward and grabbed his head. She had very strong hands. Her fingers tightened in his hair.

"And you! What were you thinking! You don't ever, *ever* go back there. We lost one son there; I couldn't bear to lose you, too. And what about Daniel! Did you think of him, if he lost you? You *never* go back there."

"Mom, please, let go . . ."

"Samuel Clemens Capra, you promise me." Her voice was a harsh whisper of fear and love.

"I promise, Mom."

She kissed the top of his head and he felt her tears trickle onto his hair. She had never shown him such raw emotion. He sat back, staring at his dad, feeling a gentle touch on his cheek from his mother's thumb. He was speechless in the wave of their love.

He felt a fool. There had been times in the awful emptiness after Danny's death when he could hardly talk to them. They were the walking wounded. He hadn't tried hard enough — neither had they — to push past the pain. Now he helped his mother to her feet and put an arm around his father's shoulders. They went into the kitchen to keep their hands and brains busy, to help Leonie finish fixing dinner, Daniel's laughter a sweet refrain.

He walked his parents home. Their residence was only five blocks distant, and Sam had bought his house to be close to them. They went inside and his father said, "I think I'm going to go to bed, son. Have a good trip to New York. I wish you were staying longer."

"Soon, Dad, I'm going to be giving up the bars. I'll be home all the time then."

"What will you do?"

"I don't know yet."

"All right. Good night. Simone, don't stay

up all night." Her insomnia was legendary.

"I won't," she said. She went to the kitchen counter, picked up a wine bottle with a cork loose in its neck, and gushed pinot noir into a big glass. She raised the bottle at Sam. He nodded and she poured him a glass.

He could hear the soft strains of music from upstairs. John Gary's marvelous, haunting recording of "Danny Boy." They'd played it at Danny's memorial service. It had been a song that their parents sang to the boys when they were young, going to sleep and scared in the foreign lands they lived in, and Sam had once asked why there was no song called "Sammy Boy" to be sung.

That's dumb, Danny had said. *It's because I was here first.*

So Simone had taken the words to "Danny Boy" and made up new lyrics for "Sammy Boy," tousling Sam's hair as she sang, and Sam would smile to have a song he could share with his brother.

Now Sam looked up at the ceiling, closing his eyes in memory.

"He'll put that on repeat until he falls asleep," Simone said.

Sam sipped at his wine. "Mom, you cannot tell anyone I worked for the CIA."

"Your father and I are like a bank for secrets," she said. "We put them away and let them grow." She sat across from him. "If they took his body away, it was for a reason. If they didn't kill him . . ."

"We have no reason to think he's alive," Sam said bluntly, trying to spare her the poison of hope.

They drank the pinot noir in silence. Finally Simone said, "He could survive. Zalmay, he was more American than Danny. He was a suburban kid. Danny saw suffering. Danny . . . and you grew up knowing how cruel the world could be. You saw disaster and mayhem and death. And I'm sorry for that, but in a way I'm not. It made you strong."

He set down his wineglass. A suburban childhood didn't sound like a bad thing at all to him — he wanted a saner, calmer childhood for Daniel. But to say so would hurt her, and so he stayed silent.

"I want you to have something," she said. "Your brother wrote it. Read it when you're alone. I've kept it for you. I thought I might never give it to you, but I think you should see it. Because if anyone could survive there . . . it's Danny."

She got up and vanished for five minutes, in the back of the house, and then returned with a large brown envelope. It was sealed, signed by his parents, marked "To be opened by Sam when the time is right."

"We sealed it up after Danny died. We don't need to read it again. Read it and then keep it or burn it."

"Burn something Danny wrote? Mom, I couldn't." It was unthinkable.

"It's not a memento I care to keep. Go home and spend some time with your little boy before you go, Sam. You will never get those hours back."

He looked at the envelope. The song, repeating, drifted from upstairs. "In sunshine or in shadow . . ."

"That song fit not only his name, but it's about a boy going off to war, and Danny was that. We just didn't accept it." She touched Sam's shoulder. "If I had known his death would make you join the CIA and put yourself in harm's way" — her voice trembled — "I would have made you read what he wrote. But I had no idea. I thought you were safe from knowing about him. I'm sorry, Sam. I'm so sorry."

The song, from upstairs: "If I am dead, as dead I well may be . . ."

Sam walked home under the moaning branches of the trees overhanging the street, the damp air of New Orleans pressing against his skin like an unwanted hug. The envelope felt heavy as iron in his hand. He was afraid of what was inside.

Daniel was still awake, a treat since his daddy was home, so Sam lay on the floor and played with Daniel, let himself relax, let himself be a father again. Let himself remember those ties of blood. He laughed. He let himself smile.

It felt like an act.

The envelope lay unopened at his feet. Daniel picked it up, tossed it aside onto the couch.

Danny let you think he was dead. Danny walked away from you all. Maybe he didn't have a choice. Maybe not at first. But it's been nearly six years. He left you. You could leave him. You have Daniel. You have a friend in Leonie. You'll be free of Jimmy. He decided not to think about Mila, but she drifted at the edges of his thoughts. He pushed her image away; Daniel eclipsed all.

But still. You want to know why. What if he's in trouble? What if he's trapped in a life he doesn't want?

Or he just wanted a new life. One without you.

Sam had hold of Daniel's foot, much to Daniel's delight. "Mmmm," Sam said.

"Toeberries. I love me some toeberries." And he pretended to pluck the toes, like ripe fruit, and made a gobbling noise. Daniel laughed and screamed and said, "Toeberries, Daddy!"

He picked up Daniel and held him close. Daniel grabbed at his nose and his mouth, giggling hysterically. It made Sam's heart full; the times he didn't call, the guilt of those moments fell on his shoulders. He had to do better by his child.

Sam let Daniel giggle and nuzzle against his chin. He was growing fast, so fast, too fast. Sam wasn't ready for it. "I'm getting out of the business." To say it, with Daniel on his lap, was a relief.

Leonie looked hard at him. "Which business?"

"Both of them." Being the bar owner, and being the pocket spy for the Round Table.

Relief crossed her face. "So. Are you going back to work for the CIA?" Her voice got quiet. He knew the question she was asking. *Do you still need me to take care of Daniel, a baby I love more than life itself? A child I think of as my own?*

"No."

He saw her sudden, bright fear. He wouldn't need her anymore.

Daniel was getting older. He would require explanations. He called Leonie "Mommy" now. She had tried once, her heart breaking, to tell him to call her "Leonie," but he was around other children with mommies, and she was the sole caretaker in his daily life. She was Mommy now. And they had to find a way to make that work, although Sam was the one with the full legal rights.

He picked up Daniel and went into the kitchen. She followed. "I'm not sure what I'm going to do for a living. I'll figure something out. But I have to finish something first. I didn't tell my parents everything," he said. "I couldn't."

"What?"

"What!" Daniel bellowed.

Sam explained about the prison, finding Danny's photo, what the Hungarian guard said. He clutched Daniel to him and told her, and she took Daniel from him. "Sam. You're squeezing him too hard."

"I'm sorry. I'm sorry." He sank into the chair.

"I cannot believe you just had dinner with them and kept this from them . . ."

"I think we had enough revelations tonight."

"Why would he do this? Not tell you he was alive?"

"He must not have had a choice." Sam looked at her. "I mean, look, the CIA loved me. Kid who grew up all over the Third World, spoke several languages, contacts and friends in dozens of countries, quick study, athletic. Danny was the same. Someone other than the CIA could have found him . . . useful. This man, likely a Russian, who took him from Afghanistan to Brazil and trained him."

For a long moment the only sound was the tick of the grandfather clock in the hallway.

"You won't give this up, will you? Ever. Even if Danny doesn't want to be found."

"No."

"He can't matter more than this little boy, Sam. He just can't. You're putting yourself in a prison. You're . . ."

Sam looked at her. "You're in a prison. We're not a couple. Daniel's not your child. But you stay here. Why do you stay?"

"Because I can't leave this child with you chasing shadows. He needs me. He needs you. He cries for you. But what do you care, Sam? You're not here to hear it."

She got up and left the room.

Daniel had fallen asleep, the hours catching up to him. Sam carried him to his bedroom and laid him down. His light hair, starting to darken into the Capra brownish-blond, curled around his face. He had Sam's nose, but Lucy's mouth, her eyes. He stared at him for a moment, this center of their lives. Danny Boy. He thought of singing the song to his child; he had a clear, bright baritone voice. He knew all the words. He thought of the last line: "I shall sleep in peace until you come to me." Was Danny sleeping in peace somewhere? He kissed his sleeping son's forehead and turned out the light.

Leonie was drinking a glass of whiskey in the kitchen. "And what happens when you find Danny?" She finished off her whiskey with a toss, and when he didn't answer she set the glass down. "Bring him home to play uncle to his namesake? Have your parents over for dinner so he can unbreak their hearts and explain where he's been for six years? Has it occurred to you that whoever he's working with, whoever has shielded him, might kill you? That he doesn't want to be found?"

"I remade my life after he 'died.' Everything went wrong, and I did all this for him."

"Because of him. Not *for* him. You think choices are forced on you. You made your choices, Sam; live with them."

"Wouldn't you want to know, in my shoes?"

Her expression softened. "Of course I would. You love him. Of course I'd want to know. But I'd let other people find him. Not you. Stay out of it."

"I can't," he said. "I have to find him. I'm flying back to New York tomorrow morning. I'm meeting with a retired CIA analyst tomorrow night. She might be able to help me."

"I just think," Leonie said, "you might not like what you find."

12

London

When he landed in London, Judge went to an apartment he kept under a different name. He made a strong cup of tea and dialed a phone number, to ring a mobile phone deep in Russia. He left a voice mail, with his own phone number, and strict instructions to return the call.

He waited five minutes. His phone rang.

"Yes?" a man's voice said.

Judge said, in Russian, "The *bol'shoy chelovek* requires your services again."

"I don't know what you mean. He's dead."

"I am the heir, so to speak, of *bol'shoy chelovek*. Should you not recall our arrangements previously, I have the financial documents to outline your earlier dealings with my friend."

The man on the other end of the line made a gasp like he was dying. "Please. No."

"I will pay you one million American dollars for what I need."

The gasp faded into a greedy steeliness. "What is it you think you need?"

Judge answered with a word, and a number.

"I must be honest with you. I am not sure I can acquire it again," the man said.

"You can. Tomorrow I will arrive."

The man's voice cracked. "Impossible! Zheleznogorsk is a forbidden city." His tone went frantic, the sound of a person certain he is dealing with a dangerous fool or a madman. "You cannot simply arrive here, idiot! You must submit first a request to the Ministry, and they can take two months to approve it. The security agencies must also approve. Then you must have a formal letter of invitation to go with your visa — that can take another week, another month. Impossible."

"The paperwork was lost. You will fix the problems with it before tomorrow. Bribe well, bribe efficiently. I travel under a Belgian passport, the name on it is Jean-Claude Cerf, and I have visited the city before." He spelled out the name, the passport number. "I am a software consultant here to discuss a proposal to enhance your satellites. My company is called CDF. You will find my website; it has my photo, my details." The Cerf alias was one he had used many times.

"You ask too much."

"And I will pay you too much. But I have little time."

"It cannot be done."

"You know what can be done? A leak, to *Pravda,* or the *New York Times,* or the *Guardian,* about your previous dealings."

"That would destroy you as well."

"No. Just you. I'll see you tomorrow."

13

Manhattan

Margaret Granger's son owned an apartment in the same building as his mother, and she had told Sam to meet her at a cocktail party there. "His place will be full of TV stars, though," she told Sam on the phone.

The Magpie was a small, slightly heavy woman, in her mid-seventies, with a pageboy of gray hair, wearing a khaki skirt and a green sweater. The chattering beautiful people in her son's Manhattan apartment were all dressed in far greater finery than Margaret or Sam. They all worked on a TV show Margaret's son starred in, and Sam had never heard of it. This did not seem a diplomatic truth to admit, so he didn't speak to anyone. The men looked refined and spotless and Sam still imagined the grainy dust of the *katchi abadis* and the Hindu Kush in his hair. He and Margaret lasted ten awkward minutes, standing in the corner, until Margaret, studying him, decided she would talk to him.

"I understand you own a bar here in Manhattan, Sam." Margaret Granger gestured dismissively at the crowd. "Take me out of here for a real drink and we can talk."

Sam helped her up from her chair and she walked over to a thin, tall man in his forties and announced, "My guest and I are leaving, sweet pea, because no one will talk to us, and I thank you for that."

The younger man rolled his eyes and kissed the top of her head and told Sam it was nice to have met him and he hoped Sam enjoyed watching the rest of the season. Margaret sighed and turned away, gesturing Sam out into the hallway and shutting the door on the party.

"Season?"

"The TV season. My God, you'd think time was measured no other way. Where's this bar of yours?" Margaret Granger's apartment wasn't far from the Guggenheim Museum of Art, near Central Park.

A cab soon deposited them in front of The Last Minute. Sam steered her toward a private room, where they could talk alone. Margaret asked for whiskey and soda. Sam had the same.

"The Magpie," Sam said. "That's an interesting nickname."

Her eyes widened. "Did you not know you weren't supposed to call me that to my face?" Her voice rose.

Sam froze and then she burst out laughing. "I kid. I was very good at finding shiny objects, bringing them back to my nest, putting them in order . . ." and then she stopped.

"The shiny objects being useful information and sources that no other intelligence officer could get."

"Information on its own is nothing," she said. "The patterns created by information are everything." She sipped the whiskey.

"You were a field officer in charge of the Hindu Kush area during the time my brother was kidnapped. I want to know what you know. Seaforth said you're a walking library."

"The question is: What do *you* know?" Her gaze was avid on his face. He thought: She wants something back for whatever she gives. Little bits of information she can squirrel away herself? Why, if she's retired?

"Did Seaforth tell you what we found in the village?" he asked.

She nodded. "He sent me a complete report so I could try and help you. I'm sorry about your brother. Truly."

"There was a box of blank DVDs there, in a packing box with an address in Pakistan. The name on the address was Mirjan Shah."

She raised an eyebrow. "What are you asking me?"

"Were there DVDs made of my brother's execution?"

She sipped at her whiskey. "For a while there was a market for execution videos. They were sold on the street in Waziristan, in the tribal parts of western Pakistan that are only loosely under government control. DVDs, showing fallen Muslims and apostates getting their throats cut. Of course, the tapes have to be sent to the people who burn the DVDs, or they have to download them from the web. Mirjan Shah ran such an operation in Pakistan selling these snuff films. I think he saw himself more as a propagandist than a film mogul."

Sam wondered if the Magpie knew that each of her words felt like a burn against his skin.

"This room where he was killed. Describe it," she said.

"A red wall behind them, canvas on the floor. Some of the blood on the canvas was blood, but some wasn't. It was potassium thiocyanate and ferric nitrate. Fake blood."

"Mirjan Shah was faking executions there for videos," she said. "He sold something like eighty different execution videos. It was like a book-of-the-month club. They showed them at extremist schools in Pakistan, for God's sake."

"Why fake?"

"Because I think he had DVDs to sell and not enough executions to feed his demand."

Cut the latex rather than the throat, with the fake blood ready to spurt . . . hold up a head and not show the face . . . match the color of the hair . . . so it could be done. Maybe they faked Danny's execution because, there, with Mirjan Shah's equipment in place, faking his death was an actual option. Not a difficult one. It made his skin go cold.

"You seem to know a lot about Mirjan Shah."

"He was one of my assets," she said evenly. "Clearly he was in touch with someone at your brother's execution site. Sending them blank DVDs that would be returned to him."

"An asset? He was an informant for you?"

She nodded. "We wanted him to stay in the business of making those fake execution films. He could tell us who was buying them, who was moving them — it gave us a list of terrorist sympathizers. So we gave him the most sophisticated equipment. The artificial heads, the latex skin that could go over the throat for the cut, at just the right thickness and consistency to look realistic . . . all that came from the CIA. He told his associates he had a friend in Hollywood who had made them for him. That's how outside experts could be tricked by his videos. Including the one with your brother, I think. Of course he edited true execution videos as well, that extremists sent to him, so we could never be sure if your brother's was real or not, and Mirjan wasn't there when they were 'killed' to tell us, one way or another."

Sam was speechless. No one had ever told him or his family there was a chance Danny's death was faked.

Margaret didn't seem to notice his stunned reaction: "Mirjan, poor fool. He died not long after your brother went missing. Shot to death. Occupational risk. You'd think he'd end up in a video of his own if they'd known he was a CIA asset."

"Would they have sent him the missing hard drive from the laptop we found? So he could edit the footage?"

Her mouth narrowed. "Normally they would just send him the file, burned to a CD. But I suppose they could have. Why?"

"I'm wondering how many takes there were of that video. Or if the executioners were ever filmed without their masks on." Sam went to the door and asked Bertrand to bring them another round.

Bertrand did, and when he left the Magpie spoke again, softly: "You know, we backed Mirjan because he hid a software code on those DVDs, each one unique for each execution video. It sent Langley, without the viewer knowing, their IP address if they watched on a laptop that was connected at that moment to the Internet. It was critical information in those early stages of the war. It gave us extremist locations to monitor, to watch, to send drones to bomb. Too many, almost — we had to narrow it down. And then Mirjan got killed. But before his operation was blown, I thought it interesting that we got signals from two unexpected places. The code indicated they'd watched a DVD Mirjan created of your brother's 'death.' And neither was in Pakistan."

"Where?"

"Moscow and New York. One was in the offices of a private security firm in Moscow. Owned by a married couple who were ex–Russian intel. Husband was KGB, wife was military intel. Now, the Russians were good little dance partners for us in Afghanistan. It's possible that there's nothing to this, that one of their people got hold of the DVD and sent it on and that it's nothing."

Another Russian connection. "But a private security firm, not government."

"The line between corporations working for the government, and the government, has gotten much blurrier, Sam. Especially in Russia. Most of the billionaires running Russia are ex-KGB. But the DVD could have been found during one of their own counter-terrorism operations, sent, and watched. It could be nothing. It was watched, only once, in the offices of Belinsky Global. Sergei Belinsky was a close buddy of the Morozovs, supposedly did dirty jobs for them, killed in a car bombing blamed on the Chechen militants. His wife, Irina Belinskaya, took over for him after she killed every Chechen connected with her husband's death."

A security operative. "And New York?"

"That was traced to an IP address in a studio in Brooklyn. An artist and art dealer who works in digital media."

"Name?"

"Avril Claybourne. She makes short films that are shown in museums and galleries, as art. Rubbish, if you ask me. But I don't know art."

"Did . . . did she use footage from my brother's video in her art?"

"She did not." The Magpie sipped at her whiskey. "We checked on her. She makes a lot of money from her garbage, but that's not a crime." She set the glass down on the table.

"Assume I'm right and Danny wasn't killed. Why would he be kept alive?"

She was silent. "Maybe . . . he was an opportunity."

"You must have had another asset in the area other than Mirjan Shah. That village seems to have been a way station at the time."

She said, "Yes. I had another asset in the area. But I cannot tell you his name."

The other informant surely couldn't still be there or be alive. He tried another tack. "They didn't let Zalmay talk on the video. Only Danny. Why?"

"Psychology analysis suggested that either Zalmay was too injured, or they did not care to risk he would say something in Pashto that would be dangerous for the Afghan audience to hear. But . . . I think that's a bit silly, don't you?" She ran a hand through her gray hair. Sam thought: The Magpie is deciding whether or not to share her shiny objects.

Finally she said, "Did you ever wonder why *they* were taken?"

"They worked for a relief agency, a Christian one."

"But if the Brothers of the Mountain weren't religious extremists . . . but smugglers, why take these two Americans?"

He gave no answer.

She tapped a finger against her cheek. "One of them was a CIA operative," she whispered.

"That can't be. The agency doesn't recruit humanitarian workers." Sam knew this from the long years of his parents' work. There had been instances where relief workers had been accused of being CIA agents — falsely — and the entire charity would find its workers expelled from a country. It had happened, prominently, with Save the Children, in Pakistan, and a few other charities. The CIA kept its distance from relief workers, most of whom were not of a temperament for covert work.

"We had a bonfire with the rule books after Nine-Eleven," the Magpie said. "You know that. And to have an Afghan, also fluent in English, on the ground . . ."

The shock nearly cut off his breath for a

moment. "Zalmay was CIA. Did Danny know?"

"I have no idea what went on between them out there in that wilderness."

He stood up suddenly from the table, furious with her. "You recruited my brother's best friend. You let him go with my brother into a war zone where they'd be prime targets. You . . ."

"Sit down. They were prime targets by virtue of being American relief workers," she said, coldness in her tone.

"Maybe they never knew Zalmay was CIA." Wrong, he thought, they knew. That's why they didn't let him talk. So he couldn't say anything in code to the agency, watching him die. They bound his mouth. They blindfolded him. He'd sat there as if asleep or drugged.

But if Zalmay was CIA, and Danny was a bystander — then Zalmay was the valuable one, to the Taliban. A greater value in propaganda and bargaining. Danny was no one.

Yet Danny lived and Zalmay died.

"I want to see Zalmay's 201 file. Tell Seaforth to give it to me. Please." A 201 file was the most complete file on any agency asset or operative.

"He can't show it to you." Slight emphasis

on *he.*

He stared at her. "You have a copy?"

"Lots of jewels in my old nest."

"What, it's in your apartment?"

She looked troubled for a moment, as if she'd said too much.

Sam gently took her hand and her face blanched in surprise. "Your other contact you had in the Hindu Kush. The one whose name you won't tell me. Who is he?"

Her eyes were bright diamonds and he realized she was a little drunk from the whiskey. "I won't tell you, because a little boy like you will end up dead. We had to work with bad people. He was . . . bad people."

"Please."

She shook her head. "What is your brother now, Sam? He could have called you. He could have come forward. He didn't. So either he's not alive or he wants nothing to do with you."

"I want to hear a reason from him."

"There is no reason that will satisfy you," she said, and he hated that she was right. But instead he said, "Margaret, I won't know that until I hear it."

"God help you," she said.

"Do you want more whiskey?" he asked.

"No, thanks," she said. "I've had enough. Take me back to the beautiful people."

14

Manhattan

Sam took the Magpie back to the apartment building. She announced she would return to her son's party, now that she was appropriately whiskeyed up to deal with her son's friends. "I need some merriment now," she'd said in the cab. Sam took her to the floor, got her settled with a fresh drink, and then went down the few floors to Margaret's own apartment.

You have a copy? She hadn't said no. And she hoarded her secrets.

The lock opened up under his picks and he was inside. The apartment itself was neat, tidy, family photos of the actor son, vintage photos of the Magpie's husband and parents. Cities across Europe, Russia, and Asia. Margaret stood alone in those.

He went through the apartment. She had a modified pocket door that had a padlock on it, like something you'd see in an old

171

factory. He knelt before it and it opened, eventually, under his picks. He slid the door open.

File cabinets, a table with papers in stacks, photos and notes taped to the wall. This was her magpie's nest. There wasn't a computer, but there was a typewriter, an old Selectric restored, and a neat stack of typewritten manuscript next to it. Old-school, inconvenient, but unhackable. The Magpie knew that the agency's eyes, digitally, might be watching her, even in retirement.

He went to the file cabinets. Unlocked. He looked for a file on Quereshi, Zalmay. There wasn't one. Neither was there one on Capra, Daniel. He pulled out a file at random to examine. And, stunned, saw it was an original. Not a copy. Everything had been digitized at Langley at some point, and these old paper files were what . . . to be burned? Serve as backups? Instead she had smuggled them out, like the famous Vasili Mitrokhin had in the KGB in the 1980s, sneaking the Soviet spy agency's greatest secrets out in his socks and shoes, stuffed down the back of his pants, then hidden in the floorboards of his Moscow home. The Magpie must have done the same.

He began searching the files stacked by

the typewriter, and three files in he found it. Zalmay's 201 file: his life, through the prism of the CIA. The file wasn't under his name, but a code name, given him by his handler Margaret: FDJETTY. *FD* was the CIA cryptonym to indicate he operated in Afghanistan, *jetty* a randomly chosen word. His family history. His education. A detailed background check of his Afghan parents, whose family had been loyal to Afghanistan's last king, Zahir, before he was deposed in 1973, and they'd come to the United States. His family checked out, impeccable.

Then his assignment. He was to make contact with anti-Taliban forces, cultivate informants, relay information back to Margaret. So he would have been looking for sources. Had one of them betrayed him and Danny to the Brothers of the Mountain?

He had used Danny for cover. Had Danny ever known?

There was a list of names, code names, cross references to numbered files. FD-THUNDER. FDPTOLEMY. FDCURE. FDGALLEON. The sources Zalmay recruited to feed him, and in turn the Magpie, information in Afghanistan.

Hands starting to shake, Sam looked up each name in the file cabinets.

FDTHUNDER, FDCURE, and FD-GALLEON were all dead. FDPTOLEMY wasn't. His real name was Ahmad Anwari, and he was alive, and he was living in the United States.

The Magpie had known his name but had said, *I won't tell you, because a little boy like you will end up dead. . . . He was . . . bad people.*

The Anwari file showed a thickly muscled man, bearded, cruel eyes, a harsh mouth with a knife-scarred lip. He had been extracted from Afghanistan a few years ago, given a new identity here, for services rendered. No details. Now he lived in Fremont, California. His new name was Ahmad Douad. He ran a nursery and greenhouse.

Ahmad had given a series of statements about his CIA work, and Sam paged through the transcripts until he found what he wanted: *They were taken by a group called The Brothers of the Mountain . . . I heard later that they kept the two aid workers shut up in a village that no one went to . . . they killed them both. They had Mirjan Shah in Pakistan edit a video for them of the deaths, he sells such things where believers don't have Internet. Zalmay was my contact and someone told the Brothers Zalmay was CIA. His friend*

174

was unlucky, a nobody, not CIA like Zalmay; they beheaded him. I arrived after the executions, about two hours; I was shocked when I saw they had killed Zalmay. I thought they would kill me but Zalmay had not talked or named me as a source. I saw both the bodies. One of the men joked with me that they had to kill Zalmay before the video was made; when his throat was cut he was already dead. I didn't understand why and he said not to ask. No one would explain this oddity to me. I thought it was that they knew he was CIA, but then they would have announced they were killing a CIA asset in the video. Or they would have kept him and questioned him or sold him to the Taliban. They took the bodies away, I don't know where. Probably burned them or threw them off a cliff or buried them where they couldn't be found. No one stayed in that village; all moved on. May I have another cigarette now?

That was a lie. No mention of a Russian, shot to death. Sam closed his eyes: In his mind's eye of the video Zalmay was blindfolded and gagged and not moving before they cut his throat and shoved him out of the camera's frame . . .

Sam wrote down Ahmad Douad's name, address, and phone number. He returned the file to where he'd found it. He headed out into the night.

Choose, he thought. He could follow the thread of the artist, this Avril Claybourne, who had watched the illicit execution DVD made by Mirjan Shah, or the Ahmad thread. Ahmad had claimed to have had eyes on Sam's brother's body — that trumped all. Sam took a cab back to The Last Minute, booking himself via his phone on the earliest flight out tomorrow morning to San Jose, feeling like he finally held a bit of luck. Even if he'd had to steal it.

15

Fremont, California

Sam's flight had left New York the next morning at 5:45 a.m., making a stop in Houston for a few sleepy travelers to disembark and be replaced by passengers holding fresh cups of coffee. He arrived in San Jose a few minutes after eleven that morning, local time. He picked up his rental car, plugged in the GPS, and headed for Fremont. He'd studied about the town on the plane, reading articles on his tablet computer — it held a large, diverse population of immigrants: Afghan, Chinese, Indian, Pakistani. Dozens of languages spoken at home. Less than forty percent of the population was native born. There was a section of town known as Little Kabul, which sounded big, but was only a stretch of one street. A few journalists had written about Fremont in the aftermath of the post-9/11 invasion, and come away saying that the

Afghan immigrants here were caught in a weird limbo: not yet assimilated, suspicious of outsiders, but trying to become more "American." Law enforcement kept an eye on the community for signs of radicalization. Among the immigrants were a high percentage of people suffering from post-traumatic stress disorder — most had, after all, fled in the face of the Soviet invasion and then the violent rise of the Taliban — but not seeking help beyond that of family. Another essayist wrote about Fremont's widening gap between the far more Americanized children of the immigrants and their parents, caught in a cultural amber. He thought these immigrants were doing far better than those trapped in the unrelenting poverty of the slums outside Islamabad.

He wondered how Ahmad Anwari, now Douad, fit into this new America. And why the Magpie was so afraid of a gardener.

The nursery was called Happy Plants. It was large, with a wide variety of shrubs, rosebushes, and trees. A few shoppers wandered through the outdoor aisles, one woman loudly ordering from a list while a nursery assistant loaded two carts with her purchases.

Sam strolled around. Then he saw the

man once known as Ahmad Anwari, inspecting fountains for sale with a buyer, who was talking and gesturing. He looked like his photo in the Magpie's file, just ten years older. More gray in his hair, the scar on his lip a bright twist of skin.

Sam ambled away from them, toward rows of brightly colored pots. A clerk offered to help him and Sam smiled and said he was just browsing. The young man, bright-faced and friendly, told Sam his name was Nur-Ali, if he needed help. Sam thanked him and the young clerk headed off to another customer.

The breeze, pleasant, smelling of roses and jasmine, stirred the air. Sam took out his cell phone and pretended to make a call, but he snapped a photo of Ahmad as he held the phone up to his ear. He put the phone back in his pocket.

The buyer and Ahmad walked back to the main building. Sam went to the fountains and watched the water dribble in the demonstration model. He waited and studied the pattern in the ripples, and ten minutes later Ahmad approached him. "Hello, sir? Are you looking for a fountain today?"

"These are like some fountains I once saw in Kabul," Sam said. He kept his voice low, his smile pleasant.

Ahmad just nodded. Waiting.

"Your nursery was recommended to me by my friend Zalmay Quereshi."

Ahmad didn't nod this time. "I don't know that name."

"I think you knew him when you lived in Afghanistan."

Ahmad said nothing. As if waiting.

"A woman who worked with Zalmay years ago sent me. We need to speak."

"About what?"

"Someone gave you a new name. Maybe they even gave you this nice nursery. But you lied to them, didn't you? You said *both* the relief workers were dead."

"That's not quite accurate," he said after a moment.

"Then what's the story?"

The mouth with its cruel scar smiled. "We close tonight at seven. Can you come back then and we can talk?"

"Yes," Sam said. "I'll see you at seven."

Once, one of Sam's trainers in Special Projects told him that the greatest terror you might face is waking up and it's all gone wrong and you're a prisoner. You're chained, you're tied. And the worst part is that you're at someone else's mercy.

You must not panic.

Sam opened his eyes. The pain rose hard, like a wave.

He remembered.

He'd left the nursery.

He'd gone to Ahmad Douad's house, picked the elaborate locks, found nothing of interest except cash hidden in a closet. About twenty thousand dollars' worth, unmarked, nonsequential bills. He'd left the house, the money untouched. Then he'd eaten lunch, tried to call Mila. No answer. No messages from Jimmy; his offer of help had become worthless. No message yet from Jack Ming, trying to find the woman who'd taken his brother from Buenos Aires. He'd looked up Ahmad Douad in the local paper at the library's online archives. Model citizen. His nursery had done well and he'd contributed plants to a beautification project at a school, donated to a local scholarship to send the kids of Afghan immigrants to college. He seemed like an American success story.

He tried to piece time back together. He'd left the library and then returned to the nursery when it closed at seven. Gotten out of his rental car and walked toward the building and then . . . then . . .

"Are you here to kill me?" a voice had asked behind him.

"No," Sam had said. "Of course not . . ."

And then the thrum of a Taser, jarring, a heaviness striking his head. The murmur of the fountains, then blackness.

Sam blinked. A blur. His head ached. Anger at himself started to burn in his chest.

Ahmad, standing before him.

He sat in a well-lit room lined with nursery supplies, bags of mulch, stacks of pots. Shears and tools rested on a table, laid out in a frighteningly surgical order.

He tried to move. Arms tied to the wooden chair. Not his feet, though.

Ahmad, speaking to him. In Russian. "What is your name?"

"My name is Sam," he answered in groggy Russian.

"And now I know what you are," the voice said, still speaking Russian.

"I just wanted to talk to you," Sam managed to say. In English.

"So let's talk. But on my terms."

"My name is Sam Capra," Sam said.

"I already looked at your wallet."

"Does the name Capra mean anything to you?"

"It's the name of a dead man." The cruel lip curled. And then he went to the table and picked up the shears. Sam had been wrong — it wasn't shears. A large knife with

182

an ivory handle. The blade had a slight curve to it.

"Do you know what this is?" Ahmad said. Sam shook his head.

"It's the one treasure I brought to America with me. I had the clothes on my back and a few dollars and my family's *pesh-kabz*. I wouldn't leave it behind so the Americans had to let me bring it on the flight. A Pashtun knife." He examined it in the light again. "Designed to pierce chain mail, that's how old it is. Imagine what it can do to human flesh. My grandfather's grandfather used it against British soldiers in the Second Afghan War. My father and I used it against the Soviets. When I was just a teenager I saw him kill wounded Russians with this knife, dragged half-burned out of their tanks or their wrecked choppers. Sometimes the *pesh-kabz* brought mercy. Sometimes it brought terror." He watched Sam's eyes.

"The Magpie, from the CIA, sent me."

"No, she didn't," he said. "You spoke Russian to me."

"Because you did. I only answered . . ." Sam stopped, watching the man's cold glare.

"They used to give me the Russian soldiers to play with," Ahmad said.

"I only want to know . . ."

Ahmad put the tip of the *pesh-kabz*

against Sam's throat. "I want *you* to talk. In Russian, in English? Which will it be?"

"Look at my driver's license. My name. Capra. Same as the relief worker with Zalmay. Capra."

"A card, with a name that is a lie? I have one in my wallet. The Russians, maybe they sent you to find me. To get close to me with your lies." Ahmad began to walk around Sam, holding the *pesh-kabz* in one hand. "The Russian commanders, well, the *mujahaddin* would let them live, because they wanted information. But they would blind them. Cut off their noses, their balls, sew them up neat so they would heal. Cut off both hands, both feet, cauterize the wounds. It was important that they live, just so they could talk. I watched. I took notes. It was like a school."

A chill descended on Sam.

"What they'd do, before they blinded the commanders . . . they'd call it 'taking off the shirt.' You sit a commander down, and you strip a Russian soldier in front of him, and you make a cut around the soldier's torso. A nice straight line, all the way around." He drew it with the handle of the *pesh-kabz* on his own chest, wrinkling his fern-green nursery polo shirt that featured the Happy Plants logo on the chest.

"Then . . . you pull the skin up, like you are taking off a shirt. All the way." He smiled, joyless. "The screams would rupture their own vocal cords. Then a bullet to the head, when the point was made. And you make the commander watch every moment." He kissed the *pesh-kabz,* then took the knife and cut off Sam's shirt, ripping the fabric free. And he switched to Russian. "Ah. You have a lot of muscle. That will make it slower. More difficult. Now. Tell me who sent you, and what do they want?"

"I told you. I'm here about my brother. I am CIA; that is why I know Russian."

He placed the *pesh-kabz* against Sam's back, halfway up between beltline and shoulders, and made a small cut.

Sam grimaced, swallowed his scream as the knife began its slow, shallow trail. He spat out the words. "They killed . . . Zalmay but kept . . . my brother alive. Why?"

Ahmad seemed amused at Sam's continued questioning. "Zalmay died because he was a CIA agent."

The pain of the cut seared across his back. "Please . . . please . . . if someone sent me to kill you, I would have just killed you. I didn't . . . Just tell me . . ."

Sam screamed as Ahmad started cutting again. "I have to give up my nice life here because you've found me," Ahmad said. "That's not fair. So I have to send a strong message to whoever sent you. Was it the big man? Is that why the questions?" But he said *big man* in Russian: *bol'shoy chelovek.*

"The big man, what's his name?" Sam said, trying to keep the pain at bay.

Shattering sound. A rock, lobbed through the storage building's window.

Ahmad stared at the window. He called out a boy's name. "Nur-Ali!" — the name of the young man who'd offered to help Sam while he'd browsed that afternoon.

Ahmad moved to the door. He called out in Pashto, fast, sharp. He stepped outside.

The fight didn't last long but Sam could hear it: Ahmad's voice, bright and sharp and surprised, and then a mechanical sound, Ahmad screaming, the impact of him landing against the building. No gunfire. The sound stopped.

If *I* could find Ahmad, Sam thought, who else could find him?

Sam felt the blood dripping down his back. The door slowly began to open.

16

The Forbidden City

Imagine a city of nearly a hundred thousand people that for years was never on a map. Never called by its name, and when it finally was, it was given a bureaucratic code based on its region and number: Krasnoyarsk-26. Only during the reforms of Boris Yeltsin was it allowed to give itself a proper name and appear on maps.

A city where people were still not allowed to enter, or leave, without special permission.

Philip Judge sat in the backseat of a Mercedes, parked before the gates of the city.

ЖЕЛЕЗНОГО́РСК, said the sign. Zheleznogorsk.

It had been a long journey. Earlier he had flown into Moscow's Sheremetyevo Airport. He had expected there to be a snafu with his visa, given his final destination, and that he was a foreigner headed to a forbidden city. But the man in Zheleznogorsk he was coming to see — Dezhin — had conjured up a next-day paperwork miracle via pressure and bribes. Corruption at its finest. A senior official with Passport Control had arrived, murmuring about a paperwork error — Mr. Cerf had visited the forbidden city before — he apologized for the misunderstanding. There were papers shuffled, stamps made, and the official consulted his phone, no doubt to be sure the bribe had arrived in his bank. After a few moments, and a few additional polite questions about the purpose of his trip, his visa, along with the permission and paperwork to visit Zheleznogorsk, was stamped; he was given the migration card he was required to keep with his passport to check into any Russian hotel; and he was on his way. He did not allow himself to sweat. He did not reflect that he had probably set a world record in navigating a corrupt Russian bureaucracy.

He had then taken a taxi to Domodedovo Airport and then boarded a four-hour flight to Krasnoyarsk, in the heart of Russia. The passenger next to him — a Moscow pharmacist, going home to visit his elderly mother — was intrigued that he was Belgian and kept asking him what the West really thought of Morozov. A spy, Judge thought, sent by Dezhin to watch me.

They landed at Yemelyanovo Airport in Krasnoyarsk, on the southern edge of the vast Siberian taiga. To Americans, Siberia conjured an image of an unpeopled wasteland, but the airport here was bustling, much busier than Judge remembered from his only visit, a few years ago. At the luggage claim he saw a blocky, thick-necked man holding a card that read CERF, and he nodded at the man.

"Dr. Dezhin has sent me to collect you, sir, so you would not have to bother with the bus or taxi to Zheleznogorsk. My name is Vladimir." He had a voice like gravel, eyes like gray stone, fists like granite.

Judge nodded. He followed Vladimir to a black Mercedes and sat in the back. *If this is a trap, it is a neat one.*

With traffic, it took a little less than ninety minutes to reach the closed city. It was, to Judge, a bit like driving backward into a time when the Soviets built cities of science to drive their missile and space programs. After the collapse of communism, worries boiled up that unemployed scientists in cities such as Zheleznogorsk would sell dangerous technologies to criminals and terrorists. The city had decided to remain closed in 1996, to keep it small, and to feed the

Russian paranoia about technology development. They did not want the West stealing their secrets.

The Mercedes stopped at the black gate at the town's entrance. A guard checked both Vladimir's papers and those belonging to Jean-Claude Cerf. Judge was conscious of Vladimir's stare in the rearview mirror. After a moment, and checked against a list, they were waved through.

The town was much nicer than one might expect of a Soviet industrial city. The crème de la crème of the USSR's engineers and scientists had been housed here. It was a reminder not of Soviet degradation but Soviet privilege. Lots of offices, lots of blocks of apartments, not very many cafés or stores, and only one theater, with the old-fashioned name of *Rodina:* Motherland. But the city felt more modern, more quiet, less blighted than other Siberian cities.

He thought of the Big Man for a moment. There were times, oddly, that he missed Sergei, the way you might miss a person who played well against you in a sport. A person who pushed you to your limits.

Vladimir drove along straight streets and turned right into a large complex of buildings near the city's edge. The town, key to developing Russian military satellite programs, had gotten new life with the creation of GLONASS, the Russian version of GPS, the global positioning system. Here new satellites were designed, built, and launched, providing both an alternative and an enhancement to the GPS system. A year after offering full coverage of Russia, the GLONASS satellites added full global coverage.

Vladimir parked the limo and escorted Judge through two rings of security. Judge's mobile phone was confiscated, to be returned to him when he left, and he was frisked. His briefcase was searched. It contained a laptop; printouts of proposals in Russian, French, and English for a security audit of the GLONASS positioning system; and a few toiletries: chewable tablets to relieve indigestion, eyedrops to reduce redness, breath mints, toothbrush in a small plastic container. These items were briefly examined but not confiscated.

Vladimir then walked him through a large design complex. Models of satellites, from the early Soviet six-winged Molniya and Kosmos 1, known in the West as Sputnik 11, hung from the ceiling. A large cubicle space held technicians and designers. Here Zheleznogorsk looked the same as the West: high-end computers on desks, bright young people working on the keyboards and screens, large computer simulations and displays flashing. No one paid any attention to Vladimir and the Belgian.

Vladimir took him into an enclosed office at the end of the hallway. "I will wait outside," he intoned in his baritone voice, closing the door behind him.

Dezhin sat at the table. It had been cleared of papers and pens, and his computer screen was dormant. He was in his fifties, with a reddened nose bright as a winter berry. His hair was white, smoothed down, and his suit was a good one, a quiet gray. But his eyes were bleary with fatigue. Judge guessed the man had not slept all night.

"Are you afraid of me?" Judge gestured toward the door. "The human mountain out there looks like he wants to kill me."

"You have made life difficult for me," Dezhin said by way of greeting. "You may speak freely here. The room has been secured against electronic listening devices. The research heads are paranoid that the West will try to steal their secrets. Like the West doesn't know how to make or build satellites. So this is where we talk to ensure we cannot be overheard."

"Thank you for making the time to see me."

Dezhin gave a brittle laugh. "As if I had a

choice. You asked the impossible."

"Yet you delivered."

"Only made possible by the fact that you had been here once before."

"I know it made for a long night for you. But a most profitable one."

"I must insist to know why you need the . . . weapon."

"You didn't ask before."

"You had a Russian with you last time. This time you are alone."

I'm going to kill your president, he thought, but instead he said, "Let me just say that my target is a great enemy of the Russian people, and the reason I can bribe you so well is because an important Russian leader wants him dead." It was all true.

"Last time I was promised the . . . weapon could not be traced to this facility. There is so little of it . . . produced each year."

"Yes, and when there was suspicion before about where the poison came from, it was aimed at nuclear facilities. Not at you. This will be the same. Listen, before, your co-operation got us what we needed to eliminate enemies who would say lies about Russia. In London, in Paris. Silenced, and dead. You did not panic then, you must not panic now."

"But after those poisonings, there are

more stringent inventory controls. Careful ones. I cannot . . ."

"You administer the inventory. Simply use less in a design test and say you've used more. It's not my job to solve your problems. That is, after all, Dr. Dezhin, what I am paying you for."

After a moment Dezhin set a vial of eyedrops down on the desk. It was the same brand as the eyedrops in Judge's bag.

"Thank you for meeting my specifications." Judge picked it up and held it to the light. "Polonium-210. Discovered by Marie Curie, who named it for her native Poland."

Now Dezhin looked at him. "Remember: You're safe as long as it's outside your body. Its alpha particles can't penetrate the skin. But if you breathe it in or ingest it, even a tiny amount . . . it is over two hundred *million*" — he paused for effect — "times more toxic than cyanide."

Judge picked up the eyedrops bottle, held it up to the light. He decided to lecture Dezhin back. "Suspected in the deaths of at least one Russian dissident in London, whose teapot at a posh hotel was supposedly poisoned with it by FSB operatives. He died, in agony, in the hospital of radiation poisoning. And of a crusading Russian journalist in Paris — put in her wine, no suspect ever identified. She drank the wine, boarded a flight to Morocco, thinking she would escape those targeting her. She died in days, also in agony. Has also been suspected in the death of Yasser Arafat. Used only in very special cases. The Big Man loved it." *Bol'shoy chelovek.*

"Unproven, though," Dezhin said.

"But once inside the body, the alpha emitters destroy cells. Rapidly. First the cells that regenerate the fastest: the digestive tract, bone marrow, hair. Baldness and agony first and then the rest of the body is eaten away. Death, in a matter of days or weeks. But that can point to many poisons, yes? Thallium. Radium. But polonium's alpha particles do not set off radiation detectors, so it can be a mobile poison. It can go across borders. It can destroy a body from inside but its emitters cannot penetrate glass or paper."

"I don't need to hear of its virtues. Just take it and go."

"Useful in the powering of satellites. Producing it normally would require a nuclear reactor, set up to bombard the element bismuth with neutrons. As you noted, it is rare: Only a hundred milligrams a year are produced, worldwide. Which is why polonium-210 always seems to point back to a nuclear facility as a source. Not a research and development station like this one."

Dezhin waited.

"Let's sit here long enough to let me complete my presentation," Judge said. He opened his tablet computer, set it on its built-in stand, and removed the stylus from its holder. He tapped on the screen and the two men sat, in silence, the fake Powerpoint presentation on Jean-Claude Cerf's tablet playing, slide by slide. Dezhin kept checking his watch. Judge kept the stylus in his hand. They stared at each other, not at the slides. And when it was done, Judge put the glass vial of "eyedrops" back in his bag.

He stood. "Our business is concluded."

"It would be better if you spent the night, for appearances' sake. I have reserved a room at a hotel here for you. Vladimir will take you there."

A trap. He was certain of it. They wanted him dead so they could take back the money and return the polonium to the inventory. Judge had no intention of staying where he was under Dezhin's power. "Unfortunately I have just received word that my poor mother back in Belgium is seriously ill. I must leave immediately. It was nice to see you again, Dr. Dezhin. We will not see each other again. Enjoy your retirement."

"I'm afraid not," Dezhin said.

The door opened and before Vladimir could step through Judge had thumbed the cap off the tablet computer's stylus and had it at Dezhin's throat. "Basically it's a plastic stiletto. Sharpened to a needle point. Doesn't alert X-ray or metal detectors. Now. Vladimir. Go stand in the corner, or I open up his carotid." Judge's hand was steady at Dezhin's throat. "I do that, then we're all in trouble, we're all in jail."

Vladimir's massive hand was in a fist. He glanced at Dezhin.

"Do . . . do as he says."

"Drop the car keys on his desk. I'll drive myself back to the airport."

Vladimir obeyed. He stood in the corner, hands on the wall, back to the other two men.

"Now. *Bol'shoy chelovek* may be gone, but I have friends in Russia. And if I do not make it to the airport without interference, they will come here. You will not see them coming and they will slip into this forbidden city with no difficulty. They will kill you both. I don't think I can be clearer. Be happy with the million dollars I've paid you."

He saw Vladimir's heavy shoulders stiffen.

"I suggest you share fairly with Vladimir here," Judge said.

Dezhin managed the barest of nods. "Go, then. Just go."

Judge drove himself back to Yemelyanovo Airport in Krasnoyarsk. He parked Vladimir's Mercedes in a lot and left the keys under the mat. The fact the two idiots had thought of betraying him was deeply unsettling, and if he hadn't been cautious enough to have a weapon hidden . . . he might well never have left the forbidden city. He got on the last flight that would make it back to Moscow in time for him to jump on a red-eye back to JFK.

He had the polonium; now he needed to penetrate the circle. He studied, on his smartphone, a story from a frothy lifestyle blog. Stefan Varro and Katya Kirova, the children of billionaire oligarchs, had been photographed leaving a nightclub in the Virgin Islands. The Kirov superyacht, *Svetlana,* had been sailing, over the past few days, from Puerto Rico to the British Virgin Islands and now to Nassau.

He would trade the cold of Siberia for the warmth of the Bahamas. But first he had to finish his final preparations. He would go to Miami.

17

Fremont

The door swung open. Mila stepped inside. Sam blinked at her in shock.

Mila held Ahmad's *pesh-kabz* and she used it, wordlessly, to cut Sam's ropes.

Then she went back outside and dragged an unconscious Ahmad and the young man inside the building. She tied them with plastic cuffs on their wrists and their feet. Nur-Ali was maybe twenty, wearing an Ohlone College T-shirt. The young man started to rouse, and she wrapped tape around his head, over his ears, eyes, and mouth, leaving his nostrils free. She carefully cut a slice in the tape over his mouth.

Then she came to Sam and set down the *pesh-kabz.*

"Let me see the damage," she said by way of hello, in the cool tone of one not bothered by blood. "The cuts are not deep. Here." She took cloth from a locker in the corner and wrapped it around his waist, stanching the blood. The incision wasn't as long as it had felt while Ahmad was making it. "I can bandage that up."

He tried not to shiver in relief as Mila helped him to his feet.

"I Tasered both the boy and him with his own weapon," she said, before Sam asked.

Sam sat on the concrete floor and she bandaged him with a first aid kit she found in the shed. "You need stitches, but that will hold for now."

He nodded.

"How did you find me?"

"I tracked your phone and your credit card. Forgive me."

"Forgiven," he said, relieved.

"Your friend is waking up," Mila said. "I'll question him. I'm not quite as . . . emotionally involved as you are. Hand me that knife. It's well-balanced. Lovely grip."

In short order Ahmad was in the chair Sam had sat in, newly tied with fresh rope.

Mila and Sam stood in front of him.

"Happy Plants." Mila leaned down toward Ahmad. "Look at me."

He looked at her, with fear in his face, mistaking in his fear her Moldovan accent for a Russian one, recoiling, thinking she was Russian and so Sam was indeed from the Russian he feared.

His scarred lip twisted, like he meant to spit in her face, and she said, "Sam's a decent person. I'm not him. I am more like . . . you. I have had a very bad couple of days. I feel angry at the world. This is your bad luck. Do you understand me?"

He nodded.

"Answer me truthfully and you will get to hold on to your fake life here. But if you lie to me" — and her voice became a warm whisper, her mouth close to his ear — "the boy, how old is he?"

Ahmad writhed, trying to see Nur-Ali a few feet away on the floor. "Leave my stepson alone. He's only twenty. He knows nothing. Please."

Sam knew Mila had no intention of taking the knife to Nur-Ali. But Mila kept her voice cold. "So even a monster like you cares about *something* . . ."

"Please, I have said nothing about the Big Man to the Americans. *Nothing!*"

"We are not with the Big Man," Mila said. "All right? We're not. We want to know the truth of what happened with Zalmay and his friend. Just tell us and I won't hurt you or the boy. Lie to me and I'll cut you worse than you did my friend."

Ahmad kept his gaze on his family knife.

"Zalmay recruited me. He wanted to know about the smuggling networks, how product was moved out of the country. There are still smuggling rings moving product into Russia, and then the Russian ends of the smuggling rings were desperate to get all their product out of the country. The Taliban, sometimes they manipulate the heroin price when their funds get short. They shut off availability and the price skyrockets for a time. Then Russians want all their product out and headed for the markets. I was a fixer of sorts, for the Russians — when they needed work done in the Afghan villages, when they needed a spy, when they needed to know what the Taliban were doing about price. Because they're in business together, but they hate each other. So I was on three payrolls: Taliban, Russian, CIA. I worked with a Russian, they called him the Big Man. *Bol'shoy chelovek.*"

"What was his real name?" Mila asked.

"I don't know. He was a big man, physically, too." Ahmad wet his lips. "Rumor was he was very high in the KGB once. He used his contacts and his skills from intelligence work to get millions in heroin out of Afghanistan and Pakistan and into Russia. Then it could move on to Eastern Europe, Japan, even America."

"Why would Zalmay care about a heroin runner?" Mila asked.

"People said that the Big Man had ties to the Russian government. Highest level."

"Morozov? Why would the Russian president be involved in running heroin? He has plenty of other sources of revenue."

"I don't know . . . It's still millions of dollars' worth of product. Maybe he wanted money the government and his friends didn't know about. Who knows why a crazy Russian does anything?"

They were silent for several seconds. "This Big Man captured Zalmay?" Sam asked.

"Zalmay tried to recruit a man who worked for the Big Man as an informant. He and his relief-worker friend were grabbed while out on a survey trip to a village. The Big Man had them brought to a place in the mountains . . . an abandoned village. And there was a man who was the caretaker of the place; when it wasn't being used, he made fake execution videos there to sell on the streets in Waziristan and elsewhere."

"Mirjan Shah," Sam said.

He nodded. "They questioned them. I was so scared Zalmay would say I was his informant. But he did not. He insisted the blond American wasn't CIA. Then . . . I don't know why, maybe a joke, the Big Man made the blond American fight for his life, for sport. Not expecting he would win. He was a relief worker; everyone knows they cannot fight. The boss told one of the Russians to fight him, and he gave them each a *pesh-kabz*. The Russian did not take the American seriously. They fought very hard, surrounded by the screaming men who were betting on them, throwing money on the ground. The American knew how to fight, how to wield a knife. He looked crazy. He chased the Russian into one of the buildings and the men followed. He wounded the Russian in the shoulder, then — I had never seen anything like this — he put the knife's edge against another man's throat, took his gun. He emptied the gun into the Russian, into the wall behind him. Then he lowered his weapons, walked to the Big Man, and handed them to him."

Sam could hardly breathe.

"Then the American said to the Big Man, *I could be useful to you.*" Ahmad's twisted, scarred lip shaped into a smirk. "The Big Man took the crazy American into another building, they talked, then he said that they would shoot one of Mirjan's videos. To explain why the men were dead. The crazy American was going to come with us. Join us. The American had ideas on how to get the heroin out. How to avoid the CIA. Like maybe he knew how to work the system because of Zalmay. He would help them. In exchange for his life. So they made the video with his death faked on it, using Mirjan's equipment. They called themselves a name. Brothers of the Mountain. Make it look like holy warriors, not smugglers. They didn't want anyone to know they were Russians. It took them a few times. They took the crazy American with them, on to Russia. That was the last I heard of him. He was supposed to be dead, so I said he was dead. If I said he wasn't, the Magpie would have said, find out where he is. They would have wanted revenge on them all for killing Zalmay. Put me at risk to find out. No. Not my job. I was just relieved not to be exposed as one of Zalmay's agents."

"What was the name of the Russian my brother killed?" Sam asked suddenly.

"They called him Anton," he said quietly. "*Bol'shoy chelovek,* he wanted a new attack dog; he got him in the American. It was like — when two people who need each other find each other."

Danny had grown up on the streets of the world's disaster zones, and he'd learned everything from knife fighting to lock picking to con games, the same Sam had. A deal to survive, and Anton and Zalmay's lives were the price. The whole history of what he believed about his brother . . . "Didn't he try to save Zalmay?"

"There was no saving Zalmay," Ahmad said. "I suppose your brother could only save himself. I wasn't there when they shot the video, but the Big Man cut Zalmay's throat himself, so I heard. It would be his style. I heard from the men who were there that it took them a few takes to film it, because the Big Man had to practice his Pashto when he spoke, with a mask on, at the beginning. He couldn't speak it with a hint of a Russian accent. When he had it right, they kept filming and then he killed Zalmay and then faked the American's death."

"The Big Man. Where can I find him? What's his real name?"

"You're really not from the Russians?"

"No. I told you. No."

"Sergei. I heard Anton call him Sergei when he was arguing with him not to make him fight the American. It was the only time I heard his name used. And the next time the CIA reached out to me — and that was that old woman, the Magpie, talking to the few of Zalmay's people still alive — I told them I wanted out. I told them about some of the so-called Brothers who'd stayed behind and said they had Taliban ties and so they got killed by drone missiles. That was enough to get a ticket here." He stopped. "But I said nothing about Russians or *bol'shoy chelovek*. The CIA would give me a new life for giving up terrorists. Why complicate it by talking about Russian drug runners or crazy Americans?" He managed to shrug.

"Give me a description of Sergei."

"Tall, around six-four. Powerful build. Light brown hair, blue eyes. Cold eyes. Nothing special about his face. No scars."

"Did you keep a picture of him?"

"A picture? No! I've told you what I know."

Sergei. The Magpie had mentioned a Sergei. Belinsky, who had been a fixer and private security consultant for the Morozov brothers and who'd watched a DVD of the fake execution back in his security offices in Moscow. Sam searched on his smartphone, found a picture of Sergei Belinsky from the news coverage when the man had been blown to bits by a Chechen car bomb in Moscow. He showed the picture on the screen to Ahmad. "That him?"

Ahmad nodded once and then looked away.

Mila glanced at Sam. We've gotten all we can out of this one, her expression seemed to say.

Ahmad looked at them both. "Are you going to kill me?"

"No," Sam said. "We're not."

"I don't care what you do to him. Whatever gets us to your brother fastest." Mila dropped the knife and walked out of the storage building.

Sam knelt before him. "Good news: I'm not going to tell your enemies where to find you. Bad news: If I ever see you again I'll lie to my CIA friends that *you* were the one who sold Zalmay to the criminals. And they will believe me."

His eyes widened. "But I didn't . . ."

"If you make a move against me, or her, or you go to the police, I'll tell that lie and this nursery will be under new management and you'll be dead. And that CIA 201 file on you will be shredded and burned."

Sam went to the table, still stanching the blood flow. He wrapped his shredded shirt around him and picked up the *pesh-kabz* from the floor. He thought of the Afghan Basti, outside Islamabad, the two men he killed there in order to survive.

208

Then he cut Ahmad free. Ahmad stood, slowly, the ropes falling away from him.

"Thank you," he said, his voice sounding stunned. He stepped away from Sam and hurried toward his stepson.

"What does Nur-Ali think you are?"

"Whatever I pretend to be." Ahmad knelt by the unconscious young man, gently took off the hood, and began untying him.

It was a question and answer for Sam's own family.

What does he think you are? What I pretend to be.

Sam walked out, flinging the *pesh-kabz* aside.

Mila took him to an emergency room, where they told a story of a mugging gone wrong. The police were called. A statement was made. Sam was singularly unhelpful and confused about his attacker. The doctor patched up his back and told him he was lucky. Sam took the prescribed antibiotics and refused to stay in the hospital.

"Airport," he said. "We can take the red-eye back to New York."

They made the flight right before the doors shut. They'd gotten tickets in first class and Mila told Sam to sit by the window in case he wanted to sleep.

Sam closed his eyes. If he thought too much about what Ahmad said — his brother killing an unarmed Russian, giving up a life with his parents and Sam to go with this murderous smuggler Sergei, who had connections at the highest level in Russia — he would lose it. The anesthetic from the cut's treatment felt like it was wearing off. He swallowed one of the painkillers. He needed sleep to heal. He had to stay healthy; he had to stay moving forward.

Don't think, do. Don't wonder what he is. Just find him.

Sergei was dead, and if Sergei trained Danny, turned him into a weapon, what had he been doing since Sergei died? But Sam still had a lead in New York: Avril Claybourne, the artist who had watched the DVD of his execution, which had sent an electronic ping back to Mirjan Shah that he had reported to the Magpie. He'd see what this artist, this Avril Claybourne, knew.

He glanced at Mila, who sat with eyes closed, breathing deeply, calming herself.

"Thank you," he said to Mila, quietly. "You saved my life."

"Oh, Sam, you would have taken that guy apart."

"No. I didn't have a way out. He would have killed me. Thank God for you." He stared into her gaze.

"You're welcome," she said quietly. "I was going to call Jack Ming about looking for this woman."

"I already put him on it."

"Oh." She seemed flustered. "Oh, that's good."

"He didn't mention he had spoken to you."

"You talked to him first, then."

"Jimmy hasn't called me. He said he'd help . . ."

"He's been very busy. An emergency."

"Is that why you said you've had a very bad couple of days?"

She tried to smile. "Nothing to that, just me trying to scare Ahmad. You should sleep now. Is that pill kicking in?"

"Yes," he said, his voice thick. He couldn't tell her, not now, that he was giving up the bars, stopping work with her. That they would no longer work together or see each other. This was not the time. The pain in his back faded, although it was too hard to get comfortable. But it was worth it. He was going to find Danny. Save him from whatever he'd been forced to become.

He slept, country and clouds passing beneath him.

Mila did not sleep. The plane's Internet wasn't secure but the phone Charity had given her would work, she was told, anywhere. She sent a message that was encoded to Charity:

> Do you have any details on ex-FSB/KGB drug trafficker in Afg. known as "Big Man" or "Bol'shoy Chelovek" first name Sergei.

The message went from the airplane, wrapped in an encoded bubble, to an e-mail that then forwarded it to nine other servers scattered across the planet, in Australia, New Zealand, India, finally landing at a server in Greenwich, in an outpost of British intelligence that no one ever talked about. Maybe they knew about Sergei. And if Sergei could give them Danny's location, then she could capture him and hand him over to Charity.

And Sam, who thought of her as his friend who had just saved his life, would see her for what she was.

Her face felt hot. But it was an impossible choice. Your lying, deceiving husband, or your one friend who has stood by you, said a small voice in the back of her brain.

She watched Sam sleep. His hand was close to hers and for an insane moment she wanted to take his hand, hold it, even though she loved Jimmy. Sam was her best friend. That was all he could be. She was married. She took her vows seriously. And even if she hadn't been . . . Sam was nearly five years younger than her, which she told herself shouldn't matter, and he was already a father and had been married to a woman who had also lied to him in the most hurtful ways. He wouldn't want her. He didn't seem to want anyone.

She thought, If I didn't love Jimmy maybe I'd love you.

She studied his sleeping face. She could not let her friendship with him derail what she had to do. This brother of his sounded like a monster, a cold killer, a version of Sam unleavened by kindness or duty to others, and perhaps it would be best for Sam if she could take Danny Capra away from him.

Don't kid yourself. What will you say to him when you've taken his brother?

You won't say anything. You will take Danny and vanish. You will never see Sam, or his beautiful little boy that you love so, again. That is the price for saving your husband.

18

Jack Ming woke Sam late that morning with a phone call from Paris. Sam creaked up out of bed, feeling the ongoing pain in his back. He dry-swallowed both an antibiotic and a painkiller as Jack told him what he'd found. "The woman who bought a ticket for herself and your brother is named Avril Claybourne."

Same as the artist who'd watched the DVD.

"She's a multimedia artist in New York," Jack continued. "She owns an art gallery."

"You genius, you hacked the database."

"Uh, no." Jack almost seemed embarrassed. "I bribed a contact who works there to access an archived file and give me the information. Ten thousand dollars. You can wire it to my account. Claybourne bought a ticket for herself and for another passenger by the name of Philip Judge. Do you know that name?"

Sam closed his eyes. "No. Can you re-search that identity, get me credit reports and such on him? A full workup. But that might have been an identity he used once and discarded, Philip Judge." Saying the name aloud somehow helped.

"I'll try."

"I'll send you an advance payment. Thank you, Jack."

"Are you OK, Sam? You don't sound OK."

"I'm all right."

Avril Claybourne must know where his brother could be found.

There was a second e-mail, from the private lab where he'd sent the bullets he'd retrieved from the wall. They came from a modified Makarov pistol. A Russian weapon. They matched the bullet Sam had taken from the corpse in the grave. Same gun. Sam staggered toward the shower.

"Mila?" he called toward the guest room. "Mila?"

She was gone.

Bertrand unlocked the entrance to The Last Minute at noon and Seaforth, already wait-ing, came in, like a man needing his first early drink of the day. Sam had come downstairs to get some lunch, dressed in his loosest-fitting shirt to ease the pain.

"You made a little trip," Seaforth said by way of greeting, pulling out a stool and sitting at the bar.

There was no point in denying it. But it was confirmation that Seaforth was monitoring his credit card usage and probably his location by tracking his mobile phone. Of course, Seaforth had no idea Sam was, in turn, monitoring his phone. *He has his own agenda and you can't let it stop you.* "I did."

"And what did you learn?"

"Why do I tell you?"

"Because I got you into Afghanistan. And we both want whoever killed Zalmay and took your brother."

Sam decided to make it look like he was giving Seaforth everything he knew. "He told me Russian criminals took my brother."

Seaforth blinked. "That is not what he told us."

"He told the CIA what they most wanted to hear. He gave you guys he could put in the crosshairs of a drone missile. What about the forensics tests?"

"The bullets in the body came from a Makarov."

"That I knew."

"I knew you had private testing done on

216

the bullet you removed." Seaforth looked irritated.

"Consider it confirmation. Who is he?"

"The DNA on the body in the grave — it's not your brother."

Sam waited.

Seaforth said, "We did a range of genetic testing on the samples. His DNA is not in our databases. The Y-DNA test resulted in an R1a haplogroup, which indicates he could be an ethnic Russian."

Ahmad had told him the truth. "Was there anything else in his belongings that pointed to an ID on this man?" If Seaforth didn't have a name, he wasn't going to help him by giving him Anton as a starting point. He needed to stay ahead of Seaforth and his misfits.

Seaforth said, "Yes, but before I share it I want to know what you're going to do with this information."

"Ahmad pointed at a Russian crime boss nicknamed the Big Man. *Bol'shoy chelovek.* Ring a bell?"

"No. But this Big Man murdered a CIA agent. He is our worry, not yours."

"He took my brother."

"And we'll make him pay for that, Sam."

Sam pretended that he didn't hear. "It would be nice to have the hard drive that was sent to Mirjan Shah. The video was on it. Ahmad said they had to rehearse the parts with this Big Man speaking Pashto. Maybe he was on the part of the video that wasn't released." Sam looked at Seaforth. "How long after that video came out was it that Mirjan Shah died?"

"Two weeks. He was shot to death, and his home burned to the ground."

"I don't think that was a coincidence. So what else did you find?"

"There was a letter in the man's pocket. Written in Russian. Not addressed to a name."

"Signed?"

"Only with an initial. It was in the pocket of a rotting corpse for six years. It's . . . damaged." Seaforth handed him a photographed copy, with an accompanying translation into English:

```
S is losing control of the [sec-
tion too damaged to read] he
should simply [section too dam-
aged to read] he checks my
phone. So burn this. I don't
think he realizes that the
brothers will kill him if he
does this. He would listen to
```

you. They must never know. A.
[section too damaged to read]

"A" likely stood for Anton. He'd written this before he died. And "S" for Sergei. But who was the letter intended for? Was this letter why Sergei didn't like Anton, ended up wanting him dead? Anton was telling someone what Sergei was doing. "Should simply" . . . do what? Did this refer to Danny and Zalmay? "They must never know." What did that mean?

Seaforth said, "We already analyzed the fiber content of the paper. It's French stationery, produced by Cartier. Did you know they make writing paper, not just watches or jewelry? Top-drawer, expensive stuff."

It wasn't monogrammed, though, which would have been helpful. *A man goes into the lawless mountains of Afghanistan . . . with fine French stationery.*

"Can you shed any additional light on this?" Seaforth asked.

"No," Sam lied.

"Ahmad Douad isn't answering our phone calls. He's vanished. I think you must have scared him." Seaforth looked frustrated.

"I'm going to keep looking for my brother," Sam said.

219

Seaforth studied him. "Are you hurt? You're moving like you're in pain."

"I slept crooked on the flight; it's nothing."

"I suppose if I asked you to let us handle the search for your brother . . ."

"You've all had years to handle it, Bob," Sam said. "I'm sorry. But you didn't."

"That's not fair. We didn't have the information that you found."

"I appreciate what you've done for me," Sam said. "Please don't think I'm ungrateful; I'm not. But I can't just stop now. Could you?"

"I would know enough to let the professionals handle this. You're a bartender now, Sam. Let us take care of it."

But he couldn't. This was his brother. "I'll think about it."

They shook hands and Seaforth left.

I'll find him first, Sam thought. The woman who brought Danny back to America. Avril Claybourne . . . He could kidnap her. Question her. Force her to talk. But that was a serious undertaking; if he made a misstep he could alert his brother. He had no idea who this woman was or who her allies were or her connection to Sergei Belinsky . . . and a more subtle approach might work better.

If he only had a way. Then he realized . . .
he did.

19

Manhattan

Mila walked down seven blocks from The Last Minute to a coffee chain store, as the text instructed her to do. She stood in a long line. The people ahead of her and the people behind her were all on their phones, texting, tweeting, reading their screens, having phone conversations via earbud, connected to everywhere except where they were.

"Do you need assistance?" the man behind her said, close to her ear. British accent, young pup, model-handsome in an excellent suit. "Perhaps . . . some charity."

"No, none," she said. The line moved forward.

He was too stupid to know to stop. "Charity expects a report now," he said, pretending to look at his phone. "Have you made any progress?"

"I am getting closer to Jimmy's . . . client."

She stepped up to the counter and ordered a flat white. She joined the corral of people waiting for their coffees. The young suit ordered his latte and then stood next to her. They both collected their coffees. She walked out onto the street, turned, and stepped into an alley between the coffee shop and a high-end hotel, the young embassy man following her.

Handsome put a sneer on his face. "An alleyway, to conduct business. How pulp fiction. Give me this client's name."

"Put my husband on the phone."

He offered his smartphone to her, with a call already placed on hold. She tapped the button.

"Mila?" Jimmy.

"Why were you meeting with him?" she said.

"I'm saying nothing."

"Did he ask you to misdirect someone? Keep someone away from him?"

He was silent.

"Give me something to find your Copenhagen friend," she said.

"He . . . he's not a client. Charity, you're wasting your time on this one."

Charity's voice came onto the line and Mila thought she might crush the phone. "Then explain the money transfer after you met with this man."

"Payment for a favor that in no way affects British national security. It was a private matter. He wanted me to keep someone . . . away from him."

Mila's skin prickled.

"James, I am wearying of your lack of cooperation," Charity said.

Jimmy said: "When you let me talk to the prime minister, I will talk."

"That's not happening," Charity answered. "You see? He won't listen to you, he won't listen to me. Jimmy seems to think this will all go away if he just waits it out. Mila, you seem to have left all the equipment I gave you in London."

"I didn't want you tracking me and interfering with me finding the client," Mila said. "You might pass that on to your New York lackey here."

"You *will* cooperate with the nice young man from the consulate."

"You tell your nice young man if he ever comes up to me for another impromptu meeting and risks burning my operation I'll pour hot coffee onto his groin." Mila hung up and handed Handsome back his phone. "Don't follow me." She walked away and hailed a cab, suspecting that Charity had another security officer from the consulate following her. She told the cab driver to take her to Times Square. She'd lose any shadow in the crowds, in the subway, and then she'd make her way back to the bar. She couldn't lead them back to Sam. She spotted a woman who'd been behind her in line at the coffee shop getting into a car behind her. No coffee in hand. Tracking her.

She'd have to lose them.

And she did. Two exhausting hours later she arrived back at the bar. Sam sat at his desk, rustling through old yellowed pages.

"What's going on?" he asked. "You vanished."

"Chasing down a lead. It didn't pan out. How are you feeling?"

"Fine. What lead?"

"This Magpie woman . . . it would be good to know if she meets with your old CIA friends or if she goes anywhere. But I couldn't get in."

He looked at her and the lie felt like a knife she'd picked up by the blade. He did not comment, and went back to reading the yellowed papers on his desk.

Danny paid my husband to keep you off his trail, once you knew Danny had been in the prison. My husband betrayed you. I'm sorry.

"Sam. You have never told me much about Danny. What would be good to know in

225

looking for him?"

Sam glanced back up at her. "My mother gave me this. It's from Danny." Then he handed her the yellowing pages, a neat, precise handwriting on the lines.

20

The Past — Burundi

Mom is making me write this. She wants to show it to a psychiatrist and I could write a bunch of lies but then they'll just drag Sam into it and he'd have to tattle on me and I'm not making him choose like that. I don't mind my parents knowing what I did for Sam. They can act like it's wrong but I did it and I was right. I followed the rules I keep in my own head. I'm not dumb. No one had to give me the rules, they're what let you live around other people and not get into trouble. That is what rules are.

My name is Daniel Webster Capra and this is about me and my brother Samuel Clemens Capra (thanks, Dad, for the dumb literary names, you could just tell people you really like reading old books, you didn't have to saddle us with those middle names. I bet Dad is a little scared now when he reads that. I'm kidding, Dad. I love you.) Mom keeps patting me on the shoulder and saying, write it like it's a story in a book. OK then, here. I want to be understood.

Sam is ten and I am thirteen. I want any psychiatrist who reads this to know we have seen a lot of bad stuff in the complete hell-holes our parents drag us to and we're old for our ages. At least I am. Sam is a baby in a way.

So this man stole Sam. The jerk lectured his friends while he did it, like this was a lesson to be learned. Like he was IMPARTING (my dad loves that word) knowledge.

"This is how you take one of them," the man said as he pulled Sam off his bicycle. He said it in Kirundi, drunk, but Sam and I knew enough to understand. Sam's bicycle fell over in the mud, and the man — tall — tucked Sam under his arm and headed for his piece of crap car.

Like he was just going to take Sam.

We weren't supposed to leave the com-pound but it's boring there, Burundi sucks if you ask me. So we were playing along the road about a kilometer from the camp, Sam on his bike, me walking, because we (Doctor, you should know this), we always, always have to leave our toys and games and books behind when we move to a new disaster zone and so I didn't have a bike, I gave the one I bought with my own money to Sam. Our parents are super busy when we're in a disaster zone and I take care of Sam.

These drunken men pulled up in a car and just decided to take my brother. For money. They think every Westerner is rich and I guess we are compared to some.

I remember every word this monster said to me, because he thought I was a nobody, a scared kid, and he was going to tell me how the world worked.

"Don't squirm, little one," he said to Sam, but in French. "No one will hurt you. You will sit at my house and your parents will give me some francs and then you will go home." He turned to his two friends and explained what he was doing. "See, you take the littler one, and you leave the older one" — he jerked his head back at me — "to go explain to the parents. Simple, yes?"

Explain to the parents, like I was his messenger boy. I forgot to be scared, I was just so mad. SO MAD. Is it OK to be this mad? Not to my mom, I guess.

He threw Sam into the back of the beat-up Citroen and turned back to me. "Go and tell your papa he gives me a thousand francs, he gets him back. Each day the payment goes up. Don't bother to say you don't have the money, the relief will . . ." and he didn't finish the sentence because I felt that old red eye open in my brain so I picked up a rock and carefully threw it at him. It barely missed him and it bounced along the Citroen's old roof.

The man smiled. "You try to be the hero. Funny."

Hero? Ha ha ha.

"Let him go!" I yelled, in French. Sam peered out the window. He looked scared.

The man's two friends hurried toward me and one hit me across the face. Blood filled my mouth and I fell to the ground. It hurt. The second one laughed and drew back his foot to kick me.

"No, not too rough," the leader said.

"If he's hurt, the parents will pay faster," one suggested. Again they spoke in Kirundi, the other popular language in Burundi, and I still understood them, even after only eight weeks in the country. I'm not dumb. Be sure my parents tell you that, too.

The leader shrugged. "Hurt him too much, they take him to a doctor, or the police, and there is a delay."

I got up from the dirt and spat blood at the man's feet and I said, in Kirundi, "You let him go." I was scared but I was madder than I was scared, does that make sense? The leader laughed at me. "Go tell your parents, bring the money to old Angelique Kobako's house in the village." He gestured east. "Leave it with her." He stumbled over his words, he was drunk. Then he shook a finger at me. "If anything bad happens to your baby brother, it's on you."

He turned and got back in the car. One of his two buddies got in the front seat and the last one got in the back with Sam.

They started to drive away and I picked up a heavy rock and threw it and turned the back windshield into a giant star. Sam tried to make himself small in the backseat, I could see him, and later he said one of the men wanted to get out and cut me with a knife for messing up the car and the leader said no. Instead the leader rolled down the window and yelled at me, "Now, mzungu, to get your brat back, two thousand francs," and then he roared off down the road, laughing.

I got on Sam's bike and pedaled hard. The road snaked through a lush landscape (as Dad called it when he took us out to take pictures after we got here) but those men were villagers and I knew back to their village they would go. There were two villages to the east, where they'd headed. A quarter-mile from where the car grabbed Sam, I came to a small clearing and a cluster of shacks. I knew the owner of one; Mom had treated the man's granddaughter last week for a bad burn on her hand. I was scared for my little brother but I was calm, too, because I had a plan.

Old Nicolas kept his prized moped inside the shack so it wouldn't be stolen. I begged him and said, "You see a car go by, with its back windshield cracked?"

Nicolas nodded and pointed toward the fork in the road past his house. "It went to the left."

I kicked the moped into life and roared it out the front door before Old Nicolas could stop me. I hollered back that I'd bring it back, with a full tank. I'm not a jerk.

I drove for five kilometers, the bike coughed smoke but kept running and I was mad at myself if it broke down, it would leave Sam with these jerks even longer. I stopped kids walking along the side of the old, rutted road — "Did you see a blue car with a busted windshield?" and the kids would nod and in the fifth kilometer a tall, lean boy my own age said, "Yeah, that's Pierre Nduwimana. He lives on the edge of Kisil town, in a house with a green roof." Kisil was another kilometer down the winding, broken road.

"Five dollars American to show me," I said, pulling the money from my shoe, and the boy hopped on the back of the moped.

What Sam told me (because Mom won't let Sam write his part because she doesn't want him to know what I did): They brought him to the house and laid him on a pallet with a dirty blanket in a room away from where they drank.

"You be quiet," the leader told Sam. "No crying. No trouble for me. We did this before, with Norwegian boy from relief group. No harm to him. We just get the money, you will be fine."

Sam nodded. He told me he didn't really cry and I'm proud of him for that.

"Now, if you try to escape," he said and picked up Sam's hand, "my friend here will show you a game with his knife and your fingers." He pulled lightly on all Sam's fingers, as if testing that they wouldn't come off. "But you don't want to play this game, yes?"

Sam shook his head.

"You'll be home soon, little man. Be good." The leader and the knife man left him alone in the windowless room and then Sam went to sleep, I guess his brain shut down cause he was scared and I'll tell you the rest of it.

The boy showed me the house and the car was parked next to it. I went and let the air out of all four tires. Not just one. Four. At the window I could hear the clink of beer bottles and I could smell the smoke of something thick in the air. They were waiting on their easy money. I picked up the biggest rock I could hold in one hand and I crawled in the window.

Now my mother keeps asking me what I specifically did and I wish she would just calm down. The first guy was asleep on a couch. I smashed the rock into the back of his head three times, very hard but carefully. Three times. He made a noise but he was facedown in a pillow because I moved his head. There was a lot of blood by the third blow and he didn't wake up. If they hadn't been high they would have woken when I hit them I guess, but that didn't happen. Then I took his knife, next to him on the pallet, and I cut his wrist, just one, and he started bleeding a bunch onto the floor. I read Mom's anatomy books, I knew where to cut. When you learn things you better apply them to the problems in life else why learn anything?

The second man was facedown on the table. He roused a bit when I came toward him and he blinked at me like a baby just waking up. He was really drunk, you could smell it on him. So I stuck the knife into his mouth, not cutting him, just telling him to be quiet. He vomited, yuck, but I put my hand over his mouth and his nostrils. I hit him twice with the rock and kept my hand over his mouth, closed off his nostrils. I'm a big kid for thirteen and he was a small guy for being whatever he was. He choked and bucked. He went still and I let go of his mouth. I hit him in the head with the stone, twice more, then I cut his wrist, too, just once. He looked dead but I don't think he was.

The leader heard the noise. He'd been lying down by the room smoking his weed. He got up and staggered toward me, and he couldn't have looked more surprised so I stabbed him in the groin and I hope I got his balls. He folded and screamed and I went and hit him with the stone three times, then opened his wrist when he got quiet.

I went in the room and Sam was asleep. Like I said he's a baby in some ways and I think when bad things happen he shuts down and steps away from it. Then I got scared that maybe they hurt him or gave him something. I didn't want him to see the knife or the stone with blood on it or the men because he wouldn't understand, he's like Mom and Dad. So I told him to keep his eyes closed and I put my hand over his eyes but I got blood on his cheek.

"What happened?" he just kept saying and I knew I couldn't tell him.

I kissed the top of his head, I just told him it didn't matter, they'd left to go drink and I'd followed him. I know he doesn't believe me but I'm not going to tell him what I did. He would freak out. I did it for him.

I led him past the men, he kept his eyes closed, we went outside. We walked past the Citroen with its broken windshield and its flat tires and to Old Nicolas's moped, where the local kid waited. No one tried to stop us. No one knew.

I told the Burundian boy urakoze (thank you), he could walk home because I needed to take Sam home and the moped would only carry two. I gave him some more money, Burundian francs, from my shoe, all pretty colors. The boy looked at me like I was a ghost and took the money and ran.

"What happened?" Sam asked again. His voice shook.

"Hush," I said. "Hush. I'll explain later." Sam climbed onto the moped and pressed his face into my back. He asked where were Mom and Dad and the security people for the relief compound? I didn't answer and I kicked the engine to life and the wind in my face felt good as we shot along the crappy roads.

We stopped at Old Nicolas's house and left the moped. I tried to give him the last of my money, but the old man would not take it. He had pulled Sam's bike out of the muddy road and we rode it home, Sam shivering on the handlebars.

I told him we'd say we got lost. He just nodded and then when we rode through a patch of moonlight he looked back at me and said: "There's blood on your shirt."

"We'll say we saw someone beaten by the side of the road and helped them. You know how Mom and Dad will love that." I didn't look at him.

"What did you do? Danny? What did you do?"

"I followed you on the moped. I asked if people had seen a broken windshield. I found where they parked it. It's not like I'm Sherlock Holmes."

"The men . . ."

"They were all drunk and asleep," I told him. "I watched them for ten minutes and then I came through a window."

"The blood . . ." Weird how Sam could sound like Mom and Dad.

I stopped the bike. "It doesn't matter."

"You got me out," he said, stuttering it out, and then he started to cry, which I hate, but OK, I let him cry. He was safe now, that was all that mattered. I held him and said into his hair that it was my fault, I shouldn't have let them take him. But he didn't need to worry about the men, they were OK, just asleep from the beer and the weed and he said "why is there blood?" and I knew Mom and Dad would find out. That he couldn't keep his mouth shut.

That if we heard about men hurt in a village nearby Sam would give it away. But that was a price I could pay. I wasn't going to let them hurt Sam. Ever.

I wiped Sam's tears away with my thumb.

"We got lost," Sam said after a moment. "But we stayed together."

That was Sam, trying to lie. He sucks at it. "Yes," I said. "The first order, remember, we don't ever leave each other behind." That is something Mom and Dad have said to us, the reason they don't leave us behind in America when they're out in the field. The first order.

He half-hiccupped, half-laughed then. He stopped crying. I knew he quit for me.

I hugged him and put him back on the bike and I thought maybe I would cry for a second out of relief that he was safe. But I didn't. I love him. When Mom and Dad think there's something broken inside me (like now) I want anyone who reads this to know I love my family, I love Sam. I'm not broken on the inside.

We got home. Our parents were furious, then relieved we were home safe. Sam kept his mouth shut. Mom and Dad figured it out because Sam had a bad dream and yelled in his sleep and then they heard about three men hurt in the village the night we vanished and Mom found the knife under my bed. The men lived but one at least wasn't going to be right again in the head I guess, well they weren't right to start with. And then someone in Kisil who works at the compound heard about two foreign boys, two rotuku, who were seen leaving the men's house and someone in the village said it was me and Sam. Rotuku means not just foreign but violent. I'm not violent . . . So Mom pressed Sam for three days of her badgering him and he kept his mouth shut, so proud of him, but I finally told her so she'd leave Sam alone. I made a deal with them: I tell them everything, they don't ask Sam about this, they don't tell him anything, he doesn't know, he slept through all the stuff they're upset about. So leave him alone. That's why I have to write this stupid essay for some doctor to look at and judge me.

Judge away. Judge, judge, judge. No one hurts my brother.

The police didn't come talk to me but Mom and Dad were reassigned to Thailand a week later and we packed in silence like I've never heard. It is weird my parents take us into dangerous areas then judge me for protecting Sam while she's stitching up people and he's making sure the money goes where it's supposed to.

They ought to just let me be what I am. I love my parents but I love Sam most of all. If that hurts them then maybe they should have to write an essay about their feelings on it, too.

Mila put down the pages. She felt cold. "You never read this before?"

"No. They decided not to show this confession to a psychiatrist. They decided they would keep it quiet and . . . manage him."

"Why didn't he just go get help like a normal person when those men took you?"

"Because he's Danny." He looked at the paper. "Judge, written three times, and Philip Judge is an alias that Jack Ming said that Danny might have used."

"And he never told you what he did to those men?" Her voice rose. "You never asked?"

"What more was I supposed to ask? He still wouldn't talk about it with me." He looked at her. "He thought it was justified in saving me."

"Thirteen years old," she muttered. "Were there any more incidents?"

"Incidents?"

"Him hurting people."

"No."

"Because, you know, you two were around disasters, suffering, and so on. People who are hurt or dying. People gone missing." Her voice was strained. "If he wanted to hurt someone again, if he enjoyed it or got a satisfaction from it . . . then he would be in a target-rich environment."

Sam looked horrified. "He's not . . . like that."

"At thirteen he bludgeoned three men and left them to bleed out. That's . . ." She hesitated. "He sounds like a little psychopath."

"How many people did you hurt looking for your sister? Maybe you shouldn't judge."

She took a calming breath. "I didn't do that when I was a child," she said. "He was thirteen and he thought this was a better choice than running to your parents and getting the police. I couldn't go to the police, Sam, and he could have. Do you think this is normal?"

"If you no longer care to help me because you think my brother's a danger, there's the door."

"Don't be rude, Sam," she said. "I'm just . . . This is upsetting. Of course I'll help you." Smooth this down, she thought. You cannot afford for Sam to reject your help right now.

"I know the name of the woman who brought him to the US. Jack Ming got it for me. I'm a little tired of waiting on Jimmy's hackers."

"We need to keep moving forward," she said. "Never mind Jimmy. Where's this woman?"

21

Manhattan

The best thing, Sam thought, about owning a bar was that you had regulars. And the regulars could often serve as an informal network of sources.

"Do we have any customers who work in the art world among the bar regulars tonight?" he asked Bertrand, surveying the well-dressed, martini-gulping crowd.

"Dominique Cross. The red-haired lady at the end of the bar, talking with the older woman. That's her mother, in from Montreal. Dominique is an art consultant for wealthy people and for corporations. She likes Tito's vodka in her martinis and she's unattached."

"You're like a bar version of an Internet search engine, Bertrand."

"I try."

"Please send Ms. Cross and her mother a round on me, with my compliments." He went upstairs and put on the best suit he kept in New York. He had to play the genial host now, and see if Dominique Cross could get him next to Avril Claybourne.

It took two rounds. Mrs. Cross — Dominique's mother — was funny and charming, but the art buyer seemed to be annoyed by Sam inserting himself into a brief family reunion.

"I've been thinking of buying some art for the bars," he said.

"And if you buy me drinks, you get some free advice?" Dominique said. There was no irritation in her tone but a bit of weariness.

"Ah, everyone wants free advice from Dominique," Mrs. Cross joked.

"I'll happily retain your professional services. But I was thinking, instead of paintings that could be expensive to insure inside a bar environment, perhaps digital art on screens that change. But sophisticated, you know. I don't want it to look like something I just downloaded from the Internet."

"Well, with digital art . . . ," Dominique said, stopping to think. It was as if now that the idea was spurred she had to play with it a bit.

"On that wall. Big, epic, a conversation

starter for when people see it," Sam prompted. "Of course, it might be best to commission work just for my bars."

The word "commission" got her attention. "There are some artists you might consider. Chang. Mbeka. Claybourne." But he noticed that she hesitated before saying Claybourne's name.

"Avril Claybourne?" Sam said, leading. "I think I've heard the name."

Dominique made a face, sipped at her drink. "You've reminded me of an unpleasant chore. She's not my favorite, but she's hosting a showing tomorrow night, and Mother and I have to go."

"Why don't you go, Sam?" Mrs. Cross said, clearly playing matchmaker.

"Mother!" Dominique said. "I told Avril you'd be there."

"I'd rather go to a Broadway show, the kind you think are too sentimental. Take Sam."

Dominique Cross looked trapped, but then she shrugged. "Well, Sam, maybe we can find an installation for your bar."

"What time's the party?" Sam asked.

22

Miami

This was Judge's order of business for this most difficult of kills, and it might have surprised an amateur.

Weapon. Usually a gun. This time it would be the rarest of poisons. If he had not been able to acquire the polonium-210, there was no point in the rest of the preparations. Now that he had it:

Escape route. Both a way to vanish and a name to frame for the kill, given that polonium was only produced by governments. He needed someone to blame, to serve as a distraction while he vanished into a different identity.

Access to target. That would come soon enough. Sergei had taught him about the circle while keeping him away from it. He had an idea of how to get inside.

But first he needed an escape route. Normally right before and after a kill he stepped out of being Philip Judge — the name he used the most — and stepped into one of the other identities that he and Sergei had built over the years. The identities Sergei gave him were ironclad, but it might be best to have a new name to slip into. So, starting a year ago for insurance, he had established another name he could assume, based in Miami.

Robert Clayton ran an online store selling used books cheaply. Clayton had his own social security number and a Florida driver's license and paid his taxes promptly. According to a hacked database he had attended public school in Miami. He owned property, and twice a year Judge had gone there, put in an appearance, met the neighbors, and explained that he had to be away for extended periods due to a parent suffering from Alzheimer's in Denver. The neighbors thought him odd but quiet and the house was well maintained by people he paid to mow the yard and fix any issues that arose, so they thought he was the perfect neighbor: rarely around yet conscientious.

But what Robert Clayton didn't yet have was an American passport. He needed a legit one, with a history already activated in the consular database. So, before leaving the country, he would need this final bit of documentation. Because Philip Judge would soon vanish forever, and he would have to be Robert Clayton. And over the next few years, he'd move the money paid to him by Firebird into accounts that Robert Clayton could access. What would make that easier, especially for overseas accounts, was a passport in Clayton's name. He didn't have time to set up an overseas identity that he hadn't used before. Clayton would have to do.

Now he had to pay a visit to the Miami-based expert who could deliver that rarest of documents: an actual US passport, not only faked, but with a history registered in a consular database. He'd had to call Shaw when he took the Morozov job, and ask him to accelerate completion of the Robert Clayton identity. He was to collect this final and most important document from the forger, Shaw, who had created Robert Clayton's entire digital footprint over the past two years.

When Judge landed at Miami International, tired, irritated, and hungry, Shaw had left several messages urging Judge to call him back.

"There's a problem with the Clayton passport," Shaw told him. "I need to meet you face-to-face to discuss options. Meet me at Clayton's house at nine this evening."

"What is the problem?"

"I'll explain when I see you. But it's an expensive one to fix. You'll need to bring cash."

He had, like Sergei had taught him, hidden resources and cash where he could easily access them. He only lived off half the earnings from his kills; the other half was hidden away, in various places, in case he needed to run. He had such a hidden deposit in Miami.

"What," Judge said slowly, "is the problem?"

"Not over the phone. Nine o'clock." He hung up.

Judge turned off his phone and walked out into the Florida rain. He didn't like problems appearing at the last minute. They were almost always human error. Or human folly.

Maybe Shaw was getting greedy. Or maybe — someone knew that Shaw worked for him.

He could call Mrs. Claybourne, ask her for help. No. The job was in motion; they were not to have contact. It was too risky for them both.

Tonight could be a trap. He'd have to treat it as such.

23

Brooklyn

The Claybourne Gallery was in Williamsburg. Avril Claybourne had bought the property three years ago and Sam had found an archived website from the sale, with the layout shown. Her offices were upstairs from the gallery. If she had information on his brother, he thought it would be there.

Mila was stationed outside, in a café down the street, as his backup. She seemed unhappy about missing the party.

But there was one big risk. If Claybourne knew Danny's real name — and he had no idea if she did know it — then she couldn't meet a guy named Sam Capra. He'd been careful to tell Dominique that he just wanted to be introduced by his first name. "Just Sam. Like, you know, it's a brand."

She'd rolled her eyes. She had brought two other clients with her, a married couple who were only a few years older than Sam and seemed very determined to let everyone know they'd made their money very young. They were eager to buy. He liked them; they would keep Dominique busy.

He snagged a glass of champagne from a waiter and drifted away from Dominique, angling through the crowd. It was probably well over a hundred people. He made out four security men, all of whom outweighed him by fifty pounds and looked very professional. He thought, It wasn't like the video art could be stolen. Maybe these men were more about Avril's security than the art's.

On giant flat screens mounted on the walls played a variety of animations, some purposely primitive but oddly hypnotic. Some mixed video from a wide variety of sources: war footage, home movies, custom shots. One screen showed a silent film hero, froze him, broke the image down into a swirl of moving pixels, and reformed it into a photo of a war hero, then a child, then a criminal mug shot. The effect was unsettling.

"What do you think?" a young man next to him asked.

"I don't know much about art," Sam said. "At first I thought this was random, but there's a pattern behind it." He might as well steal the Magpie's ideas on the world to bluff his way through this evening.

"I'm Dane; I'm Avril's assistant." He was lean, handsome, with wide-spaced piercing blue eyes and dark short hair.

"I'm Sam, Avril's potential customer."

"You might put in offers quickly. I expect everything shown tonight will be bought."

"I thought there would be more pieces," Sam said.

"Avril works primarily via private commissions. But sometimes she likes to make art solely for her own pleasure."

Private commissions. One way to account for money if this was a cover business, Sam thought. "Dominique Cross represents me. I own thirty bars. I might be interested in a different installation in each bar." He put his gaze back to the closest video.

Thirty commissions. Dane tried to keep his eyes from lighting up but failed. "You must meet Avril."

"She's busy right now and I'd rather talk in a private setting," Sam said. "Is there a private room where I could see a range of her custom work? And maybe alone — I feel awkward judging her work in front of her."

"Of course. There are samples on her website."

Sam managed to look imperious. "I'm not

going to stand here and watch them on my phone."

"Of course not, sir. There's a custom portfolio upstairs . . ."

"Could you please show me?" Sam gave him a smile.

"Sure, let's go upstairs, but just for a few."

Sam followed him, past the swell of the guests, upstairs to a combination studio/ office. A large-screen computer stood on a table, and nearby was a desk, spotlessly neat, with a laptop on it. Dane led Sam to the widescreen and activated a program, and a custom portfolio began to play.

Sam frowned, studying it in silence as the videos played. He kept a critical expression on his face, as though uncertain as to what he thought.

Dane's phone buzzed with an incoming text. He glanced at the screen. "I'm needed downstairs . . . Have you seen enough?"

"For thirty commissions?"

Dane had the good sense to look embarrassed.

Sam said, "I'd like for the portfolio to finish running. Can you come back up or I'll meet you downstairs in a few?"

"Of course." He seemed hesitant about leaving Sam, but Sam put his gaze back on the screen and let himself look utterly absorbed. Dane left but kept the office door open. The sounds of the party drifted up the stairs.

Sam went to the laptop on the desk.

Sam took the fake Audi key Jack Ming had given him in Paris. He flicked the control and the hidden flash drive emerged from the key. He opened the laptop.

It was secured, and a password requested, according to the screen.

He slid in the hidden drive. A program on it launched and began a serious assault against the laptop's password.

One minute. Two. He felt a trickle of sweat down his ribs, under his Burberry Prorsum suit.

The desktop appeared. He pressed the unlock symbol on the car key and a light began flashing. It was vacuuming up all the data on the hard drive, far faster than a commercially available drive could. Jack hadn't told him how long the drive would take.

He heard voices laughing, talking, closer than the party.

The key to his brother could be here. He couldn't leave.

More laughter. A woman's voice, clear and bright. The drive's light went green. He pulled it free, powered off and closed the laptop, and slipped the keys into his pocket as he came around the desk back to where he was supposed to be.

When Avril Claybourne came into the office, Sam stood in front of the monitor, head tilted as though studying the portfolio. The animation was a set of colored blocks, moving, shifting through the spectrum, weirdly hypnotic.

"Hello," the woman said to him. Dominique and Dane stood behind him.

"Hi, *je suis* Sam," he said. "So wonderful to meet you."

"Avril Claybourne." She didn't ask for a last name. "It's nice to meet you."

The key was in his pocket. He pulled his hand from his pocket to shake her hand. "Dane was kind enough to give me privacy to look at your exquisite portfolio."

"I'd be glad to set up a meeting with you and Dominique after the party."

"Of course. I just didn't want to waste your time, or my time, if we weren't a match."

"Of course." Avril's voice was cool.

"Well, I'm thirsty," Dominique said. "Dane, let's confab at the end and we'll find a time to meet."

"That sounds good," Dane said.

Sam could feel the weight of the stare

from Avril.

"Sam, shall we?" Dominique said.

"We'll see you downstairs," Avril Claybourne said.

Sam nodded and smiled and followed Dominique back to the party. He had to get this stolen data out of here, *now*.

Avril Claybourne glanced around the office. Nothing looked disturbed.

"He wasn't up here but maybe two minutes. Or three," Dane said.

She opened her laptop. Turned off, as she'd left it. She started it up. The screen arrived, asking as usual for its password.

"Did I do wrong? Thirty commissions, Avril, do you know how much . . ."

"Shut up, Dane." The start-up completed. She signed in and then ran a scan program. Waited for the results.

"I'm sorry if I messed up," Dane said, his voice small.

"No, of course you didn't," she said. Dane didn't know about her side business; he was just window dressing, and that was fine. "Go back downstairs. Watch him." She brightened her face with a smile. "I mean, we don't want a good catch like him getting away."

Her laptop was shielded, designed to text

her an alarm if penetrated or if an unauthorized hard drive was attached. The software didn't exist that could bypass it. Or so the Estonian hacker who designed it promised her. The scan ran. She waited.

There were no indications of a problem.

Still. She texted Dane and told him to send the security chief up to her office.

24

Brooklyn

"What the hell was that stunt?" Dominique whispered to him.

"Stunt? I wanted to see her not-on-display work. Dane showed it to me."

"Well, if I'm your buyer, then you ask me and I take care of that for you. That's part of the service, Sam. And why the sudden pretentiousness? *Je suis Sam.* Oh, please."

"I'm just trying to fit into your clientele."

She barely managed to suppress a smile. "Oh, dear."

The key carrying the stolen data felt like an anchor in his pocket. There was security at this party, mainly to keep the uninvited at bay (although Sam couldn't imagine wanting to crash this party, for the food or the company) and to keep an eye on the drunkenness of the crowd, which seemed minimal. They were well behaved. But at a command from Avril, security could take him and search him and take the key, and he'd either have to play along and risk being caught or fight his way out.

He saw Avril Claybourne come down the stairs, followed by one of the guards. Sam could see that under the jacket the man wore a holster. There were two other guards in the room, in suits, but miked up and with earpieces. If he had to fight his way out there was a busy avenue a block away. But if he had to fight his way out, then it would be on the news — violence erupts at artist's showing — and he did not want that.

But he suspected Avril Claybourne didn't want that either.

"I feel like there's a different agenda here," Dominique said, "than buying art."

He glanced over her shoulder and saw the guard Avril had spoken to watching him. He needed to get the key out of here. Off of him. In case he was questioned. A woman who worked as an associate to a man like Sergei Belinsky would not hesitate at violence. But if he panicked, he could telegraph to them that he was guilty. And he could do nothing that would put Dominique under suspicion.

He sent a coded text to Mila, thumbing the phone in his pocket. Just the number 6. Their code for *I have something to pass to you.* "I have no agenda," he said.

"My other clients are buying a piece," she said. "I've got to stay and negotiate."

He felt giddy with relief but he kept his expression neutral. "I understand. Thanks for bringing me tonight."

"You're welcome. Call me if you want to commission Avril."

"Yes. Of course." He thanked her again and headed into the night, fingers touching the key in his pocket. It could be the information that could lead to his brother.

He didn't see Mila but he knew she was close. He ambled down a couple of streets, people watching, window shopping. A man, in no hurry. He walked down Parkside Avenue toward the subway.

And spotted one of Avril's security men following him.

He considered his options. If he lost the man, Avril could simply ask Dominique where he could be found. If he let the man follow him, it might confirm to Avril that he was just a bar owner, just as described. If she could tell that her data had been copied off her laptop, though . . .

He moved through the evening crowds. He saw Mila ahead of him, on the other side of the street, closer to the subway station. He crossed the street, for all appearances heading to the subway. Mila, talking loudly on her phone to an imaginary friend, walked past him and bumped him while the shadow was navigating around a crowd in front of a bar. Sam passed Mila the key without a word; a flick of fingers and it was done.

Sam kept going. The shadow followed him down into the station. No sign of Mila. If all went according to plan she would follow in a cab or on the next train.

The shadow followed him into the subway station, past the street musicians, past the crowds. They waited at opposite ends of the platform, Sam staying focused on looking at his phone. The shadow did not move. But he wore an overcoat now, a lightweight one, and Sam imagined that he was still armed.

Sam took the Q train back into Manhattan. The shadow was in his subway car, but at the opposite end. Sam gave no sign of recognizing him from Claybourne's party.

He got off at Times Square, thick as always with tourists and tip workers in their various costumes, and started the short walk toward Bryant Park. The shadow stayed with him. On his phone. Hanging back.

Claybourne suspects you're not what you seem, Sam thought.

He ducked into one of the large, noisy tourist-catering restaurants. Servers swarmed the busy tables, waiting on families and tour groups, past four servers serenading a table with a birthday song. Sam dodged past people carrying trays and headed straight back to the kitchen. An assistant manager tried to block his way as he went into the kitchen and Sam moved past him with a shove. "That man in the trenchcoat is armed. I'm not staying here."

He saw the manager's gaze lock on to the shadow. Sam ran through the kitchen, the curtains of steam, the loud sizzle of grills, and out the back service exit. He hurried down the broad alley to the cross street. No sign of his pursuer. He melted into the crowds.

When he got back to the bar, Mila wasn't there. No sign of her.

He tried her phone. No answer.

And she had the data that could lead to his brother.

25

Miami

A block party was in full swing. A Cuban band was playing at the end of the street. Judge parked his airport rental car a street over, put on a fake smile, and walked through the crowd, nodding politely at the next-door neighbor, already well-lubricated with beer, who called out, "Hey, Robert, great timing!" He did the sociable nodding, shaking hands, saying quietly that there wasn't much difference in his mother's condition back in Denver, thank you for asking. He held up his house key and said he had to go water his plants; it had been six months. Laughter, waves, an invitation to come back out and fix a plate from the barbecue table.

He smiled and unlocked the door of his Robert Clayton house, steeling himself for unpleasantness.

As he stepped inside, he saw Shaw: a small

man, but wiry with muscle, with jet-black hair and a frown. Shaw had a key because he handled the maintenance on the house. Judge shut the door against the blare of music halfway down the block. He noticed that all the shades and curtains were still drawn.

He shut the door and the room stayed dark; Shaw hadn't put on a light. He stayed a good fifteen feet away. The front door opened up onto a living area, with a dining room next to it, and a kitchen beyond.

"You wanted to talk? Let's talk."

"Let's go in the kitchen." Shaw gestured Judge toward the hallway. Judge walked toward him.

Two other men jumped him, coming from the left, from the dining room entryway. Let's dance, he thought. It was nearly a relief to know this was a shakedown. But both coming at him at once, through a narrow passage, was a bad tactic because one was, for the barest of moments, trapped behind the other.

The first man hit him high, trying to knock him to the ground, the second reaching for his arm, to seize him before he could draw a weapon, ordering him to stand down.

The polonium-210 was in Judge's jacket

pocket, and if the bottle broke — and was breathed in or swallowed — it would kill him and them. Even a tiny amount, breathed in, would eventually kill in days or weeks. They'd commit their own murders, beating him into submission. He hated the idea of dying stupidly. And these idiots, out of greed, keeping him from twenty million.

A rage, a fear he hadn't felt since he'd faced Anton with the knife in the village of ghosts, clawed at his brain. The men gathered around him, screaming, wagering, the Russians laughing at him. *Fight, aid boy!* Sure that he would be dead in less than a minute. Their expressions had changed when he'd stabbed the Russian and then grabbed the gun. *Show us how you can fight!* OK. He'd emptied the gun into the Russian and then the wall. Walked past the silent men and given Sergei the Makarov, with a glare of defiance.

The red eye in his mind opened, bright and staring in a way it hadn't since those bastards in Burundi had stolen Sam from him.

He slammed his head into one man's nose. The man staggered back, his grip loosening, and Judge wrenched his own hand free. He clawed his fingers into the second man's face, aiming and gouging at his eyes. The second man screamed and writhed and fell back, bleeding. No mercy, Judge thought. He couldn't afford it. They would all be dead if they broke or opened the vial, and if he lost they'd search his pockets. Who knew where they'd take the poison, or if they'd leave it on his body for an innocent cop or crime-scene tech to deal with. They'd been dead men the minute they decided to strike at him while he carried the polonium. People had to live and die by their choices. He had.

He drew his Beretta, silencer capped, from a holster underneath his jacket. He'd gone to his cache before coming to the house and had retrieved both weapon and cash. He fired once into the knee of the man he'd gouged. The man screamed and fell, one hand gripping his ruined kneecap, the other his blinded eyes. The man with the broken nose slammed into him, tackling him to the floor. Judge landed heavily, felt something break in his pocket, and thought, That's it, we're done. Done. Killed by a loser, not even someone I could respect. He tried not to breathe in, in a hopeless gesture of survival.

The rage brightened the red eye. He managed to pinch the man's carotid artery and the man howled and then gasped. Then he went unconscious, and Judge could hear the feet of someone running on the hardwood floor. Shaw, who had hung back like a coward, fleeing now that the attack had gone wrong.

Judge saw him in the shadows, and he fired once as the geek reached the front door. He hit a backpack that Shaw wore over one shoulder; Shaw staggered and collapsed to one knee, still scrabbling at the door. Judge ran toward him. That little bastard — he'd feed him what was left of the polonium, make him lick the broken glass. Then they'd die here together, by the bullets, and he'd leave a note on the door, warning of the dangers. Maybe the authorities would burn the house to the ground.

For a moment he thought of his parents, and what they would think if they knew he had died this way and not in the mountains, and then the red eye opened wider in his head. He pulled Shaw back from the door before he could fumble it open. Outside he heard the Cuban music, the fireworks, the scream of laughing children. Shaw twisted the other way, stumbling down the hallway toward the bedroom, and even in the dim light Judge could get a read on him and he fired. He caught the man in the shoulder and Shaw collapsed, sobbing, scared.

Judge stood over Shaw and braced himself. Hand into pocket. He found the vial.

It was whole. Unbroken. But in his same pocket he found a gel pen, snapped, the black liquid oozing from the cracks. He stared, then smiled, and then laughed for ten seconds, and then his calm face settled back on, the red eye closed, and he grabbed Shaw between the shoulders and dragged him, blood and all, back to where the other two men lay.

"Who are these guys?" he asked.

"Friends of mine. I owe them some money . . . I told them you could double what I owe them, so they came along . . . I'm sorry, I'm sorry."

"What, loan sharks?" The pettiness of it made him shake his head.

"Yes. Albanians. I played the races a lot this year at Flagler, at Gulfstream Park . . . I needed money." His voice shook. "I can't believe you shot me . . ."

Weaknesses were so . . . weak. "So they can't tell me anything I need to know."

"They just want money from you . . . Look, I'm sorry, just get me to a doctor . . ."

Judge shot the two thugs in the head. The hiss of the silencer reduced Shaw to sobbing incoherence. Judge searched the small backpack Shaw had dropped and found a laptop in it. His bullet had missed it. "Have you activated my Robert Clayton passport in the consular database?"

"No . . . that was how we'd make you pay."

"Do it. Now." He opened the laptop, pushed it to Shaw. "Now."

Shaw managed to type out commands, mouse around the screen, run a program. The computer activity seemed to calm him. "There. It's updated. It's all good. You are Robert Thomas Clayton, according to the US passport office. We're cool. We're cool."

"Yes, we're cool."

"So . . . how am I going to explain this gunshot wound, man? I need to get to a —"

Judge shot him. Once, in the temple.

He stood there for a few seconds and the red eye closed. He checked the polonium vial again to reassure himself he was still alive. Then he put the bodies in the garage. He cleaned the floor. He would have to get rid of them tomorrow. Robert Clayton owned a nice fishing boat at a nearby marina. He changed clothes, put on a tropical print shirt he found in the closet that Shaw had stocked last year, and then he went out to the neighborhood party to enjoy the noise and to practice being Robert Clayton for a while.

26

Manhattan

Mila clutched the Audi key loaded with the data that could lead to Danny Capra, and thought, Maybe this is good enough. Give it to Charity and tell her to track down Danny Capra. I get my husband back and I don't have to betray Sam.

She could change the deal. She could free herself from being Charity's puppet.

Don't kid yourself, she thought. This is still a betrayal. You'd have to vanish. No goodbye for Sam. Just leave, walk out of his life, and know that you were the one who kept him from finding his brother.

She'd slid into a taxi after the handoff and told the driver to take her to the British consulate in Manhattan. She opened her phone and called Charity. "I want to speak to my husband." She glanced back through the windshield.

"What have you found?" Charity demanded. Did the woman ever sleep? If Charity had a life, it was on hold until this was over. "Your earlier tip on the Russian trafficker means nothing to us."

"There is a woman who works with our target," she said. "I have her data files. I can upload them to you, but I won't unless you let me speak with Jimmy." She opened her backpack and pulled out a Chromebook. She plugged the key into the port.

"Upload what you've found, and we'll talk then."

"Or . . . I could destroy the data."

"Aunt and Uncle will be on the first plane out of Sydney and back to Moldova."

Enough. "Fly them in first class. I have what you want and I'll use it how I see best. Perhaps I'll send it to the *Guardian;* they love a good exposé of the failings of governmental agencies. Or I could be good and just bring it to the British consulate."

"Don't you dare take that tone with me. You'd do well to remember you work for me."

"You'd better start thinking of this as a partnership," Mila said. "Because if you can burn me, I can burn you and the whole of British intelligence. Did your people find the hidden cameras in the Oxford house?"

"What?" Charity's breath was sharp.

"Based on a motion trigger, they upload images to a remote server. I have your photos, Charity, and that of your team." That was a lie, but let Charity spend her time tearing apart the Oxford house to prove Mila wrong.

Charity hadn't expected Mila's temper. "Fine. Please. Bring it to the consulate."

"I want to speak to Jimmy. This time without you listening. If I think for one moment you're eavesdropping I will e-mail this data, with a complete confession of my activities with the Round Table and your picture, to the *Guardian,* the BBC, and to the *New York Times.* Are we clear?"

"Hold on." She heard the click of Charity's heels, hurrying along tile. Whispered instructions to open a door — Jimmy must be under guard. Jimmy roused. "Yes?" His voice was creased with sleep.

"How nice for you that you can sleep," Mila said. "Listen to me. Is Charity listening?"

"She just handed me her mobile and walked out of the room. I don't think she can hear us." His voice sounded small.

She steadied her breathing. "I hold your future in my hands, darling, so I want answers. Do you understand, you lying piece of garbage?"

"Yes."

She had to be careful in what she said in case someone was listening. "Your meeting in Copenhagen. How long have you known that man is alive?"

"A few years. He worked with someone I had dealings with in Russia. I recognized him when you showed me the picture Sam found in the prison's ruins."

"And you said nothing."

"I said nothing."

"What is he now?"

"A hired killer. Trained by one of the best. And he will kill you if you get close to him. He will never let you capture him."

Nausea churned her guts. "They are forcing me to chase him. Because of you. Tell Charity the truth and I won't have to go near this man."

"Yes you will. No matter what I say or do. To help *him*." His loathing for Sam seemed like a physical force.

"No, I'll keep us both away from him."

"I tell Charity all I know, and I have nothing left. I just need to talk to someone above her. Talk to the prime minister. So run, darling. There's money hidden, you know the places . . ."

That was it, then. He would do nothing to help her or Sam, or anyone else. "And my

273

aunt and uncle, what about them?"

"They'll be all right in Moldova."

They wouldn't. She fought down the fury churning in her chest. "Did you lie about helping our . . . mutual friend?"

A moment's hesitation. "Yes. I would rather burn in hell than help him."

Cold anger surged in her chest. "You warned the person in Copenhagen about our mutual friend knowing he was still alive. The person in Copenhagen paid you to lie and mislead our mutual friend."

"Yes. Paid well. But I would have done it for free."

There, then. "You are the cruelest person I know."

"I suppose I am." His voice sounded dead. "I thought it for the best for the two of us. It gave me a way to get him out of our lives."

She could have asked another question about Danny Capra but instead she asked: "Did you ever love me?"

For the first time his voice broke with emotion. "Yes, love, yes. When there was a million-dollar bounty on your head, and hired killers hunting you . . . I saved you. I protected you. You don't know what I risked to save you then."

"Because I was useful to you."

"No. Because I loved you. I love you."

"Really? Do you love yourself more?"

He didn't answer, but after five long seconds, she heard Jimmy knock at a door and say, "I'm done. Here's your mobile back."

"Mila?" Charity.

"Tell my . . . husband I am doing this, but not for him. He cannot guilt me into a decision. I am making my own choice. For my family's sake. And for the sake of what I once felt for him. Tell him."

She heard Charity relay the message, precisely word for word. "He's not saying anything," Charity said. "Mila . . ."

"The data has to be decoded," Mila said. "Will it be enough to satisfy our deal?"

"No!" Charity snapped. "Not until I have a client of his in hand. *That* satisfies the deal."

"I have to go." She hung up as Charity started to yell in protest. She looked up at the cabbie, who had ignored her. The British consulate was on Third Avenue, off 52nd Street. Northeast of the bar. She moved the data off the key and onto her Chromebook. She stared at the screen. She could e-mail it to Charity; she'd been given an address. To save a husband who couldn't be a husband to her again.

Instead she closed the laptop and put it

back in her backpack, told the driver, "New destination, please," and gave the driver the address of The Last Minute.

27

Manhattan

"I broke in," Jack Ming said the next morning. "Took twelve hours, but I got inside the data."

"Thank you," Sam said.

"It wasn't so bad. I cooked a meal for Ricki while it ran. She has both cravings and morning sickness, so I'm trying to make her comfortable."

"Did we hit a gold mine?"

"No, Sam, I'm sorry. Most of the files are encrypted and I can't break those, not yet. But I did find some unencrypted files. Bank statements and money transfer records. All for Avril Claybourne's art business. They all look legit at first glance, but I'll check over them all. And a couple of others, under DBA names. Doing Business As." In case Sam wasn't quite awake yet. "Most of it is for video equipment, insurance, gallery costs. But one of the DBA accounts pays the rent on an apartment in Brooklyn that, according to a report she wrote to her tax accountant, she makes available for visiting artists."

"Where?"

Jack Ming gave him the address. Sam didn't write it down.

Mila puttered in the kitchen. He'd insisted on giving her the bedroom and he'd slept on the couch. His damaged back ached. But he could sense her watching, listening. She'd been in a strange mood when she returned to the bar last night. Edgy, anxious. It was unlike her.

"Something else. There was a draft in the e-mail file. It wasn't encoded. She must have started a reply and put it aside and forgot about it. She has several draft e-mails like that; all the rest are to her daughter who's in a boarding school in Montreal. But this one was written in Russian."

"What did it say?"

"Well, I don't read Russian but I copied it into a translation program. It reads, 'Firebird: Judge accepts assignment for the offered twenty M. He will begin once you transfer initial funds. He is aware of your rules of contact and says it will happen on American soil.' "

"What job?"

"I don't know. Twenty M might mean twenty million normally but it can't; no one pays a fee that big for anything. Judge, I assume, is that Philip Judge name you asked me to check on. Firebird sounds like a code name. So they might both be code names."

"This Judge person agreed to do a paid job of some sort for a Russian?"

"That would be one reading."

"What have you found on Philip Judge?"

"Very little. There are several dozen men with that name in the US, Canada, Australia, UK, South Africa. That's lots of various databases to crack and information to compile and patterns to emerge. I don't even know what I'm looking for, Sam."

"Is there a Philip Judge who travels to Russia frequently? Or spent time there in the past?"

"I can try to narrow the search. But if this is a false name, he could easily have more than one."

"Did she send other e-mails to this Firebird's address?"

"A couple. One says, 'I'll ask,' one says 'Agreed.' Nothing more. I couldn't find a record of what e-mails she received. She could have been answering questions posed to her in ways other than e-mail, so there wasn't a record of the conversation."

"Where did the e-mails she sent to Fire-bird go?"

"The IP address of the e-mail pointed me to a particular Internet service provider. A Russian one I've never heard of before. It's called Sekret, registered in Moscow."

"*Sekret* is the Russian word for secret."

"Well, that fits; they don't have a public website, they don't promote themselves, no online review of their service, and never profiled in the tech press. The first five hackers I contacted had never heard of them. I made some phone calls to friends who hack into Russian systems more than I do. One in Estonia told me Sekret is a satellite Internet service provider. So even though the e-mails landed on a land-based server, they got sucked up by a satellite and deleted from the server."

"Oh, no."

"Those e-mails could have been pulled anywhere . . . onto a plane, a boat . . ."

"So this is a dead end?"

Jack cleared his throat. "Hey, this is me. I am the man."

"The man."

"I found one brief mention of Sekret, five years ago, when the Russian oligarchs were diversifying into technology start-ups in Russia. It specializes in maritime ISP services. It has a very small circle of clients. All Russian, all with superyachts. The company is owned by a front, owned by another front. I guarantee you there's a wealthy Russian behind Sekret, and he's providing Internet services for his own boat and all his buddies' boats. Probably not wanting to trust anyone else with their digital security."

"So, what particular superyacht did this go to?" He would have Firebird's name then.

"The IP address that took the e-mail off the Russian server is tied to a particular satellite modem. I got a buddy who's a particular genius with satellite modems to hack it for me. He's hopeful that if he can hack his way in, we can find where that boat is. I'll let you know as soon as I hear. I will warn you now: he's expensive."

"That's fine. You are amazing. Thanks, Jack. Go get some sleep; send me the bill. Give Ricki a hug for me."

"Thank you, Sam."

Sam hung up. Mila watched him.

"Is there something going on with you and Jimmy?" Sam asked. "Because I can tell when you're upset."

"Jimmy? No. We're fine." She set down her coffee. "What did Jack say?"

He explained and she listened without

comment. He thought she would offer her interpretation of what the e-mail meant but she didn't. Instead she said, "How can I help you today?"

Sam studied her. She stared back. "This artist, Avril Claybourne," he said. "I'd like for you to shadow her."

"You stole all her secrets already. I should come with you."

"I'd like to know where she goes, who she sees. Can you handle that?"

"Of course." She had already showered and she went to prepare gear for a surveillance. He had given her no warning but . . . he thought it best Mila not be with him. What if he found Danny at this apartment Avril kept? He didn't know how his brother would react to being found. He might stay calm with Sam, but with a stranger there . . . best to keep Mila out of the way.

The moment of reckoning. He finished packing what he needed and left.

Please be there. Just be sitting on your couch, doing nothing, no trouble, and be happy to see me. What you've done won't matter. Just be there. We can get past anything if you are just there.

28

Brooklyn

Sam parked three blocks away from the apartment's address. Sam had found, in his bar, generic-looking repairman's overalls with an ID card from Metro Repair Services. A phone call to the number would reach a cell phone of Bertrand's, who would answer with the name of the business. He got out a tool kit, put on the Pelican backpack he'd taken to Afghanistan, and walked down the street to the address.

There was an electronic entry key. At the building's front door, he fed the electronic key a swipe of a card that sent an override signal and opened the door.

The account Jack Ming had found in Avril Claybourne's records had paid the rent on apartment 1245. He stopped in front of the door, took a deep breath, and knocked.

No answer.

He picked the three locks, one after

another, each one taking several minutes. High-quality equipment. Sweat poured down his back. He could hear music in a distant apartment and if someone came out and asked . . . The final lock opened beneath his picks. Calmly he stood and stepped inside and scanned the entryway for any sign of an electronic lock or alarm. He saw none.

"Danny? It's Sam," he called, very quietly. "It's Sam."

There was no answer. He didn't draw his weapon. He moved through the apartment.

No one was here. The kitchen had few utensils, and the refrigerator, while cold, contained nothing except some frozen pizzas and bottled waters. The trash had been emptied.

Maybe this *was* just an apartment for artists.

He went into the first bedroom. No laptop. But in a bureau drawer he found three guns and a box of ammunition. Sig Sauers. The numbers were filed off.

In the second bedroom, taped to the wall, there were faces, printed on four-by-six-size photographic paper, arranged in a circle around the president.

But that picture in the middle, the biggest

one, was Dmitri Morozov. The Russian president.

He felt his stomach twist. *Judge accepts the assignment,* written in Russian, *for the offered twenty M.*

Jack had laughed that no one paid that kind of money. But what kind of job would command twenty million dollars?

He took a picture of the arranged photos with his smartphone. Then he took a picture of each person. His hands were shaking and he made himself stop. Deep breath. Then he took the pictures again, to be sure the images were clear.

He unpacked the same crime kit he'd taken with him to Afghanistan. He started dusting for prints on the doorknob.

Nothing. Wiped clean. He tried the faucets, the refrigerator door handle. Nothing.

He went to the bathroom and looked for hair that might have fallen to the floor from a comb. Nothing. He checked the bedroom. It had been vacuumed. The place had been scrubbed.

But the pictures left up, like a calling card. Why? Why scrub the apartment and leave this?

He sat down on the floor, facing the pictures.

Had his brother been here?

President Morozov, in the middle. Red ink circling his face, like a mark.

Like a bull's-eye. A target.

Seaforth's voice, talking to his team: *What is Danny Capra now? What did they turn him into?*

The Hungarian guard: *Two prisoners died while he was there. . . . Both . . . were hired killers. . . . I saw they had shooting targets set up in a room . . . mats on the floor, weights. . . . It looked like a training facility of some sort. But the only two people I saw were this big man and twenty-six. When he was over there, twenty-six didn't wear chains. . . . He didn't even look like a prisoner. Then he was gone.*

The Russian connection. Sergei Belinsky, who had hidden Danny away from the world, was dead. But he had worked for the Morozovs, supposedly eliminating their enemies. Maybe he had help. A protégé he had trained. A man the world believed was dead. Who would understand the Russian power structure, speak the language, perhaps know people who could get him close to . . . He touched the picture in the center.

The Russian president, who was coming to America with his innermost circle in a week.

An innermost circle made of billionaires. Who were among the very few people in the world who could afford a twenty-million-dollar fee for . . . killing a man.

If this was an assassination plot, then Sam would expect the map on the wall to be describing motorcades, likely helicopter routes from Houston to the vice president's ranch near the city, firing trajectories. A sniper would be working out the best approaches, the weather conditions, the security cordon, trying to find the weakest spot and strike there. Creating a kill nest, a place from which he could strike without detection.

But this was . . . different. A map of relationships.

He noticed a worn, used, thin paperback on the night table. He picked it up. Shakespeare's *Julius Caesar.*

The book, with its cracked spine, fell open to the assassination scene. About a leader struck down by his closest circle. He nearly dropped the book in shock.

Danny was navigating the circle. Finding a way inside the maze of loyalty, relationships, and money that marked the Russian elite.

He took down the photos from the wall and dusted them.

A few prints appeared. He scanned the dusted prints and ran an app on his smartphone. One print was a thumb. He compared it to the thumbprint that had been digitally stored when Danny got his American driver's license; he'd gotten Jack Ming to get him the file from an archive.

A match.

Proof.

He sat down on the floor, his legs weak.

Your brother is still alive. And he is involved in a high-dollar plot involving the Russian president.

The end of the e-mail: *It will happen on American soil.*

It had to be an assassination. At the summit, in a matter of days. A confirmation sent to a boat in the Caribbean, via a Russian Internet provider.

If Sam went public with this knowledge, security forces around the world would be looking for Danny. The Russians would kill him on sight, and the CIA or FBI would alert the Russians to any threat against Morozov. But an anonymous tip with no details would not be taken seriously.

That left him one option.

You could find Danny. Stop him before he kills Morozov. Before anyone else discovers this plot.

To save him you have to stop him. The weight of what he had to do slammed into him like a bullet.

First he had to find Danny, and there was one person close at hand who could tell him the truth. He took the pictures down and put them in the backpack. He locked the door behind him.

The windows of the Claybourne gallery were darkened, as they had been for the party last night. A simple CLOSED sign was on display. Sam tried the doorknob. It turned, open.

He stepped inside the cool of the gallery and closed the door behind him. The videos that played last night had started again, images of war, love, peace, and humanity moving across the floor and the walls. It must have been keyed to the door opening, or perhaps she'd turned them on for her own reasons.

He listened and he could hear voices, two harsh ones.

He moved past the first room into the much larger gallery space where the reception had been.

Avril Claybourne had her back to him, images playing against her shoulders, her hair. Sam saw she held a Sig Sauer, mounted with a laser sight. She had it aimed across the room at . . . Bob Seaforth, who was aiming a Glock 9 millimeter at her. Standoff.

Sam froze.

"There's someone behind you," Seaforth said calmly. "So put the gun down and we'll continue our conversation."

"Please, let's not be that way," she said. Sam saw her laser dot centered on Seaforth's forehead.

Sam ducked back around the wall and dug out his Beretta from the Pelican backpack. "I'd like you both to drop your weapons and we'll have a nice calm chat."

He risked a glance around the corner. They hadn't changed positions. But Claybourne recognized his voice. "You. *Je suis* Sam."

"Moi," Sam said.

"I can offer you a deal," Seaforth said. "Whatever you've done."

"I've not done anything except protect my property against an intruder I discovered on the premises," she said.

"The laser sight on the gun will be a hard sell," Seaforth said.

Sam leveled his gun at Claybourne. "Lower it. Now."

She didn't.

"You," she said, glancing back at Sam. Moving her position slightly so she could keep him in sight. "You lower yours. Or I shoot him."

"Not how it's working today," Sam said. "You can tell me about my brother. You will."

"Brother?" she asked.

"In your artist hideaway here."

A sudden calm crossed her face. "I don't think you'll shoot me," she said to Sam. "You need me."

"I could shoot you in the leg."

"I'd still shoot your friend."

"Let's not shoot anyone," Sam said. "Let's put our guns down and talk calmly."

Her gun didn't waver.

"I know what's happening," Sam said. "What you're planning. This isn't going to work."

"I don't think we need him to negotiate," she said.

He couldn't negotiate in front of Seaforth. He couldn't let the CIA — or whoever Seaforth was with — know about Danny's assassination plot. It would most likely mean his brother's death.

"I won't negotiate with you if you shoot him," Sam said. "Where is he, right now?"

She didn't answer him. But he could see her gun waver for a moment, then center its aim again at Seaforth.

"The man you call Philip Judge. Where is

he?" Sam called.

Her voice sounded ragged. "Fine, you shoot this man and I'll tell you."

Shock crossed Seaforth's face.

"That's not going to happen," Sam said.

"All right. Fine." She started to lower her gun with a pronounced sigh and then she swung it up, her finger tightening on the trigger, and Sam fired. He'd meant to hit her upper arm to keep her from shooting Seaforth, but she stepped forward into her turn just as he fired and the bullet caught her in the throat. She dropped.

Sam screamed out a "no." He hurried to Claybourne. "Where is he?" As though asking could give her a will to live. He tried to find a pulse: throat, wrist, chest. She was gone. Her gun lay on the floor, images from the ceiling projectors playing across the spreading spill of her dark blood.

He had killed the only person who could have taken him to his brother.

Rage fired in his chest. He glared at Seaforth. "This is your fault. Why are you here, interfering?"

Seaforth had lowered his weapon as well. "Thank you," he said. "She was going to shoot me."

"She . . ."

"Get ahold of yourself," Seaforth said. He

pulled a phone from his pocket, dialed, gave instructions. Sam stared at Claybourne. *When I thought Danny was dead, he was with you. Why did he pick you over his family? Over life?*

"We'll take care of this," he said, ending his call. "My team will be here in minutes. We've been watching her today."

Mila was supposed to be watching her, too. Sam hoped she hadn't followed him into the gallery. He didn't want Seaforth to know about Mila. "We who?" Sam asked. "Why are you here?"

"You came here last night."

"You followed me."

"Yes. We believed Avril Claybourne might have useful information on your brother's whereabouts."

"Because I came here."

"Because you passed an item to an accomplice after leaving here."

"No, I didn't."

"Sam, don't insult me when I've helped you. I was searching Claybourne's office when she arrived. I chose to confront her directly. She was prepared for trouble."

Sam looked at the suitcase that stood against the wall. "She was leaving town."

"She's connected to your brother. You said Philip Judge is a name he's using?"

Oh, hell. He was in a race with Seaforth and his team now. If they found out, via Claybourne's records, what Danny was planning . . . he had to hope that Jack Ming was faster and better than Seaforth's crew. "I don't know. It might be an old one."

"How did you come across it? Whatever you found last night?"

Sam said, "I had a source."

"I searched her office. Her computer equipment, all of it, is gone."

That would slow them down, but not for long. "The CIA doesn't operate on American soil. So what are you?" He knew they were called the Church. That meant nothing to him, but he couldn't risk them finding the bug he'd put on Seaforth's phone. Not now.

"I'll tell you that when you tell me everything you're not telling me about your brother."

He heard movement in the back of the gallery, from an alley entrance, and brought up the gun, but Seaforth said, "They're with me." Two people — a woman in her early thirties, dark haired, with a slight build, and a young man in his late twenties — came into the back of the room.

"We need to scrub this place," Seaforth said. "Make Claybourne vanish. Use her phone, text her staff not to come in this afternoon, say she's on an emergency business trip. Secure the building, get rid of the body, bleach the floor. Find her Internet provider, search the mail servers, see what you can find. I want her bank accounts audited and checked. Wipe any surveillance systems. Check her purse — why did she have the suitcase; where was she heading? Her computers are already gone."

It was an impressive list of demands. Sam watched as the two — he guessed the woman was Romy and the young man was Prakash, both of whom he'd overheard on the eavesdropping app — began to work to secure the scene. Romy shot him a curious look and he wanted to say, *Yeah, I'm the crazy one, I'm the one you called radioactive.*

"I need to go," Sam said. He steadied the backpack on his shoulder. "Lock the front door after me."

"No, just wait. Let us get this dealt with" — *dealt with,* Sam thought, like it was spilled juice — "and we can talk about your brother and why this woman wanted me dead rather than talk to me."

"No," Sam said.

"Here's a phone number where you can reach me." He said it once and Sam memorized it, against his better judgment. Then he turned and walked out of the gallery. The sunlight was bright in his face.

He texted Jack:

> Can u wipe AC's digital traces? I need that all gone.

Then he turned on the eavesdropping app that was tied to Seaforth's phone. The phone was on.

Seaforth: "I want eyes on him."

Prakash (sounding stressed): "Bob, I'm not sure we can do half of what you just ordered us to do."

Seaforth: "I wanted to make an impression on Sam that he could trust us."

Prakash: "We don't have anyone. You can watch him or clean this up. Your choice. I vote we deal with the dead body in case a buyer or employee shows up in the next few."

Seaforth (hesitating): "We clean this first. I know what name he'll travel under."

No you don't, Sam thought.

And then he thought, Where was Mila? She should have been close to the gallery. Watching it, at least, seeing that Sam had entered.

He stood on the street corner, waiting for her to show herself. She didn't.

It was so unlike Mila that he grew scared. Something had happened to her. Perhaps that was why Claybourne was leaving. She'd seen Mila, hurt her, killed her — it was a roiling dark thought, a knife of dread in his brain.

No. Couldn't be it. It couldn't.

He walked on. He walked to the subway and headed back into Manhattan.

Danny took a next step when he left that apartment. He went somewhere. The answer was in the photos he'd left behind. Sam just had to figure it out.

29

Miami

His third triple kill in a few days had put him behind schedule. Messes were time-consuming. The bodies were dumped. The house had been cleaned with bleach. The men had arrived in a Toyota SUV that Judge had driven and abandoned in a dismal neighborhood with keys dangling in the ignition. He had walked until he had reached a street where a cab was readily available and then he'd taken it to within a mile of his house, and then walked the rest of the way.

He packed a bag with what he needed. He checked the passport and yes, Shaw had done as planned — there was a stamp showing entry in the United Kingdom two weeks prior. Right now, Robert Clayton was in London and no one was the wiser that he was not. He took the Robert Clayton papers, packed them inside a set of books, and overnighted the package to an address in London. For a moment he considered sending them to the man he knew as Jimmy Court. But then he decided against it. He had paid Jimmy well for another, equally important job; there was no need to confuse the issue by asking him to do more. He had another acquaintance in London who knew him by another name — a woman he had helped by ridding her of a troublesome husband, a violent criminal the police did not look too hard for once he'd vanished. She would keep the papers safe for him until he returned from Russia, with the news of his deed blazing across the world.

When he got home, he opened his laptop. It was not difficult to find where Katya Kirova was in her Caribbean jaunt — the tabloid sites were paying a bit more attention to her, what with the Russian summit approaching — and she was still in Nassau, on her father's yacht. With Stefan Varro.

Considering he'd had such a bad day yesterday, he felt he'd grabbed a bit of luck here. This was perfect. At a travel site he found his flight to the Bahamas for later that afternoon. He decided he'd pay cash for both his airline ticket at the airport and for his hotel room in Nassau. He would be Philip Judge for only a few more days. The phone call from the man who watched the village in Afghanistan made him uneasy. Eyes might be on him.

He locked up the house and headed to the airport.

30

Manhattan

No sign of Mila at the bar. Sam tried her phone again; no answer.

So he went into vanishing mode.

Sam checked into a small boutique hotel in the heart of Manhattan. On the hotel room's wall, using tape he had taken from the hotel's business center, he re-created the circle of photos. A face-recognition app on his phone identified first Katya Kirova. She was in the magazines regularly, a minor celebrity. From there it was easy to identify the rest of the players, as they all connected to her. Russia's two most powerful oligarchs — Yuri Kirov and Boris Varro — Stefan Varro; and Irina Belinskaya, the widow of the once Big Man named Sergei.

Online, he found articles and went to the Belinsky Global Security website. The firm provided security to corporate and celebrity clients in Russia, its historically allied countries, and Europe. No offices in North America.

His brother had been taken in by a Russian ex-spy who provided protection to other ex-spies turned billionaires. But Sergei hadn't been working a protection job in Afghanistan — it was the last place a Russian oligarch would go.

He unfolded his copy of the letter that had been in Anton's pocket, retrieved from the grave:

```
S is losing control of the [sec-
tion too damaged to read] he
should simply [section too dam-
aged to read] he checks my
phone. So burn this. I don't
think he realizes that the
brothers will kill him if he
does this. He would listen to
you. They must never know. A.
```

Could Anton have been writing to one of these Russians? Anton was dead. Sergei was dead. But this would have been sent to someone that Sergei would listen to. His wife, Irina, or one of his clients? And . . . did you just offer a strange man, an American living under a false name, twenty million to do a job? Wouldn't you work with

302

someone you knew of? Would these people know of Danny, under his false name, due to the Sergei connection? Or had he been Sergei's secret?

Is one of them Firebird?

In the hotel's tiny business center, he'd printed out histories and news articles on the players, trying to quickly piece together the web of relationships Danny had apparently already spent a good amount of time studying and mapping.

Anton. He soon discovered in the news accounts that Boris Varro had a dead son named Anton, vanished, never found, presumed dead. It could be his Anton. But why would a billionaire's son risk the dangers of Afghanistan?

The other mystery was Sergei Belinsky. The Russian press wrote little about him because the journalists who wrote critically about him ended up dead in elevators or poisoned with radioactive substances. One article suggested he was a private weapon for the Morozovs during the Chechen war. Sam remembered — there were a series of bombings in Moscow, blamed on the Chechen separatists but never proven. Tenement buildings in the endless gray sprawl of Moscow bombed at night, their helpless sleeping residents killed outright or smothered in rubble. There had been three in a month, and the outrage revved up Russian support for the war. One persistent rumor held that Sergei Belinsky set off those bombs to make it look like separatists were waging a terrorist campaign.

But there was never proof. And Sergei died in a car bombing, outside of St. Petersburg. It was suggested that he might have been moving another bomb when it malfunctioned. But the Morozovled press painted him as a national hero murdered by terrorists.

This was the man that Danny chose to follow, Sam thought.

He looked at the photos of the oligarchs and reread his research.

Five names: Irina Belinskaya, Boris Varro, Stefan Varro, Yuri Kirov, Katya Kirova. Danny thought one of them was Firebird. Maybe Danny was trying to identify his employer for his own protection.

Sum them up in one sentence, like he'd had to do during Special Projects briefings. Cut to their cores.

Katya was a party girl, famous just for being famous. She seemed more style than substance.

Part-Russian Stefan was trying to be the

face of the new, modern, less corrupt oligarch.

His half-Cuban father, Boris, had never quite fit into the Russian elite but was a favorite of Morozov — suave and elegant, but seen as Morozov's lapdog. Sometimes, though, a pet could bite.

Kirov seemed to hover in constant disapproval from Morozov but always managed to land on his feet. His control of oil made him powerful, second only in economic power to Morozov himself.

Belinskaya was the most feared woman in Russia, called the Black Widow. Her history after her husband's death suggested she had not flinched from exacting revenge against the Chechen terror cell that was blamed, and no jury in Russia would have convicted her.

Morozov was protected by the Russian Secret Service, not Belinskaya's private army. But these five, any of them, could pave a road to Morozov for Danny. They were all close to him.

Back in his hotel room, Sam paced. He thought. He read articles on the upcoming summit.

Then he saw it — the crack in the door. The new détente meant much more interaction for this inner circle with Americans;

there would be plenty of Americans vying to advise, befriend, earn a profitable favor with the Russians. Consultants, business-people, political advisors.

One had to be his path, too.

His gaze went to the picture of Katya Kirova. Her picture was in a lot of Western magazines and online celebrity columns. She liked movie stars, musicians, and athletes and she partied with them a lot. He found picture after picture of her in the trendiest nightclubs of Paris, Vegas, Moscow.

Bars. She liked bars. Well, he had thirty of them to impress her.

He searched her name again, with today's date. He found a news item from yesterday in a celebrity magazine. Katya Kirova and Stefan Varro, posing with two young actresses, standing on her father's superyacht in Nassau. Katya Kirova had a lovely smile but looked drunk.

Nassau, yesterday. The accompanying photo caption said that Kirova and Varro — THE EXCITING NEW FACES OF RUSSIA! — were spending time in Nassau before the summit of the two presidents.

And the e-mail to Firebird had gone to a server on a boat, serviced by a Russian ISP that specialized in maritime services. Two members of the inner circle, in the Caribbean. Who owned a boat? Both Kirov and Varro did, he quickly confirmed by searching the website of a major yachting magazine. He searched news accounts; the press were reporting on every aspect of the oligarchs given the impending summit. Varro's superyacht was in Greece at the moment. Kirov's superyacht, the *Svetlana,* was trekking through the Caribbean, making stops in Puerto Rico and the Virgin Islands, with Katya and Stefan aboard, now in the Bahamas.

He called Jack. "Has your friend had any luck in hacking that satellite modem?"

"I was about to call you. He texted me an hour ago, but I was giving Ricki a prenatal massage. He said the GPS coordinates of that satellite modem were in the Caribbean, close to Nassau."

Claybourne e-mailed someone on Kirov's yacht, he thought.

"Does that help?"

"You're amazing, Jack. Tell me what Ricki wants most of all for the nursery," Sam said, "and I'll buy it for her."

After wiring Jack money for his work and payment for the other hacker, Sam went online, found a flight to Miami with seats available and a connection on to Nassau. He didn't bother to pack; he'd pick up clothes from his bar in Miami. He didn't call Seaforth. He tried to access the eavesdropping app, but Seaforth's phone was off. *Go. Find him. You're running out of time.*

From a back corner of the lobby, Mila watched Sam leave. He stopped at the front desk, slid a key, waited for his bill to print, apologized that he'd only kept the room for a few hours, mentioned an emergency for which he had to return home.

Mila went to the elevator and went up to his floor. The housekeepers were on duty, the service carts lining the hallway. She slid a master reader card into the key slot for Sam's room and slipped inside.

She hadn't done any of the shadowing of Avril Claybourne that he'd asked her to do. Instead she'd gone to the British consulate and dropped off an encrypted file with Charity's contact there.

But it wasn't the file Sam had stolen from Avril Claybourne. It was trash. Oh, carefully done trash — account numbers and fake companies' names and money moved in interesting amounts. Jack Ming had given it to her when she'd asked him if he could provide a fake trail for someone to follow, and then lock it up very tightly.

It would keep Charity busy. Then when

Sam had called her, she had seen on the phone's app that he was close to the Claybourne gallery. She knew she'd have to explain herself, why she hadn't shadowed Claybourne.

She looked for scraps of paper in the hotel room indicating his travel plans; it was most annoying that people could price and book all that on phones now. But there was paper in the trash can. Photos, several of them.

She pulled them from the wastebasket, smoothed them flat, and studied them. Her heart began to grow cold. She knew three of the faces immediately. She held up the picture of Irina Belinskaya, the security chief.

Don't go near that woman, Sam. Her reputation . . .

She searched through the printouts again. One showed Katya Kirova in Nassau, yesterday.

That was where he would go. Either there, or Russia, and Katya would be an easier approach than the fortresses the oligarchs lived in.

The door knocked, the room cleaner's voice saying, "Housekeeping . . ."

Mila got up and walked out past the startled hotel housekeeper.

She activated a tracking app; it had last

309

shown her the location of Sam's phone. She guessed he was most likely on his way to JFK Airport. She hailed a cab.

She'd bought her Miami ticket at the counter and gone through security, her newly issued UK passport passing muster with no problems.

Sam sat in the corner, reading on his tablet. She sat next to him and leaned over. It was an academic article about the oligarchy in Russia surrounding Morozov.

"When you get close to them, don't let them catch you reading that," she said. "It'll be suspicious."

He closed the application. "I know you mean well but I need you to stay clear of this."

"I'm Moldovan. I speak Russian far better than you do. You want to work your way in with these people, you need me." She gave him a smile, put her hand on his.

"This is way more dangerous than helping me find my son. I don't know what I'll even find when I find Danny. Who I'll find. What I'll find."

And she saw fear in his eyes. He blinked and looked away.

Let your brother be horrible. He must be broken after what he's been through. Will that

310

make it easier when I take him away from you? I am convincing myself that keeping him from you is saving you, Sam. But instead she said, "I know. Please. Let me help you."

He caved, as she knew he would. "Fine. But Jimmy won't like it."

"I don't care about what he likes right now," she said.

Sam closed his eyes for a moment and he was back in the village of ghosts. An execution that had not happened — and now he had to stop one with global implications. A man forged into a weapon for a ruthless Russian — and now he had to be a weapon as well, to stop his brother.

They called the flight for Miami. He got up and headed for the gate, Mila walking beside him. For one odd moment he thought she was going to take his hand. But it was just his imagination.

One focus, he thought. Stop Danny. Save Danny.

■ ■ ■ ■

Part Two:
In Sunshine
or in Shadow

■ ■ ■ ■

31

Nassau

Judge knew it would be hard to get Stefan Varro alone; he was protected, as befitting a billionaire's son. He rarely left the *Svetlana,* and when he did, he was with Katya Kirova, and they were trailed by Sergei's widow, Irina, and her guards. Judge did not have Varro's phone number.

So after Judge arrived in Nassau, after he acquired a gun from an island contact, after he enjoyed a hearty breakfast on his balcony, watching the yacht, he waited for the *Svetlana* staff to take a break — from his hotel room he watched three workers leave the boat, dressed not in their uniforms but in casual clothes. Men, with a few hours off. He watched them amble past the confines of the exclusive marina and head in the direction of Shirley Street, a district where there were cheaper bars and weed to be bought and trouble to be found.

He followed them. They ended up drinking beer and playing pool inside a cinder block bar that was cheap but clean. Speaking Russian amongst themselves, laughing. The regulars ignored them. They were used to international crews.

He waited until two of them went off to the men's room and the remaining Russian — older, balding prematurely, with a dour frown — stood alone at the pool table.

"Hello. You're with the *Svetlana*?" Judge asked in Russian.

The bald man hadn't expected to hear his mother tongue in this bar. "Yes. What do you want?" Caution colored his tone.

Judge offered him a slip of paper with a phone number on it, wrapped up in an American one-hundred-dollar bill. "Give this to Stefan Varro. Alone. Ask him to call me."

The crewman didn't take the money or the note. "And who are you?"

"Tell him I'm Sergei's friend. He'll understand."

"Nothing more?"

"He'll understand."

The bald man took the bill and the paper and Judge paid for their next round of beers. Then he walked out into the sunshine.

■ ■ ■ ■

Two hours later, Judge stood in front of a coffee house and saw Katya Kirova and Stefan Varro walking together through the shopping district. Their bodyguards tailed them, three men in summer suits and sunglasses, clearly security. They stopped and Stefan said something to the men. One shook his head. Stefan shook his head and gestured.

The three men, along with Katya, headed back toward the marina. Stefan walked past Judge and headed for the beach. Judge followed.

He sat, as instructed, on a bench before the sand, watching the water. Judge sat next to him. Children screamed and played in the surf. Tourists wandered the beach and locals wandered after them, selling hair braiding and souvenirs.

Stefan Varro glanced at Judge as he sat down.

"Who are you?"

"I was Sergei's assistant." It was an odd thing to tell the truth. "One he kept out of sight."

"Sergei is dead." Stefan put his gaze out over the beach, the blue of the water.

"Sadly. Yet I have carried on his work whenever needed. I am needed now before you all go to the summit."

Stefan glanced at him again. "I heard he had a pet . . . weapon. How do I know you're telling the truth?"

"Sergei did favors for your father — and for you. I need a favor in return."

"I don't know you; I knew Sergei."

"But I know what Sergei did for you. The journalist in Moscow that was going to expose your father's dealings with the Morozovs. That prosecutor who wanted to investigate your company. The girlfriend in St. Petersburg, Nadia, who made tapes of your pillow talk to sell to the Western papers to try to expose corruption at your family's companies."

Stefan's voice quavered, ever so slightly. "Ridiculous. I don't know what you mean."

"There was a final message Nadia left for you before Sergei killed her. Sergei played it for you at your family home at the Nebo retreat outside Moscow, when you paid him the final installment of the contract for killing her. He asked her if she had anything to say to you before she died. You and I and Sergei are the only ones who ever heard it and you deleted it, told Sergei good job, and paid him." Judge put on a high-pitched pleading tone: *"Stefan, don't, don't, we will go to Sochi together and forget all this, please, Stefan, let's go back to Sochi, please . . ."*

And Stefan's face went pale. Judge explained, "I held the recorder while Sergei held the gun on her and she tried to bargain for her life."

"My God." Stefan Varro ran a hand over his face. It was the detail only someone present at her death would know.

"Do you accept my credentials?"

"Yes, OK, what do you want?" Stefan Varro spoke with impatience. Judge had noticed that people with money were often impatient, as if they had less time than the rest of the world. When he had his twenty million he would be kinder than that.

"I need you to bring me into the inner circle before the summit. I need to be at the launch party when Morozov and you all leave for America."

"Why?"

"There is someone close to the circle who is a danger. Who might expose every crime Sergei committed for you all." The lie felt fine in his mouth.

"No one in Russia will care. It will be seen as foreign propaganda."

"I think the press who is so eager to take your photo with Katya and proclaim you

319

the 'new kind of Russian' would be interested in the fact that Sergei killed your mistress."

"It would be seen as a lie."

"Stefan. Sergei was the Morozovs' hired gun. He knowingly murdered a CIA officer in Afghanistan," Judge said.

"What?" Stefan visibly jerked in reaction.

Judge kept his voice cool. "Did you not know that? I think your father does. What would be the American reaction to that news? You think you have seen sanctions now? You want your president and your father and the men who run Russia to be seen by the world as common thugs? Someone knows about this and is going to tell the Americans. I need to be inside in the summit."

"Who is this traitor?"

"It's obviously not you or your father. Or I wouldn't be talking to you."

"Who, then? Kirov? That drunken bastard . . ."

Judge held up a placating hand. "It could be any number of people. Sergei did much work, and he could have been spied upon. And now, at a moment in history, someone could seek to ruin that. I know this because of an informant I have in the US government. One who worked with Sergei. But we can stop it before proof is produced."

Stefan shuddered, his face turning red with rage.

Judge put a calming hand on his arm. "You do nothing except help me get inside. We strike at the wrong person, then we alert the traitor."

He could see that Stefan did not do well with being told no. Judge said, "You let me handle the problems, as Sergei did. That is the only way the system works."

"I have to think. Where have you been since Sergei died?"

"I stay quiet. In the shadows. I act when needed. I don't act unless there is a threat. For me to come talk to you shows the seriousness of this problem."

"All right."

"You'll know me as Philip Judge. An American investments counselor. Someone you have hired to diversify your portfolio in the stock market. We'll say that you've known me for five years; we met in New York."

"If you worked for Sergei, why not just go to his wife if you need a cover?"

"Sergei's widow never knew about me. No one did. He preferred it that way. Will you help me?"

"Yes," Stefan said after a moment. "I'll

pretend to be your friend so you can find this traitor."

"Thank you. You'll be a hero to Morozov after this."

"What do you need?"

"Is Katya Kirova hosting one of her parties on the yacht this week?"

"Yes, tonight."

"Add me to the guest list. I want to suss out all these people who have contact with the Kirovs and the American investors. I need a key to open every door on that yacht."

"The doors are all electronic; they use a card key. I'm not sure I can . . ."

"Stefan. You are smart and resourceful. You can. I'm staying at the Hotel Sebastian. And are you returning to Moscow before the summit?"

Stefan nodded.

"You will give me a ride on the private jet if I need it." And he would.

Stefan said, "Fine. Philip Judge. All right."

Judge handed him a slip of paper. "That is our history together, if you are asked. Where we met, how long we've known each other, how much money I handle for you out of my New York office. The account number is real; it's in your name, should anyone check. Memorize it, and then burn it."

Stefan finally nodded.

"Go along and this will all go well, and you'll be a hero. I know the Kirovs and some of the other oligarchs have sneered at you, Stefan. That you and your father are not Russian enough. No one will be able to criticize you if you help me."

Stefan tried again. "Tell me again who you suspect."

"Stefan. Don't be curious. Be patriotic. I'll see you tomorrow." Judge got up and left and walked back to his hotel.

32

Nassau

From his hotel room Sam watched, with binoculars. The *Svetlana* was the largest yacht Sam had ever seen — he guessed its length was over 250 feet. It was docked at Nassau's most exclusive marina. There was little traffic off and on the ship; a catering service truck arrived, and men loaded a shipment of what looked like liquor and fresh produce. A young couple — or at least a man and woman that he thought might be Katya Kirova and Stefan Varro — lounged briefly by the yacht's pool. Another woman stood at the stern and shot skeet over the water.

Sam suspected shooting wasn't allowed in the marina, but no one came to the boat to complain. She had red hair, tied back with a stylish scarf, and he realized it was Irina Belinskaya. She did not miss a single skeet. When she was finished she handed the rifle to a crew member and went below deck.

He called Jack Ming in Paris. "Were you able to get Katya Kirova's credit charges?"

"Well, yes, but it's not even in her name. Katya is too rich to bother signing credit slips. Usually one of her bodyguards signs for everything, using a card in her father's name. I had to look at them all to find hers, and her father has two dozen different credit accounts. Her most frequent charges in Nassau have been at a nightclub called Bright, a bar called Jean-Claude, and a clothing boutique called XK." He gave Sam the addresses for all of them. "She spent six thousand at the boutique the first day, another two thousand the next. Her charges at the bars go into the hundreds. Highest-end stuff."

"She's an adult; she doesn't have her own card?"

"I think Papa Kirov keeps his daughter under close watch. She used to, though. So maybe he feels he has a reason to keep his eye on her."

Sam thanked Jack, hung up, and watched the yacht.

A couple of hours later two women, both in brightly colored dresses, one in orange, one in emerald, walked down the gangplank from the yacht. A heavyset man in a summer suit walked behind them at a respectful distance. He could guess from the red hair that the woman in the green dress was Irina Belinskaya, and the dark-haired one was Katya Kirova.

"We have an expedition," Mila said. "Girls' afternoon out?"

Bodyguard, Sam thought. He watched them walk in the direction of the Jean-Claude bar, where Katya Kirova had been photographed a couple of nights ago. But they went past the bar, to the higher-end shopping district.

"Put on your best linen suit," Mila said. He did as she asked. When he was done changing in his room, she emerged from the adjoining room dressed in a fetching pale yellow dress.

"Go to the Jean-Claude bar and wait for me. If it goes well," Mila said, "I'll bring them to you."

Sam sat in the Jean-Claude bar. It wasn't very busy yet; it tended, Sam guessed, to attract a more late-night crowd. But the cocktail Sam ordered, a rum punch, was properly mixed, the bar was spotless, and the servers professional. A small-built man in a good suit spoke quietly to the bartender and nodded at Sam, and Sam said, "Nice place. You ever think of selling, Jean-Claude?"

"Is it so obvious I'm the owner?"

"I'm a bar owner myself. I'd like to think we can spot each other."

"Ah. No, sir, I am not thinking of selling. Even though owning a bar in the Bahamas is not quite as glamorous as it sounds."

"It never is," Sam said. "I own several bars." He took a sip of the rum punch he'd ordered. "New York, Miami, LA, Moscow, London . . . so my question was serious."

"I get asked to sell every few weeks," Jean-Claude said. "But by tourists who have too much to drink, not an actual businessperson."

Sam slid him a business card. "If you ever change your mind," he said.

Jean-Claude pocketed it with a wry smile.

Forty minutes later he turned toward the door, hearing the flood of Russian being spoken at high speed. Mila walked in, laughing, with Irina and Katya. My God, she's the best, Sam thought.

Mila waved at him as they commandeered a table and gestured him to join them. Jean-Claude rushed over to make sure they were comfortable and to take their orders. They were carrying shopping bags and Mila held a birdcage . . . with a canary in it. The canary seemed annoyed, chirping and fluttering.

Katya Kirova was laughing, and chirping at the bird. She was prettier than her pictures, dark-eyed, brown-haired, curvy. The bodyguard, following at a distance, seemed bemused. He stood off in the corner. Until Sam walked toward them, and the bodyguard — six foot six, and built of muscle — interposed himself between Sam and their table.

"It's OK. That's Sam, my American business partner," Mila said, in Russian.

The bodyguard said, "I have to frisk you; sorry," in polite English. The bodyguard quickly and professionally checked Sam.

"We're worried about recording devices," Katya said, in English. The bodyguard, done, stepped aside and Mila gestured at the chair across from her, between Irina and Katya. "There are news sites that will pay for recordings, just for the clicks."

"He speaks a little Russian, not much," Mila said as an aside to the others. She switched to English. "Sam. I have acquired two new friends. And a bird."

"That's my bird," Katya said, laughing.

"Sam, this is Katya Kirova. And this is her security chief, Irina Belinskaya. Sam,

Katya is famous so she needs protection. Ladies, this is Sam Capra, my business partner."

"Partner only?" Irina asked. She was polite but not as friendly as Katya.

"All business," Mila said. "I am married. Sam is not, though."

He shook hands with them both and sat down with his rum punch. "Lovely to meet you both. Does the bird have a name?"

"Sadly, no. Mila stole him," Katya said, with unalloyed delight, "from a horrible woman. Heart darker than a coal mine."

"We are thinking of freeing him," Mila said. "I do not know enough about whether he could survive here, though. Are there hawks? Will he be eaten?"

"The dress shop where we met had this songbird in it, and he was chirping, and the horrible woman complained that the bird would not be quiet," Irina said. Sam guessed that she was in her mid-thirties. She gave him a sly smile. "So she wanted quiet, we gave her quiet."

"She might want her bird back," Sam said.

"Petr!" Katya called to the bodyguard. He came forward. "Go back to that horrible woman and give her a hundred dollars for her bird. If she complains, you can go up to two hundred. And ask that nice man for our regular bubbly." She winked at Sam. "We spent two thousand there; she will not complain."

"They did," Mila said to Sam's raised eyebrow. "Not me."

Katya laughed. Her smile was bored. Sam's new friend, the owner, arrived with a chilled bottle of Dom Perignon and a glass of club soda for Irina. "Would you mind if we practiced our English with you?" Katya said.

"Yes, please," Irina said. Her English was nearly unaccented. She gave Sam a steady stare and he smiled back, then she glanced over at Katya. "Katya wants to expand her vocabulary beyond designers, cocktails, and rap lyrics."

Katya laughed. "In the changing rooms we heard Mila speak Russian to us when I told Irina we needed to rescue that poor songbird. She suggested we form a criminal gang to commit bird-sleeping."

"Bird-napping. Like kidnapping," Mila corrected her with a smile.

"English, ugh," Katya said. "It makes you think too much."

Irina took a sip of her club soda. Sam noticed she kept a steady watch over who came and went from the uncrowded bar. "Yes, fortunately Katya did pay for the clothes, if not the bird."

"Irina even let me buy her something," Katya said. "That cannot be worn with a gray suit, which is her normal look." She made a mocking, grim face. "Irina takes her job very seriously."

"I would have rather gone to the bookstore," Irina said. "I've read every book on that yacht."

"Mila said you are looking for nightclub properties here. I suppose you have to check them out when they are busiest, at night," Katya said.

"True," Sam said. "I asked Jean-Claude, but he doesn't want to sell."

"Don't you dare buy this one. I adore Jean-Claude." Katya wiggled fingers in a wave at the older man. He blushed and waved back.

"Mila said you own many bars, including the Tsar Lounge in Moscow," Irina said.

"Over off Tverskaya! I know it," Katya said, clapping her hands in delight. Tverskaya was a prominent shopping and dining street, not far from Red Square. Sam felt the doorway to the circle begin to open even wider.

"Hip," Irina said, "but not hipster."

He wasn't sure what he had expected from Irina but this warm, attractive woman

331

wasn't quite it. He had expected cold calculation, fierce professionalism. She had a big and difficult job but she seemed at ease. She was a surprise to him.

"You should open a cool bar like that here," Katya said.

"We have to think about what would work for the patrons here. Each town has its own requirements. Although," he said, worrying that he was playing a card too early, "I wouldn't mind taking the Tsar Lounge concept global. I think it could work in different cities. A Russian-themed bar in the West. Maybe here in Nassau — I'm not sure yet, but more likely New York or London. I have to run numbers, see what draws."

"There is a whole science to running a bar," Mila said. "Costs per drink, per plate, earnings per seat."

"Where I sit earns the most," Katya announced.

"Undeniably so," Irina said.

"It's true. People pay me and my friends to come to their bar openings," Katya said. "I turn around and give the money to charity."

"You're famous?" Sam asked.

Katya laughed, then stopped when she realized he was serious.

"Do you not know who I am?" Katya

smiled. "How refreshing."

"I will teach you a new English word, Katya. Mortified. It means deeply embarrassed, which is what Sam has made me," Mila said.

"I don't know anything," Sam said. "Except to ask when I don't know something."

"Sam, like me, is someone busy with his work, Katya," Irina said. She refilled Mila's and Katya's champagne glasses and waved off Jean-Claude when he tried to bring her an empty glass.

"What do you do?" Sam asked. "Forgive me for not knowing."

"I am friends with famous people. It's very demanding work," Katya said. Her smile was genuine, though, indicating that she wasn't offended. "I don't really do anything. If I could find a job, Irina, what should I do?"

"Personal shopper," Irina said. "Except you would bankrupt the clients."

"And what about you, Irina?" Sam asked. "You said security. Are you a bodyguard of sorts?"

"Yes, I keep Katya out of trouble," she said quietly. She didn't elaborate.

"It's a full-time job!" Katya agreed.

Irina's phone buzzed with a text. She pulled it from her purse. "Duty, in fact, calls." She downed her club soda. "Our time away from the mother ship is expired, Katya. Your father wants us back."

There was no argument, no protestation, although Katya was a grown woman.

"It was nice to meet you both," Mila said. "Thank you for the champagne."

"I am having a party tonight on the yacht," Katya said. "I hope you will both come. I'll have your names added to the invite list."

Sam saw a momentary look of consternation cross Irina Belinskaya's face. There but gone. "That's very kind of you . . . I did need to go check out the bars I was interested in buying, though."

"Oh, do that tomorrow night. Even that as work is dull. There will be leading Bahamians there . . . They can probably help you in deciding which bar to buy."

Sam snapped his fingers. "Hey, you could just leave your yacht docked here always and I could turn it into a bar."

"Then I will have a job," Katya said. "Captain Katya. It was fun to meet you, Mila and Sam; we will see you both at the party, yes?"

Mila and Sam shook their hands and watched them leave, the canary in its cage under Irina's arm. Petr, the bodyguard, nodded at them and followed Irina and Katya out.

Sam and Mila stayed in their roles, finishing their drinks, the owner teasing Sam a bit that the price on the bar had gone up since he had such rich friends. Sam and Mila laughed and made their way back to the hotel.

"Petr took our photographs with his camera phone," she said. "We'll be checked."

"I assumed we would as we got close to their orbit."

"I think Irina was interested in you."

Sam glanced up. "Why?"

"A hunch. She'd been rather talkative with me at first — my English is better than Katya's. The moment she saw you her attention shifted."

"She's assessing threats, constantly. It's her job. You're imagining things."

"Sam." Mila waited until Sam glanced at her. "I know Lucy made you feel like women see you as radioactive. They don't."

For ten seconds Sam had no idea what to say. "I'll be nice to her at the party, then."

"These Russians live with constant security around them. Irina has an entire security team that travels with them, all ex–Russian intelligence or army. We'll be watched.

It wouldn't surprise me that tonight our room will be searched while we're at the party."

"*Someone* in that circle is Firebird."

"Katya doesn't seem likely."

"She's in the circle; she can pay his fee and not blink. We need to figure out which one benefits the most."

"Are you going to tell me what you think your brother is here doing?" Mila asked. "Are you ready to trust me with the whole story?"

He sat her down and began, from when he'd found his brother's apartment.

33

The Svetlana, Nassau

Katya Kirova, who loved meeting new people, and Stefan Varro, who did not, had been told by their fathers and mothers: *Widen your circles. Befriend Americans. Find some nice, easily understood investment opportunities. We need pretty, shiny Americans standing next to us, endorsing us, showing we are not so different from Americans. We all love money. We all want to make money. We are like you, America.*

So, a parade of new faces, and it was Irina Belinskaya's job to check them out. Today there were forty-seven. The first batch of names on the list included a friend of Stefan Varro's, Sam Capra and Mila Cebotari, and seven American potential business contacts flying in from the States who were invited by Stefan or Yuri Kirov. The rest were musicians, film actors, writers, the semifamous, flying in for the party. Poor

Katya never had business contacts. Except this bar owner, who'd so casually mentioned he'd want to take his Russian bar as a franchise. He was fishing for investors. He was likely to be disappointed. But if Katya wanted to throw money at something — well, a nightclub chain was a likely match.

He was a handsome one, though. There was a leanness about him, like a knife. Katya would wrap him around her little finger, no doubt, although she wasn't quite so sure about Mila's assertion that they were just business partners . . . There was something between those two, Irina thought, that transcended business.

Shame, she thought. Sergei had been gone for so long . . . yet she did not permit herself a man in her life, not beyond a single night. It was a liability. Her reputation did not attract the kind of men she wished. It was not fair but simply was what it was. But Sam, with his nice smile and his lovely eyes . . . he is too young for you, she thought; he was at least five years younger than her. That shouldn't matter at all, these days. One could look, though.

She thought of Sergei. She had loved him so much that his death had been a cancer that lingered and grew and ate away at her for the first year he was gone. Then it had subsided to a dull throb. Unrelenting. And when she saw a handsome man, a man like Sam Capra that she might have enjoyed having dinner with, or talking books with . . . the ghost of Sergei rose in her heart and she pushed desire away.

She turned her attention back to her computer, to check on this bar owner and his partner. She was thorough. Belinsky Global Security employed some of the best hackers in Russia, and they had written programs to let her access financial, travel, and banking records. She found nothing suspicious in their digital lives. He really did own many bars.

She moved down her list to the next name, a friend of Stefan Varro's whom he had done business with in America for several years. Philip Judge. She checked the man's credentials, credit history, and more. He seemed clear, and Stefan personally vouched for him. She moved on to the next: a software CEO flying into Nassau for the party. She had several more names to check, and she would not give this job to an assistant. She liked to be thorough herself.

Because if she found a problem among these people, a liar, a false face, it was best she deal with it quietly and directly.

34

The Svetlana, Nassau

Philip Judge arrived early for Katya's party. He was disturbed to see that there were paparazzi outside the private marina, but they ignored him as he arrived. He was not famous. He was cleared through the gate, was cleared through the security stations. A security man confiscated his phone, his wallet, everything. He expected this: He knew the inner-circle paranoia. He came aboard the yacht, where the crew and servers were finishing loading tables with food and drink. Every inch of the deck was in use: the pool had been covered by a durable retractable floor, the helicopter was gone from the yacht's helipad — in its place an apparently famous progressive-house DJ was setting up for a concert later.

Stefan nodded at Judge, came forward, and greeted him heartily in English. "Philip! How good of you to come." Playing the part to the hilt. Judge was relieved.

He and Stefan grabbed the first pair of champagne flutes off a tray.

"You're early," Stefan said.

"I can't stay long." He noticed a red-haired woman approaching them. Irina Belinskaya. He thought: If you only knew.

"Irina, this is my old friend Philip Judge."

Judge shook her hand. She was attractive, fit like a well-honed athlete, a redhead with piercing blue eyes. Her gaze was shrewd.

"Irina Belinskaya."

"It's a pleasure to meet you." Sergei was right about his wife. She was smart, poised, beautiful. *Irina is my weakness,* Sergei had once said, in Brazil. *My only weakness.*

Will I ever meet her? Judge had asked.

No. Never.

"I heard you say you can't stay long?" Irina said. "A pity. For an investment counselor, the decks will be thick with potential clients here."

"I come more in friendship for Stefan than in commerce."

"Then you're a better friend than most here," Irina said.

Stefan laughed. "You'll see Philip again — I am giving him a ride to Russia."

Other guests began to stream past the marina entrance; they saw the flash of paparazzi lights. "Excuse me. Other guests are arriving." She nodded at Philip Judge and stepped away.

"Let's go to your suite and talk privately," Judge said. He followed Stefan down into the yacht's depths.

In the cool of the evening, Sam and Mila walked down to the *Svetlana*. It was massive. Security men stood ranged along the dock. He recognized some of the people in line: a film actor, a journalist, a pair of sisters who had a reality TV show and who were, like Katya, greatly skilled at getting the paparazzi's attention. At the boarding ramp stood a portable metal detector and a man with a checklist. And, on the boat's highest deck, looking down, was Irina Belinskaya, surveying the operation with a careful and practiced eye.

"Sam . . . ," Mila said. She saw her, too.

"Yeah," he said in answer.

The couple in front of them were Americans, a little drunk already, claiming that Katya had most certainly invited them. Their names were not on the list. The guard was unrelenting and sent them on their way, not kindly.

Sam and Mila stepped forward. "Hello, darling," Mila said to the guard. "Mila Cebotari and Sam Capra."

The Russian scanned the list, written in Cyrillic. "Ah. Yes. Thank you and welcome aboard." He gestured and another man, dressed as a ship's steward, stepped forward.

"I'll take you the next stage of security, Mr. Capra, Ms. Cebotari." His English was excellent.

The next stage? "Thank you."

They walked through the metal detector and then across a small, festively decorated gangplank and were led to a second staging area, inside the yacht itself.

"Sir, please empty your pockets again," the young steward said.

"Pardon me?" Sam asked, in Russian.

"The Kirovs are very protective of their privacy. They do not allow . . . the selfies during the party." The young guard smiled and produced a velvet-lined steel box. "Your phone, your belongings will be returned to you when you leave the yacht."

"I don't mind giving you my phone, but my wallet?" Sam raised an eyebrow.

"It will be under lock and key, sir, entirely safe."

Sam emptied his pockets and Mila removed her small phone and wallet from her purse. "You can't mean for me to surrender my makeup." She kept her clutch close.

"Of course not."

The steward smiled politely, closed the steel box, and took it out of sight.

"Don't we get a claim ticket?" Sam asked.

"Not necessary, Mr. Capra. It's my personal responsibility. Ms. Kirova asked me to let her know when you arrived . . . This way, please."

Five minutes later Irina Belinskaya was searching through the steel box with Sam and Mila's belongings. She and her team would search every guest's pocket clutter, looking for listening devices, hidden cameras, weapons, anything that indicated a threat to her clients. There was always a chance that foreign agents — she particularly worried about the US, the UK, Germany, and Israel — would try to infiltrate one of Katya's parties. Kirov, and the entire circle around Morozov, had many enemies. Or an independent operative, backed by Chechen rebels or Ukrainians or disloyal Russians. Kirov was very close to the president, so he was a target.

She picked up the phone. Two minutes later one of her operatives left the yacht, heading toward the hotel where Sam Capra and Mila Cebotari had their rooms.

■ ■ ■ ■

"What do you want to talk about?" Stefan asked. He set down his vodka on the bedroom table. Judge took a small, polite sip of his beer.

"Did you get me what I needed?"

Stefan handed him an electronic card key. "It has master access. I took it from the housekeeping office. It should open any door. So you're thinking it's Kirov, or a crew member?"

"I am saying nothing, Stefan, and please make no assumptions. I want you to stay here for ten minutes. I'll be back."

"Where are you going?"

"I'll be back in a few." Judge slipped out the door.

Stefan waited. Should he say anything to his father? He dug out his phone, torn with indecision.

I need the perfect hiding place, Judge thought. He wished he'd had more time to scope out the yacht, but one had to improvise at times. Soon as he was done he'd leave the party behind. From the upper decks he could hear the sound of music, of revelry, of laughter.

He went down to the lower deck. Smaller cabins for the crew and conference rooms. A server room. Irina Belinskaya's office.

He studied the doors. Choose wisely, he thought.

The party was building toward full voltage — chattering celebrities, pre-concert music from the DJ played low enough that the famous could hear what they were saying, gourmet Russian, American, and Bahamian cuisine being eaten, champagne gulped — when Irina's operative returned later. He found Irina near the stern of the yacht, conferring with the security detail. She wanted the alchohol consumption monitored; right before the summit, this didn't need to turn into a vodka-fueled disaster. She also kept a careful eye on the reporters who were here, writing for American magazines. And the crowd beyond the marina, who was excited to hear the famous progressive-house DJ.

The only problem was Yuri Kirov, who hated his daughter's parties and was absent. The reporters had already asked where Yuri was. She and Katya both smiled and put them off. He had meetings before the summit; he had not been feeling well . . . The Kirovs needed a good face to put forward, so where the hell was Yuri? She would have to send someone down to his stateroom to bring him up.

"I searched the hotel rooms of Capra and Cebotari," he said to Irina, leaning in close to her. "Nothing of interest. Those two appear to be exactly what they say they are."

Then the sound of gunfire exploded across the deck.

35

The Svetlana, Nassau
Gunfire.

Katya had made her way over to Sam and Mila, working the crowd, telling Sam he needed to meet every celebrity so he could invite them to his various bars. She had also announced that he should invent a drink in her honor, the Katya, when the ripple of explosive sounds tore across the yacht. Sam spun toward the noise and Mila pushed him and Katya into the doorway of a large room off the main deck.

Fireworks. Sparkling across the deck, people fleeing and running away from the brightness. A stampede starting at one end of the boat as the security lines were rushed by a sudden mob heading down from the marina entrance. Protesters, suddenly unfurling banners and raising peace signs.

"Not gunfire," Sam said.

The roar of the party suddenly grew, and

Sam turned to see six of the uniformed servers tying thick plastic cuffs and fastening themselves to the boat's railing at the front of the bow. Sam saw the security people sprinting toward them. A banner was quickly hung along the side of the yacht.

"No partnership with Russia! Freedom now! Freedom for Ukraine and Georgia! Protect Estonia! Freedom for the Russian people! Down with the oligarchy!" This was yelled together and in precision, as practiced as a choir. Some of the crowd that had gathered to gawk at the party along the pier rushed toward the boat, some waving flags they'd pulled from under shirts; others here for the music snapping photos with cameras and phones. Recording the reaction of the security team toward the people attaching themselves to the yacht. The partygoers themselves seemed to be caught between panic and amusement.

Irina held up hands and spoke into the microphone that connected her to her team. "This has to be a staged provocation. The world will be watching. Stop them, but do not be violent. Non-lethal weapons only — use beanbag rounds. No bad publicity." The security team's guns were useless — the protesters had judged, accurately, that they would not be employed. However, the team had both Tasers and beanbag guns — which fired soft projectiles that stung and stunned but did not hurt. Half the Belinsky Global team began to deploy around the VIPs, the other half ushering off the intruders.

"I hate these people!" Katya screamed. "Look at that sign!" One on the deck proclaimed useful hashtags for social media: #KATYAGOHOME #NO2RUSSIA. Sam saw the #NO2RUSSIA sign on banners heading toward the yacht.

"I give to American cancer charities! I don't do bad things!" Katya yelled. "Who are these assholes?"

Protesters began shimmying up the ropes tying the superyacht to the pier, waving at those filming them, calling out that the videos were being uploaded to social media. The security team members scrambled, trying to stop the protesters from attaching themselves to the *Svetlana.* One bodyguard returned on deck, armed with a beanbag-round shotgun, and began firing warning shots at the protesters dangling on the side of the boat. They began dropping into the water, angry but unhurt.

Katya, outraged, stormed out onto the deck, pleading with the protesters, Irina sticking close to her, two other guards rushing to her side, trying to get her belowdecks.

She waved them off like an outraged cza-rina. She stopped a protester and began talking to him, gesturing wildly.

Sam whispered to Mila, "Stick with them. I'm going down below to see what I can find." She nodded and followed, hurrying toward Katya's side.

Sam went down a spiral staircase to the next deck. A wide hall led each way to heavy doors. He tried the first one. Locked. He tried the next. The door was ajar, caught open by having fallen against the open dead-bolt.

It was a beautiful stateroom, appointed with rare hardwoods and fine linens. He stepped inside and turned on the lights. A Russian passport on the table, next to keys and change and a charging tablet computer.

He picked up the passport. This was Ste-fan Varro's room. There was a glass of vodka and a half-finished beer on the table, still cold to the touch; Stefan had had company, perhaps just moments ago, drawn out of this room by the noise up on the main deck.

He searched it, not even sure of what he might find. On the table were a number of printouts, proposals for investment from American companies. Nothing else of inter-est.

He heard another boom of firecrackers,

and screams and chants up on the decks. The music ominously went quiet. He swept through the room, heard voices out in the hall. The security team, coming up from below, or employees. A yacht this vast must have a sizable retinue of cooks, cleaners, and support staff.

He noticed there was a door, leading to the next stateroom. He tried it. Locked. He pulled a lock pick from the stitching on his jacket hem, one designed to pass a security search. The lock was simple and he was through the door in thirty seconds.

This was a woman's room, clothes tossed carelessly on the back of a silken chair. English newspapers on the table, a stack of paperback novels in Russian and English. *I've read every book on that yacht.* Irina's room, he guessed.

He checked the closets. There was a small safe there, the kind you would find in a hotel, and those were not a challenge for Sam.

The safe door opened.

Inside was Irina's Russian passport. Also oddly inside here was Katya Kirova's passport. Perhaps Irina kept it for her. Nothing else.

He put the passports back and closed the safe.

There was an adjoining room, the door already ajar. Carefully he pushed it open. He guessed immediately this was Katya's room. Her rescued canary fluttered in its cage. Some of the brightly colored dresses she favored were laid out on the bed, as though she'd debated over which to wear. On the desk was a box of stationery, some neatly written cards addressed in Russian and English. The box said Cartier on the side.

The same stationery used by Anton in writing his letter about Sergei in Afghanistan.

In the small closet there was also a safe, and he opened it to find . . . a Glock 9-millimeter gun inside, capped with a silencer.

He expected this in Irina's room. Not Katya's.

He didn't touch the gun. He saw an ammo clip next to it. There were also some pieces of jewelry, and a spare phone pushed back in the corner.

He checked the phone. It was the first cell phone from any of the Russian circle he'd gotten his hands on, and phones were often treasure troves of data. Locked. He attempted to guess the code: her birthdate, the birthdate of family members — numbers he had memorized when he'd studied the circle. Her phone was a different type than Seaforth's, and he didn't have a software pry bar of sorts to force his way in. No luck. Someone like Katya probably had multiple mobile phones. He put the phone back inside the safe and shut it.

Shallow-acting Katya was a surprise. Why did the party queen need her own suppressor-capped gun, surrounded by security? And what did the stationery mean?

He heard police sirens going on the dock. He assumed the Royal Bahamas Police Force was arriving swiftly to arrest the protesters. He heard splashing and looked out the small window. Protesters escaping the boat and the pier by jumping into the water. In the water he saw some of them clambering into waiting boats that turned and sped away.

Sam slipped back out into the hallway. He saw another suite, the door slightly ajar. He pushed open the door and, too late, heard the soft buzz of a television. This was a larger stateroom. He ventured into the entryway. He saw feet, in expensive shoes, resting at the edge of a bed. He almost turned back. But he decided to risk walking forward into the room.

"Hello?" he called in Russian, turning the

corner into the bedroom proper.

The man on the bed aimed a gun straight at his head. "Get out, protester."

"I'm not a protester," Sam began, and the gun fired.

36

Nassau

The chaos of the protesters had been a good cover for Judge's departure. He'd finished his errand on the lower deck and returned to Stefan's room, where Stefan paced and fretted. They were riding the elevator up when he heard what sounded like gunfire. He'd made Stefan hang back until he'd realized they were fireworks and a protest, not an attack on the yacht. Then he'd pushed his way past protesters and security alike, hurrying from the marina. The press photographers and curiosity seekers, chasing the protesters, rushed past him and then he was in the Nassau night, the crowds behind him. He got away as the Royal Police sirens began to sound, reinforcements arriving to quell the disorder.

It was done. Now he just had to wait for his ride to Russia. He had to play out his role on the stage of history, and then retire.

The tension of the past few hours seeped out of him and he nearly felt dizzy with relief. The plan was going well. Despite the setbacks, despite the dangers. He picked up a newspaper and started walking back to his hotel room for dinner and a shower and much-needed sleep.

He glanced up, by chance, and saw a face that tickled the back of his memory. A man, sitting alone at a café, sipping a beer. A face he knew.

He did not slow. He did not turn back. The man had not seen him, he thought. He'd been glancing at his phone.

Sergei had files. Dozens of dossiers on people: potential enemies, foreign agents who could pose problems for the Morozov brothers, operatives of other governments. Sergei had been given the mandate by former KGB officers to act like a private KGB on their behalf and that included intelligence, taken or funneled from the Russian agencies to the president and then passed on to Sergei. That man . . . that man was a chief in CIA Special Projects, in Eastern Europe, based in Warsaw. Robert Seaforth was his name.

Special Projects. No. *No.* It couldn't be.

But he was sure it was the man. He had studied Sergei's files, both before and after

Sergei died. Especially those relating to the most secret and hidden back corner of the agency. There he had a special interest.

Maybe they were here for the Russians. Watching the Kirovs, Stefan Varro. Yes. That must be it.

Are you willing to take that chance? What if they're here for you?

He could vanish. But he couldn't disappear yet into the Robert Clayton identity; those papers had been sent to London, awaiting his arrival.

He'd been cleverer than he needed to be.

Panic, for the first time in a long while, kindled and burned in his chest. He had to stay calm. He could try to call Mrs. Claybourne . . . and then he realized that, in his haste to leave the yacht, he'd left his wallet and phone behind on the *Svetlana.* He wouldn't go back there tonight. No, not with the chaos of the protests. Too much risk.

But he had his gun. He took it from the hotel room's safe and loaded it. From his balcony he watched Bob Seaforth sit at the café, watching, waiting, wondering, a tremble in his chest. Deciding, weighing the risks and the benefits, trying not to let fear win.

37

The Svetlana, Nassau

The two shots went wide of Sam, peppering the wall.

"*Bozhe moi!*" the man yelled in surprise. He dropped the gun and the bottle he was holding in his other hand. "The safety was off!" he said in Russian, shocked.

Sam jumped onto the man's legs to keep from fighting him and seized the gun. He recognized it as a PB — *Pistolet Besshumnyj,* "Silent Pistol," an old KGB favorite, a Makarov design with an integral suppressor that made the barrel look long. The gun looked old, in need of care. Sam unloaded the gun, thumbing the magazine release at the base of the grip, then ejecting the bullet from the chamber. He set the weapon and the ammo down on a table.

"Don't do that," Sam said in Russian. He kept his voice calm. Old KGB. A common feature in the inner circle's job history.

"The safety was on. I thought . . ." The man pointed at the two holes he'd made in the wall. "That paneling came from rare woods in Brazil. Costs a fortune."

The man was around fifty, soft-looking, balding, and very drunk. Sam picked up the now nearly empty vodka bottle as it softly gushed onto the carpet. The man — Sam recognized him as Yuri Kirov, Katya's father — wore a suit as though he had dressed for the party.

"All that gunfire. They're coming for me. Where is Katya?" He must have decided Sam was no threat. Or was an employee of Irina's.

"They were fireworks and no one is coming for you. Katya is fine."

"There are strangers climbing on the boat. I saw them out the window."

"They are harmless. You don't need a gun."

"Do I look all right?" Yuri asked, straightening his suit.

"Fantastic," Sam said. Owning bars had given him more patience with drunks.

Yuri curled into a ball, gestured at the bullet holes. "Will you dig those bullets out before Katya sees? She'll be mad at me."

Russia's most powerful oil baron, drunk as a lord, on his gigantic yacht with a hundred VIPs on the decks. "I probably shouldn't have a gun," Yuri said in Russian, slurring his words. "I might kill the wrong person."

Is there a right person you want to kill? Are you Firebird? Sam wondered. Then Yuri Kirov said, "So protesters are on my boat. I take it you are not a protester, because where is your sign?" At this he laughed, a broken sound.

"I'm a friend of Katya's. Do you want me to get her for you?"

Yuri Kirov focused, with great effort, on Sam's face. He stood up from the bed and very formally offered his hand to Sam to shake. "Most of Katya's friends don't speak Russian. You have an American accent but you speak well."

"I own a bar in Moscow. So I decided to learn."

"A bar. Wonderful news. I could use a drink."

"Do you want me to bring you coffee? A glass of water?"

Yuri wagged a finger. "I am not drunk," he insisted, and then he nearly fell, and Sam steadied him back onto the bed. "I'll just rest a moment," Yuri announced. He peered hard at Sam's face. "Have I seen you be- fore?"

Sam thought, Have you perhaps seen my brother's picture?

He blinked again. "Eh, they showed me pictures of everyone who was coming tonight. Irina always does. I am supposed to care."

Yuri attempted to retreat into dignity. He straightened his tie. "An American who speaks decent Russian. A rare thing."

"Your daughter is interested in investing in my bars. Bringing Russian-themed nightclubs to the United States."

"I want to go see these protesters now. Help me up, please." Sam got Yuri to his feet, straightening his suit again. Sam slipped the gun and the ammo into his own jacket pocket.

Yuri Kirov moved out of the room, slowly, staggering, leaning on Sam.

The police sirens outside were still loud. He pressed the elevator button but it didn't respond and Yuri Kirov huffed with impatience. So Sam helped the older man up the spiral staircase.

They had reached the large dining room that faced out onto the main deck. The security forces and the Bahamian police had the situation under control. The protesters who had attached themselves to the railing were gone, now sitting handcuffed on the dock itself. Irina Belinskaya's security team was in command, back on perimeter, the guests milling about, watching, chatting. A Bahamian police captain appeared to be in conversation with Irina Belinskaya. A table of food had been knocked over and the yacht's workers were clearing it up.

Irina and Stefan Varro were farther out on the deck, supervising the return of order from the chaos, Stefan trying to keep the guests from leaving, reassuring them that all was fine.

Katya saw her father standing in the doorway, Sam behind him. Kirov handed Sam his phone, as if he was a functionary, and as much as Sam wanted to steal it for five minutes he saw Katya watching, so he slipped it back into Kirov's jacket pocket. Kirov didn't seem to notice.

Sam caught Katya's eye, shook his head, pointed at Yuri, and frowned.

Katya hurried over to him, a forced smile on her face. Mila followed her. "Papa, go back downstairs. It's nothing."

"Who are these losers?" Kirov asked, gesturing at the handcuffed protesters on the dock.

"Troublemakers," she said. "Ignore them."

"Shoot them," Kirov said to no one, gesturing down the line.

"We can't do that, Papa, honestly." Katya looked at him with real concern.

"I suspect," Mila said, "that you'll see a lot of this at the summit. They're just the opening act."

Her theory was greeted with uncomfortable silence. Katya glanced at Sam. The alluring glance she assumed for the photographers was gone, replaced by a steely suspicion. "What are you doing with my father?"

Yuri laughed. "He took my gun away. Give it back to me; I'll solve this problem." He made his fingers into a gun and aimed it at the line of protesters, and Katya slapped his hand down, glancing back at the busy photographers.

"He fired a gun at me downstairs," Sam said mildly. "I have his gun and ammo in my jacket pocket."

"Papa!" Katya went pale. "Are you crazy? You're not supposed to have a gun."

Yuri wiped his mouth with the back of his hand. "You don't make the rules. Is it your boat? No."

"It's all right," Sam said. "He didn't come close to hitting me and I took it from him."

Katya's face flushed and she touched his arm in apology. "I am . . . I do not know what to say, Sam. I am so sorry. Please, don't tell anyone."

Yuri moved away from Sam and Katya and stared out at the protesters being escorted out of the marina by the police, who had descended on the scene in force.

Katya said, "Papa, go back downstairs. You must not be photographed . . . looking this way." Now she shot Sam a pleading glance. Sam, who also preferred not to be photographed, gently steered Yuri Kirov back inside. He didn't resist very much, but his mouth twisted in a petulant frown.

"You see, it's OK now," he said to Yuri.

"Yes," Yuri said and then turned away. He walked to the elevator, instead of the staircase. Sam went in and saw Yuri hadn't pressed the deck button; he was just staring at his feet, waiting. As though he were so used to others doing things for him that he needn't bother.

Sam pressed the button for a lower deck instead of the button for Yuri's deck. Yuri, eyes closed, didn't notice. It would give Sam an excuse to see what was on another deck.

"No one is going to take away what I have," Yuri said. "That's what they want to do. The Americans. Morozov. Varro. That little creep Stefan. Take what's mine. Take it all, and I won't let them."

"That would be wrong," Sam agreed.

"Are you dating Katerina Yureyevna?" Using the formal name for his daughter. "Are you one of them?"

"Them. What them?"

He started to speak but then shook his head, as if sad. "I don't want her dating Stefan. That boy . . . he is not a good person. Not a good man to women."

"I thought your families were old friends."

"Friends, no longer." His thought seemed to trail off. "That man was here. That man. I saw him. He didn't see me."

That man? "What man?"

Yuri shook his head. The elevator pinged and Yuri Kirov lurched out, heading for what he thought was his door. It was marked, in Russian: SERVER ROOM. KEEP DOOR SHUT. The yacht had its own communications hub, using secured satellite Internet. The e-mail servers would be inside. Sam hurried down the deck, as if confused, saw that the other rooms were marked, such as CONFERENCE ROOM 1 and so forth. This deck included offices, to conduct business of Zvezda Oil when needed, converted from the suites. The server door, like many others, had a lock that required an electronic card key to open. He saw one door marked SECURITY CHIEF. Irina's office.

"This is the wrong deck," Yuri called. "My boat is so big it is confusing you."

"Sorry, my mistake." Sam guided the man back onto the elevator and went to the correct deck. He led Kirov into his room. The man tumbled onto his bed. Sam undressed him down to his undershirt and boxers. He made him drink two glasses of water and take some aspirin, like a sick child. Sitting there, small and sad, he did not look like a former KGB chief or an oil tycoon. He just looked like a scared man who had had too much vodka.

"Thank you for your kindness," Yuri said after the second glass of water. "I'm sorry about nearly killing you. I'm glad I didn't kill you, I mean. What was your name again?"

"Sam. *Samuil.*" He gave it the Russian pronunciation.

"And your father's name?"

"Alexander."

"Samuil Alexandrovich, then. We will pretend you are a Russian with such a fine name. You own bars, so you know how to pour vodka, yes? Pour me one more."

Sam did, just to keep Kirov placated. "Who are you afraid of, Yuri Ivanovich?" He handed him the tiny amount of vodka he'd poured him.

"Loneliness and death. All men fear that. Go back to the party. You are too young to worry about either one." Kirov gestured with the glass of vodka, sipped, and then curled up onto the bed, looking like a drunken ruin.

Sam considered the map of the *Svetlana* he'd built in his mind. He realized directly below Yuri's room was where the server room would be. The scrambled e-mail that had gone from Avril Claybourne to confirm the kill to Firebird had landed back here.

He needed to get into that room, and uninterrupted time to get into its systems.

He needed to become a guest on this yacht.

Sam glanced back at Yuri Kirov. Yuri Kirov was asleep. He was tempted to pick up the man's phone and look at it. But he had pressed his luck tonight, and if the man awoke with Sam pulling his phone out of his pocket all would be undone.

What was the man afraid of?

That man. Maybe someone who frightened Yuri Kirov. Or someone he hated.

Sam went out the door, shutting it behind him.

38

Nassau

Midnight. Seaforth — the Special Projects man — got up from the café table, still alone, carrying a book he tucked under his right shoulder.

That could be a sign. A tradecraft sign, meaning he might expect someone watching him to get the signal.

Or he could just be walking with a book. What if he was simply here on vacation?

You know that's not true. He's here. Maybe looking for you.

Judge hurried down to the street. He followed Seaforth, a half-block behind. Judge thought Seaforth was going to turn into another hotel, but he walked past it. Judge closed the distance.

Seaforth pulled out a phone and began to talk quietly into it. He turned into an alleyway, a small cut-through between two restaurants that led to another street and another block of hotels.

He was halfway down the alley when Judge shot him, the suppressor on the gun making a hard *tweet*.

He'd turned just as Judge fired, a sense warning him perhaps, the sudden sharp scream of experience. The shot caught him hard, and he fell, blood on the front of the linen jacket; and at the other end of the cut-through came four women, laughing, talking loudly about grabbing a cab to Cable Beach and going to the casino. Judge turned and hurried away, head down. He was already out of the cut-through when he heard one of the women scream as she spotted Seaforth sprawled on the ground.

He's dead, he's dead. He never saw you.

He wiped the gun, jerked off his blazer with no tags to identify its origin, dumped it in a trash can, then turned and hurried into a hotel lobby. Cheesy island music blaring from the bar. He worked his way into the crowd, ordered something touristy, waited, sipped at the overly sweet concoction.

Seaforth was probably here to watch the Russians. Nothing else. But now he couldn't be a risk to Judge.

Thirty minutes later when he walked back out to go to his own hotel, the police had

370

cordoned off the area.

"What's going on?" he asked one of the hotel doormen, swaying slightly.

The doorman didn't want to say a shooting; it was a forbidden word to say to a tourist. "Not sure, sir. Perhaps someone ill — ambulance came, roared off."

In a hurry meant Seaforth was still alive. Not good. He should have taken more time with his shot. But there was nothing to be done now.

He went back to the hotel. He tried to call Stefan, to bring him his wallet and his phone.

There was no answer.

The tattered remains of the *Svetlana* party wound down earlier than expected. The protest had drained the party of its life. The celebrities, most of them, retreated to a posh nightclub at a nearby major resort. The crew began to clean the yacht. Irina and one of the bodyguards — Petr, the one with Katya when they'd met her — offered to walk Sam and Mila back to their hotel.

"Just in case," Irina said, "you are accosted by any of the protesters. I doubt they've faded into the night." But Sam wondered why they rated such treatment.

Their walk was unmarred by anyone with

a sign or a grievance against Russia. There was a police tape up past an alley as they walked toward their hotel, officers milling about, the danger — whatever it was — long past. Mila prudently dropped back and chatted with the guard, leaving Irina walking with Sam.

"Mr. Kirov is not what I expected," Sam said.

"I presume you expected him sober," Irina said. "Katya told me about the gun. Thank you. We would all appreciate your discretion, Sam. To have it known he was firing a gun at an American guest while drunk . . . before he has meetings with American oil executives — it would be a disaster."

Ah, hence the special treatment. It was good to have a little power and to use it wisely. "I gave his gun and ammunition to one of your team once I had him back in the room. I have no desire to embarrass him or Katya. Or you."

"Thank you."

"He seems a bit afraid, to be frank."

"He is. Russia is changing. He is not ready to change with it."

"Sure," Sam said.

Irina seemed to study him, measure him. "Yuri Ivanovich has been kind to me. When Sergei died — we lost so much business.

The security consultant who is murdered with a bomb? It gave an impression that he was not competent. These people pay great sums for confidence they will be safe. So when I relaunched the company . . . when I was ready . . . Yuri Ivanovich was the first to hire me again."

Sam thought, Maybe they didn't hire you because you were supposedly hunting and slaughtering everyone you blamed for your husband's death.

Irina went on: "So . . . I want you to understand, he's a danger to no one. He's functional, most of the time. You could look at him and think he has more money than he'll ever be able to spend in ten lifetimes, so why drink so much? But Russian presidents have thrown oligarchs in prison before and stripped them of all their billions, taken over their businesses, run their families out of the country. I think, despite all his advantages, he feels very unsafe. Being wealthy in Russia now sometimes feels like being an aristocrat back before the 1917 revolution. Except it's not the Bolsheviks who will murder you, but the other aristocrats. It's not a healthy way for anyone to live their life." Her voice was almost bitter. "Did you know half of Russian men die before they're fifty? Can you imagine that in America or Britain? I . . ." and then she fell silent.

"Irina, meeting you today has been the most interesting thing that's happened to me in a long while. And not only because I hope Katya will invest in my bars. Just because it is."

Now she smiled and brushed a lock of lovely red hair back from her face. He wondered, unprofessionally, what it would be like to kiss her. The thought almost jarred him.

He changed the subject. "How did the Kirovs make their money before oil? I mean, they had to have some initial capital to invest in oil."

"Ha, well, our Yuri's ex-KGB. He doesn't have an MBA."

Sam raised an eyebrow. Irina shrugged. "It's not a secret. The KGB had millions secreted around the world for their operations against the West — untold millions. Stashed in bank accounts, in safe deposit boxes, in vaults, in basements — and it was the bureaucrats and agents like Yuri who could access those funds who could use them to buy up assets like oil operations."

First they were spies dedicated to tearing down the West; then they were robber barons.

"Stefan kept talking to Mila during the party," Irina said. "You're sure you're not a romantic couple?"

Sam wondered if she was asking out of more than curiosity. Even as busy as she had been, he had felt her gaze on him. "We're not."

They reached the hotel. "The *Svetlana* sails tomorrow morning," Irina said. "But first, could you and Mila come early for breakfast? Katya asked me to invite you both. You could tell her father and Stefan your ideas about the bars — they are looking for investments. Say at eight?"

"Thank you," Sam said. "We'd love to."

Irina gave Sam a handshake — her fingers lingered longer than Sam thought they would — and then said good night to Mila.

He and Mila rode up to their room in silence. He was going to ace that presentation tomorrow, and be on that yacht when it sailed, and access that server room. Firebird was close — he had to be. And when he had Firebird, he could send his brother a message that appeared to be from Firebird:

Job delayed. Do not act. Will still pay. Meet me here.

No assassination, and then he'd have Danny exactly where he wanted him.

Inside the hotel, Sam and Mila did not speak to each other except to say "that was fun," and for Sam to relay the breakfast invitation.

"Was Stefan flirting with you?" he asked.

"A bit." She shrugged. "Harmless, though."

Sam was pointing at his jacket pocket, where his phone lay, and at her purse, where her phone was. She nodded. They had to assume, now, that their cell phones had been interfered with in the way Sam had interfered with Seaforth's. They had been invited back, which only meant closer scrutiny.

Now, Sam thought, they were not Capra and Court on a job. They were two actors staying in character.

They said their good nights in the hallway and went inside their respective rooms.

He checked his room. He was sure it had been searched; a hair he'd left across the closed zipper of his bag was gone. So Irina's people had been here and they were good but not good enough. He showered. Then he turned on the TV and lay on the bed. Irina had brushed his arm twice while they walked and maybe that was accidental or maybe not. He could not let himself be fooled by her, the Black Widow. She was a dangerous woman.

He had to make sure that when the *Svetlana* departed tomorrow, he was aboard.

39

The Svetlana, Nassau

Irina heard music playing softly in Katya's room. She stuck her head in through their shared door and saw Katya lying on the bed in her party dress.

She curled up on the bed next to Katya and touched her hair. "What's wrong?" Sometimes it was hard to think of Katya as a client; she had become like a little sister.

Normally a party energized Katya. Now she seemed tired, sad. "Papa. He fired a weapon tonight at another person, Irina. What if he's losing his mind?"

"It was just the vodka. We need to watch him more closely. He just needs you."

Katya coughed. "The protesters upset Papa. He thinks the next protest could turn dangerous. He doesn't want me to come to the summit. In America. Where I am the famous one. He is too silly. He wants me to fly back with Stefan tomorrow to Russia."

"I'll go with you."

Katya shrugged. "No. I'm staying here with Papa. You stay here with us; don't go back with Stefan. You can have fun with our brave Sam. I saw how you looked at him."

"I did not!" Irina sat up. "Now you are the silly one."

"Not you. Never you." Katya managed a smile.

"Don't be ridiculous," Irina said. "You'll go back to Russia before the summit?"

"Yes. But I want Papa to get right before we go back to Russia. He can't be like this back there, and then go to the summit. You'll stay here on the yacht and sail up to Washington?"

"Unless you need me to come back with you. I can help you . . ."

"No." Katya turned onto her back. "I'm fine now. Thanks for cuddling up with me. I'm going to sleep."

Irina went back to her own room, shutting the door. Katya was lonely, despite all the attention the world gave her. Irina understood.

She lay down and thought about the long nightmare of the evening. The protesters should never have gotten so close. The clients would be upset. Yuri Kirov might fire her. But she needed more people, and this wasn't Russia, where factors could be more easily controlled. She would have to draft new plans for the rest of this trip, meet with her security teams, have strong words with the marina management.

Before she fell asleep, she thought again of Sam. And for the first time, Sergei's ghost didn't intrude into her thoughts.

Katya held the old gun that had been taken from her father and opened up her room safe. She put it in there, next to the other gun she'd taken from him a few days ago. She hadn't realized he had this keepsake from his KGB days on the yacht. She would need to search his room.

You have a problem. He is losing his grip. And maybe it's your fault.

Then she noticed . . . the spare phone wasn't where she'd left it. She was careful about always putting it flush against the back right corner. Always. Her heart thrummed in her chest. She inspected the spare phone. She tapped an app marked with a smiley face.

The smiley face app wasn't for cheery notes or a game. It silently and secretly took a time-stamped picture of whoever entered in a wrong access code on the phone. She checked.

It was a picture of Sam, peering at the phone, during the time of the protest.

He had been in her room, trying to access her phone.

Was that when he heard her father being a drunken fool? She hadn't thought to ask why he was entering her father's room.

Katya Kirova felt a sharp shock, then anger. He was nothing but a dirty little spy. Acting nice to her drunken father, pretending to be interested in Irina, acting like he wanted to be her friend.

You know why he's here, she thought.

After a moment she put the phone back in the safe and locked it. Sam was her specific problem now, and she would have to find a way to deal with him. She could run back to Russia. Or she could deal with him tomorrow. Give him a warning. And if that did not work . . . she had Papa's guns. Accidents sometimes happened with old guns.

40

The Svetlana, Nassau

The first words Yuri Kirov said to Sam at breakfast were "Don't think you have sway over me because you saw me at my worst last night." He didn't look good, but he was up, showered, dressed, and drinking a very large cup of hot tea.

"Papa," Katya said, sounding mortified, "Sam helped you."

Sam smiled and offered his hand, which Yuri shook. "I'll hope that today is your best, Yuri Ivanovich. We'll cover the whole spectrum in our first two days of knowing each other."

Five seconds ticked by in absolute silence. "Sit down, Samuil Alexandrovich," Yuri Kirov said, but there was less heat in his voice. Katya and Stefan laughed at the Russian-style patronymic given to Sam. The tension lifted. Fine, Yuri was embarrassed. Sam could help him with that.

So, through breakfast, they negotiated their way to a place where Yuri Kirov was no longer embarrassed. After his initial bluntness, Sam was respectful and Kirov asked smart questions about his bar business. Katya did as well until her father silenced her with a wave of his hand.

You ought to listen to your daughter, Sam thought. She knows this business better than you do.

"Oil and liquor," Yuri said. "I suppose we deal in the two basic liquids that make people happy."

"Yes," Sam said, and the tension truly eased. Kirov and Stefan and Katya looked carefully at Sam's spreadsheets, at his projections for expenses and growth with the first three Tsar Lounge franchises in Seattle, New York, and Las Vegas. He planned an exit strategy should the franchise have a shelf life of hipness — as many bar concepts did. He also outlined how he would keep the Russian theme fresh and new, introducing Westerners to Russian cuisine in Western-palatable, high-end bar style. He had math on how much each drink would profit them, how much each seat in the bar would generate in a night, a day, a week, a month, a year. He commandeered the bar by the pool, raided the yacht's kitchen, and made them samples of signature cocktails he'd feature, with bold new takes on vodka and *kvas* and Russian staples like beet or salted cucumber.

He made one cocktail he called the Katya, which he handed to her with a flourish. Her smile was thin and he wondered why she might be cool to him this morning. Yuri applauded and took a small taste of the drink.

Sam wanted them to see the potential Tsar Lounges as a highly profitable business to be plundered. Because plunder was the name of their game. He knew Yuri's company, Zvezda, produced as much energy as Norwegian and British oil companies, but at a decidedly lower profit margin because the Kirovs and the other oligarchs with fingers in the oil pie took their share long before any stockholders saw money. But on that point, he stayed silent.

"These are interesting numbers. Small, as far as my investments go, but I would like to bring this to America," Yuri said.

"Sam," Irina said, "I wonder, I know that Stefan is flying back to Russia today, but could you and Mila stay on the *Svetlana* and you two and Yuri could hash out more of the details?"

Sam kept his expression neutral. "Aren't you sailing for the States in an hour or so?"

"Yes."

Stefan said, "I know you came here shopping for a bar to buy here, but this is a bigger opportunity. If all comes to agreement, it could be one of the many investments President Morozov announces as part of the summit." He gave Sam a thin smile.

"Just hang out on the boat and refine the proposal? Mila, OK with you?"

"Of course. If we have time to go back and get our bags. I don't want to get shipwrecked wearing just what I've got," Mila said. Everyone laughed politely.

"Unless . . . ," Stefan said. "One of you wants to come back to Russia with me, and the other stay here. There might be other investors back in Nebo" — Sam knew Nebo was the name of the inner circle's private compound outside Moscow — "who would like to invest as well." He gave Mila a sudden smile.

"What a thoughtful invitation," Mila said. "But I think it would be better if we could both work on the proposal here."

"But you could take Stefan to the Tsar Lounge in Moscow," Sam said, just as sharply. "Give him and his father a tour, show them what we're envisioning. I can work on refining the numbers here." He thought Mila could be valuable around the

385

rest of the circle. Perhaps she could find out who was Firebird there, if he couldn't find it here on the boat. And if he found where Danny was, it would be better to approach him alone.

Mila didn't argue. "Yes, Sam, of course."

Stefan said, "I'd like to see the numbers with a more aggressive expansion. There is about to be goodwill toward Russia again in the West. We should think of openings in Montreal, London, Los Angeles, Miami, as well. I think . . . what is the term? Strike while the iron is hot."

"Yes, Miami," Katya said. "It is the night-club capital of the world, Sam. We should open there first."

He had thought of that but he'd thought it smarter to let them suggest it and be invested in the idea. "That's a great idea, Katya. I'll work up those numbers first."

He was in. But Mila's smile, he knew, was forced.

"What's the problem?" he asked on the walk back to the hotel. Both of them had turned off their phones so they couldn't be overheard if hacked. "Is it Stefan? Are you afraid of him?"

"I can handle a blowhard like Stefan Varro," she said. "But I don't think we should split up. Finding your brother . . . he's dangerous, Sam, yes? He could be dangerous even to you."

"If I can talk to him, I can stop him."

"He has twenty million reasons not to talk to you."

"He has one to talk to me. I'm his brother."

"Sam . . ."

"It will be fine."

She hugged him, there on the street. Her breath hot against his neck. This wasn't like her. Normally she was steely; he was the one to bend in the storm of emotion. She trembled in his embrace.

"What's the matter?" he whispered.

Because if I find him, you never will, Mila thought. The enormity of what she was going to do overwhelmed her for a moment. But she had to.

"This gives me a little more time to find out who Firebird is," Sam said. "In that server room is the answer, I think. And if I find out who it is, and he's in Russia, then you're there. We're a team. We can do this."

"Even if we find Danny . . . he may not listen to you."

"I know my brother," he said.

Yes, Mila thought, and you probably think you know me, too.

Mila packed. She walked down to the hotel desk and retrieved a bag that she had checked into the hotel safe, away from her own room. Inside of it was a prepaid phone. She sent a text to Charity.

Heading for Moscow on private jet departing Nassau. Strong likelihood target is currently in Moscow. Need team on ground to extract target at my call in next few days. Plan to have team to meet me at Tsar Lounge, near Red Square, posing as customers. I will have to brief them on target grab and they must handle extraction details. TARGET IS EXTREMELY DANGEROUS. I am watched constantly. Do not respond; I am destroying this phone.

At least if she found Danny Capra in Russia, she was prepared to make him vanish. And perhaps it would be better this way, with Sam here and unable to interfere. She tore out the SIM card once the message had gone, crushed it, walked down the hallway to where one of the housekeeping carts stood, and stuffed the remains of the phone into the garbage bag hanging on its side.

A limo picked her up ten minutes later, taking Mila to the airport. Stefan wasn't in it and she felt a sense of relief. She'd be stuck with him long enough on the flight.

From his balcony, Sam watched her leave. He'd picked up a newspaper from the stand downstairs and now he scanned its headlines. Most of the news was about the protest at the Russian yacht last night, but there was also mention that an American had been shot in Nassau. Wounded. It did not give his name or condition.

Sam packed his bag and walked back to the *Svetlana.* It would be sailing out into the Atlantic in less than thirty minutes.

41

The Belinsky Global team searched Judge more thoroughly than he was searched on a commercial flight. It was a good thing he'd dumped his gun after shooting Seaforth. He only had the one bag. The searchers even checked the seams of the suitcase. The two men pawed through his toiletries: the eyedrops and the deodorant and the toothpaste. He didn't twitch, didn't react. They were thorough but then they put everything back in his toiletries bag and zipped it up.

They used a portable X-ray scanner on his bag and his laptop. He stood there, as if bored. The laptop was special in a way no one suspected . . . but it passed their muster. They handed him back the laptop. He thanked them in Russian.

"Forgive their caution," Stefan said, as if they weren't following orders. He'd brought Judge his wallet and phone that morning, and Judge had told him, *I'm flying with you this morning to Russia. Make it so.*

"No worries," Judge said.

"And now that you've been thoroughly groped, let's have a drink," Stefan said.

"Thank you. But I'm not much of a morning drinker," Judge said.

"A small one then. It's a long flight."

"Don't you have to check my passport or something? Like when you board on a commercial plane?"

Stefan smiled. "No. I am an honorary consul for the Russian Federation. To . . . I forget which country. Maybe Rwanda." He shrugged. "It means when I come back — when we come back to the States — I have a diplomatic passport; I need not mess with customs and I'm basically waved back inside. Lots of people close to President Morozov have this title. It's convenient."

"Do I get waved through, too?"

"You will in Russia, for sure."

He already knew Stefan and the inner circle had diplomatic passports. There had been an article in a now-shuttered Russian newspaper complaining about the privilege. If he were lucky, there might not even be a digital or paper record that he had entered Russia. He could hide in a dark corner of their own convenience.

The Kirov jet was big, a Gulfstream V Global Express, suited to carry eighteen. Sitting in a chair by a window was an attractive woman in her late twenties or early thirties.

"Philip, this is Mila Cebotari, also a new friend whose work we are investing in. Mila, this is Philip Judge, an American investments advisor. He's worked with me for the past few years, off and on."

The woman stared at the sight of him. Judge thought her skin paled, her mouth quivered. It was the barest reaction, one no one else would notice. But Sergei, and experience, trained him to register such reactions. But she put on a firm smile and stood and shook his hand. Why the reaction? He studied her face. He had seen it before. Where? Where? Not another Seaforth. He wondered if he could run.

He said, "Hello, Ms. Cebotari."

"Hello, Mr. Judge."

"Mila is a partner in several bars and nightclubs around the world. She is involved in one in Moscow and we might be investing in it," Stefan said.

Bars. He willed his smile not to tighten, his pupils not to dilate. He could give no sign he recognized her. But he knew then that she knew who he was, that the truth that James Court had whispered in his ear weeks ago was real. *Your brother knows you're alive. He's looking for you. Pay me and I'll make sure he never finds you.* He'd seen this woman, once, two years ago, with James Court before; she knew Court; so therefore he had to assume she knew Sam. She could only be here because of Sam.

She knows who you are.

"It's so nice to meet you," Danny Capra said to Mila Court. He offered her his hand and she shook it. Her gaze didn't leave his.

The guards closed the plane doors.

Why is she here? Is she here to confront me? Stop me? Deliver a message?

Stefan insisted on vodka; Danny could not refuse, although the last thing he wanted to do was to drink, especially in front of this Mila.

So he drank minuscule, polite sips of the Baikal vodka Stefan poured and counted the hours. He ignored the woman as best he could. She spoke little and sometimes watched him and sometimes closed her eyes and just listened as Stefan blathered on about the challenges of running businesses in Russia, in competing with Western companies. Russia was full of internal enemies, devils, who would try to bring the country and its leader down. Danny nodded and made sympathetic noises. He could do nothing about her now; he would have to deal with her upon arrival. She would seek him out, if she had an agenda.

Then he had to do this quickly. Kill Morozov as soon as possible, vanish. Before the summit. Dead was dead, American soil be damned. He had the polonium-210 and now he had to force the opportunity. Before this woman brought his brother to him.

And do what about her? If he were alone with her — the red eye in his mind might open.

"How did you meet Stefan?" Mila asked him.

"In London. I was doing investments consulting there."

"Ah. London is full of Russians. Like three hundred thousand of them," Mila said. "They could be their own large city."

"Yeah, I'm pretty sure there aren't three hundred thousand Americans living in Moscow," Danny said.

Steel went into Stefan's gaze. "Is that a judgment against Russia?"

Danny shook his head. "I meant no offense, Stefan. No, just an observation. It seems like a lot of the Russians in London are making their lives there with no intent to return home."

"People," Mila said, "should always consider returning home."

In the long years he had not encountered anyone who knew him for who he was. He could not look at this woman. So he looked at the vodka glass.

"I wouldn't mind living in London, but my father feels we should live in Russia." Stefan sipped at his own vodka. "Sometimes my father is tiresome."

"Fathers forget what it is to be young," Danny said.

"He means well. My father came from nothing in Cuba. Russia gave him a home so he thinks he must stay forever. But . . . if you are not all Russian, Russia can be hard." Stefan shrugged.

You want to be accepted so badly, Danny thought. The thought rushed into his brain: Could Stefan be Firebird? It wasn't just the oligarchs that had access to the money. It was their children as well. He remembered the figure he'd seen. Russia had a population just over 143 million. But only a hundred families controlled a third of all of Russia's wealth. The wealth, so concentrated, was staggering. It wasn't just the small, tight circle around Morozov that could fund the assassination. Maybe a younger person would want to make a murderous change. Grab power for himself.

"It must be difficult," Mila was saying. "To have so many enemies."

"Enemies killed my brother Anton," he said.

"I'm sorry," Mila said.

"He was . . . he was in Tajikistan, on a trip for President Morozov, and he vanished. Never seen again. We had to assume he was dead."

Silence fell hard between the three of them. Danny knew this was the story fed to the world. Anton had been with Sergei. Danny had stabbed and shot Anton to death. Best not to mention that.

Mila broke it. "Do you have much family, Philip?"

"No," Danny answered, his voice steady. "My parents are dead."

"I'm sorry." Knife twist. "No sisters? Or brothers?"

"I'm an only child." The plane had started to feel very small. They had hours and hours of flying to go.

What did she know? Was she just here simply because his brother was looking for him . . . or did she know the real reason he was here? He had to assume she knew.

"So maybe just don't mention Anton to

Uncle," Stefan said. "He is sensitive about Anton's death still."

"Uncle?" Mila asked.

"President Morozov. The kids of his closest friends call him Uncle," he said, almost embarrassed. "So, he's like family, our godfather, you know. If something happened to any of our fathers and mothers, he'd take care of us. He always gives us gifts: watches, religious jewelry, fancy stationery to use so we will write him because he does not like e-mails or texts. So. We called the first Morozov Uncle and then when he died we called the second one Uncle, too."

"That's nice," Mila said. "Family is so important."

She knows, Danny thought. What would she do when they landed? Call his brother? He couldn't let that happen.

Maybe she was here to deliver a message from Jimmy Court. If she was, she would live. If not . . . in a back corner of his mind he thought how he would make Mila disappear.

42

The Svetlana, The Atlantic Ocean

Sam had gotten settled into his room on the yacht in short order. He had not had to surrender his cell phone this time, but Irina had told him, in a voice tinged with regret, that there would be no personal cellular service available once they sailed. The satellite phone system would be available should he require it. He stood on the sundeck and watched as the *Svetlana* headed out of Nassau, aiming toward Florida. He went to the lower deck, found an empty conference room, and worked on refining his proposal, adding in numbers and details from the breakfast meeting. Waiting.

There were other guests aboard: a film producer looking to get Yuri to finance a picture, two software moguls, a vice president from a major retailer, an executive from an aviation firm. Kirov wanted to work on the investments announcements with them all before the summit. They were holed up in their cabins as well, coming out to confer with Kirov in the room that had been set aside. Katya spent time up on the sundeck with the film producer and an actress from a TV show Sam didn't know. Yuri was sober and had not produced a firearm since the party.

Something happened to get him drunk, to get the gun. A trigger, a source of fear or panic. *That man,* he'd said. He saw someone. Did Kirov know what had happened in that village of ghosts? Had Danny really been close?

He worked until after lunch, which was brought to him by a steward. No one was looking for him. Now was the time to access the server room. He'd noticed card keys on the belts of crew members. He'd seen one of them, a bald man with glasses, talking to the software moguls about how the ship's Internet satellite system worked, and how reliable it would be at sea. He'd seen the man point up to a small satellite dish, attached to a mast, aimed at the sky.

Sam bumped into the crewman as he left the conversation, ogling up at the satellite dish, and apologized profusely in Russian. The crewman apologized as well and headed toward the bridge.

Sam, the man's card key now in his hand, lifted as delicately as if by a Charles Dickens pickpocket, headed down to the lower deck. He would have to hurry; the man might notice at any moment that his card key was gone.

The server room. He glanced along the hall. No sign of a camera, but he drew from his pocket a mini camera detector, which could track either wired or wireless cameras. In a minute he determined the hall was clear. Kirov did not want to be spied on by his own security people.

He slid the card key along the reader.

The door clicked open. He stepped inside. He used the camera detector again — no telltale electronic signature. He put it back into his pocket.

The room was cool and windowless. A server array stood along one wall, with a hookup to a satellite Internet system. A soft, varying hum rose from the cooling fans of the different devices. A glow of red and blue lights from the machines illuminated the darkened room.

He spotted the server equipped with a pullout keyboard, eased the keyboard out, and lifted the folded LCD screen. Below it was a label with the admin password. This most common of security holes was truly international. He typed in the password on the label, which was . . . Firebird1991.

He felt cold. Firebird.

The system opened up. Where to start? He clicked on a device management icon.

First he saw a navigation system that showed every device on the *Svetlana,* on every deck, that was accessing the server. Each had a unique serial number — Jack had told him these were called MAC addresses. He could see a cluster of the devices in the conference rooms where the Americans working with Yuri were updating their investment presentations. A couple on the upper deck aft, one on the bridge, a phone in the residential staterooms on the main deck.

So anyone given access to the satellite Internet connection could have sent or received e-mails on this yacht from Claybourne. It most likely was Yuri Kirov . . . but it didn't have to be.

He jumped to an e-mail management tool. The e-mails delivered to the *Svetlana* went first to a land-based server, which then waited for the *Svetlana* to gather them when her systems used a satellite to connect to the Internet. The e-mails were then deleted from that land-based server and moved to the *Svetlana*'s server.

He found the list of e-mails currently on the server. In the search bar he typed the e-mail address used by Avril Claybourne. Nothing. He searched for Firebird. Nothing.

This couldn't be. *It came here.*

He paged through. There were e-mails pertaining to business deals, financial transfers. He had memorized the time stamp on the e-mail from Claybourne's system — the first financial transfer would have been after that, probably very soon. Would there be a confirmation e-mail? He searched along the parameters of an hour after the e-mail was sent by Claybourne.

He looked for encrypted e-mails. There were none.

Someone had scrubbed the server of the incriminating e-mails.

He heard voices in the hallway. Footsteps, laughter. If he was caught he had no reason to be here. The voices grew closer. Then passed him.

He fought down a wave of frustration and panic. If there was a conspiracy to kill Morozov, maybe there were other e-mails, related to the plot, not sent to Claybourne. Like instructions to move funds. He searched for "instructions" and saw a cluster of e-mails — sent by Stefan Varro. They were instructions relating to the buying and selling of foreign oil stocks. Stefan and Boris Varro were placing sell orders by the millions, but only if the stock price rose into a certain window, a good ten dollars above what the current price was.

Did . . . did the Varros know that Morozov had been marked for death? His death might well send oil prices climbing; political uncertainty in a major energy producer tended to drive prices up. Were the Varros setting up to profit off his death? Firebird, perhaps, was not one Varro, but both of them.

He looked for e-mails to banks or other financial institutions. Kirov was moving money, but it was for investment in these software and retail ventures for which the entrepreneurs were here. Nothing unusual.

He searched for Capra. Found one, an e-mail from Stefan's laptop to his father in Russia. It was an attachment, with Sam's PowerPoint for the Tsar Lounge. In Russian it read, "This is an easy investment; he speaks fairly good Russian; it will undergo much less scrutiny than investing in technology or a more formal business."

Again, voices in the hall. He froze: he waited. He thought about what Irina Belinskaya had done to the men she blamed for

her husband's death. Out here on the ocean
— they could make him disappear and not
even alert the other guests. He could not
stay here any longer.

He had failed. This was a dead end. But
Firebird1991, as a password — it *had* to be
Kirov. Yes, the firebird was one of the most
famous of Russian stories and images . . .
but coincidence only went so far. 1991?
What could it mean? After a few moments
he realized that was the year the Soviet
Union collapsed.

Was that why Yuri was drinking with a
loaded gun at hand? Because he'd ordered
an assassination, and the fear and worry of
it were eating away at him like an emotional
acid? What would the pressure be like for
such a man, who had billions at stake in
always staying in Morozov's good graces?

*You have your answer. Now what are you
going to do about it?*

He logged off. He made sure everything
was as he'd found it.

He turned and then he noticed the door
in the corner. RESTRICTED, it read in Russian. He tried the doorknob. Locked. He
tried the card key. The light on the reader
stayed red instead of flashing to green. He
put an ear to the door to listen, but he could
hear nothing over the hum of the cooling

404

fans in this room. Could there be another server in there, one holding the information he needed? Or something else? He could try and pick the lock — but forcing a door equipped with an electronic key would likely set off an alarm.

He'd have to find another way.

He checked the hallway. It was empty. He stepped out and eased the door shut. He did not dare take the card key with him; it would soon be missed, and they might check to see if it had been used. He dropped it on the floor by the door to create the illusion it had simply been dropped on the deck.

He took the stairs to his room's deck. He opened his door.

Irina sat in a chair, waiting for him.

"Uh, hi," Sam said.

"I couldn't find you. Where were you?"

"Down in a conference room. I thought I'd find some table space to spread out my data and refine my proposal."

"Come up on the sundeck. I have my own proposal for you."

43

Miami

The sky was bright and blue. It would take a few more hours at their cruising speed to reach the coastal waters off Florida, where he assumed the yacht would settle into a long track up the East Coast. The sun was starting to set. He and Irina were alone on the deck. "You could help me with something important," Irina said.

"What?" Sam stared up at the clouded sky. He braced himself for the accusation.

"I need to pick up a package from Miami. And I'd prefer there not be a record that I was there."

He stared at her. "What record?"

"An entry point in my passport. It's watched. And I don't want a record that I was here."

He waited.

"I need to retrieve a package. The *Svetlana* will anchor several miles off Miami. We could take the Vikal limousine tender boat — it's down in the yacht's garage — go to Florida, get the package, get back. No one knows we've gone to land."

"You want us to illegally enter the US, pick up a package, and bring it back to the *Svetlana*."

"Yes, that's it."

He laughed and she laughed. She said, "Also, there will be a party. Did you bring a suit?"

He stared up again at the sky. Something illegal? This could be the fast road to finding his brother, if it gave him more information, a final confirmation that Kirov was Firebird.

"I don't take stupid risks," he said, ignoring the historical catalog of stupid things he had done.

"Neither do I."

She was asking him to break the law. If they were caught, it could end his search for Danny. Being questioned by the police would force him into an impossible choice: let the assassination proceed or put a target on his brother's back. But he had to go with Irina. He remembered the family saying: The first order is you don't leave your brother behind.

"Yes," he said. "I did bring a suit."

■ ■ ■ ■

The night had fallen, the stars aglow in the clear sky. The *Svetlana* dropped anchor, and Irina and two crewmen launched the thirty-one-foot Vikal limousine tender from its garage. The *Svetlana*'s garage held the Vikal, an array of jet skis, and a wall of snorkeling and scuba equipment. The Vikal was a handsome boat in its own right and Irina handled it like an expert. They pulled away from the *Svetlana* and rode through the choppy waves toward Florida. One had to navigate multiple patrols, he knew. The Coast Guard kept an eye out for two hundred miles from the coast. Customs, twelve miles. The state of Florida, three. But despite those rings of security, no one stopped them.

Seaforth, he wondered. *Is he following me? Does he know I'm here?* Watching from afar, and maybe letting this play out since he covered up Claybourne's death? Or maybe he and Irina were just lucky. He hoped the luck would hold returning to the *Svetlana*.

They pulled into a private marina next to a beachside high-rise. A membership card was produced from Irina's clutch purse, and they docked. Well-dressed people mingled on the back terrace overlooking the stretch of the beach. A party was going on at the club facility on the ground floor of the high-rise and an invitation to the party — written in English and Russian — was also produced from Irina's purse. No one asked for a passport or ID.

They illegally set foot onto American soil in well-made shoes.

"I've never quite arrived at a party this way," he said.

"Never say I'm not fun," Irina said back.

It was hard sometimes to believe what he'd heard about her — that she had hunted down and killed the families of the men who had blown up Sergei. He remembered that murderers could smile, too.

They went inside. No one paid special attention to them but he saw a few people nod toward Irina, one a tall man with a shaved head and a gaunt face.

"Friend of yours?" Sam asked.

"Not particularly," she said, and tension strained her voice.

Sam snagged them both glasses of champagne offered from a server's tray. He heard as much Russian in the conversations as English, and Sam realized then they were in Sunny Isles. He had been here before, an area north of Miami Beach with a high percentage of Russian immigrants. He had made a mortal enemy here his last time, and he glanced around to be sure he did not see a bent, broken man in a wheelchair. But there was no such man. No one gave him a glance.

"I do love a good party," he said. "But why are we here?"

"We're not staying," she said, smiling over her glass of Moët.

He could see that many of the émigrés were older, people who had grown up under communism and then escaped it once the walls fell. The other group consisted of younger people, some of them dressed subtly and tastefully, others trying too hard to impress or cajole or seduce.

Maybe one of them is Firebird? He realized with a shock that his brother's funder could easily be an expatriate American who might want Morozov dead, not one of the inner circle. An Americanized Russian — especially in Miami, where the CIA had once operated an office that treated the city like foreign soil during the long secret war with Cuba — might have the connections and the drive to rid Russia of Morozov. Not because he was a tyrant of sorts but because it would be good for Russia, and Russian business. He might have horribly miscalculated. If she was bringing him to Firebird — he wasn't ready. He wasn't armed and he had no resources here to force Firebird to recall his brother from his job. He'd have to improvise.

"Let's go," Irina urged, and she and Sam walked into the lobby, using an electronic passkey she drew from a beaded clutch to access the elevator. The guard smiled at them, but with their passkey he didn't challenge them or ask for ID.

Irina turned to him. "Kiss me."

He didn't ask why. He took her into his arms and gave her a gentle kiss, not too showy, just to show affection while they waited for the elevator. Her fingertips touched his jaw, her other hand curled in his dark blond hair.

The elevator arrived and they broke apart and boarded, the only passengers. The doors slid shut.

"That was for the benefit of the guard," he guessed.

"Yes, and you did well," she said. "People who kiss in a place look like they belong. He'll remember only that he saw a couple." Her face was slightly flushed and she wasn't looking at him. "You're a good kisser; you should have a girlfriend."

"I should," he said.

The elevator arrived at the penthouse floor. He followed her to the doorway of an ocean-facing room. He tensed, wondering if Firebird might be on the other side of that door.

She unlocked it with a key.

The view was spectacular. The door opened into a large living room that faced out onto the bay, silver steel in the clouded moonlight. She walked to an alarm pad and entered a code, and a soft beeping that had started the moment the door opened stopped.

Guard downstairs, card key to elevator, alarmed room. A lot of security.

Elegant furnishings: clean, modern — lots of white, black, and silver — filled the room. But the air seemed stale. She turned on lights and walked through with purpose. There was a kitchen, large, with an elaborate island. Then a hallway, with bedrooms. All were furnished with magazine-level taste. But they had an emptiness to them, as though people had never lived in their calculated beauty.

He saw no pictures of people, no photographs, no papers, nothing to indicate who owned this place.

He followed her to the master bedroom. She opened a closet that was empty of clothes. Inside the floor of the closet were two large green duffel bags, the kind a long-term traveler might take on a trip.

She picked one up — it was clearly heavy — and gestured at him to pick up the other one. He did. The bag felt as if it weighed one hundred pounds.

"What's in here?" he asked.

"The money to invest in your clubs," she said. "American cash."

"No. Really."

"Really," she said, and she met him with a hard stare.

"What, I unzip this and it's stacks of cash?"

She nodded.

"It's highly illegal to take large amounts of cash out of the country without declaring it."

"I know, but there were no customs forms on the Vikal." She stepped close to him and tried a smile.

"What is this? A test? If I say no, no investment?"

"The Varros and Kirovs like to know that they can trust their business partners, even with delicate matters. That you can keep your mouth shut. There's all the money here to turn your dream of launching the Tsar Lounges into a success, Sam. This is how they work."

If he had sense he would say that he wasn't comfortable with this. But this could get him to Danny. So he had to do it.

"All right," he said. He stepped closer to her. He could smell her skin, light floral perfume, a slightly salty smell of the sea. "I understand how they work. I work the same."

Her eyes seemed fixed on his mouth and she started to nod, but then her face went blank as she looked over Sam's shoulder. He turned.

In the bedroom doorway there stood a man with a gun.

44

Miami

"Rolan Igorovich," Irina said. "No need for the gun."

He stepped forward and Sam recognized him: the balding man from downstairs with the gaunt face, who'd watched them arrive at the party. "I thought I'd help you with your pickup," he said in Russian. He told Sam, in accented English, to raise his hands. Sam obeyed, because the gun was pointed at him. He searched Sam but found nothing but Sam's phone, which he put in his pocket. Then he searched Irina, and took her phone from her purse as well.

"Stop this, Rolan Igorovich," she said.

"This is not your place to be, your money to take."

"I have my orders."

"You do not mind if I ask you to sit and wait while I make some phone calls."

"I do mind. Sometimes I am told to solve

a problem without being given the reason. You know what the Kirovs and the Varros are like."

He stared at her.

"If you interfere, you will be the one in trouble. You are making a mistake. It's not your concern," she said. "Because of what this money is meant for."

"I know what you've been doing," he said. "And you're . . ."

He wasn't expecting Irina to throw herself toward him. She went straight for his eyes, fingers hooked into claws, and he yelled and slammed an arm across her shoulders, knocking her hard into the wall. With his right hand he kept the gun up, aimed at Sam.

Sam charged him, leveling a kick hard into the gun. It was an unexpected move and Sam followed it up with a barrage of muay thai blows — sharp, fast strikes to eyes, jaw, throat.

Rolan took two hard hits but parried the other blows. He retreated. He seized Irina by the hair and brought her in front of him, trying to use her as a shield. Sam stopped and Igor aimed the gun at Sam's head. Irina elbowed him hard in the face; blood spurted from his nose, and Rolan hammered the gun across the back of her head and she went down.

A cold fury filled Sam. As Irina fell, Rolan lost his shield and Sam threw an item at hand — a small, sad vase of artificial flowers — right at Rolan's face. Rolan tried to dodge the blow and now Sam wrenched the gun out of his grip, grabbed Rolan by the throat, and threw him into a wall.

"Irina? Are you OK?" Sam called. He didn't want to risk a backward glance.

No answer.

"You know about this money?" He jabbed the gun against Rolan's cheekbone, just below the eyes. Rolan's throat tensed in terror.

"I keep watch for Mr. Kirov on his Western properties. He owns this condo. Through a holding company."

"And he hides cash here?"

"Yes. And she's been taking it all."

"All? He has other houses . . ."

"Yes. In the Bahamas, in the Virgin Islands, in Puerto Rico. This week. Please, put the gun away."

The places where the *Svetlana* had cruised this week. "This same amount?"

"Yes, usually."

"Maybe three to four million. It's not much to them," Sam said, almost to himself. "These are all billionaires with dozens of

417

accounts in places like Switzerland and the Caymans. They can hide and move money how they like. They . . ."

Except a payment that could *never* be tracked. Like the one that Firebird was making to Danny. Twenty million . . . the money to pay Danny for Morozov's assassination was being put, kept, and amassed on Kirov's yacht. A place that could move the money easily internationally, to wherever Danny might need it delivered over time. In bits and pieces, because a twenty-million wire transfer moved out of a Russian account in the days before or after Morozov's death would be a huge red flag.

It meant . . . yes, finally: Kirov was Firebird.

He turned Rolan so he could see Irina, past the man's shoulder. She was sitting up, groggy, dazed. Did she even know what this was for? She'd said it was money for his bars. Did she know the truth or was she just Kirov's errand girl? Sam, or any investment, might be a convenient lie.

Kirov is paranoid right now for one simple reason: He's behind the hit on Morozov. And his nerves are shattered. Maybe I can use that.

Sam stuck the gun into Rolan's mouth and spoke in Russian. The man shuddered.

"I am not as nice as Irina. If Mr. Kirov wanted you to know about this, and what it's being used for, he would have told you. Do you understand me?"

"Yes."

Where on the ship was she hiding the money? Did anyone besides Kirov know? Did Irina know what this was for, or was she paid to turn a blind eye? She was no doubt loyal to her customers, but she was loyal to her nation, too, and Morozov was Russia to many of his countrymen. Her husband and Morozov had been close. So he had to think what to tell Irina.

Sam took back his and Irina's phones and pushed him away. "Leave. Clean up your nose. Go back to the party. Be a good employee and keep your mouth shut."

Rolan left. Sam kept the man's gun.

He went to the kitchen and found a cloth and wet it with cold water.

"I cannot believe I let him . . . take me down . . ." she said. "How embarrassing. Are you all right?" she asked him, as if forgetting she was the one lying out on the floor.

"Yes. How do you feel?"

"My head hurts."

"It's not cut badly. You'll have a lump on your head." He gave her an improvised field concussion test, using his hands and asking her questions, and she seemed all right but shaken. "I think you're fine, but you need a doctor."

She waved off the idea. "I'll be fine. Where is . . ."

"Rolan, was that his name? He left," Sam said.

"You let him leave? He . . ."

"I told him to mind his own business. I have friends in Miami, too."

"He means well but he's an idiot. What did he say?"

"He thinks you are stealing money from Kirov's houses. And he either wants to stop you or he wants a cut."

"He truly is a fool."

"Is this money for my bars?"

"Yes."

"Why do you think I'd take dirty money?"

"It's not dirty. Just hidden. Because of the sanctions. Cash on hand, in case they needed to leave Russia, and not in a bank account where it could be frozen. Or they needed money to spend in America. This way it's already here."

When you had billions and billions you needed escape routes, he thought.

She sat up slowly. She managed a smile. Then she leaned over and unzipped the bag and he saw the bills, in neatly organized stacks. He picked up a stack and paged through it. The bills were not consecutively numbered. The bills were not new. This money had been collected, and kept, maybe over a long, long while.

Assassin's pay. Money that could not be traced. A nondigital financial trail. Because when a Russian president dies on American soil, the Americans investigate as well, and the financial trail would be the first place they'd start.

So don't leave a trail. Money that no one would miss. Slowly collected, hidden aboard Kirov's yacht. It was a variation on the old KGB trick of how the men like Kirov raided the spy agency's overseas cash reserves, hidden troves of money spent to buy up Russian industry. History, repeating itself, on a smaller scale — but with possibly more devastating results.

"That's a lot of money, Irina."

"What kind of consultant were you in London? After your time at Harvard?"

He smiled. "You checked up on me."

"We had to."

"I was a security consultant."

"And where did you get the money to acquire all these bars?"

He was silent.

"Sam?"

"My mother's family has money. An uncle left it to me."

"So much money for so many bars, owned by front companies. Did it really come from a dead uncle?" She sounded like she didn't quite believe him.

"No," he said after a long pause, which was the truth. But it was good for her to believe they knew each other's secrets. It bound them. This was why she'd picked him for this. To see if he was comfortable beyond the borders of the law. "I help you get this money back to the yacht, then what?"

She put her face a little closer to his. "We invest in you and your bars, and all your dreams come true."

"Will we go to Russia soon?" he asked.

The question seemed to surprise her. "Yes."

He took the damp washcloth and again cleaned the scrape on her scalp, the smear of blood drying in her beautiful red hair. Hair like fire. "Did you kill the people that killed your husband?"

The sheer shock of the question made her eyes widen. But she stayed close to him. "What do you think?"

"I think you are capable of it. But I don't think you did it."

Her gaze lowered for a moment. "I wasn't capable of much right after Sergei died. I was too distraught. He was everything to me."

"And revenge came in a matter of days."

Now her gaze fixed on him. "That was the Morozovs. They used government informants, hired guns; *they* exacted Sergei's revenge on the Chechens."

"Did the Chechens kill Sergei?"

"Of course they did."

The circle, he thought. Or the Morozovs. What if Sergei outlived his usefulness? And what had Danny done after his sponsor, his mentor, was blown apart in a car bomb?

"And the Morozovs spread the word that was you taking revenge. The Black Widow."

"Of course not. You cannot have murders so closely connected to a country's leader." She touched his jaw again, soft as silk. "They needed me. And it was an insult to some of the Chechen leaders that a woman could hunt them down. If I could have I would have. But I wouldn't have killed their wives and their children."

"That happened?"

"That happened. They began to whisper that it was me, and the whispers turned to fire. No charges would come and Sergei was avenged."

For a moment he thought of kissing her. He didn't even know why. She looked at him and said, "Thank you for tending to me."

"I'm sorry he hurt you. Are you sure you don't want to see a doc—"

She kissed him. He held perfectly still for a moment then kissed her back, gently. Her lips nibbled his as he pulled away.

"You just took a blow to the head," he said. "This isn't a good idea."

"Old Russian cure for headache," she said. Reaching for him, kissing him.

"Vodka?" he asked, laughing.

"No," she said. "This." And she kissed him again, pulling him toward the bed.

An hour later, he heard the soft hum of a shower running, and he looked inside the duffel bags while Irina was in the bathroom: stacks and stacks of hundreds, nothing smaller. If they were all hundred-dollar bills, and each bill weighed around a gram, then a million dollars would be a bit north of twenty pounds. This might be four million total here. The thought made him dizzy.

He joined her in the shower, and afterward they dried off and dressed. They carried the bags out of the condo. He watched her lock the door and slip the passkey into the outer pocket of her small purse.

They walked past the guards and the partygoers of Sunny Isles. The party was louder, more crowded. No one seemed to notice them. He did not see Rolan. They loaded the bags into the boat.

"I wish we could stay here longer," she said. "Just the two of us. There are no ghosts here." Her voice was low. She gave a little laugh, because it was impossible to stay. She touched his jaw again and he kissed her hand.

For a moment he wished it as well, but then he thought: She has her own agenda.

He brushed a windblown strand of red hair from her face. "On the yacht . . ." he said.

"I can't appear to be distracted by a romance," she said. "Not now. I am always on duty."

"I know the feeling," he said. "I understand."

"When this is over . . . the summit . . . when you're spending time in Moscow, or when Katya comes to New York to open the Tsar Lounge there . . ." She didn't finish the sentence.

He kissed her again, for two reasons. First, he wanted to. Her fingers tangled in his hair again. His hands ran along her ribs, her waist, and gathered her to him for a few delicious moments.

They broke apart. He waited until she turned away to guide the limousine tender out from the marina to stuff the key he'd lifted from her purse into his pocket — the second reason for the kiss.

No one stopped them. He kept expecting for a Coast Guard chopper to swing low over them, bathing them in headlights, but the sky stayed dark. Twenty miles out was the *Svetlana* and all her lights were ablaze.

The Vikal tender was brought aboard the *Svetlana*. Two of Irina's men took the duffels and left. Irina handed them an access card from her purse and told them to bring it back when they were done. The card key had a purple tag on it. Like the card key lock on the restricted door in the server room.

The room he couldn't get into. *The money's there.*

Sam and Irina, still dressed in their party finery, went up to the deck. Aft stood Yuri Kirov, watching them, face blank.

Sam watched him. *You are collecting the money to pay my brother to kill Morozov. Maybe you want him dead so you can be president soon. You would risk war for your*

426

own greed. You look frail and drunk but I think that's an act, Mr. Kirov. Tonight, when everyone's asleep, you're going to tell me how to contact my brother. We're going to call him. And you're going to fire him from this job.

Sam knew he couldn't open the tender garage while the yacht was moving. He remembered there was a small Zodiac tender stored up on the sundeck, used by the crew when needed. That would probably be easier. He needed a plan. Because he was going to kidnap Yuri Kirov right off his own boat.

45

Nebo, Russia

Stefan studied figures on his computer, then slept for the last part of the flight.

Eventually, Danny slept, too. Mila watched him; his slumber was a mark of confidence. Because he knew at that moment she could do nothing to him. If Danny knew her husband . . . did he, in turn, know who she was? Surely not. Jimmy had kept his life so compartmentalized. But she had made two cracks about family, letting her emotion trump her judgment. She hated Danny. For what he had done to his brother, who deserved so much better. For being the leverage that she had to have.

Mila thought: Maybe Danny thinks you're here on Jimmy's behalf. Or maybe Danny will try to kill you as soon as you're alone with him because anyone who can expose him is a threat.

Mila closed her own eyes and slept, surprisingly, and she awoke as the plane began its descent. She looked out the window at the compound. Ten large estates, all extraordinarily grand, a couple of them ridiculous, built like miniature castles. They all sat along a long, winding loop of road. At the end of the oval was the grandest: the Morozov house. Each house sat on smaller acreage than you might think — as if they wanted to be closer together. Additional buildings were along the perimeter — other slightly smaller grand houses called *kottedzhi,* for visitors and support staff, a helipad, a conference center, a stable and riding center, an enclosed swimming pool, a spa, and more. Dense, untouched forest divided many of the houses from each other, giving privacy, and from the three runways.

A town, fifty miles from Moscow, just for Russia's brightest and best billionaires. They called it *Nebo:* the Russian word for heaven.

She needed a way to get out of heaven, with Danny Capra as her prisoner. Quickly, and quietly.

The plane landed on the compound's smaller runway. Nearby was a larger runway that Morozov had added, capable of handling the larger jets in his fifty-plus-aircraft presidential fleet.

Mila walked off the plane. Everyone

stretched in the cold morning air. She stepped away from the group, scanning the massive villas of the circle. A buzz of activity at every house, even in the early morning — people, security details.

So much security. Far more than she anticipated. She saw cars with government emblems on the side. More security than the private Belinsky Global teams. Her heart sank. Getting Danny Capra away from here was going to be difficult. She had no weapon, no transportation. So she'd have to use Stefan.

"Many important guests here already," Stefan said. "Many prominent Russians, and Western friends, for the departure party and to prepare for the summit. This is a big moment in history for us."

You have no idea, Mila thought.

The man calling himself Philip Judge followed her. "Impressive houses," he said.

"The first president Morozov," Stefan said, coming up behind them, "had a nearby village bulldozed to make room for our homes. The village had been there since 1308. They had survived the Mongols, the Germans, the Communists, everything."

"Except the billionaires," Mila said. She smiled to soften the blow, to make it seem a joke.

Philip Judge smiled, too, and she thought that smile would soon be gone. She had to get in contact with Charity's team here in Moscow, extract him, get him back to London.

And he wouldn't easily walk into a trap.

Stefan laughed and started texting on his phone. "I should tell you that you can sleep for a bit, but for you, Mila, the rest of the day is meetings. Interviews. I have a full workday myself."

"What?" Mila asked. "I thought . . . we'd go to the bar, in a couple of hours." That was still her best way of getting Danny Capra to Charity — get him away from Nebo, where he could be grabbed off the streets of Moscow. She had zero intention of waiting around here. She put a hand on Stefan's arm and mustered a warm, inviting smile. "I was so looking forward to us going to Moscow together."

He gave her a smile, as if reassured that she could be interested in him. "As soon as we can; I have other meetings today," Stefan said, in a tone that suggested perhaps she had forgotten that the Varros were investing in more than her bars. "I'm afraid any investment must go through scrutiny before being announced. Mila, our lawyers will wish to speak to you about the bar project. There will also be a detailed security check on you and Philip by the presidential security forces." He gestured toward the security teams they could see in the distance, in perimeters around the houses. "With the president expected soon . . . and so many foreign dignitaries, last-minute guests like the two of you must be cleared. Also, there will be press here. You are not to speak to them without permission. You'll be given a badge that allows you access to certain areas of Nebo — my house and the common areas, such as the conference center. It is security. You understand."

"Of course," Mila and her enemy said together, and then both politely laughed. Inside she fumed. She was sure her UK identity could stand the scrutiny — but what if Danny Capra was caught in that security net? He would be gone from her. He looked utterly confident.

Parked by the runway was a Dartz Black Shark, the highly armored Latvian-built, Mercedes-engined SUV the Russian elite preferred.

Stefan looked up from his phone. "OK, Philip . . . I'm sure we can get a meeting with my dad. And then tomorrow, Mila wants to take us to the bar in Moscow. That could be fun."

"Fun, of course," Danny made himself say. Of course she wanted him away from all this security. All these witnesses. He could tell she hadn't expected the crowds here for the pre-summit preparations.

He needed Mila gone, and his brother left with no avenue to pursue him. Could he get rid of Mila at the bar? Or en route? An accident? They would be surrounded today by lawyers and security personnel. He had to find a way. "Sounds great," he said to Stefan. Stefan was clearly interested in her. That could be a problem.

And he could use this time to figure out the security situation here. He must get close to Morozov tomorrow night, before he left. Today would give him that opportunity to find a path.

He caught Mila looking at him. He smiled at her. She was trapped, helpless, a fly in amber here. But he was not.

He had an idea. It meant she would die. Regrettable, but it would be necessary.

Mila's stare locked on Danny. Then she turned away and climbed into the Dartz.

Stefan got in next to her, Danny on the other side. "I know you're disappointed,

Mila. But we'll have tomorrow," he said, trying to smooth over her unhappiness. "Your club is supposed to be fun, according to Katya. Too bad Sam isn't here with us."

Danny kept his face neutral at the word *Sam* but inside he felt his chest crack, like a shovel had powered through the bone. Actual pain. He swallowed and it went away. He felt a sudden betraying sheen of sweat on the back of his neck.

Danny stared out the window. So this is what a neighborhood of billionaires looks like, he thought, looking at the houses to push away every thought of Sam.

There had been reports that they were all planning to build an even bigger, billion-dollar compound in the warmth of Sochi. This was their one set of homes where the inner circle could easily be all together. It was their Ground Zero.

And he was going to walk into the heart of it and kill the target.

The Black Shark pulled past several security checks. The security officials — government, not a private force like Irina's people — knew Stefan and his two bodyguards on sight, but checked carefully, more than once, the American passport of Philip Judge and the British passport of Mila Cebotari. Stefan explained more than once that Philip and Mila were friends, who had been cleared by the investigative teams at Belinsky Global. That apparently carried weight.

Then, the shock.

One of the guards, talking to Stefan's driver, mentioned that President Morozov was at Nebo, having arrived late last night. Hence the greatly expanded security. Everyone got quiet in the limo; Mila's face went pale. Danny noted that Stefan didn't call Morozov "Uncle" in front of the government security forces.

He's here, Danny thought. And you have to find a way to him.

The motorcade pulled into the vast driveway of the Varro dacha. They got out. Danny was searched, as was Mila. Another guard inspected his baggage, right there on the driveway. A third guard studied the screen on his phone. Danny suspected it was an electronic report on him, probably provided by Irina Belinskaya. He stood and was careful to keep a polite, understanding smile on his face.

The searches turning up nothing of interest, the guards thanked Danny in rough English and he and Mila followed Stefan up to the dacha. A woman in a housekeeper's uniform nodded at Mila. "Ms. Cebotari, Katerina Yureyevna asked that a room at her home be prepared for you. And then Mr. Varro's lawyers will be here later to talk to you. Why don't you come with me and we'll get freshened up."

"I'll see you tomorrow, Mila. Enjoy your day," Stefan said.

Mila forced a warm, inviting smile to her face. "Tomorrow, then. Or earlier, if you change your mind." She followed the housekeeper across the street. Two bodyguards, one male, one female, followed them.

Danny watched Mila walk away. "How soon do you think I can meet President Morozov?"

Stefan stared. "Do you need to see him? Do you know who the threat is . . . ?"

"No. Not yet. I prefer he not know my connection to Sergei. It's better that way. Deniability." He needed to deal with Mila first. Then he would be free to act, as he had planned, and to walk away to his twenty million.

Stefan nodded. They went inside the Varro house. An elderly servant greeted them. A suite had been prepared for Philip Judge. He went up to it, following a manservant carrying his bag, and it was bigger than Claybourne's loaner apartment back in Brooklyn. Stefan told him that Morozov would be at the Varro house tomorrow morning for a meeting.

"Fine. I need to see anyone here who was also on Sergei's list of enemies. I need access to walk around the compound. Can you get that for me?"

Stefan nodded. "There's a special pass. I'll see you get one."

Danny closed the door behind him. The bathroom was spectacular. All granite and marble. There was a medicine cabinet, pre-loaded with Russian brands of lotion, shampoos, toothpaste, eyedrops, painkillers, breath mints.

He unpacked, showered, and dressed, and then he called a number in Moscow, hung up after the third ring, waited, called again, and hung up after the fifth ring. He sat by the window. The phone rang.

"I have a job for you," he said.

"What?"

"I am bringing a woman to Moscow tomorrow. To the Tsar Lounge, off Tverskaya. Do you know it?"

"I know that entire area well."

"I need her dead. She's petite, blond. She'll be the only woman at my side. I need her shot, preferably on the street. If not on the street, inside the bar itself. One shot, dead. She cannot survive. Stefan Varro will be with us. Don't hit me, or anyone else."

"This is extremely short notice."

"I'll signal you when I know when we're heading to Moscow."

"Not how I work."

"And I'll pay you one million US." It was exorbitant but worth it to him.

He heard a soft sigh. "I accept. Half up front."

Danny realized he could not let his desperation show. "Fine . . ."

"I thought you didn't work in Russia anymore."

"I don't. I'll be in touch. I'll e-mail you a picture of her."

He decided to stretch his legs with a walk. He wanted fresh air after the long flight, and he wanted to start studying the ring of protection around Morozov.

Because he planned to make a mockery of it.

46

The Svetlana, The Atlantic Ocean
Kidnapping was harder than murder. A homicide could be done with a single shot — walk up to victim, kill, walk away. A kidnapping involved control of a desperate person, escape, concealment, refuge.

A kidnapping at sea, snatching one of the world's wealthiest men, under the nose of a highly trained security team . . . Sam knew if he overthought it, he'd lose his nerve.

He needed a few items and he could not be found collecting them. He already had the key to the condo in Sunny Isles he'd stolen from Irina, where he thought he could take Yuri. This could be very civilized. A Yuri threatened with exposure was a Yuri who could be counted on to abort the assassination.

That afternoon he went belowdecks, announcing his curiosity about the engine room. One of the crew took him through

439

the *Svetlana*'s engine room. It was all computerized and he discarded his idea to shut it down somehow, leave the *Svetlana* adrift as he escaped with Yuri. On the way back up, one deck up, walking alone, he found a maintenance room, unlocked. Inside he found a large roll of duct tape. It would be fine for binding Yuri's mouth and hands.

He next needed a satellite phone. He found a loaner left in one of the business conference rooms, where the software moguls had been working on their proposals. He picked it up and slipped it into his pocket, turning it off in case anyone called it looking for it.

Now for the riskiest act of all. He went up to the sundeck where the Zodiac crew tender was kept. A crewman was up there, watching him. He glanced into the boat; it was an emergency tender, and so did not require a key. He realized the crewman was still watching him. Sam smiled and moved on, peering out at the sea.

Next, to the infirmary. In the salon he saw the ship's doctor, who seemed to do very little on the *Svetlana*, playing cards with one of the crew while Yuri sat companionably with them, reading on a tablet computer. Sam hurried to the small infirmary.

The door was open. The pharmacy cabinet was locked but he picked the lock quickly. He found a sedative, loaded a syringe. He was in and out in three minutes. He passed two security guards on his way back up and nodded at them and one gave him a crooked smile. Did they know about him and Irina? Or suspect? Surely not.

Now for a weapon. The security team wore their sidearms — he'd seen Glocks and Russian-made GSh-18, a 9-millimeter semiautomatic with an 18-round capacity. There was an armory on this ship. But he had no way in, and there might well be a guard stationed there. It was likely on the tank deck, where the crew slept, and a passenger had no business down there.

Katya had a gun, though. She had that spare one in her safe, the unexplained one with the attached suppressor. He also had no way into her room, unless he could access Irina's room. That could be done — but Irina had told him to keep his distance on the *Svetlana*.

Instead he took the path of least resistance. He went up to the bar on the main deck and let his experienced eye go across the bottles. He asked for a Pavlova Supreme — crème de cassis and vodka. The crewman tending bar had to go down to the galley to retrieve the required liqueur.

So while he was gone, Sam stole the very sharp knife the man used to slice limes. He slid it up his long-sleeved shirt, and when the crewman brought the crème de cassis and made his drink, Sam smiled and sipped it, the weight of the steel cool against his forearm.

It would have to be enough. Now he had to wait for night.

Dinner was a quiet affair. Several of the investor execs worked through dinner, having the meal delivered to their conference rooms so they could continue to refine their presentations. Yuri found this work ethic uncivil and told Katya, Irina, and Sam he found American workaholism a sign of cultural decay.

Sam agreed and poured Yuri more ice-cold vodka. "No more," Katya said. "Too much is bad for you, Papa, especially now."

"I have insomnia," Yuri said. "I have many worries. If I don't have a little vodka I'm awake half the night, fretting about business."

"No, Papa, please," Katya said and Yuri, with a grunt, pushed the glass away. Irina and Sam said nothing. Sam waited for Yuri to say something about Rolan and the cash run to Miami, but he said nothing, and also said nothing about Sam's investment.

After dinner Sam excused himself to his room to work on his proposal. Irina gave him a contemplative look but nothing more. No one, he thought, could guess of their special hour in Miami. She was too discreet.

He slept for a couple of hours, the stolen knife under his pillow. He awoke and lay in the darkness. He listened to the ship growing quiet. But then — there was a swaying. The *Svetlana* was turning. Away from Florida. He went to the window and got his bearings with the stars. The ship was making a wide, lazy circle, moving away from the Florida coastline.

Back toward the Bahamas. Something was wrong.

He went up on deck. No sign of Irina or Yuri or Katya. Everything seemed quiet. He could go to the bridge and ask the captain what was going on, but he didn't wish to draw attention to himself.

He'd watched last night and the security team patrol was minimal at night; being boarded in the ocean did not seem a major concern. He'd seen two guards last night patrolling the yacht, walking the upper and lower decks. Two guards he could deal with, quietly.

He returned to his room and lay down, very still and quiet.

Then he got up when it was past midnight and got the knife. He taped the knife's handle to the small of his back, and stuck the roll of duct tape and the satellite phone in the back of his pants. He hid the capped syringe in his sock. He put the Sunny Isles penthouse key in his pocket. He got the complimentary bottle of vodka left in his room and figured he would offer Yuri a drink, say he couldn't sleep.

He went out into the hallway. He knocked gently on Yuri's door.

Then he felt the weight of the gun, the barrel of the suppressor, against the back of his head.

"Don't move. Don't speak." It was Katya.

She pulled up the back of his shirt. Removed the roll of tape and the satellite phone, stripped the knife from his skin.

"Drop the bottle and step back from the door," Katya said. "Slowly. Don't speak."

He obeyed.

"Back to your room," she said.

She had the gun perfectly placed against his skull. He did as she told him, moving steadily and slowly. She could have screamed for security. She hadn't.

Inside his room she shut the door. "Lie

down on the floor. Hands behind you, in the small of your back."

He obeyed.

"Do you have another weapon?"

"No," he lied. "What are you doing, Katya?"

"Why are you coming to my father's room?" she asked.

"I wanted to talk to him."

"With weapons and tape, in the middle of the night? Who sent you?"

"No one sent me."

"You tried to access my spare phone. The one in my safe. Why?"

How did she know? "I . . ."

"Don't bother denying it. You're an American who speaks Russian but you're not of Russian descent. Are you CIA?"

"No," he said.

Her voice was a bare whisper. "Did Seaforth send you?"

Seaforth. "Are you really going to shoot me or can we talk plainly?"

"You were sent here to spy on me. By Seaforth. What does he want with my father?"

She was Seaforth's spy: He saw it. He remembered what Seaforth's team said in the conversation he'd eavesdropped on via the phone bug: *Speaking of the Russians . . . what says our source there?*

445

Katya made total sense as a recruit. She was the most high-profile Russian constantly in the West, but had her ear close to the Russian leadership. She met with many people, and it never raised suspicion. Seaforth and his so-called misfits had made a brilliant stroke. But now something had gone wrong between her and Seaforth. Trust was gone.

"I didn't shoot him," she said. "Is that why you're here?"

"Who?"

"Seaforth. He was shot in Nassau. Don't pretend you don't know."

"Shot?" He remembered the police tape across the alley, down the street from his hotel.

"He sent you."

"No . . . I came on my own."

"I'm supposed to believe that."

"Believe what you want." He risked turning his head so he could see her. Eye contact was important. "Your father is financing an assassination against Morozov during the summit. Irina and I picked up the money from his house in Sunny Isles."

Her mouth trembled.

"I have . . . leverage with the assassin. If I can talk to him I can stop it. I want your father to tell me how to get in touch with

446

the assassin."

She stared at him. "Why would Papa kill Morozov?"

"Anyone close to him whose standing is always at risk to the president's whims must have his reasons. Your father, the Varros, any corporate leader in Russia."

"Who is this assassin?"

"He's not here. He will have to get close to Morozov, and your father is helping him." Sam cleared his throat. "You alone could stop it, Katya. Get your father to call off the hit. You could persuade him."

"And how do I tell him that I know of this? Tell him I . . . have been working for the Americans? He'll kill me. Or worse, disown me." She gave a sick, feeble laugh.

"If he's found out, they'll kill him. They'll kill you if they know you've reported to the CIA. You'll both be dead."

"Do you think anyone — Irina, the tabloids, the people like Stefan who have known me my whole life — would believe that I spy for the Americans?" She shook her head. "They do not take me seriously. I am . . . what do they say, the party girl. It has always been that way for me. Seaforth saw I had a brain. That I had a contribution to make. I'm not giving my father to you. I will" — and he spun out under her, his legs catching hers, and she fell heavily.

He put a hand over her mouth, dug in his sock for the syringe, thumbed off the cap, injected the sedative into her. Her eyes widened and she went limp.

"I'm sorry, Katya." Change in plan. He could not leave her to explain how she stumbled across Sam's plan, and he could not take Yuri captive while carrying an unconscious Katya. So Katya would have to be the bargaining chip. Take her off the *Svetlana,* call Yuri on the satellite phone, force him to call Danny and call off the hit. Or what? He'd threaten Katya? Would Yuri Kirov believe him? Sam would have to make Yuri believe him.

He picked her up, settling her over his shoulder. He went out into the hallway. Darkened, silent. He risked the elevator. He rode it all the way up to the top deck. The doors slid open. The salon was dimly lit. He exited the elevator and along the dim lights of the *Svetlana* he could see a lone guard walking the deck below.

He watched the man move along the deck. Away from the Zodiac. In the sea breeze, Katya stirred, and groaned in her sleep.

"Hush, Katya," he said, gently patting her back. She stilled. He moved out onto the deck. The guard, patrolling, had gone inside. It was boring out on a boat at night, nothing but darkness all around them. A sheet of stars above, watched by the bright eye of the moon. He hurried toward the Zodiac. He set Katya down on the deck; she groaned again. To lower it with the crane and cables would be too noisy. He thought he could pull the inflatable over the side, then jump in with Katya. No other choice.

He lifted the Zodiac, shifting to push it over the railing. As he moved to push the aft end he saw Irina, and a guard behind her, each with a pistol leveled at him.

"I can explain," he started to say and Irina fired. He tried to go over the railing as she did; he spun, in agony, and he fell. The stars retreating, then the cold water closing over him.

Darkness. He kicked up toward the surface, even as he thought, They could shoot you when you come up. He stopped short of the surface but in the dark he couldn't guess how far down he was. Couldn't be far. But he'd hardly had a chance to gulp in air. He stayed down, his lungs aching, his shoulder blazing.

Finally his lungs rebelled and he surfaced. The *Svetlana* had kept going, past him, its lights now aglow.

Sailing on. Leaving him behind.

He shuddered. Alone, in the vastness of the ocean. The waves picked him up and lowered him; he rode the swells, watching the yacht continue.

Survive. He tried to conserve energy, floating on his back. He realized with a jolt that if he was bleeding he might draw sharks. Or was that a myth? His brain felt a jumble. *It can't end like this. Danny. Daniel. Mila. Leonie. Mom and Dad. It can't end like this.*

Plan, he told himself. He had no plan. He tried to focus on the stars, find the constellations, determine which way was west. Land — Florida — would be somewhere to the west, yes? How far? They'd been twenty miles offshore but then the boat had turned, heading back toward the Bahamas. Freeport was fifty miles from the Florida coast, was that right? And he was between that, or was he farther north? Could he swim it? He almost laughed and the salt water hit his mouth and he choked. He coughed and went back on his back, floating.

You aren't going to make it. This is it. His mind refused to accept it, his son's face crowding out every thought of fear.

Then he saw it. The Zodiac, cutting toward him, a searchlight gleaming on and raking the waves. Looking for him.

He dived into the darkness, a cold black emptiness. He heard the boat buzz above him, saw the track of the light. He risked rising to take a breath, and heard a man yell in English, "We're trying to help you."

Right. They didn't need him alive, except for questioning, and he thought of Ahmad Anwari carving up his back. He breathed in a lungful of air, dived back down, felt the water part close to his feet. Firing at him.

The boat kept circling. He swam hard, to its left, but after thirty feet his lungs begged. He burst into the air again and turned, and he could see the boat closing hard on him, the searchlight's glow showing Irina in the prow, a shotgun with a bright orange stock to her shoulder. She fired.

He felt the blow on his neck and head before he could submerge, and then the adrenaline drifted out of him, and he sank under the black waves.

47

The Varro Estate, Nebo, Russia
Danny had spent Monday checking out the security details and avoiding Mila, whom he had not seen again since their arrival. She had clearly said nothing about the assassination plot; but that could be Sam's influence. Sam would try to find him and stop him if he knew, but without telling the authorities. That was pure Sam, and Mila must be sticking to his play. For the moment. But he could not risk her keeping silent.

Now it was Tuesday morning, and he awaited Morozov's arrival at the Varro house.

You could learn a lot about a man you needed to kill by watching him walk where he felt safe. Like the two young Germans of Marianne's on Long Island.

He'd noted yesterday that Morozov and other officials were closely guarded by government agents; the Belinsky Global teams, guarding the wealthy families, were smaller. There were teams assigned to each family and their guests. Stefan had arranged for Danny to have free rein to wander in Nebo, but he'd noticed other guests with color-coded badges that only gave them access to certain areas. He assumed Mila, being a relatively unimportant contact of Stefan's, was similarly limited. Yesterday he had walked the runways, the estates, the exits from the compound. He did not go near the Morozov estate, but he walked the path from it to the plane that stood ready to take the president and the chosen few to America tonight. And he studied the schedule of pre-summit events slipped under his door, which had Morozov's schedule for the day.

The plan he'd formed began to refine itself in his mind. He hated smoking, but Russians did it in large numbers still, and he'd offered cigarettes to the security guards posted near the plane. Chatted with them, told them he was supposed to be on the flight tomorrow. He shared cigarettes; they shared gossip.

Now, from his bedroom window, Danny watched President Morozov and his security team get out of their cars in front of the Varro estate. He watched the man walk, talk, move, laugh, and knew that he controlled that man's fate. Here, at Nebo, Morozov was overconfident. He got out of the car at the same time his guards did, something he would not do in Moscow or New York.

Danny had put on his best suit, and he waited for Stefan to come fetch him to come downstairs when it was time.

Thirty minutes later, Danny stood before his target. Usually when this happened the target was dead seconds later. He didn't have the polonium with him, but it didn't matter. Right now this was about staying in the circle, to plan for the right moment.

The president of Russia was smaller than he looked on television. But then, Danny thought, most actors were. Morozov had a full head of ginger hair starting to gray, and eyes the clear blue of a cloudless winter sky. His suit was dark gray, bespoke, and he wore no tie. Security guards were posted at the door, but not in the vast den where he and a man Danny recognized as Boris Varro stood, holding a glass of orange juice. Morozov held a tall tea mug, with a presidential-looking double-eagle emblem on the side. He was a man of careful and controlled habits, and he preferred tea — Russian-style, with jam stirred into it —

instead of vodka.

The double-eagle mug was an important detail Danny filed away. *Dmitri has a favorite mug,* Sergei had told him once. Like a king with his golden goblet.

The FSB agent shut the door behind them. The two men over on the other side of the room glanced over toward the two arrivals, with no interest.

Danny glanced over at Boris Varro. Half-Cuban, half-Russian. He had black hair, shot through with early gray, and wide shoulders. Dark brown eyes, a half-smile that Danny thought, from his photos, might be his default expression. He wore a dark suit as well, but wore a tie of dark blood-red. His mouth twitched, slightly, Danny noticed.

I killed your son, Danny thought. I killed Anton. It surprised him when I did it.

"Son," Boris Varro said, nodding toward Stefan. "I was telling the president about the unpleasantness in the Bahamas."

"A minor protest. Hello, Uncle."

President Morozov did not respond at first. His glance at Danny turned into a measured gaze, and for a moment Danny could see him as the old KGB functionary, the security man taught too well never to trust anyone. "Hello, Stefan, good to see you. Who's your friend?"

You never ask a question you don't already know the answer to, Danny thought. "Hello, sir, I'm Philip Judge. It's a pleasure to meet you." He said this in his best Russian.

Morozov set down his large tea mug and offered and shook his hand. "An American investments advisor, I hear."

"Yes, sir. And a prop for Stefan."

A silence that Danny didn't expect fell on the room. He looked at these men and he thought of that long-ago night in Afghanistan, being afraid, being forced to fight Anton Varro for his life. He didn't like the silence. "But I'm happy to be a prop. If it helps Russia and America to a better relationship."

"Ah. So you can tell the world to invest in Russian industries?" Morozov asked.

"Of course, sir. They're sound investments. I'm preparing a report on it for American brokerage houses." Danny paused. "Would you or your staff — naturally, you are too busy, sir — be interested in seeing it when it's done?"

"Yes, I would. And we should have a marketing campaign for this," Morozov said. "Do we? To encourage American investors to buy into Russian companies, should all go well at the summit?"

"I'm not aware of one . . ." Boris Varro said with a small laugh.

"Then spend several million in the American newspapers or websites. Invest in Russia. Varro, see to that. Philip, Stefan Borisovich, include that data in your report to me."

It was an awkward silence. *Did he just order Varro to spend a few million of his own money for Morozov's whim?* Danny tried to imagine an American president or a British prime minister snapping orders to the captains of industry. *Go invest in this odd business idea, because I want you to do so.* It felt like the other side of the mirror.

But Varro made no objection. He just gave another small laugh. "I'll see to it."

Maybe this is why Firebird wants him dead. Danny said, "I would be happy to work with Stefan Borisovich on such a project, Mr. President. He's full of great ideas."

"Truly?" Morozov couldn't help but sound vaguely surprised. Stefan reddened but kept his smile in place. "Well done, then, Stefan Borisovich; you help your American friend. Hire an agency there, your father will see to the details." And it was done.

Stefan gestured to him and the two younger men took their leave. Danny thought: The Varros don't fit in. His father laughs like the kid who can't believe he gets to hang with the cool kids and Stefan just tries too hard. They think they will, but they'll never fit in. They're not Russian enough.

Stefan was giddy, smiling. "That went well."

"Well?"

"He let me do this. He . . ."

"He told your father to spend his money."

"We must at times, for the president and Russia. It's a privilege, not a burden."

The price of belonging to the club.

But then reality caught up with Stefan. "But . . . you're not an investments person. It's not for real."

"You don't need me for that. You know the Russian companies and an ad agency will do the heavy research and lifting. I'll make some phone calls and we'll share the credit. Thank you."

"Why didn't you tell the president you were Sergei's associate?" They were walking away from the house. "He loved Sergei."

"I will. First we find the traitor who wants to derail the summit. Deal with them quietly and privately, so there is little attention. I spent yesterday surveying the terrain, as it were. Seeing who came and went."

"You said this person could outline Sergei's actions." He didn't seem to want to say *crimes.* "That's a small number of people who knew what he did."

"True, but someone may have told someone else in the years since. Remember your problem with your talkative mistress."

That silenced Stefan for several steps. "Now what?"

"This afternoon," he said, "we go to Mila's bar and have a bit of fun before the party tonight." And when Mila was dead in a couple of hours, it would be easy to blame her for being the spy he'd lied about to Stefan. He could say he simply eliminated her as a threat and it would be unquestioned and Stefan would be silent. Two birds, one stone. And he had a second reason to see Morozov: to deliver this report, his excuse for working with Stefan.

It would be the next and last chance he could be sure of being close to the target. In his room, he opened his luggage. Inside was a laptop, wrapped in a protective sleeve. The Russians had scanned it back when he flew from Nassau, seen nothing unusual. He opened the back of it, took off the housing — it had been modified so this could be easily done. On the motherboard, in its own notch, was the circuitry for a basic cell phone. He took it out of its notch. On the

459

side that presented to the X-ray machine was the circuitboard. On the other side was a very primitive screen that showed text in green letters, a simple speaker, and a rudimentary keyboard. The phone could be easily crushed and broken. It was untraceable and only to be used in communication with Firebird.

He texted the number Claybourne had given him for Firebird:

What I need from you is this — during the departure party, the front lounge of the plane, where M rides, must be cleared at some point before M's departure. I only need five minutes.

There was no immediate answer.

I have my way to kill him now, Danny thought. Just have to deal with the Mila problem, and I'm done.

A few minutes later, there was an answering text from Firebird.

I understand. I will notify you when it is clear.

He dismantled the phone, replaced it in its camouflage in the laptop's motherboard, and then studied himself in the mirror. He was going deeper into the cave, closer to the dragons now, and he could not risk a mistake.

Sam will know you had her killed. He'll know it in his heart.

Danny texted his friend, the assassin, an estimated time of arrival at the Tsar Lounge, attached a photo of Mila he'd managed to snap, and wired him the half-million.

48

The Church HQ, New York

Julian and Romy had flown Bob Seaforth to New York, on a medevac jet loaned from the agency. The bullet was out of his shoulder and he told the doctor on the jet that he could not be given sedatives; he had to stay awake.

He had no way to contact his source. If he had been attacked, what had happened to her? And to Sam Capra?

He had slept, finally, in the hospital bed in the Manhattan brownstone. A doctor and a nurse, both former Marines, tended to him. He was staring at the ceiling, wondering how long the pain would last, when Romy and Julian entered.

"Hey, how are you?" Romy asked.

"Fine," he said, sitting up. In the doorway the nurse, a broad-shouldered man, lingered and Seaforth waved him off.

"Any word from Raven?" Seaforth asked.

That was their code name for their source on the *Svetlana.*

"No. No contact," Romy said. "After you were shot, the *Svetlana* departed, headed to the Florida coast, then moved back toward the Bahamas. Kirov had a private helicopter fly to his yacht, and then it headed to Nassau Airport."

"I thought they were going to cruise up to DC."

"So did we. Change of plan. A private jet belonging to Yuri Kirov was prepped and it left Nassau a few minutes ago. We didn't have eyes on it but we monitored the flight departures. It's headed for Moscow, with a refueling stop in Lisbon."

"Is Raven aboard?"

"I think it likely she is. Our attempts to contact her have failed."

"Sam Capra went to Nassau; where is he?"

"Capra has fallen out of sight. He checked out of his hotel the morning after you were shot" — Romy managed to make this sound suspicious — "but we have no record of him leaving on a commercial flight. A plane registered to a company owned by Boris Varro left that same morning."

"So the *Svetlana* doesn't sail to Washington and the Kirov and Varro jets race home." Bob leaned back against the pillows.

"And no song from our Raven."

"What do you want us to do?" Julian asked.

"Find out when the Kirov jet is due to refuel in Lisbon. Get the police on there; if Sam's aboard, pull him off — say there's a problem with his passport."

Julian and Romy stared at him. "What painkillers did they give you, sir?" she asked.

Julian added: "Kirov — and his daughter and all that circle — every one of them has diplomatic status."

"They're not diplomats!"

Romy shook her head. "They all have cultural attaché–coded passports. They don't go through customs. And the Lisbon police aren't going to storm a Russian plane without good cause."

He nodded. Romy was right. "Where did they say they would land in Moscow? Sheremetyevo?"

"No. Private airstrip in Nebo, the oligarchs' retreat outside Moscow. All the oligarchs are departing on Morozov's jet from there to come to Washington." Romy crossed her arms.

Seaforth cursed softly. "Do we have any informants inside Nebo?"

"Our office? No. Langley might, but they won't share. They'll want to know what we're doing. What *are* we doing?" Julian asked.

For a moment Bob Seaforth didn't have an answer. "What's the situation with Claybourne's vanishing?"

"Prakash is on it. Claybourne's daughter has been texting her. We control the text app tied to her phone number; we haven't responded. Her daughter hasn't reported her missing, though. As far as she knows her mother took a sudden trip to Seattle for a project and hasn't been in touch. This is not unusual with Claybourne — she once went three days before answering her daughter's texts and e-mails. But we'll run out of time there."

"What about her involvement with Danny Capra?"

Romy glanced at Julian, as though not wishing to bear bad news. "From what we've pieced together from her computer files, she has created an entire tangle of front companies and offshore accounts. She's had years to build this up and we can't untangle it all in a couple of days. We need a forensic accountant to sift through it all, Bob, and we don't have one. But I think the only explanation is that she was brokering some highly illicit services. High-dollar ones."

"For the Russians? They're connected to this somehow."

"We're trying to start there . . . but Bob, there's three of us and we're busy trying to cover up a murder. One that you let Sam Capra walk away from." Romy's voice was tight.

"He saved my life," Bob said.

"Well, he saved you and ruined our hopes of easily breaking through her cover," Julian said. "If you can get us a forensic accountant, we can start to make progress."

"Get me . . . to Helsinki. I can call in a favor to get an agency plane. I want us to be ready to extract Raven. She knows to run to Finland if she needs an out and can travel without our help. That was our agreement. And if Sam Capra is there . . . ready to extract him as well."

Romy shook her head. "Sir. Please. You're not in a condition to travel."

"I'll . . . be fine. Bring Dr. Alvarez and Nurse Joe along. I want us close to Russia."

"Do we ask the agency for help? We're supposed to be clear of them . . . ," Romy said. "We don't have any people in Russia; we're not set up for this."

"I'll handle that. Just arrange the flight."

"Bob, seriously, you're not well," Julian said.

"No, I'm not. I'm worried sick. Big money hidden, a presidential summit, a guy who's been presumed dead for years and wasn't . . . this is trouble."

49

The Kirov Estate, Nebo, Russia
Monday had been a nightmare for Mila. The lawyers for Stefan Varro had been boring and detail-oriented and Mila passed the long hours of the meeting explaining bar economics while imagining ways to kill them. Then she was questioned for an hour by FSB agents protecting Morozov. The identity created for her by Charity was rock-solid. A South American ambassador was also staying at the Varro house, and he'd pestered Mila about having drinks with him. She'd put in an appearance at a party for visitors at another mansion, but no sign of Danny, no sign of Stefan. A schedule of events for the elite at Nebo was slipped under her door: a talk with the Russian ambassador to America, broadcast on the Internet; a Hollywood director giving a speech on why Russian and American studios could work together; a panel on

joint military exercises the countries could try. All a warm-up for the summit. And all of it a chain around her ankles, keeping her here.

Her plans lay shattered. She had no weapon, no car, no leverage. Guards stood at the ends of the hallway. The guests were watched. Security was everywhere. To act in haste would get her caught, arrested, or killed.

She tried to text Sam again and got no answer. This had been a mistake. At least her room was grand. The four-poster bed was elaborately carved. The fabrics in the curtains and the sheets were modern but exquisite. In the bathroom there was also a stocked medicine cabinet, with everything she could need: lotions, eyedrops, hand-milled soaps, high-end perfumes from Dior to Chanel. This was a gilded cage.

She ate a breakfast delivered to her room, showered, and dressed in her best clothes. She went to the window. She spotted a guard stationed outside the house, one in the expansive front yard, one by a fountain, and another in the street that divided the Kirov estate from the Varro estate. She'd tried to find out where the central garage was, hopeful she could steal a car. But every plan she began to formulate quickly fell apart.

You cannot take Danny prisoner here. Make the call.

A knock at the door. Stefan, smiling at her. She was almost happy to see him. "Everything OK? How was your day yesterday?"

"Fine, thank you."

"It'd be great if you and Philip and I could go to the bar this afternoon. A fast trip, before the party tonight."

"Of course," she said. "Let's do that." She must not show the relief she felt.

"I guess we could wait for Sam and Katya, but they're still many hours away."

"What?"

"Oh, Irina called and said they will arrive for the party tonight."

She was under a countdown now. She had to get Danny Capra extracted from this compound before that plane touched down. The two Capras could not meet face-to-face. She had to call Charity.

"Let me make some calls . . . some arrangements at the bar. We'll make it into a proper party." She forced herself to smile.

She followed Stefan outside as he headed back to his own house. "May I just walk along the road in front of the house? I need to stretch my legs," she asked the guard in Russian. The guard nodded.

She waited until she was well away before she pulled out her phone.

50

Kirov Jet, En Route To Russia

The jet arced high over the Atlantic. In the small, pressurized cargo bay Sam Capra lay, bound in chains, both feet and hands cuffed. He stared up at the ceiling. His mouth tasted sour with chemicals. He ached where a bullet had creased his chest, and where Irina's beanbag round, fired from a shotgun, had slammed into his neck and his skull. He'd woken up briefly to see Irina's face above his, and at first he thought they were back in the bed in Sunny Isles, gasping with pleasure, but no, she wasn't smiling, and she jabbed him with a needle, and then nothing again. He woke up on the plane, inside a huge duffel bag that had been unzipped.

He tested the chains. Double-locked. Both his hands and his arms were bound. The compartment panel, in the ceiling, that led into the main cabin opened. Irina, dressed in jeans and a dark turtleneck, eased herself down next to him. She said something to someone behind her, and the door was shut. She knelt by him.

"Hello, Sam. How do you feel?" she asked.

"Confused."

"Physically, you're fine. The bullet grazed your chest. The beanbag rounds did no lasting harm. Although if I fired several into your ribs at short range, it could send bone splinters into your heart." She said this as if considering it as an idea.

"Where am I?"

"The Kirov jet. We are bound for Russia."

That was not good news. "And I suppose you want an explanation?" He could not betray Katya. They would kill her, and she was Seaforth's agent. He'd stick to the code as though he was still in the agency. Never betray another.

"I trusted you when we went to Miami. I trusted you . . . in many ways."

"Which is why I suppose neither Yuri nor Katya is hearing this discussion. You'd lose your job."

She shrugged. "Perhaps. Where were you going to take Katya?"

Sam said nothing. Irina waited. Finally she said, "It's an exceptionally long flight. And there is no in-flight movie. Why don't you tell me a story, full of intrigue and action? Maybe no romance, though. I don't believe in it."

He stayed silent for five more minutes, and she said, "Let's try again. There is a cargo bay door. You are lying on it. It would be a long, long fall."

He was going to have to make a gamble with both his and Katya's life. "What has she said?"

"You want to hear her story first?"

"I want to know if she's lied about me."

"She said she found you at her father's door, acting suspiciously, and she saw you had a knife. You took her back to your room, where you knocked her senseless with an injection."

Katya had done the smart thing: She had told the basic truth of how they had encountered each other. The truth was good, if it didn't hang you. "That's correct. I was going to take Yuri. I wanted the rest of the money. I figured out from Rolan that you've collected quite a bit of this cash. But Katya got in the way, and I thought it would be better to take her and force Yuri to tell me where the money was."

"This seems a stupid move."

"Especially now. I was going to take her to Sunny Isles. I wanted her to show me where the rest of the money was."

"You think there was more?"

"Yes. A lot more. He's a damn billionaire who's worried about Morozov turning on him. He's got to have cash hidden all over the world."

"So you decided to jeopardize your entire future by kidnapping her."

"I wouldn't have hurt her. What was he going to do, call the police for me stealing his illegally hidden cash?"

She studied him. "I think you're lying to me. I think there's more. You're many things, Sam, but you are not stupid." She leaned down, ran a finger along his jawline, like she had several times in the past couple of days. "I really like your face. If I give you over to Petr, he'll make sure no one ever likes it again. He will beat you to a pulp. What do you think men like Kirov or Varro do to men who try and steal from them?"

"I'm an American citizen, you can't . . ."

"You're an American citizen that America thinks is still in the Bahamas. And will never know otherwise." She put her finger along his lips, moved a hand into his hair. "We're going not to Moscow, but to the private compound the most powerful families in Russia call their own. You don't have long to convince me of what you were trying to do. Sergei used to take people to Nebo. There is a house there, smaller, away from the others. No law, no passport can protect you there. There is no law there except power. I have never had to use it. But I will."

Sam said nothing for several moments. "What will happen to me there?"

"Well, we're arriving at a busy time. You'll be in my custody. I will question you. If you don't satisfy me with answers, I might turn you over to the actual police. But that then would create a public record. They would have to acknowledge that you were on Russian soil, in their custody, right before the summit begins. It would be a bad start."

He waited.

"But . . . worst case, we say you fell off the boat. No one saw you or realized you were missing for a day or so. We put a DO NOT DISTURB sign on your door. No one will disturb you."

"That seems unpleasant."

"Or . . . you can arrive in Nebo, not in chains, but as a guest, of sorts." She shrugged. "Because, after all, Katya is unhurt. Even though Yuri wants your blood."

He had no room to negotiate. If he told her there was a threat to Morozov, she would turn him over to the federal police immediately, and if Danny was close, would he be caught and killed? . . . It was a simple choice. It was better to stay silent.

"But maybe you can do me a favor," she said quietly. "And I can do you a favor."

Room, perhaps. "What?"

Her voice went low. "Why am I talking to you here, instead of up in the cabin like civilized people? The Kirovs."

He stared.

"Someone on the *Svetlana* has been in touch with the Americans. Katya, I think, because she's young and foolish. I believe she has been in touch with the CIA."

He could not let himself give a reaction.

"And now, now Kirov is gathering all this money he's kept stashed. Maybe to pay off the CIA, to leave his daughter alone, forget they ever recruited her?" Irina's gentle smile went crooked and he could remember what he'd said to her: *I don't think you killed those people but you'd be capable of it.* She would. He could see it in her, the cold calculation to survive.

"Do you know, Sam?"

He lied with a shake of his head.

"I mean, what would happen if Katya was exposed as an informant for the Americans? Kirov would be ruined as well. Morozov would take Zvezda Oil away from him. They

477

would lose billions. If she was sent to a Russian prison I don't think she would survive long, do you? I think she played at being a spy, played at being an American girl, and now she's tired of it. You came here to take her back. Was it a rescue in your mind? I think you are CIA, Sam."

"I swear to you that I am not," he said.

"Then you're what? A money-grubbing kidnapper? Is that better? Should I just give you to Kirov then?"

"Millions-grubbing," he said. "Weren't you ever tempted by that cash?"

"I think you were sent to fetch her. Did she not want to come?"

He met her gaze. "What if I told you this all had something to do with Sergei. With his death."

Anger flushed her face. "Don't . . . don't bring him into your lies. Don't try to manipulate me. That will only make me mad." She studied his face. "When we get you to Nebo, we keep you hidden for a while. To see how best to use you. I wish to test the waters. But I think with you in our hands, the Americans will be more deferential to Morozov's demands. More willing to bend. A CIA agent sent to kidnap a billionaire's daughter, a girl who is like family to the president? We could trot you out onto every TV screen in the world."

This could not have gone more wrong. "You'll destroy the Kirovs, too."

"No, I think we will work out a story that protects them. That's what they pay me to do: protect them. We can paint Katya as a hero who resisted the CIA's requests. They will follow along with any plan I suggest to them that keeps them in power." She put her fingers through his hair again.

He turned away from her touch.

"Tell me, Sam. The wounds on your back. Someone took a knife to you recently. I noticed when we . . . were together; I noticed when we stripped your clothes off you when you were pulled from the ocean." She touched his jaw again. "What happened to you?"

"It doesn't matter. But do you think the CIA sends an injured operative on a job like this? I'm not with them."

"Then why are you here?"

He didn't answer. She got up and left him in the cargo hold and she opened the hatch to the main cabin. For a moment, he could hear Katya sobbing and Yuri Kirov bellowing in anger.

She slammed the hatch door shut and he lay in darkness.

51

Near London

"I'm bringing you the target," Mila said by way of greeting to Charity.

"You better not be lying to me. That computer drive you sent me was garbage."

"It was encrypted; how could I know?" Mila said. "Are you still wanting this target or not?"

"I'm listening," Charity said.

"In a few hours we will be at the Tsar Lounge, Moscow, off Tverskaya. Have an extraction team ready to grab the target. He is a trained killer, so we need to use maximum force. Also there will be a bodyguard contingent, probably a half-dozen. Also the son of one of Russia's most prominent billionaires will be with us. Please don't kidnap him by mistake."

Silence for five seconds. "Are you serious?"

"One other thing. They cannot extract me.

I stay behind."

"I don't understand."

How to explain Sam? She couldn't. "If I'm taken, then an ally of mine is left behind to face much suspicion. So you grab the target, you leave me, and my ally and I will get ourselves out. It's the only way."

"And risk *you* being questioned by the Russians? Absolutely not. If I leave you behind then there will be no cooperation from your husband." Charity hesitated. "A trained killer in league with one of our top men. Who are they planning to kill?"

"No one, now," she lied.

"Are you saying this man could point Jimmy to an assassination plot?" Charity's voice rose slightly.

I need you to grab him and take him, Mila thought, before Sam gets here. So she had to put the spurs to Charity, so to speak. "Possibly."

"I'm looking at a Google street map of this bar," Charity said. "You get the target outside the alley behind it. I'm not getting in a firefight with private security in a bar in the heart of Moscow."

That was exactly what Mila wanted to hear. "Fine. I'll get him alone. But you must be ready, and take him then. You *must*."

She put up the phone and walked back

toward the Varro house.

"Location on that phone," Charity said to the tech.

"She called from Nebo, in Russia. The very exclusive retreat for President Morozov and his ten closest cronies."

My God. Charity put a hand on the back of her chair. What disaster had James de Courcey gotten himself into? President Morozov? Nebo was a security nightmare; no wonder Mila wanted them taken at this nightclub. She studied the map. She imagined the headlines if things went wrong in the heart of Moscow. She decided not to call the prime minister. Not yet. This was still an internal matter, one where she could claim to be pursuing a prime suspect in a case of treason. She had the right to make the call.

She called her team in Moscow, and the plan, altered to Charity's liking, was put into place.

There had long been a sense that British businesspeople in Moscow could be targeted by Russian gangs. There were also informants working for the British in Russia. Any of them might need evacuation or rescue.

In short: There were kidnapping plans and protocols put in place by Charity's team.

They wanted to get the target out of Russia, but they could also hide him in a safe house until any police search for him had ended. And then across a border of their choosing, preferably into Finland or one of the Baltic republics.

Mila wouldn't be happy, Charity thought. But she'd have to be happy with what she got.

52

En Route To Moscow

Stefan, Mila, and Danny piled into a limo. Small Russian flags flew on it, as if they were officials. An armored Dartz Black Shark SUV, filled with Belinsky Global security, followed them.

The car drove on private roads out of Nebo, past the ruins of another village, the buildings already starting to be overgrown with grass and ivy. Mila wondered why the remnants of the village had been left standing. As if the circle around Morozov wanted to be reminded of their own power, their ability to reshape Russia.

Danny was sitting on one side of her, Stefan on the other. A guard sat in the front seat next to the driver.

We'll get to Moscow, she thought, and I'll get everyone settled with drinks, and as exhausted and jet-lagged as they all are, I'll get them plastered in a private room. Spike the guards' sodas or water as well with grain alcohol. Then upstairs with Danny by saying I have a message from Jimmy for him, we must talk, and as soon as we're up in the office and seated at the desk I shoot him with the tranquilizer pistol Sam has kept at every safe house. Then drop him out the window into the alley, into the waiting arms of Charity's team. And thus is the killer made harmless. I say to Stefan that our friend Philip stayed out in the bar, talking to a beautiful woman. Then he's gone off somewhere. Stefan will freak but Stefan has other concerns in the next few days. Then back to here, for Sam. I can't leave without Sam. Too much suspicion on him if I did. He'll think the Russians figured Danny out and took him. And that's a problem I'll deal with tomorrow.

Danny Capra smiled at her. It wasn't a smile at all like Sam's. How could they be brothers?

They had crossed the private security perimeter surrounding the compound. Now they headed down a ten-kilometer road, heavily wooded before it reached a village and a main highway to Moscow.

"So, Mila, what shall we drink at the Tsar?" Stefan asked. He put his hand on her knee.

485

Mentally she timed how long it would take to break all his fingers. "Oh, I think the finest champagne. Only the best for you, Stefan." She smiled charmingly at him. She could feel the weight of Danny Capra's glare on her.

Stefan's smile went crooked. "I think this is the start of something beautiful —"

The gunshots blasted the tires of the lead car and it veered into the ditch. Seconds later a gas canister was blasted into the car's window, shattering the bulletproof glass.

Flash grenades exploded around them and the limo driver cursed. A concussive shock sent the limo veering off the road. The limo flipped, throwing its passengers together, upside down, right side up, then upside down again, on its roof, halfway down the incline. For a moment Mila was stunned and blinded. They all were. She saw herself and Danny and Stefan, grasping at air, trying to grab back sight and sound.

Charity had changed the plan. Taking Danny and her now, leaving Sam behind to face the consequences.

The guard and the driver were yelling frantically into their mikes on their jackets, and she heard an eruption of gunfire hitting the limo.

She had only one choice. Fight the team

that was trying to save her. She would not leave Sam behind to face the private cruelty of the circle's justice.

She saw the expression on Danny's face: He knew what this was. Arrest or death.

Chaos. Mila heard gunshots, the thud of something heavy hitting the car, the guard in the front seat yelling that they were under attack, a door opening, then more flash bombs. Stefan, shielding his eyes, opened a holder in the back of the seat. A gun. She tried to grab one but he got it first . . . and shoved it into Danny's hands.

Cold terror flooded her. "Wait!" she yelled.

But he didn't shoot her.

Instead Danny kicked her in the head as he wriggled out the door, dragging Stefan with him. Stunned, she fought back, trying to grab Stefan's feet, but Danny pulled him away.

She heard voices yelling in Russian, with English accents, telling men to throw down their weapons or be killed. Weapons fired. Then screamed demands to stop. Weapons fired. Both the men in the front seat, hanging upside down by their seat belts, unconscious.

Voices screaming in Russian and English to stop. Through the broken window she saw Danny Capra running into the woods, through the towering pines, a bullet ricocheting off a trunk by his head, him returning fire, shoving Stefan Varro away. Hands pulled her free of the limo, out the door on the other side. "Go, go, go!" she heard someone yelling in English. More gunfire. She breathed in the odd-colored smoke, felt woozy.

Smoke and sky, strong hands dragging her, forcing her to her stumbling feet, making her run.

She screamed for Stefan, for the guards. She tried to wrench away; she threw a punch at one of the men dragging her along; he shrugged it off.

Where was Danny? No, they *had* to have him. She was shoved into the backseat of a car that wheeled hard down the road, a hand keeping her pushed down, the car accelerating so fast she felt her stomach twist.

"Where is he? The target? Where is he?" she screamed.

"He got away. They've radioed for help. We can't wait, we can't go back."

"No!" she screamed. "No! You have to go back. You weren't supposed to do this yet!"

"Be quiet." The man had a heavy Scots accent. "Nothing to be done." He handcuffed her with zip ties as she coughed out the smoke.

Charity. She would kill her for this. *You are dead, woman. Sam. Sam.*

She looked up at the Russian sky through the window, and then the car drove up into the belly of a cargo truck — and darkness fell upon them all when the doors were shut behind them.

"Let me go back," she said, and they told her no, and she raged and screamed at them. She screamed a name at them but they didn't know who *Sam* was. She felt the truck rumble along, taking her away from Danny, from Sam, and this was worse than betraying him, she thought: This was helping to murder him.

53

Near Nebo, Russia

Five minutes after the attack, Danny Capra emerged from the woods, helping Stefan Varro, who held his nose, bleeding. Cars from the circle's compound raced up to the scene. The guards in the Black Shark were still bleary from the chemical gas jetted at them. Gas misted the air like smog.

The driver and the guard stood by the wrecked limo. Rubber bullets lay underfoot, fired after the windows were shattered. Whoever the attackers were, they'd tried to make the attack nonlethal.

"They took Mila!" Stefan said. "Why . . . why would they take *her*?"

"For ransom? They might think she's your girlfriend," Danny said. That was close. So close. Stefan leaned hard against him. "Stefan, clearly you were the target."

Stefan accepted this without question. "What will they do with her? We have to

490

call the police, find her . . ." His voice trailed off. "Don't they know who we are? They can't . . . they can't . . ." He didn't do frustration well, as though it were an alien sensation.

Danny gripped Stefan's arm as the security teams put him and Stefan in a car and rushed back to Nebo. "Let me do the talking. Do you understand? This is the work of the traitor. Say nothing."

"Is my nose broken?" Stefan asked. "Will it look OK?"

A war council quickly gathered. And Danny found himself, again, in the same room as the president of Russia.

The president's security had taken command of him; Belinsky Global had taken command of the crime scene. It was remote; no one else had seen the attackers arrive or depart. Teams combed the village nearby, looking for the cars involved in the ambush. But the attackers were gone.

Morozov looked hard at Stefan and his father, Boris. Then at Danny, who met his gaze for a moment and then modestly put it down. "We will *not* publicize this. Not before the party tonight, not before the summit. It will cause confusion and fear. The road must be cleaned now of debris

491

and evidence, before the departure party. The injured men can be treated here at the private clinic. The cars junked here and replaced. Is that understood? I give no weapons to our doubters."

"Stefan is hurt," Boris Varro said. "They took his woman friend. And we do nothing?"

"His nose isn't even broken."

"And Mila, what about her?" Stefan said, nose clogged with gauze, eye already bruising.

Danny sat at the table, calmly. "May I say something?" he said in Russian.

"You are the one who got out Stefan, yes?" Morozov said. "Well done."

Danny gave the barest of nods. "Thank you, Mr. President. They took Ms. Cebotari but obviously they used nonlethal weapons. So they may release her, unharmed. Or they may ask Stefan for a ransom. I do not think they will just kill her when they could ask for a ransom."

"Ransom? Why would we pay for her?" Boris Varro said.

"To avoid embarrassment," Morozov said. "Because she was your guest and it was your duty to protect her. Sometimes you are not very Russian, Boris."

Boris Varro's face went red with shame

and fury.

"You said she has a partner. Another American?" Morozov said.

"Yes. We met in Nassau," Stefan said. "Kirov and I are investing in their project."

"Can he be trusted to keep his mouth shut and not make a fuss?"

Stefan shrugged. "I believe money may help there. We are investing in his business. If we can persuade him to let us handle this . . . and we can handle it quickly."

Met in Nassau. Danny kept his expression neutral. Seaforth had been there. Sam had been there. *My God.*

"Are you all right?" Stefan whispered to him.

Danny nodded wordlessly.

Morozov said to one of his men, "I want word put out, immediately but discreetly, to the criminal underground in Moscow that we want this woman back, unharmed. Compliance will bring a financial reward. Failure will bring the entire wrath of this government on their heads. Find who did this. Now."

Morozov and Boris Varro and the police security chief took over the conversation. Stefan glanced at Danny, and Danny barely nodded, just once.

The meeting broke up. Morozov was

493

bundled up by his formidable security team and left. The last glance he gave was for Danny, curiosity and suspicion mixed together. Stefan got himself a glass of water from a pitcher and swallowed another pain-killer.

It was only Danny and the Varros still in the room.

Danny thought about the extremely expensive hitman waiting near the bar. No job now. A canceled job could create problems. Damn this woman. And then, even if Sam was in Nassau, the Russians could come after him. What if Mila had told Sam that he was here? He needed a way to shield his brother. Part of his brain said to leave it alone. The other part said, *Do something to protect him.*

He had to do this. There was no choice but to save Sam. "Stefan has been assisting me," Danny said. "I was taught my work years ago by a master. His name was Sergei; we worked together closely. We protected you all. I am still protecting you."

Boris Varro turned and stared at him. "Who are you?"

The lie came easily, polished in his mind for when he needed to tell it. "My name does not matter. But there is an internal threat here. A problem, possibly, with the

Kirovs. I am unsure who is behind it. Threats have been made to expose Sergei's crimes to end the summit."

"Crimes."

"Sergei killed a CIA operative in cold blood. It was this operative who killed your son Anton."

"What?" Stefan said.

Boris held up a hand. "Hush, Stefan. Let him talk."

"The killing was done as a faked execution video, but Sergei cut the operative's throat. I learned an enemy has acquired footage from then. It shows Sergei unmasked, the kneeling agent next to him. I believe it was stolen from a hard drive Sergei used. He is clearly the same man killing the agent. Now. The Americans will not take kindly to Morozov's right-hand man killing a CIA agent on tape. They will not want to buy oil or gas from his billionaire friends. So. I need your help. I need to be close to the Kirovs. I think one of them is the traitor."

"Yuri could never . . ." Boris began.

Danny held up a hand. "Yuri has been acting very strangely."

"He was drunk and shooting at a guest. He missed," Stefan said quietly.

"And we must not have further incidents.

I was suspicious of Mila and that was why I wanted her away from Nebo. I would have handled her in Moscow — taken her for questioning. Her American partner — I have studied him, as has Irina, I am sure, and there is no suspicion attaching to him. He is innocent; he poses no threat. Mila is Moldovan, even with that British passport. I think Mila was working with someone looking to embarrass the families. There are many Russians in London who would love to hurt you, hurt Morozov, in the public eye. This person who got the evidence against Sergei could well be one of them, and have gotten help from the Kirovs. If Morozov falls, the premier elected with him falls as well. Yuri could rise."

The Varros stared at him. "How do we know you worked with Sergei?" Boris demanded.

"He knew things, Father. Things only Sergei could have known," Stefan said. "He speaks true."

"When does Irina arrive?" Varro asked.

"In a few hours."

"Radio the plane. I want to talk with Irina," Varro said. "Put out feelers. I want to know everything about this Sam and this Mila. Someone in Moscow knows about him."

"Sir. Irina does not know about my work with her husband. Few people knowing about me is the only way I have been able to work and to survive. Please, do not tell her."

Boris Varro studied him. If either Stefan or Boris was Firebird, he thought, they would play along and protect him. If not, they might well tell Morozov this very moment who he was.

Risking it all for Sam's safety.

Stefan picked up the speakerphone and got connected to the Kirov jet. Irina Belinskaya's voice came over the speakerphone. "Yes?"

They told her about the attack and the taking of Mila. Nothing was said of Philip Judge, or Sergei.

Now I know who you are, Firebird. The both of you.

Irina was, he thought, strangely silent, until she said, "I understand." And the conversation ended.

"I am glad," Boris said, "that we have come to understanding."

Danny nodded and left.

Danny Capra sat alone in his room. Thinking.

So the immediate problem was fixed. He

felt a sense of sharp relief. Whoever had taken Mila — he was sure it was her husband's organization, the Round Table, which he'd had a few dealings with — had managed to take all the heat off him. He looked, more than ever, like an ally and friend to the inner circle. He had saved Stefan. Morozov had nodded approval at him. They would close ranks now, and he was well inside the ranks.

And he had protected Sam. He had told the Varros that Sam was nothing to fear. And even with Morozov dead, Sam was thousands of miles away, and Mila was gone. They could be suspected of being troublemakers, but not of murder.

Sam and Seaforth both in Nassau. Sam would be protected by his old employer. He would be OK. Danny repeated it, like a prayer.

He closed his eyes. Morozov would be dead soon enough. And he himself would be gone, into Finland, soon enough. He would take a car — they had an actual large pool of cars here for their use — and drive the M10 to Moscow, get another car, and drive to Finland. He had a cache of money and a different passport hidden in Moscow. It had been a caution that Sergei Belinsky had taught him. Always have papers, always have cash, hidden where you could get to them. The closest border crossing between the European Union and Moscow was Latvia, but he thought it would be watched more closely. Plus, he had a friend in Finland who could hide him. He'd made a few friends over the years. Then he'd get to England, become the Robert Clayton identity he'd established, and life would be a fresh new adventure.

He would vanish, the shadow that never was. When they went looking for Philip Judge . . . they would find nothing. And what would Sam say? *Oh, that was my brother, who killed the Russian president.* Of course not. He would keep silent. The rest of the world would think maybe he'd been a man who looked like Danny Capra but no one would make the connection anymore. Mila and Jimmy would say nothing. They themselves were criminals of a sort; they would never go to the police.

And it didn't matter. He could get to London; he could step into being Robert Clayton.

Because he was going to be smart about how he did this. That was the problem with killers of heads of state. Rarely were they daring enough to be smart.

He looked at his watch. A few hours to

go. He lay down on the bed to calm his thoughts, to close his eyes.

He slept, and he didn't hear the buzz of the Kirov plane approaching.

54

Irina unhooked Sam from his chains. "There's nowhere for you to run," she said. "If you run, I'll shoot you in the kneecaps. And not give you to a doctor for a full day. Do you understand me?"

He nodded. She helped him up into the main cabin. Two of her men were there. Katya sat, looking miserable and sick, food untouched before her. Yuri Kirov stared at him but said nothing.

"Katya," he said. "Are you OK? I'm sorry."

She nodded. For a moment she looked at him. But she said nothing.

"I don't think you speak to my daughter again," Yuri Kirov said. "Sit there and be quiet."

Sam sat. Irina nodded at the two guards; they went into the back area of the plane, which had been fashioned into a small,

501

separate room, and shut the door.

"Sam. Mila has been taken."

"Taken?"

"Kidnapped. It looks like they were aiming to grab Stefan, but he escaped. The attackers took her instead."

"Who is *they*?"

"We don't know. Doesn't she work with you? Perhaps it is your friends at the CIA, making sure they get out at least one of their agents."

"Neither Mila nor I are CIA," he said. "I told you that already."

"Was Sam your CIA contact?" Irina demanded of Katya.

Katya stared at him. And then she nodded. "He works for them, too," she said, very softly. Saving herself. And maybe saving him, he thought, because they needed him alive if he was CIA. "I told the CIA I couldn't help them anymore, and he came for me. To force me, or persuade me."

"I understand," Irina said. "Thank you."

"Katya has given you what you want, Irina," Yuri said. "Use Sam how you see fit. But leave us out of it."

You are Firebird, Sam thought. Is this why you want Morozov dead — to protect your daughter?

"All right," Irina said. "This is what we're going to do."

55

Moscow

The extraction team had taken Mila first to a safe house, on the outskirts of Moscow. They hurried her up the stairs, turned on a few lights, sat her down. The room was bare, just a table and three chairs. They left her alone for a long while after making sure she wasn't injured.

"You screwed up," she said when the leader came back into the room.

"So you told me," the team leader said. He had a broad Scottish accent.

"You've made it impossible for me to go back there," she said.

"That was the idea."

"No, the idea was that you extract the one target I told you to. You've killed a man."

His phone rang. He went into the other room. The four others watched her. She watched them.

The Scotsman came back into the room.

"The Tsar Lounge. You wanted us to grab the target there. Why?"

"I could control things there. It's friendly territory."

"Is this bar your husband's base of operations when he's doing dirty jobs on the side?"

Then she saw a way out. "Yes, it is," Mila said.

"Is information there on his operations?"

Mila nodded.

"We're going to this bar," the Scotsman said. He gestured at the one woman on the team, standing near Mila. "You'll come with us."

"I was supposed to go to that sendoff tonight for Morozov," the woman said. "And report back on what the feeling was at the party. There's been nothing on the news about the incident so far." Mila realized the woman must have diplomatic cover in Moscow, at the British embassy. All the diplomats had been invited.

"Obviously this takes precedence," the Scot said. "Let's go."

The assassin, waiting for the man he knew as Philip Judge and a woman in an e-mailed photo, kept waiting. He'd fashioned a quick kill nest in a building across from the Tsar

Lounge, being remodeled into office space. It had been a lucky break to find a roost to give himself such a clean shot. But Judge was badly overdue. No contact. Something had gone wrong.

Then he saw her, walking with another woman and a broad-shouldered man, jumping the early line to get into the Tsar Lounge. It was a bar that got busy early. He scanned the crowd. No sign of Judge, who had specifically said the woman and Stefan Varro would be with him. He knew what Stefan looked like; everyone in Russia did who read a paper. Normally he would simply leave. Judge wasn't here, so the job must have been aborted. But . . . this was a million dollars. A million. Far beyond what he was normally paid. And he already had half.

Shouldn't he deliver?

He put his eye back to the scope, adjusted the rifle.

They arrived at the Tsar Lounge. A well-dressed line to get in stretched along the sidewalk in front of the club, and Mila went up to the bouncer, spoke to him in a low voice, and he spoke into his headset. After a moment the bouncer told Mila that Galina, the manager, was in and Mila and the Scot and the English woman were waved through. Mila heard an annoyed woman curse at them for jumping the line.

Inside. He'd hesitated and they'd gone inside.

The assassin decided he'd wait. What if Judge was dead or captured by the police? There was no advantage in doing the kill then; he would not get paid.

He put his eye back to the scope, a million dollars a number that kept crowding out thought, logic, sense.

Galina Berg, the bar's manager, hurried down the stairs from the apartment above. She was in her early thirties, dark-haired, immaculately dressed.

"Mila?"

"That's all right," Mila said quickly, cutting her off. "These are some friends of mine. I'm taking them upstairs for a bit."

"No one's supposed to go up there," Galina said. "You know that."

"It's all right," Mila said. "I promise. Sam is coming soon. We'll wait for him there."

"All right," she finally said.

Mila led the Scotsman and the woman upstairs. At the top of the flight was a door, marked PRIVATE NO ENTRANCE in five languages. Mila opened the door and they stepped inside a well-furnished apartment/ office. In one corner there was a desk, with a laptop. The Scotsman had drawn his weapon as they came through the door and he checked the room, the kitchen, the two small bedrooms. All was clear. There was one door that was locked.

"What's in here?"

"Storage," Mila said. The room stored weapons, false IDs, and a cache of money, but she did not volunteer that information.

"Open it," he said.

"As I am not the owner, I don't have the key."

He listened carefully at the door and heard only silence. "I'll shoot off the lock."

"Do what you must."

He did and after he shattered the lock he kicked in the door. Searched the room. Found the weapons and the cash. There were no false IDs in the drawers and Mila felt a surge of relief.

"This is your husband's home roost when he's working for the Russians."

"He's not working for the Russians," Mila said. "He's working for himself."

"Let me see the laptop," he said.

"It's encoded," Mila said. She sat down at the desk, unasked. "Do you want me to type in the password?"

"No!" he said. "You might activate a fail-safe and destroy the data. Get up from that desk." He'd holstered his gun and stepped toward her.

She pulled the gun that was hidden under the desk. There was one such weapon holstered at every desk in every bar Sam Capra owned. She leveled at him and fired. It didn't make a blast, but a pocking sound, and he dropped. Then she shot the English woman, who didn't have time to scream.

She waited until they went still, and pulled out the darts. They had been injected with a heavy dose of veterinary tranquilizer. Then she put the gun back where it was. She pulled both of the unconscious agents into the bathroom. She zip-tied their hands and feet. Then she sat down at the laptop that Sam used when in Moscow, which had nothing to do with the bar's business, and entered in a command to destroy the hard drive. It wound and ground and made distressed noises.

She took the Scotsman's gun. She took his car keys and the phone. The call log showed that the number he'd just received a call from was the same one she had for Charity. From the woman's purse, she took an ID — she had brown hair, was about

Mila's height — and the bar-code bracelet that was the entry into the farewell party back in Nebo. She kept a dress suitable for each bar in the spare bedroom, and it would be fine for a cocktail reception that was a farewell to the Russian circle before they boarded their planes. She put on the dress. She found a brown wig that wouldn't look stylish, but would serve to pass muster as the English woman should there be a physical description tied to her bar code at the security checkpoint. She took the woman's glasses off her and put them on herself and made a final check in the mirror. It would have to do.

She went downstairs. "Close the bar," she told Galina.

"What?"

"Close the bar. Pull the fire alarm. I don't care. Shut it down after I leave. In about a half hour, there will be British agents coming here. Once you've shut down, leave. Don't go upstairs. I left my friends there. They'll wake up in about three hours but I think the Brits will be here before then."

Galina nodded.

The assassin waited. He was a patient man. The line had thinned as more people had gotten in. Only a few left. A group of laughing women, a few couples, a brown-haired woman in a hurry. He kept the scope aimed at the front door.

He could not help himself. The million — how would he spend it? A new car. A better apartment for his mother. He could take her to that theme park in Paris, or even the one in Orlando. He could . . .

And then a crowd began to spill out of the bar, the distant whine of a fire alarm. Far too many people leaving. Far too many.

The job was ruined. The assassin raged in his head, trembling with frustration. A half million was better than nothing. But a job that had gone wrong made him uneasy. Perhaps it would be good to leave the country for a while, until he found out what had happened to his client.

He packed up his gear and went home, where his mother asked him if he'd had a nice day.

Mila went to the English woman's car, noticed it had diplomatic plates. That would be useful. She got in and tossed her purse on the seat.

She drove out of the lot and headed for the highway that would take her to Nebo.

56

Nebo, Russia

At the edge of Nebo, the airfield lights showed the president of Russia's Ilyushin Il-96 aircraft standing on the runway. Torches and streamers covered the walkways, the roads. Hundreds of guests thronged the spaces between the houses, and the grandest house of all belonged to Morozov.

The evening party was on.

They had taken Sam to a modest empty house at the edge of the compound. The house, he supposed, that Sergei had used for his interrogations. There was a guard outside. Sam stood at the window and watched the distant crowds, the illuminated jet. He had failed.

He thought his brother would try to strike here because as intense as security was it'd be even greater in America. Hundreds of guests. Danny might be among them. And he still had no way to stop him, no idea of how his brother might strike.

Sam loathed Morozov and all he stood for, but he couldn't let him die. But he couldn't say to the guard, *A man fitting this description is going to try to kill the president when he reaches America.* They would gun down Danny on sight. Or arrest him, and he'd never be free. He'd die in a Siberian prison or before an execution squad.

If he could *prove* Kirov was Firebird — that there was an active plot against Morozov — then the trip might be delayed. Or if Danny's employer was in custody, Danny might abort the mission, considering he wouldn't get paid. And he'd need to run, because the Russians would be looking for whoever Kirov had hired.

But no Russian would believe him when they heard he'd tried to kidnap Katya. Irina, fond of Katya, was still trying to protect her. And Sam was the trump card to be produced once Morozov was in America. The agency would eventually have to acknowledge he was a former employee. No one would believe the *former* part. He'd be a criminal, a rogue, a talking point, blamed as part of the assassination if Danny pulled it off. Irina was setting him up for far more than she imagined.

But he could talk. *You'd be putting your own brother in their sights.* Sam ran his fingers through his hair, torn, angry. *And if they learn an American killed him, it could be war.*

He looked down the loop. At the end was a house that no one came from or went to. This struck him as odd; the rest of the estates were bathed in light, people drifting among them.

A knock at his door. The guard opened it, looked at him, closed it, and locked it.

Sam turned back to the window. He saw more helicopters landing — dignitaries fetched in from Moscow. The hundred families who controlled thirty-five percent of all of Russia's great wealth were here in force. The copters were landing, though, close to the empty house. People streamed past it or were ferried down the road in limos.

He heard a voice, softly speaking, pleading, then ordering. The door opened.

Katya stepped inside. The guard stood there, watching, gesturing Sam to sit in the chair. He did. The guard told him in Russian to put on the handcuff attached to the chair. Sam did. The guard stood in the doorway, but hung back, watching.

She whispered to Sam. "The guard

doesn't speak English. So say nothing in Russian."

He nodded. Sam said, "You look gorgeous." She was dressed for the party, and for the photographers that would be swarming around her. She was stunning in a dress of emerald green, diamonds at her ears and throat, dark hair swept up like a czarina, the picture of modern Russian glamour.

"I cannot believe you have a kind word for me."

He shrugged.

She said, "Thank you. That's my job for them all here. To look. Not to think." She continued, not looking at him: "Why did you try to kidnap me?"

"I couldn't take you and your father. I thought he would do what I wanted if you were with me. And then you would also be safe from him, from Irina. From this. You know what Morozov will do to you if he finds out."

"Yes. I might . . . once I am in America . . . stay for a while."

As in forever. She meant defection. "I think that's a wise course."

"You said why my father was taking the money . . . but you said nothing to Irina about it."

"She has her own theories. She thinks Yuri

515

wants to use the millions in cash he hid in the Caribbean to pay off the CIA to let you go and never reveal you spied on the circle for them. I know the truth. You won't like it."

"Tell me."

This was it. His only hope was to gain her help, and the only way to do it was to trust her. "The killer I'm hunting here is my brother."

Her gaze widened.

"Years ago, Sergei Belinsky trained him as his protégé. As a hired killer. He saw Belinsky kill a CIA agent, he . . . witnessed Anton Varro's murder. Sergei kept him as a secret. Now your father has, misguidedly, hired him to kill Morozov. Probably in an effort to protect you and to protect his holdings. That's who the cash is for."

She paled.

"I think he's here tonight. I have to stop him — for the world's sake, but for your father's sake and your sake, too, Katya. If he sees me here he'll abort the kill, I'm sure of it. But if he kills the president, you're going to lose everything. So will your dad. So will I. Help me."

She seemed to need to steady herself. "You want me to take you out to the party? Irina won't allow it. She said you have to be kept out of sight."

"Only this guy, another guard, Irina, and your father even know I'm here."

"Listen. You're wrong about my father. I asked him about the money; he didn't even know it was being brought on the ship."

"He's lying. Of course he knows. It's his money and it's his boat."

"Sam. You saw what he's like . . . the drinking. He said it was because he suspected what I'd done with the Americans. He has been watching me. Normally he pays me no attention . . . but now he has. He was upset over that." Her voice broke. "He said Irina moves money for the Varros, for him, for others who are her clients. It's an old trick from their KGB days, cash hidden in the West. So maybe she's doing this for the Varros, stealing money from Papa, to make him look bad."

An old KGB trick. That had been how the oligarchs had gotten their initial cash to invest in denationalized companies in the looting of the Soviet Union.

"She said she was told it was for me."

"Stefan could have told her that. She works for both families. Maybe Morozov was behind Anton's death? Is that it? Is that the motive?"

"The only question that matters is, do you

517

let this terrible night happen, Katya? I can do nothing without your help. It all depends on your choice."

She weighed her decision. Her gaze met his.

"Follow my lead." Katya turned and made an obscene gesture at Sam. The guard smiled. Then she went up to the guard and formed her hand into a fist and punched him once, sharply, on the nose and then the jaw. She was strong and the man was so surprised he stepped back, blood coming from one nostril.

Sam sprang. He was still handcuffed to the chair but he pivoted on his leg, swinging the chair with him and bringing it down on the man's head. The guard staggered back and Sam hit him again with the free hand.

The guard went down. Sam clubbed him again with the chair, four more times; the legs splintered and the guard was unconscious.

"Don't get blood on his shirt," Katya said, calmly. "We need to dress you as him."

They used the guard's key to unlock Sam's cuff. He stripped out of his clothes and put on the guard's suit. The man had an ID clipped to his pocket and an access wristband, like that of the guests. He had a pair of sunglasses in his pocket and Sam put those on. It was night but it was the best way to disguise his face, and the grounds and the houses were flooded with light for the partygoers. They bound the guard with his own handcuffs, gagged him, and tied his feet with knotted strips of sheet.

"No going back now," he said to Katya. "Thank you for your decision."

She nodded. "If Papa has done this, he has to be stopped. And if he hasn't, then your brother still has to be stopped."

"Let's see if he's here."

"If he's not?"

"Then I leave. I'll find a way out of Russia."

"Seaforth told me . . . if I was suspected, or scared, and had to get out of Russia and could do it myself, head to Helsinki. He would get me safely to America. So you might try there."

He nodded. "Katya, the fastest way for you to get out of here is to play along: go on the plane with Morozov, like you're supposed to."

"You don't think your brother put a bomb on the plane?"

"No. Not his style. He'll kill Morozov alone, not innocent people."

"And if your brother is here?"

"Then I'll stop him."

57

The Morozov Estate, Nebo, Russia

Sam and Katya walked into the seething, happy, celebrating mass of people surrounding the Morozov estate. He walked one step ahead of her, sunglasses in place, scanning the crowd. She touched his arm lightly as he navigated the party. The signal both of them gave off was clear: He was her personal security. He waved off those that were approaching her, saying in Russian, "Later. Later. Katerina Yureyevna is late for the photographers." Admirers stepped back and settled for a wave. The rest of the guards only gave him a cursory glance. He had taken the guard's earpiece and he could hear the chatter of their communications on their network, reporting in that all was well. The guards who scanned at the entry gate let them pass without scanning wristbands after a peremptory word from Katya. Her wrists were dripping with diamonds and she did not bother with bar codes. She was *Katya.* They entered the grand hall.

If he found Yuri Kirov, he could confront him and whisper in his ear: *I know you hired a man to kill Morozov. Katya knows, too. Tell me where he is. And I'll be silent forever about what you and Katya have done.*

Crowds of media, both the Russian press that did not dare openly question Morozov, and the Western press that did but that he often ignored, were in the main hall. Photographers, and the security assigned to them, rushed toward Katya. And Sam stepped away in the crush, as Katya had told him to do; the press fawned over her and no one paid him a bit of attention.

The house was vast. He moved through the ballroom, the kind you'd expect in a five-star hotel.

He saw Kirov, surrounded by a group of fawning admirers, women in elegant gowns, men in tuxes and suits. To his left, Boris Varro, in a group across the room, laughing and talking loudly. Gesturing. Katya was sure Firebird was the Varros — what if she was right? This was a gamble if he was wrong.

Sam didn't see Morozov anywhere. He thought the president would naturally draw the biggest crowd.

Then Sam saw Irina, talking to Stefan Varro, both talking to another man. Sam turned away before they could see him.

He slid into an adjoining, smaller salon. From this angle he could see Yuri Kirov in the big ballroom . . . and then Katya came to her father and hugged him. She saw Sam and began to steer Yuri toward the smaller salon. Yuri spoke to the man standing across from him, perhaps making apologies, with his back to Sam.

And then that man, turning, looking straight at him, was his brother Danny.

It was as if time froze. Sam felt as though he slid out of reality, then back into it, a strange shifting of focus. As if the past six years had been a dream, and this was the true world that he had suddenly awakened to. No Lucy. No CIA career destroyed, no Daniel, no Mila, no Jimmy, no abandoned village in the Hindu Kush, no horrifying video.

His brother, back to life. There was the theory of it, a hope like a knot in your heart, and there was the fact of it. Sam heard the rasp of his own breath over the giggling and murmur of conversations.

He stared and Danny stared — so much for being professionals of the subtle arts — and Katya noticed. Sam walked toward them. Yuri looked surprised and uncertain. Katya put on false enthusiasm. "Sam! I am glad you are here. I thought perhaps you did not feel up to the party."

He forced himself to breathe. Danny, here. Danny, alive. Danny, looking at him, the great lie of his death turning the air between them into an unseen storm.

Sam forced himself to smile and nod. "Hi, Katya. Hello, Yuri." He forced himself not to look at Danny. Sam thought he would suddenly burst into tears if he did. He never cried in front of his brother after Burundi. Ever. Danny didn't permit it.

Katya's voice was like silk. Reminding him that other people were around. "Sam, have you met Ekaterina Vaslova? She is a very famous writer."

Sam nodded and said hello in Russian, shaking the woman's hand. "And this is Marya Antonovna Romanova, one of Russia's most famous actresses, as I am sure you know. Sam owns the Tsar Lounge in Moscow; do you know it?"

"Ah, of course." The actress gave Sam a warm smile. "There's a very stylish crowd there."

He'd waited for Danny to flee. Danny stayed. Now, in the group, Sam looked full into his brother's face. Danny looked

524

slightly different. The cheekbones more prominent, the nose a bit narrower, the lips heavier. Just enough calibration, Sam thought, to fool the cameras for passports, to dodge the facial recognition software. Danny's hair was darker. It was the strangest thought Sam could have had, but the slightly altered face was part of the reality of his brother.

Sam wanted to hug Danny. Sam wanted to strike him. Sam wanted to hate him. Sam wanted to forgive him. It took every bit of his training, of his strength, of his desire to keep his brother alive, to keep his composure.

"And this is Philip Judge. We also met him in the Bahamas."

"Hi. Sam Capra," Sam said. He offered his brother his hand. Danny took it. Shook it. The flesh of Danny's palm was dry.

"It's nice to meet you, Sam," Danny said. His voice rang steady, same as Sam's.

Sam knows why you're here, Danny thought. He knows. He knows, because he isn't just looking for you. He is keeping his mouth shut. He felt like his heart might shut down.

What are you going to do about him? Because he can't interfere. He will get you both killed.

"So what do you do, Philip?" Sam said, studying his brother's face. He couldn't believe the polite words spilling from his mouth. Everything he thought he would say to Danny — *I forgive you, tell me why, are you all right, thank God you're alive* — fell away from his brain, dead leaves on a windy day.

"I handle investments for Stefan Varro," he said.

Varro. Sam thought of the oil stock sell orders he'd seen on the yacht's e-mail server; the price of oil would skyrocket when Morozov was killed. Maybe I'm wrong, Sam thought, and maybe Katya is right. Or maybe they're just normal sell orders and have nothing to do with the assassination. Investors place those orders all the time.

"I'm badly in need of investment advice. I'm going to get a drink; would you like to come with me?" Sam could not believe the calm in his voice. "Excuse us for a moment, Katya, Yuri." He put a hand on his brother's arm and Danny gave in, letting Sam steer him toward one of the bar stations. They walked together, smiles frozen on their faces.

If Yuri tells Irina I'm here, I have three minutes. Maybe less.

They went through the crowd, past the bar, outside onto the huge stone patio. Clumps of dignitaries moved, in laughter, in conversation.

"Get out of here. Now," Danny said in a low voice.

"That's what you say to me?" Sam said. "You're alive. You're alive and . . ." He felt heat light his eyes, his cheeks, his throat. To see him. To see him, right here. Six years. He'd missed him every day. And his grief had been a needless lie.

"I'm trying to save you. Again. This isn't the place for you, baby brother." He put his hand on Sam's wrist. "I need you to go."

"You're not going to k. . . do what you're planning to do to Morozov," Sam said, low, barely a whisper.

The words stopped Danny.

"You'll never, ever get away with it," Sam said. "Never. They'll hunt you down. They'll find you. And they'll kill you."

"I'm a dead man. No one hunts a dead man. Except you." He tried a smile and Sam had to look away. "I should have known you'd come looking for me. You're tougher than I thought you would be. You're not like

Mom and Dad. They sail in and fix the aftermath of the disaster. Not you. You go after the problem at the root. You're like me."

"How would you know what I'm like now?"

"Because I've watched. I've kept tabs on you. From a distance. I know about Jimmy Court and the Round Table. About those bastards in Nine Suns who tried to take you down. I know about your ex-wife. I know about my nephew. Thanks for naming him for me."

"We can discuss what you know and what you don't know about me later." Sam tried to make his voice firmer. He felt his control slipping away. He had to get Danny away from this huge crowd, someplace where they could be alone and talk. Reason with him. "But tonight isn't going to happen." Sam scooped up a glass of dark red wine for each of them from a passing tray, pushed one into his brother's hands. He could see over Danny's shoulder Katya, standing at one of the French doors, watching them for a second, realizing who Danny must be.

"I've already gotten away with it," Danny said.

"Really. I thought it was supposed to happen on American soil," Sam said.

Danny drank his wine. "Come with me."

He was suddenly afraid of Danny. "No."

"Or what, Sam? You'll tell them who I am? And who you are? You won't and we both know it." He turned and walked away, and Sam followed, tagging after him, the old habits and relationship still defined and unchanged. The night air felt good and cool, the moon and stars hidden behind the cotton and silk of the clouds.

They walked past the small groups gathered on the patio and the vast lawn beyond. Away from everyone. Sam realized the presence of others was the most powerful cork on his emotions, his relief, his anger. There was far more relief than anger. He still loved his brother. He could not comprehend what he had done, but love didn't erode.

"Danny." He said his name for the first time.

Danny froze him with a stare. "Don't."

"You lied. The worst lie imaginable."

Danny started to walk away from the party, toward the Varro estate. "I cannot do this right now. Go to the airport in Moscow. Get out of Russia. Now. I'll find you . . . later and we'll have a long talk."

"You don't have to do this. You witnessed Morozov's right-hand man killing a CIA officer. You tell that to the world, Morozov is done in regard to the United States."

"No one would believe me, and no other witnesses are alive."

"The hard drive. From the village, sent to Mirjan Shah. You took it. You killed Shah and you took it, and it's got Sergei's face on it, before or after the video was shot. For insurance."

Sam could see the truth of it all in Danny's face. He could fool the world but not Sam. *If I knock him out, where do I hide him? How do I explain to the guards that I attacked someone?* Sam turned back toward him. "I know who Firebird is. He'll kill you."

Danny almost broke stride. "It doesn't matter." He laughed and he put an amiable arm around his brother's shoulders as they went past a couple of party stragglers, laughing and merry. "I need you to do exactly what I say. Exactly. Go back to your room, wherever you're staying . . ."

Sam pulled away from him, his voice a harsh whisper. "What are you? What are you now?"

"I'm your brother."

"My brother couldn't have done what you've done. Mom and Dad have suffered horribly. I joined the CIA because you were killed the way you were, and I wanted to fix the world . . . I reshaped my entire life

530

because of what I believed about you, and that's all been a lie . . ."

Danny turned his face away.

Sam slapped him, hard, forcing Danny's face back toward him. "You don't get to ignore me."

Danny's voice was flat. "Jimmy was supposed to keep you away from me. Don't trust him or Mila when all this is done."

Sam couldn't even form the words *You know Jimmy and Mila* when a voice hailed them.

"Philip?" Stefan Varro hurried toward them. He smiled uncertainly at Sam. "Is everything OK?"

"Yes," Sam said.

"It's fine," Danny said to him. "We're having a wonderful chat."

It seemed to satisfy Stefan. "Um, all right. Philip, I need to borrow you. Come with me, please."

"Now?"

"Yes, my friend, now; come on."

"Go," Sam said. "I'll catch up with you later, Philip."

The dismissal seemed to surprise Danny. And Stefan gave Sam an odd glance. But they went, vanishing back into the crowd, Danny glancing back at Sam.

My friend, Sam thought. Odds were

Danny was staying with Stefan. He turned and sprinted for the Varro house.

"What about Sam?" Stefan said, panicked. "What do we tell him about Mila?"

Danny kept his voice reassuring. "It's all fine. Katya Kirova brought him. He was told Mila wasn't feeling well and had gone to Moscow. He accepted it. He is eager for his investment. He knows nothing."

Let this lie work, Danny thought. For Sam's sake.

58

The Varro Estate, Nebo, Russia

Most of the staff at each of the estates were busy assisting at the party. Sam smiled and went through the Varros' kitchen entrance. An older woman glanced up at him; she was brewing tea — still the Russian national drink — in a large samovar and putting it onto a cart. All the kitchens, he guessed, had been pressed into service.

"Apologies, madam," he said in Russian. "The American that is staying here with Stefan Borisovich — Mr. Judge? He asked me to fetch him a document from his room." Then he gestured up, shrugging. "Which room is it . . . ?"

"Ah. Second floor, third down. I can show you . . ."

"No need, madam, you are busy. I'll find it."

He went up the stairs closest to the kitchen. The floor was grand, the hall wide, and fine paintings hung on the walls. A Picasso, a Monet, a Frida Kahlo. Fresh flowers filled vases on marble-topped tables. He found the door the woman had indicated, and opened it. It wasn't locked.

He shut the door behind him. The weapon must be here. Danny presumably was not going to kill Morozov with his bare hands. The weapon had to be small, had to be disguised as something else. Danny had to get it on a plane. He would be watched closely by the Secret Service, as part of the presidential entourage, and it would be difficult for anyone to pass a weapon to him or him to collect it.

Think like him.

And he had to kill him in a way that would give him time to escape. Danny was no martyr.

How could you kill a world leader and walk away? How do you kill without the weapon in your hand, and yet you survive? How did you do it so you struck here yet he died on American soil? A delayed death. He had to keep it close at hand, for fear of it being discovered by someone else. It had to appear innocuous. It had to get past the presidential security. Had he gotten it in the Bahamas or here?

He started to search the room, his mind racing.

You will know it when you see it. You will know it when you see it. You will . . .

59

Nebo, Russia

It was a mistake. If one of the primary orders of Danny's business was never to break cover, he had obeyed that personal commandment and yet he had made a mistake. He had erred in walking away from his brother because Stefan told him to, and when two minutes had passed listening to Stefan's purred assurances, as they worked their way past the crowd, that these financial reporters needed a good story, he thought:

Sam won't wait for you to come back. What if he's off searching your room, looking for the weapon?

The thought froze his brain.

If he finds the polonium . . . if he breathes it in, he's dead.

That unhappy possibility occurred to him just as Stefan introduced the financial reporters and Danny immediately forgot their names. Danny put on his best, most sincere smile and said, "Let me get you a summary that will help explain Stefan's investment plan in America. Please, I'll be right back."

"Philip . . . ," Stefan started, clear annoyance in his voice.

Danny left Stefan and the two reporters staring as he barreled back through the crowd. He walked briskly, not running to avoid attention, toward the Varro house. The lawn seemed to stretch forever. He nodded at the front door guards, who nodded back.

He went inside and up to his room. He opened the door — had it been unlocked? — turned on the light, and let his gaze scan the room. Was everything in its place? He didn't have much to search. His laptop was open, a printout of the faked investments report for Morozov next to it.

No sign of his brother.

He went to his toiletries bag and pulled out the eyedrops bottle, still double-sealed in his plastic bag.

There it was. Where he'd left it.

He looked at himself in the mirror.

Maybe Sam took his advice and was headed to the airport in Moscow. Or maybe he'd gone to get a cell phone to call their parents. The thought, insane but possible, rocked him. What if Sam came to him with a phone, with their mother on the other end of the line? Or to call his friend Mila, who was no doubt back with her husband? No. Sam couldn't betray him, would never betray him.

The phone in his pocket, assembled from its hiding place in the laptop for the last time, stirred.

A text, sent untraceably, scrambled from server to server:

It is clear for ten minutes. You will have access. Go. Now.

Firebird, speaking directly to him. Fulfilling the final request he'd made.

Danny Capra put the eyedropper bottle in his pocket along with his fake financial summary and headed out the door.

60

The Presidential Ilyushin

The Morozov Ilyushin Il-96 modified wide-body, the preferred presidential plane out of the unusually large Russian presidential fleet, was guarded, of course. But Philip Judge was an expected passenger, scheduled to fly to America with the Russian elite.

Philip Judge was passed through security, with his credentials, and walked through the portable scanner that checked for metal or any chemical trace of explosives. He was patted down, politely but thoroughly. He smiled and nodded at the guards, who waved him on.

Danny thanked them and hurried up the portable stairs that led up to the massive plane, departing with smiles from the guards. He glanced back; no sign of Sam running toward the plane.

He entered the grand main cabin. Part of the plane had been preserved for regular seating, but here was a larger seating and working area where Morozov liked to spend the flight.

Maybe two minutes left.

The crew was gone, farther in the back of the cabin, and he could hear Irina Belinskaya's voice outlining and reviewing the departure protocol for after the reception, to get the passengers flying to the West aboard and settled. Some passengers might be drunk, and would need to be reminded of security requirements, and not to bother the president or Mr. Varro or Mr. Kirov or his daughter during the flight . . . There was scattered laughter from the crew.

While they were all watching her . . .

He saw what he needed, ready for him. He walked up to the samovar, a reconstruction of the one used by the last czar, ready to serve the man who was czar in all but name. And there sat next to it the double-eagle mug, larger than the others for Morozov's favored tea.

The same tall tea mug he'd seen Morozov use when they'd first been introduced at Boris Varro's house.

The only one here. Just for the president.

He took a deep breath and opened the eyedrops vial. A single drop of the saline, containing an almost invisible speck of the

540

polonium, in suspension, dropped in the cup, awaiting the tea that would be served even before takeoff. Resting in the bottom of the cup. Awaiting its chance to shape history.

The exposure to the microdose might make Danny sick, days from now. Or whoever handled the cup in preparing the drink or washing the cup. But he believed he'd been careful enough so that the dosage would only sicken those who handled the contaminated cup, and kill only one man: Morozov, who would drink his own tea.

Twenty seconds later he set the financial report down on the single leather seat that bore the double-eagle crest, where Morozov sat during flights. The note attached on the cover read: *Stefan is being bold here in his investment choices. I hope it meets with your approval,* written in both English and Russian. He had been careful not to leave prints.

Irina's voice droned on; the crew laughed again.

A minute later he was down the airplane steps, heading for the party. Soon he found the financial journalists. He was a little out of breath. "The president wanted my report!" he said, by way of apology. The journalists smiled. "So I can't comment on it until he has read it; I'm sorry." The smiles fell.

He apologized and moved off.

He still had the polonium with him and he needed to get rid of the poison. He'd have to do that soon. But first he needed to find his brother and get him away from here.

Sam watched Danny come down the plane's stairs, from the cover of a grove of pines close to the Varro house. Danny had been carrying a document and nothing else, and now he was empty-handed. Walking with purpose.

And then he saw Irina heading toward Danny, with two guards bracketing her.

They stopped Danny. Irina spoke to him. Then they moved off. Away from the party, away from his position in the trees. He realized after several moments that they were angling away from the estates, toward the empty house Sam had escaped from.

Sam started to follow, and then between them and him came a dense crowd, led by music. Morozov's security team leading the way, Russian and American and British and French and Japanese flags waving, someone with a giant peace sign, some of them a bit drunk, the press recording it all.

Sam watched them. When the bulge of the

crowd had passed, the military patriotic songs fading as the crowd reached the Ilyushin, there was no sign of his brother, or Irina.

61

Nebo, Russia

The car Mila drove was licensed to the British consulate, so it did not undergo the normal security check search. Such were the perils of diplomacy. She was grateful for this, as the extraction team's gear was hidden inside the trunk. Stun guns, a gas canister, rope. She thought she might need it all in dealing with getting Sam out and capturing Danny Capra. But Sam, she decided, was the priority.

And the moment she was spotted by anyone who recognized her, she would be facing an uncomfortable questioning from the security details. Irina Belinskaya would be unrelenting. She had to hope the crowd would be a suitable camouflage.

You don't even know what they've done to Sam. He could be a prisoner. He could be dead.

Mila — or as the invite read, Alice Devere

— parked in the sprawling diplomat's lot. There were a number of limos waiting but many of the more junior diplomats had driven embassy cars.

"You've missed most of the fun," one of the guards said, scanning the admission bracelet. She was past the first obstacle — the man checking invites hadn't seen her when she was here before. The party was winding down, a few arriving late, more heading out before the traffic thickened.

She nodded and shrugged and moved through the thinning crowd. Morozov and the oligarch circle were gone, presumably already headed toward the Ilyushin. Those who weren't boarding the flight — the majority of the guests — had turned out to watch, some sitting on the grass of the expansive lawns, drinking and laughing. Russian flags, American flags, flags from many other nations. That such a festivity was the sendoff for the president and his cronies would send a decided message to the West: that the Russians felt they were to be respected, to be equals, not arriving on bended knee. At least one journalist was parroting this Morozov party line directly into a camera as he broadcast from the gathering. She turned her face away as she moved past the camera.

She navigated the crowd and saw Irina Belinskaya and Danny Capra walking into the woods, and then saw two burly men following him closely. She had no idea where Sam was. The security teams that had been close to the plane moved off.

The music swelled, a medley of patriotic Russian tunes. A loudspeaker announced that the plane would soon be departing. She hurried forward a bit.

They were walking toward the house she wasn't sure who owned, smaller, set away at a distance. Only a single light gleamed in a window. She hung back.

She saw Danny Capra get close to the house, saw him turn back toward Irina and freeze. He stopped walking; Irina didn't. She said something to him. Then, the two guards rushed him and took him, hooding him, securing his hands with zip ties. He didn't fight back.

Mila melted back into the shadows in her dark dress, watching. They dragged Danny off. She wondered why he didn't fight back.

But a few moments later here came Sam, following them.

She hissed his name to him. He scanned the woods and she stepped out from behind a thick tree.

She thought for a moment he was going

to embrace her, but he simply touched her arm. "Are you all right? What are you doing here?" he said. "They'll arrest you if they see you."

He doesn't want me here, she thought. Does he know? "Most of those that know my face are, I think, on Morozov's plane. I have weapons in the trunk of a car I brought."

He watched the woods. "Why did you come back? It's way too dangerous."

"Because you need my help."

"Is Jimmy here, too? To help?"

He knows. "Sam . . ."

Sam said, "I think Danny's been made. Irina's people are taking him to that abandoned house on the edge of the compound. The road curves back toward it. Drive the car down there and wait for me."

"You can't go in alone," Mila said.

"I can and I am. I need you standing by to watch if anyone else comes and be ready to get us out. They'll search your car, though, if they know that there's trouble brewing. So I can't let Irina or these guards raise an alarm."

Mila said, "They won't search. The car has diplomatic plates."

He didn't ask for an explanation. "He's done their dirty work and now they need to make sure he doesn't talk."

"Done it . . . you mean he killed Morozov?" She looked confused.

"I'll explain later. Please go get the car and get it as close as you can to that house without being seen. Please, Mila."

She hurried through the grove, toward the road. She'd seen, in the extraction team's escape van, a map of the satellite imagery of Nebo, and she had an idea where in the nearby woods she could put the car. She skirted the Morozov mansion this time, nodding at the guards on the perimeter, asking one of them the way back to the parking lot. He politely told her and she thanked him. She got into the car and drove not toward the exit, but toward the empty house.

One of the security men on the roadway stopped her. "Stop, please; the exit is the other way."

"I know, I know," she said in her perfect Russian. "So embarrassing. A stupid friend of mine had too much to drink and went wandering and passed out over by that smaller house. I don't want to make a fuss; he just started at the embassy and our boss will be so upset. The lane is just a giant circle, yes? Can I go get him and circle back that way?" She made a circle with her finger and gave him her most pleading, harmless smile.

After a moment he nodded and waved her ahead.

Mila drove, and when she reached the farthest bend in the road she killed her headlights. She pulled into the woods closer to the empty house and popped open the trunk, considering her options. Sam needed backup. She selected a Glock 9 millimeter and a combat knife and hurried toward the house. Lights gleamed from the first floor, no sign of guards, no sign of either Capra.

62

The Empty House, Nebo
Danny felt a foot prodding him. A hood
covered his eyes and his hands were bound.
He tried to sit up. "Be still and be quiet."
Irina's voice. He lay on cold concrete. He
wriggled toward the foot.

"Be still," Irina said. So he lay still.

He remembered their conversation after
he left the plane:

*There's a problem, Philip. Would you please
come with me?*

What's the problem? Thinking: Kill her if
you have to and make a run for it.

*It involves that man you were talking to
before. Sam.*

I only just met him.

*We have a problem with him and I need your
help. Please.*

A problem with Sam. He could not walk
away. Danny felt a mortal fear take hold of
his bones.

They'd walked through the woods toward the empty house on the edge of the compound, and when he'd looked back the two men seized him, gagged and handcuffed him, and dragged him, hooded, through the woods and into a house. He didn't fight back because . . . Sam. They had Sam. Down a flight of stairs and then across concrete.

He lay on the floor and then he heard footsteps leaving, the door shutting.

Then silence.

"Hello?" he said to the quiet.

"I'm still here," Irina said.

"What's happening, Irina? I don't think the president or Stefan will appreciate my being treated this way."

"Morozov isn't going to have a lot of worries for long. Thank you for that."

He kept still. "I see."

"You've fallen under my suspicion for being an enemy of the people and the state. Not that it matters as much as being an enemy of the inner circle."

He struggled against his bonds. "Irina . . ."

"You're just going to sit and wait here for a while," she said. "We're going to let your wonderful plot with the polonium play out. I figured out your method. It's very . . . Sergei."

He bit his lip. "You think they won't connect me to you?"

She let five long seconds tick by. "I'm quite sure of it."

"You're Firebird. Not Kirov or Katya or Stefan or his father."

"Sergei called me that. His nickname for me, because of my red hair. I was his firebird."

He tried: "I didn't poison him. I didn't have the chance. You have to let me get on the plane . . ."

"I hope you're a better killer than you are a liar. I know you were on the plane. I made sure the lounge was cleared for you."

"Irina. Listen to me. I knew your husband. Sergei. I was loyal to him . . . He saved my life. I don't know why you want Morozov dead . . ."

"You killed my husband," she said.

He was silent. "I didn't."

"You tampered with the bombs. At the Morozov brothers' orders."

"You're wrong." His voice sounded oddly flat.

"Don't lie to me. I know what you are. My husband's secret weapon. The one I was never supposed to know about. The one who turned on him."

"The Morozovs never ordered me to kill

him," Danny said. That part was true.

"Then you're just unlucky."

"So what happens now? Morozov falls deathly ill to the polonium about the time he lands in America and you put my head on a stake?"

"I'll have been the one suspicious of you, who caught you," she said.

She shut the door behind her and he heard four bolts click into place.

Get out of here, Sam, now, get out of here.

63

The Presidential Ilyushin

Midnight. There was a grand procession to the plane. Morozov, Kirov, Varro. Stefan and Katya and their entourages. Journalists. People that they did business with in the UK, Spain, Canada, the United States, Switzerland, Japan. Members of the press. Members of the American diplomatic corps. Waving, the cameras rolling.

Names of those flying to Washington, DC, were checked off the lists displayed on the tablet computers held by both Belinsky Global Security personnel and the Russian federal agents charged with protecting the president on the plane, before arrival in the United States, before the Americans took responsibility for his safety.

The security man checked off the name of the last boarding passenger — an American software CEO — and then glanced at the list on his tablet computer. One more,

Philip Judge. Suddenly the Judge name was stricken from the list. Must be a last-minute cancellation, he thought.

He tapped and sent the finalized list to Irina Belinskaya, who messaged him back her thanks and told him to proceed. As the oligarchs would be protected by American security personnel while on US soil, she would not be accompanying the group on the plane.

Everyone who was supposed to be aboard was, and the guard helped the ground crew wheel the stairway away from the plane.

On the plane, Katya Kirova found a seat. Her hands were shaking and she folded them in her lap. She would call Seaforth's people once they landed. Her father sat by her for a moment. He patted her arm.

"I need you, Katya. You stay with me when we get to America. All the time."

"Yes, Papa," she lied.

In the front of the Ilyushin, the steward told an aide that the tea in the samovar was ready, as per custom for the president. The aide filled the double-eagle mug, stirred in a teaspoon of jam, and brought the hot, dark brew to Morozov. He toasted to their journey, to their success in going to the West.

They raised their cups and they drank.

Morozov took a long sip from the cup and smiled for the journalists, who snapped his picture in the toast. He waved.

Then he noticed the investment report script in his seat. Ah, the pushy, oddball American investor friend of Stefan's. Morozov liked him. This investor, leaving him something to read on the plane, thinking he had no other concerns. He admired, however, his persistence. Such people got what they wanted. He handed the report to one of his assistants and told him to put it in his briefcase.

Then he finished his tea and listened to the chatter of his staff around him.

"More tea, sir?" the cabin steward asked. The man had been trained well.

"Yes, another cup. But make sure no more alcohol is to be served. If anyone has overindulged then get them tea or coffee."

"Yes, sir." The steward took the mug to the samovar and refilled it. He added a generous dollop of jam, stirred it into the hot tea, and brought the mug back to Morozov, who took another sip. This mugful tasted better, he thought, than the first one.

He sat down and closed his eyes for just a

moment, as those around him chattered and settled in for the long flight. He could sleep in the double-eagle chair. He had already heard from the Western press that the "party plane," as they had dubbed it, suggested that the Russian delegation would arrive in DC looking much the worse for wear and at a disadvantage. He was ready to prove them wrong.

A few minutes later the Ilyushin speared the night in a thunderous rise, flying on a northern trajectory, toward the United States, winging toward its destiny.

And Morozov sipped his tea.

64

The Empty House, Nebo

The guards stood inside the entry hall of the small house. Sam could hear them, speaking softly in Russian. One he recognized as the guard he'd beaten earlier, freed and back on duty. Then the two guards went back to the kitchen.

He considered his nearly nonexistent options.

He circled the mansion, staying below the windows. He listened at each of the windows, best that he could, the noise of the crowd and the music of the farewells drifting on the wind.

He didn't hear Danny. He didn't hear anything.

But he did hear the engines of the presidential Ilyushin power up. He hoped Katya was on it, escaping to America. The takeoff would be loud, momentarily deafening as the jet soared above Nebo. It might give him a chance.

He tried the back door. It was locked. A window beckoned. He broke it, softly, using his suit jacket to shield his hand and the roar of the departing jet to mask the sound. He listened. No sound of an alarm from the house.

He shoved up the window and crawled inside, into darkness.

He was in a study. A sofa, a desk, comfortable chairs.

He moved quickly through the house. No sign of Irina or the two guards. Irina detaining Danny after his visit to the presidential plane, without turning him over to the police — it could mean only one thing.

She was Firebird.

He didn't know why but if Kirov didn't know about the money, then she was stealing it from where she knew the oligarchs had hidden it. She was robbing them to pay Danny. Hiding it on the yacht, in a secured room. She wanted Morozov dead for some reason. Why didn't matter. He just had to find Danny and get him out. Their only advantage was that if Morozov wasn't dead yet, she could hardly raise the alarm without implicating herself in the plot.

And with Mila's car maybe they could

make a run for Latvia or Finland. Seaforth had told Katya to try for Finland, and so would he. The border was over twelve hours away by car, but the police normally wouldn't stop a car with diplomatic plates. Unless ordered to.

A thought, borne of his love for his son and his parents, crept into his mind: You could leave right now. With Mila. He's made his choices. He's caught. He walked away from you. He chose to let you think he was dead. He was cruel. You owe him nothing.

The first order, remember, we don't ever leave each other behind. Whispered in Burundi. Long ago. Still true.

He moved down a hallway, into the empty kitchen. Beyond was another room, a dining space for the staff, he guessed, and he heard a muted conversation between the two guards. The kitchen was well-appointed, and he took a cooking knife off the magnetic strip that hung above the stove's granite island.

The guards were checking in with the wider network. Sitting in the chair, drinking water, was the guard he'd beaten earlier. "Echo Two, Echo Three, at small house, per orders." The guard on the right said, "All clear," and the time code and copy, signing off. They walked into the kitchen, one stripping off his headset. Sam was behind the island as one came around. Sam rose and put the knife to the man's throat as he turned.

"Freeze or I'll cut his throat," Sam said and the second man — the one Sam had beaten with the chair — froze. He looked at Sam with a burning fury. Sam pulled the first guard's gun — an MP-443 Grach pistol — from its holster and gestured the second guard to lie flat on the floor, hands behind him. The man obeyed.

The guard with the knife at his throat was older, grizzled, head shaved bald, in his fifties but thickly built. He said, "You've made a very bad decision."

"I know," Sam said, "but it's mine. On the floor." The bald man obeyed. He relieved the second guard of his holstered Grach, keeping the gun aimed at the back of the first man's head. And as he did so the second guard — younger, face contorted with anger at having been surprised — tried to grab at his legs and yelled something in Russian at the bald guard.

It was like a coordinated play from a coach. The younger guard kicked out Sam's legs, catching one. Sam fired and missed, the bullet hammering into the floor. The bald guard jumped to his feet, trying to wrap a meaty arm around Sam's throat. Sam slashed at the man's arm with the knife and the bald guard grunted but didn't cry out. These were tough men, hardened in Chechen service and Russian intelligence.

The younger guard barreled into Sam before he could shift position for better advantage. Sam's head snapped back and hit the kitchen counter. He leaned back, spinning free of both of them, fighting to stay on his feet, raising the Grach to fire again. The younger guard sent a hammering blow into Sam's temple.

He fell, and the bald guard stood on his hands, forcing first the knife and then the Grach from his grip, and then the younger guard started hitting him. Four hard blows.

At some point the man stopped. Sam heard them arguing over whether or not to kill him. Irina's name was mentioned. Then the men dragged Sam down the basement stairs.

65

The Empty House, Nebo

Sam opened his eyes to grogginess and pain, feeling the touch of fingers on the pulse in his throat. His brother lay next to him, staring into his face.

"Are you all right?" Danny asked.

Sam stared at him. "Yes." He struggled to sit up. He was bound with zip ties. He could see Danny was bound as well. His face hurt and he was bleeding from his nose and his ear.

"Not long now," Irina said. Sam blinked. They were on a concrete floor.

He tried to sit up; he couldn't. "What . . . what have you done?" Sam said.

"Are you asking him or me?" Irina said. She knelt by Danny. "Thanks for doing your job so well."

Danny closed his eyes.

She glanced at her watch. "We just need to wait a few hours."

"*You're* Firebird. Not one of the oligarchs," Sam said.

"Shut up," Danny told him.

Irina said nothing. She ran a fingertip along Sam's jaw. "Little fool." Then she slapped Danny. "Murderer."

"Are you going to kill us?" Sam asked.

The most important question garnered a response from her. "It's important, for history, for justice, for the people of Russia, that you be captured trying to escape the country. So in a bit, we'll go for a long ride. Security forces will catch up with you just before you cross the Latvian border."

"Captured and killed," Sam said.

Irina shrugged.

"You're framing us."

"You can hardly call it a frame when Philip here actually has poisoned Morozov."

Sam looked at him. She didn't call him Danny. She didn't know they were brothers. "With what?" Sam asked.

"Polonium-210. It was in an eyedrops bottle. I put a drop in a tea mug only he uses."

She held up an eyedrops bottle she'd pulled from Danny's jacket. "We'll put this back in your jacket once you're dead."

Danny was silent. So was Sam.

Irina crossed her legs and picked a bit of

dust off one of the heels. "Look at our guilty parties. Our two noble players on the stage. A man the world presumed dead, and a CIA operative who attempted to kidnap a Russian heiress whose father was collecting cash to pay the assassin. You're the icing on the cake, Sam. The Americans will look very, very guilty. Killing poor Morozov just as he came to make peace with the West."

"Maybe Morozov ordered Sergei dead, but I didn't do it," Danny said.

"I heard a rumor, more than once, that he had a man he'd found in Afghanistan, trained, made into his weapon. When I asked him about you he denied it. But others told me you existed. And then Sergei was dead. And you were the only person he trusted. The only one who could have gotten close enough to kill him. It took a long time to find you."

Danny said, "This is personal. I mean . . ." He said it almost in shock.

"This isn't an assassination," Sam said. "This is a small-town murder, just on a big stage. *You* want him dead. Not for politics. For simple revenge." He wriggled in his bonds, trying to sit up, his mind clearing while his body ached from the punches he'd taken.

Irina said nothing.

Sam said, "Sergei ran the heroin smuggling out of Afghanistan. He was the Big Man. But why is an FSB agent running heroin? Why? It's because he was doing these side jobs for the Morozovs: arranging murders of enemies, buying off officials; the heroin money funded all these dirty jobs." He twisted to look at Danny. "Am I wrong?"

Danny stared at him, then closed his eyes.

"There was a letter in Anton Varro's pocket in that village. He wrote it to you, Irina. Who else would have had influence over Sergei in his dealings with the Morozovs? Trying to warn you about what Sergei had done, asking you to reason with him. That he planned to kill a CIA agent." He realized now the brothers referred to in the letter weren't the Brothers of the Mountain; they were the brothers Morozov, who could not have kept a man close to them who'd killed a CIA operative. It was too politically dangerous if the truth came out.

She looked confused. *Of course.* She'd never seen the letter. It had never been sent.

"Sergei killed a CIA agent?" she asked.

"Yes," Danny said. "And I have photographs to prove it was him. If you don't let us go, they'll be published."

Sam wondered if that was a bluff.

But Irina laughed. "Thank you. So kind

of you. When it comes out that Morozov's right-hand man" — she choked a bit as she called Sergei this — "killed a CIA agent," she said, "and that the CIA was trying to turn Katya, and sent an agent after her . . . no one will look at me. And Morozov will have paid for what he did to Sergei. He'll be dead and his memory ruined."

She glanced at him but knelt down by Danny. "I'm tired of confessing. Although it is a relief. I'm more interested in your confession."

"I have nothing to say."

Irina stood. "I have to go deal with the guards and the remaining guests. Presumably there will be news soon from the plane, bad news. Thank you for that." She turned and left.

Silence.

"I'm sorry," Danny said. "I'm so sorry."

Irina went upstairs, talked to the two guards, and gave instructions. She put the eyedrops in her pocket, although carrying them made her nervous. Then she walked out of the house, took a steadying deep breath on the steps, and headed toward the presidential mansion.

From the shadows, Mila moved forward.

66

The Empty House, Nebo
The cellar door opened. Mila.

"Mila," Sam said. "Irina and her men are upstairs."

"The men are not a problem. They let their guard down once you arrived."

"Hello again," Danny said.

Mila cut Sam's bonds with a knife that already had blood on it. She made no move to cut Danny's.

"Give me the knife," Sam said.

"He's not just your brother," Mila said. "He's a paid assassin."

"It doesn't look like I'm getting paid," Danny said. "Does that make a difference?"

"Shut up," Mila said. "I do not want to hear a word from you."

"Please give me the knife," Sam said.

Mila's voice was ice. "Listen to me. We are surrounded by Russian security. I'm guessing most of the guards aren't in on this little capture because they'd all be here, taking in the scene. For Irina the fewer who know, the better, until Morozov can't be saved and she blows the whistle. We're going to put him in the trunk, still tied up," Mila said. "And drive out."

"If we have to fight our way out we need him," Sam said.

"If we have to fight our way out we're already dead," Mila said. "I told a guard on the road I was driving down here to retrieve a drunk friend. Act drunk. Your face looks like crap, by the way; we need to clean you up."

Danny lay in the darkness of the trunk. They perhaps had only minutes before the dead guards were discovered. But they had been off on their own, doing work for Irina that needed to be concealed from the rest of the force. If her own security teams knew that Irina was behind the slow-motion murder of Morozov, they would turn on her.

His only comfort was that there were weapons here in the trunk with him. Mila and Sam were riding in the front. He heard Mila say, "I found my drunk friend, taking him back to Moscow" in her impressive Russian, and the guard telling her good night and to drive carefully.

As long as Sam gets out. He did not want to die. But he did not want Sam to die, and Mila could absolutely not be trusted. His concern as the car accelerated onto the road was how upset Sam was going to be if he had to kill her.

67

En Route To Moscow

"We have to ditch this car," Sam said.

"It's too valuable; it has diplomatic plates. No one can stop us."

"We are at least twelve hours away from the border. Irina will find the dead men long before that. And as soon as that guard who tried to keep you from driving away reports you as having headed toward the empty house, they'll know to look for this car. Diplomatic license plates aren't going to save us. Let's not head for Latvia. That was where they were going to stage our capture, nice and far from the oligarchs' circle, escaping the country. Head for the Finnish border."

She drove toward Moscow. Traffic, late, was thin and the sky was clouded.

She tuned the car radio to a news-and-talk station in Moscow, and it was full of reports from the reception and the departure. All good news so far.

This, she thought, was a terrible silence.

Sam said, "He knew about you. And Jimmy."

"Jimmy took money from your brother to give you false information for your search, so you'd never find Danny. I'm so sorry. I had no idea."

"And when did you learn this?"

She glanced at him, quickly. "In New York City."

"Why didn't you tell me?"

"I couldn't."

"Where is Jimmy?"

"I don't know."

"Mila."

"I honestly do not know where he is — somewhere in England, hiding, and I don't care to know. He and I are over."

"I'm sorry," Sam said. "Please pull over and let my brother out of the trunk."

"This is not the place for a family reunion."

"Please do as I ask."

"Sam. He just killed the Russian president . . ."

"No. He didn't," Sam said.

"What?"

"He was going to poison him. It was the only logical weapon I found in his room.

Eyedrops. I replaced them."

"How . . ."

"Each room had its own stocked medicine cabinet, you know, like a stocked fridge in a hotel. Eyedrops, toothpaste, deodorant, aspirin, all the basics."

Mila nodded; her room had been the same way.

Sam said, "So I took out the eyedrops bottle in his toiletries, which was double-bagged, and replaced it with the one from next door. I emptied the replacement eyedrops and filled it with tap water and put it where the poison had been. Danny came back to his room and I watched him leave to go to the plane. I checked his room again. The eyedrops from his bag were gone. That was his weapon. So technically, not knowing the dosage Danny used, he's probably expecting Morozov to expire in flight or shortly after landing. On American soil." Technically, he thought, satisfying the requirements of the contract. "But Morozov just got a little extra tap water and saline residue in his drink."

"Sam. Thank God you had the presence of mind . . . so where's the actual poison?"

"In my pocket. I've not opened it because I suspected it's something like polonium-210. Highly radioactive but contained by plastic or paper, he had to get it past the security here — you just can't let it get in your body. It takes a long while to act — for him to get to America — and it makes you very sick. Very hard to get. It takes a government to produce it because you need a reactor." He smiled. "It's been a Russian weapon in the past, so its use might well point back to Russia. Danny might have chosen it as a precaution to point guilt back here, regardless of where Morozov died."

She let out a sigh. "But still, how could he have gotten access . . ."

"Irina might have cleared the cabin for a pep talk to the security team or the crew. She would have made it easier for him. That's what she's been doing all along. She wants revenge on both Morozov and Danny and this is how she gets it."

"So you saved Morozov," she said in a flat voice.

"I saved us from an international incident that could have led to war."

"You saved your brother."

"No. Irina's teams — the top private security in the world — will be hunting us. They probably already are. We have to ditch this car."

"Do you know why I don't want to ditch the car?"

"Why?"

"Because that will involve letting your brother out of the trunk."

"He's in the trunk with weapons. I saw them. That should make you uneasier."

"What are you going to do, Sam? Announce to the world that his death was faked and he's been in hiding the past six years, doing the dirty work of the Russians and then being a freelance killer? He'll go to jail for the rest of his life."

"He could vanish. Into a new life. Daniel and I will vanish with him." He stared out into the night.

"Is that fair to Daniel? To Leonie? What about your parents? Shall they vanish, too? Trust me, that is far harder said than done with older relatives." Her voice nearly broke.

"What do you want me to do?" Sam asked.

"I want you to stay who you are. I don't want you to vanish."

He let five seconds tick by. "Your husband is buying out the bars. Your help and his help on finding Danny was the price. He said I have to get out of your life. His life. He wants me gone from the Round Table. Now."

"I'm going to offer you and your brother a new deal," Mila said.

575

Then they began to hear a thump from the trunk. Danny, wanting out.

68

Nebo, Russia

The last of the diplomats had left the estates. They were the unimportant ones. A crew had begun to sweep through the compound, cleaning up the reception house and the grounds.

Irina Belinskaya was waiting in her office for a phone call. But she wouldn't have to wait for long, she supposed. No telling how much of the polonium was in the dose that Danny gave to him. It might take hours. Alexander Litvinenko, assassinated in London, had not fallen sick until the next day. She hoped Morozov would sicken quickly.

She scanned the cameras that monitored the periphery of the compound. The party had gone well. There had been no incident. Except of course for the odd behavior of the American Philip Judge, which had resulted in arousing her suspicions, as the press would be told later. She had already sent texts to her two subcommanders. Philip Judge acted oddly at the party and did not board the flight, which was a considerable honor.

Shortly after the panicked call would come from Morozov's security, then the search would begin for the American who had not boarded the plane. She would have to wait for her security team to take them to the M9 highway that led to Latvia and a team near the border would be alerted to intercept them and kill the hired gun and the CIA man.

She checked her phone and listened to the radio chatter on the private network. A drunk young man, a relative of an ambassador, had been put up in a guest room at the Varro house. Another diplomat had had car trouble, but it had been fixed and he'd been sent on his way. All calm.

But nothing from the two guards at the house. They had been very well paid, one Sergei's nephew, the other an old trusted friend. When she had told them she was sure Morozov ordered Sergei's death they had sworn to help her avenge him. However long it took.

She'd given the older guard a burner phone. She called it. No answer.

She headed out of her office. "I'm going

to walk about," she told the assistant on duty. "Let me know if we get any calls from the plane."

"I'm sure they're all sleeping off the champagne and vodka." The assistant laughed.

Irina forced herself to smile. She got in her car and drove down to the small house. It had all been in the timing. Once she discovered the CIA had seduced Katya, it was the time to strike. She could steal the money from Kirov for the assassin's payoff, and he could not complain because she could expose his daughter as a traitor. She needed a scapegoat, and when she got one she moved forward. The cash from Kirov would be moved off his yacht to a new hiding place, where she could replenish the five million she'd paid from Belinsky Global accounts to initially hire Philip Judge. It had taken a while to find him, too, and the woman who served as his handler. But she had been patient.

She walked into the house, feeling very good about the evening.

The bodies of the guards lay sprawled on the kitchen floor. Downed with one shot each to the head. Not execution style, taken by surprise. She frowned. She drew her GSh-18 from her shoulder holster. She had miscalculated. They had reported all was well.

Her phone vibrated — it had been modified to have an entirely silent mode — and she nearly leaped out of her skin. She continued her sweep. She went through the house. No sign of the assassin or the CIA agent.

She fought down panic. She could raise the alarm. But if she contacted the police, the two men might be taken alive. Live men could tell their tales. That she could not risk. She called in and asked the security at each house to check the few overnight guests that were staying. Was anyone missing from their room?

She chimed into the network. "Did anyone clear anyone for driving down to the small house?" she asked.

She waited for the response; it came quickly. Her assistant came on the line. "One of the street guards said a woman asked to drive down there to retrieve a drunk friend. She was in a car with British diplomatic plates. We found her on the entrance security tape."

"Description?"

Except for brown hair, the woman fit Mila Cebotari's description. She came back. Amazing, Irina thought.

The assistant continued: "She came in using credentials given to Alice Devere, an embassy attaché. She left with a man who did appear to be drunk, in the passenger seat."

"Just one man?" Irina asked.

"Yes."

"Check the surveillance system. I want to know when Alice Devere's car was checked out of the lot."

Diplomatic plates. My God, the woman — maybe she was British intelligence, and she had been here, and she was taking Irina's pawns out of the country. *No.*

"We need to find that car. I want a feed on every traffic camera between here and Moscow." Such feeds were only available to the FSB, but she had her own hackers who had found their ways into every government database in Russia.

"Find them now." She had been far too careful; this could not go wrong now. She would not let it.

69

Toward Moscow

They had pulled off the main M7 road, down a side road, into darkness.

Sam opened the trunk. Danny climbed out. "We need a new car. The police will be looking for one with diplomatic plates."

"I wonder if Irina will call the police," Sam said. "She won't want us talking to the police."

"I took this car from an extraction team," Mila said. "They wanted me out of the country."

"Is that your new deal? You extract us?"

"No," she said. "You and me. He's on his own."

"I'm not leaving him," Sam said.

"You should go with her," Danny said. "If she can get you out . . ."

"You don't seem to understand what I have been through to find you," Sam said. "I said no."

"Mila," Danny said, "I know you have no love for me. But you care about Sam. Please take him. Sam, go with her."

"No."

"Sam, our pictures will be on the television in hours, if not minutes."

"It's the night. No one's looking for us. And they don't even know that we're three people. They'll look for two men," Sam said.

"If guards remember me, they'll know we're three," Mila said.

"We should split up then," Danny said. "Mila one way, us the other."

"I don't know if that's a good idea," Mila said.

"That's true. Sam, look, take this weapon." Danny leaned down into the trunk and picked up the Taser and before Sam could stop him he fired it into Mila. She jittered to the ground.

Sam tried to seize the weapon. "Stop it! Stop it!"

Danny grabbed him and shoved him against the car. "She's with British intelligence. I recognized one of the guys in that extraction team that tried to grab both her and me. He's MI-6, used to be in Berlin. That is who grabbed her. Not her husband. The Brits. That's who she's going to hand us over to. She doesn't come with us, Sam."

"Let go of me."

Danny said, his face close to his brother's, "Say you will listen to me."

Sam nodded and Danny released him.

Sam knelt by her and pulled the Taser needles out. "Mila, are you all right?" He held her hand while the effects subsided. When she could form words she gestured at him to lean close and he did.

"Shoot him," she whispered, barely managing the words. "Shoot him in the leg and let . . . let the team take us out of here."

"Why are you working for the British?"

"They spotted Jimmy talking with Danny in Copenhagen right before all this started and they knew Danny paid Jimmy. They want Danny as a client, to figure out what Jimmy did." The words came out in a spill.

"What does Jimmy do, exactly? The Round Table?"

"There are six or seven of them. Jimmy was one. High-ranking officers in intel networks — British, US, German, Japanese. They help each other, without official sanction, when one needs something done. And they make deals under the table with each other. To share information, to do jobs for hire under the cover of their regular work and split the money."

"Oh, hell." If you needed something

stolen, who better than a professional spy? "Did you know this?"

"Only recently."

"So what happens when you give my brother to the British?"

"They leave my aunt and uncle alone. What they do to Jimmy — I don't know. I'm not sure I care. They would question Danny about the past six years, I'm sure. If he killed anyone in London . . ."

"Let's go," Danny said.

Sam stood up. "I won't leave her here."

"She," Danny said, "can call her British friends, who will be happy to get her out of the country and to safety."

"You're not half the man your brother is." She bit her lip and wouldn't look at him, only at Sam. "Don't do this."

Danny said, "Give her a phone, and let's go. They'll pick her up."

"Maybe they won't," Sam said. "She turned against them."

Danny shook his head. "They won't want her falling into the hands of the Russians. That would be worse."

"Sam," Mila said, "I may not see you again."

"C'mon, Sam." Danny pulled at his brother.

"Sam. Give your son my love," Mila said.

"Tell him I love him."

Sam's chest hurt. He had thought he was ready to pay any price to find Danny and now . . . "Mila, please."

"I'm not coming with you and you won't come with me. Done, finished, Sam. I did what I had to do. You do, too. That's who we are. It's who we'll always be." Her voice hardened.

"Call your people now and let me know that they're coming for you," Sam said.

She called Charity's number and gave her position. The backup extraction team said they would be there within an hour. She turned off the phone and shrugged. "Café back at the highway. So I'll go inside and have a coffee and if my face appears on the TV screen I'll wait outside. Goodbye, Sam." She turned.

"Mila . . . ," Sam said, and it was as though his world had collapsed into one word.

She stopped, but didn't turn to face him. "I was going to screw you and Danny over to save Jimmy. We played the game, you won. Have a good life."

And she walked toward the crossroad for the café, looking in her evening gown not like an undercover agent but a woman who'd spent too long at a party.

Sam watched her go and a core deep

inside him, past bone and heart, broke.

"Sam. I'm sorry. But get in the car. Now," Danny said.

They drove into Moscow in a painful silence and abandoned the car near Moscow State University. They took the subway to a parking garage not far from Red Square. Parked in a back corner in the garage's top level was an older-model black Mercedes, with the key under the bumper. Inside Danny had a new passport, cash, and two guns. "Do you have another passport?"

"Yes. At the Tsar Lounge, but I don't know if it's been compromised or not."

"We'll try it."

He drove over to Tverskaya. The Tsar Lounge was closed; it was now the middle of the night, but one light shone upstairs. And a man Sam didn't recognize stood near the front door.

"The Scot I recognized," Danny said. "She could have warned us. She didn't."

"Keep driving," Sam said tonelessly. Mila had exposed the bar as a safe house to her British masters. There was no point in stopping. "They'll probably learn about all my bars. That part of my life is over, too." Mila. The bars. What else was he going to lose tonight?

"Then we'll just have to figure another

way to get you across the border."

"You won't leave me," Sam said. In the tone of that child he'd once been in Burundi.

"No, Sam, I won't leave you. You didn't leave me just now. That's the first order of being brothers, still." He tried to smile but it didn't quite work.

"Stop with that first-order garbage," Sam said. "You left us for six years."

Danny had no answer to that. They headed out of Moscow, onto the M10, heading northwest toward Finland. Fourteen hours of driving lay ahead. It was easy to forget the vastness of Russia until you had to travel it.

"Well we always wanted to take a road trip together," Sam said.

Danny laughed, an odd, broken sound. "Not this way."

"You had an escape route out already."

"Of course."

"Did you have that in Afghanistan?"

Danny didn't answer.

"Why?" The one word that lay between them like a mountain.

"I wanted to be me."

"Be you."

"I could do what I was best at."

"Killing people. I read your account of

saving me in Burundi."

"I don't just kill people. I eliminate problems. Did I go after those men in Burundi? For sport? No. They hurt you. They took you. The rules were off."

"Danny —"

"I know you don't understand how I think. Fine. But I wanted to be good at it. Sergei was the best."

"You told Irina you didn't kill him. But you did."

Danny glanced at him.

"I still know when you're lying."

"He was blowing up apartment buildings full of sleeping people for Morozov, to justify crushing a breakaway republic. Kids, old folks, families. So, I found my line I wouldn't cross. Sergei was moving a bomb to be planted in Moscow. I fiddled with the wiring. Problem solved."

"Irina thought Morozov ordered him dead."

"I don't think Morozov wept much, but . . . the decision was mine."

"We have to think about how to get out of here," Sam said. "I don't think I can risk my passport. The border, where there aren't guards, is electronically monitored on both sides. And another problem." He paused. "You didn't kill Morozov. I switched the eyedropper bottle. I have the one with the polonium. It's in my pocket. The one Irina took off you is . . . eyedrops."

Danny said nothing for several long seconds. Sam expected him to explode in fury. Instead he said, quietly: "Sam, for God's sake . . . we need to get rid of it."

"I'm not dumping it where an innocent person could find it and poison themselves."

"Thanks for spoiling my job. I thought I'd been rather elegant about it."

"Except for being set up and played," Sam said, "you were."

"Even with Morozov alive, Irina has an excuse to hunt for us. Her men are dead."

Sam said, "I assume you had a plan to get out."

"When we get past St. Petersburg, I know where we might get a way out of Russia. Into Finland. You said you wanted to go there."

"What's this way out?"

"I'll show you."

"There's a man I could call. CIA. Bob Seaforth. He's helped me, under the table, in the search for you. I know how to reach his people." He wondered how his brother would react to the name.

"No. No CIA." Danny shook his head. His tone was insistent.

"They can protect us."

"I shot Seaforth. In Nassau."

Sam jerked to look at him. "Why?"

"I recognized him from when you worked for them. I thought he was tailing me. Maybe he saw my face, maybe not. But no CIA for me." He glanced at Sam. "I witnessed the murder of a CIA operative and never came forward. Aside from shooting Seaforth, I won't be their favorite person."

"Oh, Danny. I don't know if he's alive or dead."

"I have a photograph of Sergei, from the video. He forgot to keep his mask on when he was practicing his lines; he didn't realize the camera was filming. You can tell that it's the same man who kills Zalmay. That video could be worth something to the CIA. Leverage over Morozov. I lied to Irina, though. No one's standing by to publish it if I don't make it out of this mess."

"Where is it? We can use it to make a deal."

It took him thirty seconds to decide to answer. "If I don't make it, it's at a home owned by a guy named Robert Clayton in Miami," Danny said. "But I will get you out of here. You and me, we don't need anyone else."

"Thinking that way has gotten us into this

mess," Sam said. "I can call someone. I can get us out."

"No. We're doing this my way."

"Why? Because you're the oldest? You walked away from being my brother. I just . . ." Sam had no words. He thought seeing Danny would fix everything, make his life whole. But the fracture ran too deep. Fix the fracture when they weren't being hunted. He stared out at the night. "Let's get clear of Russia. We have hours to go. Let's not lose our focus."

"Focus, yes," Danny said. "That's what we're good at. Taking care of each other. Getting out of trouble."

"We, together, are not good at anything, Danny."

Danny said nothing for several minutes and Sam had resigned himself to a night of silence. Then his brother said quietly, "It's a long drive. I want . . . I want you to tell me all about your son. And that pretty ex-forger that lives with you." He paused for a moment. "And Mom and Dad. Tell me about Mom and Dad."

70

St. Petersburg, Russia

Nine hours later, the Mercedes pulled up in front of a modest apartment building on the southern outskirts of the city. Danny went to a seventh-floor apartment. The rent and taxes on it had been paid regularly for many years, from an account in a bank in St. Petersburg.

It was morning and Danny used the tire iron from the car's trunk to pry open the lock. He stepped inside and saw a small alarm pad asking for a code. He entered the code Sergei had given him for his safe houses . . . and it still worked. It hadn't been erased. Relief swept over him.

The lockbox was in the closet. He pried it open with the tire iron. The keys, two of them, on a hoop, were inside. He scooped them up. There was cash there as well, and two Makarov pistols, and two passports, one with Sergei's face and one with Irina's, both

Finnish, along with a set of entry and exit stamps for Finland and the Baltic states. He didn't bother to reset the alarm. He closed the door.

In the Mercedes, Sam waited. He made the impossible choice. He watched his brother go into the apartment tower and he pulled out his phone. He called the number Seaforth had given him as they spoke in Avril Claybourne's gallery, her lying dead on the floor.

"Yes?" Seaforth's voice.

"You're alive. Thank God."

"How did you know . . ."

"I'm in trouble."

"Where are you?"

"St. Petersburg. I have no way out of Russia. I can't use my passport. We are headed for the Finnish border."

"We."

"My brother is with me. We are being pursued by private security, but it could go public at any time. Frame-up. My brother is using a safe house once used by Sergei Belinsky; he says he has a way out but he won't tell me. He forbade me to call for help."

"I'm nearly to Helsinki," Seaforth said. "I came here looking for you. We knew they took you off their yacht. I can get to the border . . ."

"Irina Belinskaya is after us, with all her security force. We have info that could bring down Morozov. We're only maybe two or three hours from the border. Can you track me on this phone? I want a deal for my brother. Protection for him in exchange for cooperation."

"I agree. Yes. Leave it on . . . and I'll . . ."

"He's coming," Sam said, and he slipped the phone into his jacket pocket.

The Mercedes wheeled out and headed north.

71

Irina was airborne, in a Zvezda Oil jet. A call to Yuri Kirov aboard the presidential Ilyushin jet ensured that she had full access to all his air fleet. She had simply told him that he would give her all logistical assistance, and he agreed. Yuri made no mention that Morozov had fallen ill. Patience, she thought. You've waited long enough.

Thanks to the Belinsky Global hackers, who had infiltrated the extensive street camera network in Moscow, Irina knew the British diplomatic car had been abandoned near Moscow State University. Then subway cameras showed the two men traveling toward Red Square, entering a parking garage on foot. A few minutes later a Mercedes and a BMW left. Both were being traced. There was no sign of Mila.

Fifteen minutes later, she knew the BMW was a legitimate car. So it was the Mercedes. Philip Judge was very good, she thought. Prepared. Like Sergei had taught him. Your greatest creation, Sergei, she thought, and I'm going to destroy him.

Then they made a mistake. The old apartment in St. Petersburg. She'd kept it because you never knew when a place to hide or a place to run would be useful when you were contemplating, for years, an assassination. She had not been there in two years. But when the entry code was entered, she got an alerting text.

She hadn't known Sergei had told Judge so much. It irritated her. It told her they were in St. Petersburg now. Two hours or so from the Finnish border. Or perhaps they would try for Estonia.

But why would they stop? If Philip Judge had the foresight to have a Mercedes, he would have stored cash, documentation, and more in it. The stop was needless. Unless . . .

The keys. He knew about the keys. The amount Sergei had shared with this man staggered her, as if it was an intrusion on her marriage.

She called an operative in the Belinsky Global St. Petersburg office and told him the address, and what to look for. But she knew the keys would be gone, and she knew exactly where they were going.

She told the pilot to head north. She told him to arrange a car and a Zvezda helicopter for her upon landing at a private airstrip near Vyborg, close to the Finnish border. Then she got on her phone and started calling in every favor. Irina knew every forger, every money launderer, every fence who could be a help. Sergei had given Philip Judge all his contacts, all his knowledge; had given everything to his weapon. Those would be the people Judge would turn to.

Her message was the same: *I need these men found. If you see him, hear from him, I need to know. He must be found. Whatever he pays, I will triple it.* Nothing bought loyalty like money. It had been true even in the old Soviet days.

I need these men found.

72

Finland

Like Irina Belinskaya, Bob Seaforth had gone begging. He was riding toward the border not in a CIA chopper but in a borrowed helicopter from a Finnish phone mogul eager for American government contracts. Bob Seaforth told Julian, "I want to break into the Belinsky Global communications network."

"We don't have a way in."

"Find a way. Hit them with a worm, find a vulnerability. I want to know what that woman is saying, who she's talking to."

"I'll do my best."

"Put Prakash on."

"Here, Bob."

"You are tracking Sam's phone?"

"Yes, sir. He's on the A127. But his battery is dangerously low and we could lose him at any time. We picked up intel that the Russian border stations are watching for a black Mercedes. There was an anonymous tip. Highest priority."

"Tell Julian to get me on Belinskaya's phone. Now."

73

The Border Zone, Russia

The border zone stretched five kilometers into Russia. The border itself with Finland — eight hundred miles of it — was maintained by electronic surveillance and guarded crossings. Landmines had been laid during the Cold War, according to rumor, despite Finland's carefully managed neutrality. Finland was a European Union country, but not a NATO country. Here there was a carefully controlled peace, almost a politeness.

But the Russian Air Force had made four incursions into Finnish airspace in the past three months, so the studied peace was at risk. Tensions were higher.

Near Vyborg, at a former Soviet airfield turned into a private airport for the use of the Russian elite, Irina Belinskaya stood by her jet and waited. At the end of the runway a helicopter landed. It was a small Zvezda

Oil chopper, owned by Yuri Kirov.

She had armed herself with an assault rifle, two pistols, and two of her top men who had flown up with her from Moscow.

The pilot waved her toward the small chopper. She boarded and told him to head for the border. The Border Service was a division of the FSB, and the agent in charge of this stretch had been told to give full co-operation and not ask questions. There was a promise of an excellent job for his soon-to-graduate-university son at a Kirov company. He was glad to comply. He told his team to ignore any electronic signals or triggers activated by Irina and her team. It was a matter of national security, and he considered himself a good Russian.

"Where exactly are we headed?" one of her men asked.

"I'm going to tell you a secret," Irina said. "There is a short tunnel that goes under the Finnish border. Built by our clients, years ago, in case they needed a secret way out of the country, into a neutral state, without making a border crossing. The tunnel goes from a weather station owned by a subsidiary of Zvezda, the oil company owned by Yuri Kirov. It then reaches to a house in the Finnish border zone owned by a Finnish subsidiary of a Russian bank, owned by

Boris Varro."

The man whistled. "And you know they're coming here how?"

"They stole a pair of the keys that open the tunnel doors. Let's find a position. I want them taken alive if possible. I need to know what they've been doing the past fourteen hours."

She needed to plant the polonium on Danny and Sam once they were dead. And her men could not know about it.

Bob Seaforth listened to Irina's words. Julian — devious and brilliant — had managed to access and activate the microphone in Irina's phone. He heard what she said to the operative and he ordered Romy and Prakash to find every house owned by a Finnish subsidiary of Varro's bank that was close to the border.

Ten minutes later Romy called him back. "There are three of them. First is ten kilometers away from the second one, then the third one is a further four kilometers."

He couldn't be in three places at once. He had to choose one. If he picked wrong this could be a disaster. The pain from his bullet wound felt like a building tsunami. He hadn't slept, hadn't eaten, and now he was playing a game of Russian roulette with Sam

Capra's life. "Give me the coordinates for the one closest to the border. Even if it's just five feet closer. Give me that one."

He was alone, and Irina Belinskaya wouldn't be. And he could not allow two brothers, one with CIA ties, to be captured in Russia for murder. Not today. Not ever. He loaded a full clip into his gun. He had to have enough to deal not only with Belinskaya but the Capras. Danny Capra was dangerous, and Sam might be if his brother was threatened.

Sometimes the best way to end a problem was to clean it entirely.

In Washington, the Russian president's plane had arrived, to flags and music. Morozov came down the stairs, stern-faced, until he touched American soil and then he broke into a wide, warm grin and waved for the cameras. He felt great. It was going to be a wonderful day.

74

The Border Zone, Russia

Sam and Danny pulled off onto a side road close to the border zone itself. Signs warned them against trespassing and that the zone was patrolled and that crossings were allowed only at official stations. But one sign was marked PRIVATE ROAD ZVEZDA ENERGY WEATHER STATION NO TRESPASSING.

"Kirov's company," Sam said.

Danny held up the keys. "A tunnel."

"A tunnel."

"Sergei and I used it once before, when he needed to get me out of the country after a job for him. They built themselves a bolt-hole, in case there's another Russian revolution and they need to get out. It comes up just across the other side of the border."

"Irina knows about it then." Sam glanced into the woods.

"Irina doesn't know we're here."

"Don't underestimate her," Sam said. "She's here. Or she'll have sent someone here."

Danny considered. "Then this is what we'll do."

They argued, but Danny was at the wheel and a few moments later, he barreled down the road as soon as he heard the whine of the helicopter.

"There! There!" Irina yelled at the pilot. Their helicopter was a Russian model based on the American MH-6 Little Bird, designed for special operations work. Capable of carrying four, not armed with fixed weapons, fast and maneuverable, a standard of private military contractors. Seated behind her and the pilot were the two Belinsky Global operatives, now armed with AS Val assault rifles.

Irina felt a thrill of victory. Judge and Sam had made the mistakes she needed them to make. Now on a private road, away from public view, she could deal with them and write the history of the past few days as she saw fit. And she would survive.

They opened careful fire, the back of the Mercedes windshield shattering, bullet marks pocking the trunk. The Mercedes fishtailed, spun, accelerated but stayed on the road. Both sides of the road were covered in thick pine forests, with only infrequent gaps.

"That is not a border patrol chopper; that is Irina," Danny said. "Open your door a crack and be ready to run. We're abandoning the car. They can't see us in the forest."

"They can reach the weather station before we do."

"We risk it." He shoved the keys for the hidden tunnel into Sam's hands. "Hold these for me. Go across if I don't make it."

"I'm not leaving . . ."

"Shut up."

Sam cracked the door open. Danny did the same.

"On your mark . . ."

Danny sluiced the car under the cover of the pines. Sam opened his door wider and Danny shoved him hard. "Run for it! Get to the station!" And he shoved Sam out the passenger side, Sam tumbling in the dirt.

And then the Mercedes roared back out onto the road, a target, U-turning and heading back the way they'd come.

Leading the chopper away.

"Danny! No!" Sam yelled. Tricked, he thought; he tricked me.

Through the pines he could see the agile

little helicopter make its sharp turn, following the damaged Mercedes.

Sam had a knife in a leg holster he'd taken from the trunk before, a Makarov pistol, and . . . the polonium, in the eyedrops bottle. Still in his pocket.

Think.

"Don't let him get back on the main road!" Irina ordered. The helicopter chased the Mercedes, hunting a gap in the forest cover.

"There! Drop!" The chopper dipped down, dropping behind the car, opening fire on its tires. They shredded and the Mercedes spun out, stopping sideways on the road.

Danny scrambled out the opposite side, opening fire with a VKS Vykhlop large-caliber silenced sniper rifle, firing 54-millimeter special subsonic ammunition. The bullets were STs-130VPS armor-piercing rounds.

The chopper dropped to the road so the two operatives could chase Danny on foot.

Danny aimed the Vykhlop at the copter's rotors. The little special-ops choppers were agile but vulnerable.

The two security operatives jumped from the helicopter, advancing on the car, making careful shots, keeping him covered. The chopper rose and roared over him, nearly sideways, and Danny made the shots of his life, two bullets hitting the rotor assembly, shredding through the metal, and the chopper spun.

Irina saw Danny's face in a blur as the chopper shot past and she screamed in fury.

He fired again at the back rotor, destroying it. And then the rifle jammed. In rage, he threw it aside and drew a pistol from a holster on his hip.

The pilot brought it down into the pines in a controlled spiral, Irina bracing herself for impact. Then they were down, jarringly hard, but level. Irina jumped from the chopper moments after it hit the ground, drawing her pistol, running toward the side of the car where Danny was pinned. She took cover behind a thick tree trunk.

"Lay your weapon down and surrender, or you die."

He was caught between her and the two security operatives. He stared at her for a long moment and then, taking his time, he threw out his pistol, which clattered in the dirt.

"Hands up!" she ordered. He obeyed.

She looked in the Mercedes. Sam wasn't in the sedan. "Where is Sam?"

"He slowed me down," Danny said. "I killed him."

"I don't believe you," Irina said. "Get him up. Bind his hands."

She sent the two operatives into the woods, searching for Sam. The pilot's leg was slightly injured and he wanted to radio for help, but she said no. He limped along beside her, Danny in front of them, hands zip-tied, bleeding from a cut from the shattered glass of the car.

The two operatives vanished into the woods, armed with assault rifles.

"I think Sam got out of that car," Irina said.

"He wouldn't have had time."

"You didn't know we would be here."

"I had my suspicions."

"I don't think Sam would leave you. He's shockingly softhearted."

"Don't think that when he puts a bullet in you, Irina. Which he will." He thought, My only hope is to get her to walk into whatever trap Sam is laying for her.

"Where is he?"

"I guess you need us both dead so you can accuse us both of making an attempt on the president's life?"

She glanced at the pilot, who showed no reaction to Danny's statement. "You are a remarkable liar," she said. "Accusing me when I am the one capturing you." She was still miked up to her team. "Report."

Both replied there was no sign of Sam.

"He must've run for the weather station. Really no reason for you to come all this way and then veer away from it, to engage us. You were buying him time."

"He's not with me. If he was I would have gotten him closer to the tunnel and then made my stand," Danny said.

"Sam!" she yelled into the woods. "Come out and we can make a deal. Otherwise your partner dies."

"This is Burundi," he said, and she had no idea what he meant. "Just in reverse."

Sam waited in the quiet of a slight depression in the forest floor, quickly covered in dirt and leaves, and when the operative came by Sam jumped up and tackled the man. He clamped a hand over his mouth and slashed his throat. Special Projects had taught him this silent killing in fieldwork and for one second his stomach pitched at what he had done. But this was war, and he took the earbud off the dead man and put it in. Then he dragged the body into the slight depression in the earth he had used. He took the man's weapons. He had no idea what voice procedure Irina's team used in their signals. He needed to find the other operative and the pilot — he had no idea how many might be in pursuit of him, but he knew that model of chopper didn't carry more than four. He had no idea if she had summoned a team to the weather station.

But he wasn't going to Finland without Danny.

"One, two, report," Irina said.

"One, clear," the first man replied, and it was echoed a few moments later by the second man, panting slightly. "Two, clear."

"You know why she only brought three of you?" Danny said to the pilot. "Containment. She can't have the world knowing she tried to kill Morozov. So she'll either pay you very well or she'll kill you. Or you'll kill her, if you're smart. You have a gun — shoot her. That's my advice. I'm dead anyway, so what does it matter to me?"

"The lies of a desperate man," Irina said.

"Ask yourself: If you're chasing two men who have tried to assassinate a president, do you only send four people?" Danny laughed.

The pilot said nothing — didn't reach for his gun — but he glanced at Irina.

"Sam!" she yelled again. "Come out, now." She stepped forward and held up a knife. "Or I start cutting pieces of him off! Do you hear me?"

His voice was steady, utterly calm. She wondered if this quality of his was why Sergei had made him into his secret weapon. "Sergei slept with a lot of other women. And he would tell me things about you. Annoying habits. Times he wished he'd stayed single."

"Shut up," she said. She decided as soon as they were at the weather station she would shoot Philip Judge in the knee. She didn't want to bother dragging him through the woods.

Sam didn't hear her clearly as the mike wasn't active when she yelled her ultimatum. He was too far distant, but he heard a garbled cry. Irina had made a simple mistake in asking both operatives to respond, which told Sam there were only two and he'd killed one. He wasn't sure if there was a pilot or not; he thought there must be but the helicopter had gone down: He'd heard the slash of the rotors smashing into the trees. His brother had managed to bring down a chopper. Three remaining hostiles, and Danny. If Danny was still alive.

"Target acquired," he said in Russian, "fifty meters off weather station. Running northeast from the road." And he let fly two shots and waited.

The second operative appeared on his left and Sam shot carefully, with the AS Val. Its integrated suppressor kept the noise down. He did the pattern shot he'd been taught at the agency, head, head, chest. The man dropped.

"Target acquired," she heard reported in the mike, and then shots.

She glanced at Danny. "I think they've killed your sidekick."

And she shot the pilot in the head. He fell.

"That's your fault, with your stupid accusations," she said. She shoved the gun in Danny's back and pushed him toward the sound of gunfire.

Danny said nothing. And then the flutter began in his brain. He'd shuttered the red eye back at the Mercedes because they would have killed him if he kept fighting. And he wanted to live. He wanted time again with his brother, the only person who'd understood him. He wanted life again, a life without secrets. He had thought he did not care, that it did not matter, but now it did.

The imaginary red eye in his brain

opened.

"Irina." Sam's voice came into her earbud. "Your men are dead. I've killed them both. And I'll make a trade with you."

"What?"

"The eyedrops you took off Judge aren't the poisoned ones. I have the polonium. Judge never poisoned Morozov. You bring me Philip Judge and I'll give you the polonium."

And if he was telling the truth? Then she could kill Morozov later. If he was lying, she would kill them both. All she needed was the two of them dead, with the poison. Fine. "Where are you, Sam? I'll be happy to trade you."

"Come to the weather station. To the tunnel."

Irina ran through the woods, and the assassin did not try to slow her down. Now, now, she would have the end of the story she needed. The CIA agent, Sergei's killer, a poison that could only come from a government facility — and Morozov, finally dead, with the CIA clearly responsible for it. Her long game had paid off.

She ran toward the weather station, pushing the bound assassin ahead of her.

Sam reached the weather station. No sign of life. The door was locked. He used one of the keys to open it. If this was a bolt-hole then he thought there might be something helpful inside: a phone, a laptop, another clip of ammunition. What was here? A bare desk, a computer, meteorological equipment, a bookshelf. A bathroom. Spray cleaners, toilet paper.

Where was the tunnel? The bookshelf. He yanked on its side and it pulled away from the wall, revealing a steel door. He opened it with the other key and pushed the door open. Dim, eerie lights flickered in the darkness, offering patches of light and longer stretches of darkness. He couldn't see its end.

The moment they were in the tunnel, she thought, she would kill them both. They would be trapped, exposed, on the long stretch. She could fill the tunnel with gunfire. The Russian government would say the CIA knew about the tunnel, maybe even through Katya's treachery. And the polonium, if its container broke when she shot Sam full of bullets, could be contained in the tunnel safely. Two American assassins, radioactive with the same poison that had killed the president — it was like a gift.

"Irina?" Sam's voice called to her from the open tunnel. She positioned Judge in front of her.

"Yes, Sam?"

"Why was Anton Varro writing you a letter about your husband?"

The question startled her, turned a knife in her heart. "What?"

"The letter I found on Anton's body. I think it was for you. He writes you about what your husband is doing — perhaps telling you he's taken prisoners that he shouldn't, warning you of the consequences, so you're ready. On fine French stationery that Morozov gives as a gift. He was spying on your husband for you, wasn't he? Did you ask him to? Did you win him over the way you won me?"

"Shut up," she said.

"Anton wrote about the brothers, and I didn't realize at first that he meant the Morozovs."

She was silent.

"I asked myself, in the middle of a very dangerous stretch of Afghanistan, the son of a billionaire with him, running drugs to fund illegal operations the Morozovs don't want traced, and he pits Anton against a defiant prisoner. He lets Anton die. He recruits that prisoner to be a private weapon that only he knows. Why does he do those things? Because he knew you and Anton were spying on him. His own wife."

"That's not true."

"He covered up the truth about Anton's death. And we have the letter he wrote," Sam said. "Betray us and it will be published in the States. If he knew Anton was spying on him for you and died for doing so, then I think the Varros will react badly. I think the other families will abandon you." A bluff — the letter didn't hold enough specifics to hurt her. But she didn't know that.

"I only have your word this letter exists."

"But you know he wrote it. Because he was writing you. How else do I know about the Cartier stationery he used?"

A hammer hit her gut. "I . . ."

"That very expensive stationery that Morozov gives all his friends' kids. Found in a grave with a body that a DNA test will confirm to be Anton Varro and a dead CIA agent. I wonder what the world will think of Morozov then," Sam said.

Irina was silent.

Sam's voice softened. "Irina. Come with us. You can't stay in Russia. They'll kill you.

Morozov isn't poisoned. I replaced the polonium with water. He isn't going to die."

"You're lying. You're lying."

"He's not," Judge said to her. "Come with us. I think the CIA will happily give you asylum."

"I'll trade you your partner for the polonium. That's my only offer," she said. She felt a stark hatred for this young man. It was the only way to draw him out. She needed them both dead now.

"Fine," Sam said. "Send in my . . . partner."

She shoved the bound Danny forward, keeping the gun locked on his head, into the doorway leading to the tunnel. It was a dimly lit black pit. Thin light flickered from a few bulbs down the tunnel. She saw in the uncertain glow Sam had his own gun aimed at her.

"Set the polonium down," she said. She wondered if she could shatter the container with a bullet while he held it. That would kill him and make his body radioactive.

"Let him go. He walks into the tunnel, and then I set it down for you," Sam said.

"All right," Irina said.

"Come on, Danny," Sam said.

Danny didn't move.

Danny, Irina thought. His real name. I

never knew his real name.

"Come on, now. I know what I'm doing," Sam said.

Danny gave Irina a final glare and moved down the stairs into the darkness.

"Now the poison," Irina said.

"I'm going to put it on the steps at the end of the tunnel, on the Finland side, as we leave."

"No. Here."

"No, you might come after us. I don't think you'll risk exposure to it if I take it with us until we're safe on the other side."

"You've killed all my men."

"Good reason for you to come after us."

They heard the sound of a helicopter. Sam thought, She's got reinforcements coming. But the sound was to the west — Finland, very close. Close enough to be the end of the tunnel. Seaforth, maybe? Figuring out where he had gone, tracking the inner circle properties along the border. He'd given him enough information to make a serious attempt before the phone died.

"Put it down now," she said. The arrival noise of the helicopter seemed to unhinge her, as if she knew their escape was close at hand, and everything she'd done was ruined.

She needed it in his hand. If it was in his

hand she could destroy it and him; then she would be free.

"No. At the end of the tunnel. We shut the door on the Finland side; you take it and go back to Russia. Try again to kill Morozov, if you like."

"You could cheat me."

"I won't. I just want him. Irina, I'll give you my word I won't cheat you."

"Then show it to me," Irina said. "Prove you have it."

"All right," Sam said. "All right." Slowly he pulled the eyedrops bottle from his jacket pocket.

Her gun was aimed at the back of Danny's head as he moved forward. Then he stopped.

"Hold the bottle up," she said. "I can't see it."

Sam did and the moment he raised his left arm she fired. The bullet tore through his forearm and he dropped it. He went to one knee, aimed past Danny, and returned fire. He shot her in the leg as he fell.

She went down to one knee, screaming, but aiming again. Danny reversed course and barreled into her, before she could shoot at Sam or the polonium bottle again. Her gun sputtered as it fired into Danny. He wrenched away from her, pulling the gun from her grip.

"You shot Sam," he said. "You shot him." He seemed to not realize he'd been shot himself. Blood burst from his mouth.

"Danny, don't!" Sam said, from the floor. They fought for the gun and Danny fired another shot into her, into her thigh. She screamed.

"Run," he simply said again, leveling the gun at her head.

Irina turned and staggered, the blood pouring from her leg in sharp pulses, staggering up the stairs.

Irina fell into the dirt outside the weather station. She scrabbled for the cell phone in her pocket . . . She needed a doctor. Her fingers fumbled with the buttons. It wasn't working. It wasn't . . .

She saw him, then, as blood from her femoral artery watered the soil, coming through the birches and the pines. Sergei, smiling, walking toward her on the wind.

"Come on," Sam said, "come on." He could see now that his brother had been shot in the side and the chest, and was bleeding profusely.

Sam carried Danny down the rest of the tunnel, his own arm afire with pain and blood. He just ignored it. The tunnel to Finland seemed to stretch forever, like a long concrete tomb. "Don't die," Sam said. "Don't die. Don't leave me."

"I don't want to," Danny said. "Not again."

"The tunnel is giving us forever to talk," Sam managed. His arm was a blaze of agony. He had to keep his brother moving. And pray that it wasn't Irina's people waiting for them at the end of the tunnel.

The long game that Irina had played. The long game should be life and living it, not manipulation for a pointless revenge. So talk about life, he thought. Make him want to keep it.

"I want you to come to New Orleans. Play with Daniel."

"Don't sing that song to Daniel," Danny said. "*If I am dead . . . in sunshine or in shadow.* It's all too sad; what was Mom thinking?" His voice went ragged. "Sleep in peace . . . You came to me . . ."

Sam pulled him up the stairs. He sang: *"Danny Boy . . . I love you so."*

"I love you," Danny whispered. "Tell Mom and Dad . . . I'm sorry."

A spill of light showed the stairs, rising. The door. Finally, the door. Finland. Freedom. Unless Irina's team was on the other side. They'd die together.

He set Danny down on the floor. His brother touched his cheek. "Sam. You got me out."

"Hold on, hold on . . ."

"I had one more day with you." He tried to smile. "One more day . . ."

Sam stood, his shot arm thundering with agony. He opened the door with the other key, nearly collapsing. He tried to push and it didn't budge. Then he yanked and the door opened toward him. Another bookcase on the other side, one house a twin to the other; one a place of death, this one a place of hope. He pulled hard against the bookcase, his arm aflame with pain. Through the windows he could see, fifty yards away, a private helicopter, three men standing . . . and one of them was Bob Seaforth. He unlocked the front door and yelled for help, that he needed a doctor. The men ran toward him, Seaforth following slowly, waving.

Sam stumbled back down the stairs.

"It's OK, it's OK," he said. But Danny was so still. Quiet. He touched his brother's throat. He wasn't supposed to leave him again. Sam said his brother's name, from whisper to scream, and it echoed down the empty blackness of the tunnel.

75

Northern Virginia
Two weeks later.

Sam Capra paged through the newspapers from Russia.

The summit had gone well, marred by the news that Katya Kirova had dropped out of sight shortly after arriving in the United States, and had reportedly eloped to Mexico with a film star. The paparazzi waited at every major nightclub but she did not turn up, and eventually her father and the other Russians returned home without her. The Kirov yacht sailed through the Panama Canal and headed north, toward Baja, where Katya had last been reported. Sam wondered if Yuri would somehow get his daughter those millions in cash hidden in the server room, so she could live out her life out of the public eye.

Irina Belinskaya, the security chief for the inner circle, had gone missing as well, as had five of her employees. Initial reports suggested foul play. A search of her office aboard the Kirov yacht yielded a shock — a small amount of polonium-210, in a marked vial, a highly lethal poison only obtainable via nuclear facilities. Shortly thereafter, the bodies of two of her employees were found in a basement at the Nebo compound, and she and her men were found dead near the Finnish border. All had been shot to death. It was decided that the conspirators must have turned on each other and killed each other. Why they were heading to Finland was left to conjecture.

There was no mention in the press accounts of Sam Capra, Mila Cebotari, or Philip Judge. Or the long-ago murdered hostage, Danny Capra.

The inner circle, desperate to avoid blame or connection, cleaned up very well after themselves. Stefan Varro quickly bought a majority interest in Belinsky Global, and he promptly renamed it Varro Security.

Dmitri Morozov left the summit, with his inner circle now ready to make deals with their American counterparts, heralding a new era of closeness. But he noticed that the American demands got a bit stiffer in the following weeks. He got irritated. Finally the words he had long dreaded, like a dark shadow, the truth he thought had died with Sergei, came to him, carefully delivered by private message from the United States embassy.

Our intelligence service knows that your trusted associate Sergei Belinsky murdered a CIA operative named Zalmay Quereshi in Afghanistan and killed the son of one of your closest associates, Anton Varro, while conducting drug-running operations to fund murder and bribery on your behalf in Russia. We have physical proof. Consider your actions carefully should you wish not to have this information become public.

The accompanying photo showed Sergei Belinsky, a balaclava mask shoved up to his forehead, standing and glancing down at Zalmay Quereshi. The proof had been found in a house owned by one Robert Clayton, in Miami.

The relationship between the two countries, formed on this new trust (in that *I will trust you not to ruin me*), seemed to strengthen. A few pundits said President

Morozov seemed far more amenable to the Western overtures and offers than he had before the summit.

Sam closed the papers. He missed Mila. He missed his son. He missed his brother.

Bob Seaforth came into the room.

"I don't much like hospitals," Sam said. "I thought I could go home."

"We're flying Leonie and Daniel up here to see you. We thought it best to wait."

Sam looked at Bob. "We need to talk about the Round Table. I'm ready now."

"Our sources inside MI-5 have already told us. Your patron, James Court . . . he's finally talked. They cut him a deal. You're free of him."

"What will they do to him?"

"He'll resign from Her Majesty's Secret Service. He'll take a quiet pensioned job in a government backwater and turn over every contact he had to them. He did some very good favors for the Allies. Some were questionable. But he is cooperating. I understand his finally getting to see his wife face-to-face was the trigger for his talking. They should have tried that in the first place."

"His wife."

"I understand they are honoring whatever deal they gave her. Citizenship, the security of her family."

"I doubt she will want to see me." He thought: What if I never see her again?

Seaforth said: "My understanding is that the, um, marriage between Mila and de Courcey is not . . . surviving the strain of this, um, situation. But that is rumor, not a fact I can confirm."

"De Courcey? His name is Court."

"His real name is Lord James de Courcey, third son of Henry and Georgina, the Duke and Duchess of Avondale."

Sam was silent.

"The Avondales are not very stereo-typically aristocratic. There's a family estate, though. His parents are heavy into organic farming, green energy, natural textiles, and they very much stay out of the public eye. But . . . still a duke and a duchess. James was taught at home before going to university in Wales and majoring in history. He got a job working for MI-6, much to his father's displeasure. But under the name James Court he runs a small software consulting firm in London. That's his cover that you and your, um, friend know."

"Mila . . ."

"As I said, I hear the marriage is over. The Brits are not at all eager to advertise that a spy who is also the son of a duke was pulling intel jobs on the side — especially one that eventually led to MI-6 attacking a member of the Russian inner circle outside Nebo. It would be deeply embarrassing. Each intelligence agency has dealt with their Round Table member in their own way. There has been a spate of quiet resignations."

"I can't resign."

"True. You weren't an actual intelligence officer during your time working for Mr. Court. So. We're prepared to be . . . forgetful of this period. Thanks to you, we now have Morozov in our pocket."

Sam said nothing. It was thanks to more than him.

"But pockets get emptied." Seaforth risked a smile. "The analysts suggest that if Morozov keeps acquiescing to our demands, his popularity will be slipping. We have him, but who knows if he'll survive in power. Morozov could be gone soon enough, and then one of them perhaps in his place. We'll have to put pressure on the next president. Or maybe we'll get lucky, and so will the Russian people, and they'll have an actual choice."

Sam said nothing.

"Your brother . . ."

"I know."

"Sam. This was started because a CIA agent used very bad judgment in taking your brother along when he shouldn't have. Zalmay put them in a situation where they both might have been killed. Foolishly, and thoughtlessly. The agency never should have recruited Zalmay. But . . . whatever else your brother did, he gave us a leverage with Russia we've never had before."

"So he's a hero."

"Is he one to you?"

"I knew him better than anyone else. Yet in some ways he was still a stranger to me. Our business is to know. I didn't know my wife. I didn't know my brother. I don't know who I want to be anymore."

"What will you do now?"

"You mean like a job? I . . ."

"Those bars are still in your name. With the Round Table gone, there's no one to contest your ownership. Certainly none of the intel agencies want a legal fight over them. They're yours."

"I'm not sure I want to keep them."

Seaforth cleared his throat. "I know you and the agency did not part on the best of terms."

"True."

"You fixed this. You took on tracking a man who could have killed Morozov and sent this world into a dark and dangerous place. I need fixers, Sam. I need people who can do what you just did." He sat across from Sam. "Would you come back, work for me in a special capacity? The bars would still be your cover. And I would only ask for you in times of trouble. You could have some normalcy in your and your son's life."

"A normal life."

"Any crimes you committed working for the Round Table, they're gone. Full immunity." Bob Seaforth took a deep breath. "I've freed you, Sam. Would you like to work for me? Help me fix the problems no one else can touch?"

"You? And what are you that you can cover up Avril Claybourne's murder and get me and my brother out of Finland with no one the wiser?"

"I've left the agency. I now work for the Federal Intelligence Analysis Office."

"What is that?"

"Officially we help agencies understand their data better. Unofficially we do far more."

"You call it the Church," Sam said. He remembered the code name from when he'd eavesdropped on Seaforth's meeting with his team. "You have a team of misfits: Romy, Julian, Prakash."

Seaforth stared. "How do you know that?"

Sam shrugged. "I'll tell you someday."

Seaforth cracked an astonished smile. "Well. Then you know I've recruited people who don't always conform to the rules. I've had my eye on you for a while."

"I'm not sure I can handle doing CIA work again."

"We're *not* the CIA. We are an experiment. Trying to do our work the old-fashioned way, depending on humans gathering information directly from other humans. You are exactly what we need."

"May I think about it?"

"Of course."

Second chances, Sam thought. What will you do with yours?

ACKNOWLEDGMENTS

Special thanks to Mitch Hoffman, Jade Chandler, Lindsey Rose, Jamie Raab, David Shelley, Ursula Mackenzie, Deb Futter, Beth deGuzman, Brian McLendon, Matthew Ballast, Karen Torres, Andy Dodds, Jo Wickham, Andrew Duncan, Anthony Goff, Thalia Proctor, David Palmer, Kimberly Escobar, Jane Lee, and all the amazing teams at Grand Central Publishing and Little, Brown UK.

I am blessed also to work with Peter Ginsberg, Shirley Stewart, Jonathan Lyons, Holly Frederick, Eliane Benisti, Kerry D'Agostino, and Sarah Perillo.

For their generosity and expertise I thank Sherrie Saint (Director of Investigations, Alabama Department of Forensic Science); Nick Slavik, who shared his experiences in Afghanistan; Ed Lasher and Yachtcomputing LC; Kerry Kingery of the United States Coast Guard; Zsuzsa Megyeri, my editor at

Jaffa Kiado, for Budapest advice; Paige Pennekamp McClendon and Marianne Fernandez, for Miami expertise and the please-forgive-me borrowing of names. I would also like to acknowledge the late Dr. Gale Stokes, my Russian history professor at Rice University, who inspired a lifelong interest in Russia, and who thought writing crime novels was a fine use of my history degree. Any misrepresentation of facts, or bending of time or geography to suit the purposes of the story, is my responsibility.

Special thanks always to my family, Leslie, Charles, and William, who are my anchors during the writing and rewriting of the books.

Russia is a complicated land, and this book presents an entirely fictional take on the political and economic leadership of the nation. However, it is true that (a) much of the country's vast wealth has been concentrated in the hands of a few and (b) some of those business leaders are former KGB. Those facts served as a seed for the idea of this novel. There is no oligarch compound in Russia called Nebo, and the abandoned airfield at Vyborg remains abandoned. Zheleznogorsk exists and remains a forbidden city, and polonium-210 was identified as the poison used in the 2006 murder of

Russian dissident Alexander Litvinenko in London. One scenario of how he was poisoned suggests that the polonium, possibly taken from the Avangard reactor in the closed city of science, Sarov, was introduced into his tea at a London hotel.

ABOUT THE AUTHOR

Jeff Abbott is the *New York Times* bestselling, award-winning author of sixteen novels. His books include the Sam Capra thrillers *Adrenaline, The Last Minute, Downfall,* and *Inside Man,* as well as the standalone novels *Panic, Fear, Collision,* and *Trust Me. The Last Minute* won an International Thriller Writers award, and Jeff is also a three-time nominee for the Edgar Award. He lives in Austin, Texas, with his family. You can visit his website at JeffAbbott.com.